Tricia

A Gardener's Daughter

By

JB. WOODS

(Previously published as 'Tricia' by Jennifer Woods)

Conversations written in Harrington font are when the characters are speaking French

This novel is a work of fiction and the author's imagination and any resemblance to actual persons living or dead is entirely coincidental.

The author also willingly admits to having stretched local geography to suit his own ends.

The right of JB. Woods, to be identified as the author of this work has been asserted in accordance with the Copyright, Design and Patents Act 1988

© 2023
New Edition 2024

Cover design: Brian Platt
Hunter Valley Sunsets courtesy of Appellation Australia.
Other pictures from Clip Art
Published by JB. Woods

Dedicated to Patricia Cartwright with whom I had a relationship until I made the young naive decision to end it all. A decision I lived to regret until the arrival of Jenny my beautiful wife.

Other books by JB. Woods

The Hunter trilogy:
1) REBOUND
   2) Below the Belt
   3) UPSTART (Wyskochka)

   19th Century historical dramas: STOLEN BIRTHRIGHT

   Children's book: Henrietta – Tales from the farmyard
   Short story collection: Gems from my pen

In search of Happiness

Part 1

A young Mill girl

PROLOGUE

1842

The Right Honourable Judge Beakly placed the black cap on his head with due solemnity and through the mists of cataracts peered over his pince-nez across the court towards Lord James Kearsley, who, with a slight nod of the head, signalled his approval.

With bored complacency, Beakly turned his attention to the man in the dock. 'Edward Cartwright! It is the sentence of this court that you be taken to the prison from whence you came and hung by the neck until dead.'

There was an audible cry from the spectator's gallery as Cath Cartwright buried her head in her hands only to look up in surprise when the woman alongside her gave her a nudge. Justice Beakly removed the cap from his head and to Kearsley's dismay, continued, 'However, using the powers bestowed upon me I commute your sentence to that of no less than fourteen years transportation to the colonies. Take him down!'

A dull rumble of thunder murmuring its disapproval at the severity of the sentence reverberated around the building as a late summer storm passed overhead and an audible sigh of disappointment went around the gallery as the bloodthirsty citizens of Lancaster, equalled only by *'Les tricoteuse'* of the French guillotine, were denied one more victim by the infamous *Hanging Court*. Instead, another name was added to the roll call of transported Empire builders.

Ted Cartwright, a tall, barrel-chested man with thinning hair looked at the Judge dispassionately before glancing across the courtroom towards his wife, Catherine. He only had time to shout, 'I love you,' over the hubbub before he was bundled unceremoniously down the steps to the cells below.

The whole procedure had taken only seven minutes and Cath, who had hitched the twenty miles to Lancaster, stifled a sob. She had no time to reply to his parting and did her utmost to suppress the fear that rose in her breast at what lay ahead for her and their only child, Patricia.

~~~~~

CHAPTER 1

1839

Tricia Cartwright had been working in the Kearsley Hall kitchens for eighteen months when one October Sunday afternoon while taking a welcome break her Mam opened the door at the bottom of the stairs, and shouted, 'Tricia!'

Her call was not in love or sorrow but with a tone that demanded attention.

There was no response so she called again, a little sharper this time, which left her daughter in little doubt that she was serious.

'I'm coming, Mam,' came the complaining response, but without the accompanying sound of movement.

Cath leaned against the doorjamb for more support, and looking up the stairs she bellowed. 'Patricia! Get your nose out of that book and get down here now or it will be a sore backside for you, young lady.'

Tricia, tall for her age with grey eyes and her waist-length coal-black hair tied in a ponytail enjoyed her free time after working fourteen hours, six days a week in the Hall kitchens but her mother had used her proper name and that meant she was in trouble.

She carefully marked her place in her newest book '*Pride and Prejudice*' and made her feelings felt by her solid progress down the stairs before the loud—*Clack*—of the door catch, heralded her arrival.

'What is it, Mam?'

Cath gave her a look of disapproval, and said, 'Come here, madam. We have visitors. I hope you're tidy?'

'I'm tidy.'

'Good.' She put her arm around Tricia's shoulder, led her across the room, and introduced her to a serious, but pleasant lady and two children. 'You will have seen them at work, Tricia, but let me introduce them properly. This is Miss Hardcastle the Governess up at the Hall and this is Harry and Stephen, Lord Kearsley's grandchildren.

Tricia viewed the two children with barely disguised disdain and inwardly she thought, "Harry should be alright, but Stephen looks a bit posh." Outwardly, she smiled, and said, 'How do you do?'

'Very well and how do you do?'

"These two are going to be fun," Tricia thought.

'Tricia, Lord Kearsley would like you to be a companion to Stephen and Harry so run along and show them around. Take Tess with you and be back for tea and don't go near the river.'

'Yes, Mam, but can't I finish me book?'

'It's 'my book' and, 'No you can't. Now get along with you.'

Deep down Tricia resented these interlopers into her private world hidden in rural Westmorland. She grimaced, and said, 'Alright,' before reluctantly adding, 'Come on you two, if we're going anywhere follow me.'

Tricia, at eleven and a half years of age, took the lead. Harry, on holiday from Eton, a few months older than Tricia was the same height but stockier with wavy dark hair and was beginning to show the ruggedness of his father. Nine-year-old Stephen who was slight with the refined good looks of his mother brought up the rear picking his nose. Tess did what sheepdogs do and ran backwards and forwards between them as they edged their way past the carriage at the gate and in single file went down the track through the woods towards the river.

At the bottom of the slope where three tracks met, she stopped and pointed to her right. 'That way goes to the river.' She pointed over her right shoulder. 'That is the lower track back to the Hall.' She pointed to her left. 'And that path follows the riverbank to Fishy Bridge and the back gate of the estate.'

'Fishy Bridge,' piped up Stephen, 'there's no such name.'

'There is so, 'cos I named it.'

Harry spoke for the first time. 'Why Fishy Bridge, Tricia?'

'Because when you look into the water it's teaming with fish.'
She pointed down the track that led towards the river.
'What's down there,' Stephen asked petulantly.
Tricia sighed and her eyes flashed in a brief show of anger, she was not going to like this Stephen and his childish curiosity.

They set off down the track and after a hundred yards it petered out to a barely visible trail and Tricia wandered off into the vegetation. 'Follow me,' she called over her shoulder.

She pushed on a little further with the others following closely when she stopped by a wild gooseberry bush. 'Here we are. Try one of these, they're juicy.' She grabbed the largest pale green fruit she could find and bit into it. 'Umm… Lovely!'

Stephen grimaced. 'Ugh! They're green, I'm not doin' that, you'll get ill.'

Shut up,' scolded Harry as he picked a modest one, wiped it on his trousers and gingerly bit into it. 'They are delicious, Stephen, try a little piece of mine. Look, I'm not ill.'

Stephen took the morsel, put it into his mouth and immediately spat it out again.

Tricia shrugged and shook her head in dismay and against her mother's advice decided to take them down to the river.

When they arrived there, Tricia and Harry removed their boots and paddled at the water's edge by the rapids and Tess ran in and out of the water barking at her reflection.

Stephen, who they teased because he wouldn't paddle sat moodily on the stony beach when Tricia sensed something wasn't right. Before she could react Stephen rushed by and into the river.

'Stephen! We didn't mean it. You're not a scaredy-cat. Please, come back.'

Harry joined in. 'Stephen! Stop!'

'I'll show you who's scared,' Stephen shouted as he pushed further into the fast-flowing current. Step by slow step he forced himself forward. The rushing water created a wave against the resistance of his legs and churned itself into a frenzied froth. Legs braced apart he pressed on. The water came up to his thighs, trying to topple the slender obstruction in its rush towards the sea.

'Stephen,' Harry yelled, 'Come back at once!'

Suddenly frightened by the power of the water, Stephen, unsure of what to do muttered to himself. "That's scared them, I'd better go back."

He twisted away from the current to face downstream and turned once more to face the way he had come and took a careful step towards safety. His foot slipped on a loose stone, which threw him off balance. While he swayed crazily backwards and forwards with his arms flailing trying to remain upright the river seized its chance, plucked him up, and hurled him downstream, a tumbling piece of human flotsam.

'HELP!' he screamed as he disappeared into the maelstrom of frothing rapids.

Tricia and Harry stood dumbstruck for a moment before Tricia sprung into action.

'Harry! Run up to the house and get help. I'll follow the river bank and watch where he goes.'

Harry wasted valuable time when he sat down and put his boots on before running back up the track and Tess, sensing the urgency of the moment, ran in front of him barking the alarm.

Tricia meanwhile ignoring the pain ran barefoot up the pebble beach and into the woods and followed a barely distinct track that she knew would bring her back to the riverbank

Brambles pulled at her skirts and slashed at her ankles. Broken twigs and tiny stones cut into her bare feet. Branches tried to hold her back but she forced herself through disregarding her discomfort in a desperate race to catch up with the unfortunate Stephen.

At last, she reached the point where the river slowed and the current pushed into the near bank.

'STEPHEN!' she shouted repeatedly. 'STEPHEN!'

There was no reply and fearful of the consequences she searched and peered through the overhanging branches into the dark water. There were old logs and many twigs and leaves dragged into the bank by the winter floods, but no sign of Stephen.

'STEPHEN!' she yelled again in desperation. 'Ooh… Stephen, please be all right.'

She picked up a broken branch to prod down into the water and jetsam below her. Poking, calling, and working her way around overhanging trees she progressed slowly along the bank.

A flash of grey caught her eye. 'What was that?' Stephen had grey trousers.

She slashed at the branches and her heart pounded with excitement when she saw the inert body trapped by a branch face down in the water with the backside of his trousers ballooning with the air trapped inside the heavy material. Tricia jabbed at him with her stick unsure what to do next.

'Aah!' She cried in dismay as her prodding loosened the grip of the overhanging branches and Stephen floated away. 'Oh dear, someone help me. Stephen!'

She hurried further along the bank keeping a watchful eye on the motionless floating figure through the undergrowth and she could hardly suppress a cheer when another low branch snagged the unconscious boy.

'What do I do now,' she uttered.

Lowering herself to her knees, she reached out. It was no use. Stephen was too far below her. Sobbing at the futility of her efforts, something snapped within her.

Without a moment's hesitation, she jumped into the eddying current alongside the helpless figure. She bobbed up and grabbed a branch. Thrusting her free arm under Stephen's chin she pulled his head out of the water and shouted as loud as she could, 'Help!… Someone help!'

It felt like an eternity but it was only minutes before she heard voices calling her and Stephen.

She called out again. 'HELP! We're down here!'

'Tricia, is that you?'

She recognised her father's voice and called out. 'Daddy, daddy,' and then watched in fear as they ran past.

'Down here in the water, daddy!

Tess hesitated, turned back and barked. Ted and Cath, with Harry in tow, stopped and then ran back.

'Good heavens, lass. What are yer doin',' her Dad shouted?

Dropping to his knees, he reached down, but he was inches short of Tricia's outstretched hand.

'Mother, hold onto my legs.'

He lay on his stomach and wriggled to the edge. Further and further, he leaned out, easing himself forward a little at a time.

'Ted, be careful,' Cath, cried out anxiously.

'I am. Lie across my legs. Come on, Harry, you as well.'

They did as they were bid and he was able to reach down and grab the collar on Stephen's shirt.

'You hang on to that branch, girl,' he said to Tricia.

Wriggling backwards and pulling with his arms, he hauled the hapless Stephen onto the bank.

'Same again, mother. Come on!'

They repeated the exercise and pulled Tricia to safety.

He then ran over to Stephen, grabbed him by the feet and lifted him into the air.

'Slap his back, mother.'

Cath slapped, and Ted shook the ailing lad. After half a minute, Stephen coughed, spewed water, and began gulping huge breaths of air into his starved lungs. Ted lowered him to the floor and massaged his back.

Looking up at Tricia, he said, 'Right lass, you've got some explaining to do.'

Thus came a changing point in her life.

☐

The following day Tricia and her Mother were summoned to Kearsley Hall.

In their best clothes, Cath with her grey hair tied in a bun and Tricia's hanging loose between her shoulders, they waited nervously in an anti-room before they were called into Lord Kearsley's office.

The room was wood-panelled with maroon drapes at the long windows. Shelves stacked with all manner of books hid one wall and midway along another wall was an open fire. Behind a large ornate walnut desk sat the homely personage of Lord Henry Kearsley. His thinning hair was grey, but his sparkling blue eyes showed his intellect was unaffected by age.

Harry and Stephen with their father, James, Kearsley's eldest son, and his attractive wife Juliet, stood to one side.

Cath and Tricia took two paces into the room.

'Come forward, Mrs Cartwright. Let me have a closer look at our heroine.'

They obediently took two paces forward and Tricia kept hold of her Mam's skirt for moral support.

'Don't hide, young lady,' said Kearsley in a homely manner with a lilt of North Country accent. He threw a sidelong glance at James. 'I don't bite like some I know.'

Cath put a hand around Tricia's shoulder and gently eased her forward.

Henry picked up a paper-knife and pointed it at Tricia. 'That's better. You young lady are Patricia, I take it?'

Tricia bobbed and looking directly at him, said, 'Yes, sir, but my friends call me, Tricia.'

Cath nudged Tricia in the back. 'Don't be cheeky.' She directed her next words to Kearsley. 'I am sorry, sir. I tried to bring her up nice, but she's a little wild.'

'Have no fear, Mrs Cartwright; I like spirit in a child.'

James opened his mouth to interrupt but his father cut him short. 'Now young Tricia, I'm told you jumped into the river and rescued Master Stephen. Is that correct?'

Tricia half-turned to look at Cath, who mouthed, 'Go on.'

'Yes, sir,' replied, Tricia, confidently, 'I couldn't reach him so I jumped in. There was nowt else I could do.'

Kearsley smiled benevolently, 'That was brave of you was it not?'

'I dunno, sir. As I said, there was nowt else I could do.'

Kearsley rubbed his chin before replying. 'Such humility is rare even in a child.' He stopped in mid-sentence and paused thoughtfully for a couple of seconds before continuing. 'Mrs Cartwright, an act like this deserves some reward therefore, as of today, Tricia will cease her employ in the kitchens and become a companion for Stephen where she will join him in his schoolwork, but not before she has completed whatever punishment you meted out for her indiscretion. I will give you a small allowance to improve her wardrobe and Miss Hardcastle will advise you on the necessary arrangements. Is there anything you wish to say?'

James interrupted. 'Father, I must protest.'

'You always do, that goes without saying. However, that is my wish and let that be the end of it. Mrs Cartwright. Have you anything to say?'

'Only thank you for your kindness, sir. She is keen to learn and won't let you down, but may I ask of one favour, sir?'

'Yes, Mrs Cartwright, what is it?'

'That I be allowed to take Tricia's place in the household for a few hours a day?'

'Yes, glad to hear of it. Eight 'til four but on her pay is that understood. Now make sure Patricia is here soonest. That is all, you may go now, and Tricia—Thank you, again.'

Cath half curtsied and backed out of the room pulling Tricia with her. Mercifully, the butler had anticipated their move and the door was open.

—

Tricia missed the outdoors, exploring and playing in her secret place under the big fir tree adjacent to the cottage and a couple of days into her punishment she was sulking while she swept the last of the ashes from off the hearth. She wiped her brow with the back of her hand before she gave the range a quick flick to remove the last of the wood ash clinging to it.

It would be another hour before she finished black-leading, and she mumbled, 'It wasn't my fault the stupid boy fell into the river.'

She picked up the ash bucket, carried it outside and tipped the contents on the garden path, screwing up her eyes as a gust of wind swirled the fine dust around her.

She dropped the empty bucket by the back door and spoke to Tess.

'It's alright for you.'

Tess wagged her tail and gave her a doggie smile of pleasure when a call from Cath interrupted her thoughts. 'Tricia! Where are you?'

'Out here. Coming!'

She sighed and trudged into the house.

'Ah...! There you are. What are you up to?'

'I've just done the ashes, Mam, and now I'm going to black-lead the grate.'

'You've worked hard today, Tricia, just give the range a quick wipe and then you can go out to play. Don't tell your Dad, mind.'

'Thanks, Mam.'

She dashed into the living room and started rubbing vigorously and ten minutes later she was back in the kitchen.

'Finished, Mam, can I go out now?'

'No, you can sit there and have something to eat.'

Cath cut the end crust off a cottage loaf, spread it with dripping and gave it to Tricia along with a mug of milk.

Tricia gulped the milk down and rushed out of the door still chewing on the crust.

'Tricia!' Cath called after her, 'take Tess.'

'Aah... Mam, I don't want her today,' and she ran off before her mother could argue.

At the front gate, Tricia stopped and thought for a moment. She was suddenly aware of the rattle of harness coming down the track from the direction of the Hall and wondered who might be calling at this time of day.

A two-horse roadster jangled down the hill and pulled up. Stephen jumped out.

'Tricia,' he called as he ran towards her, 'What are you doing?'

'Nothing, but I'll race you to the bottom of the hill.'

She didn't wait for an answer but took off in a mad dash leaving Stephen scrabbling in her wake.

When she reached the junction, she stopped suddenly and Stephen crashed into her. They both tumbled into the long grass on the verge in a tangle of arms and legs breathless. While they both laughed hysterically, Tricia pulled the little fellow to his feet.

'Which way,' they shouted simultaneously.

Tricia was surprised to see the change in him without the presence of his elder brother.

'We can't go down to the rapids,' she said, 'but we can go to Fishy Bridge and into the meadows on the other side of the river.'

'Let's do it,' and it was his turn to shout, 'I'll race you,' as he scampered off.

Like frolicking jackrabbits, they raced along the cart track that followed the river below the cottages.

—

It was two hours later when they arrived back at the cottage. Stephen jumped into the carriage and Tricia waited until they had disappeared around the bend in the track before running inside full of excitement.

'Mam, you'll never guess what we've been doing?'

'Oh, there you are, Tricia, where have you been until now?'

The stern voice of Ted called from the living room. 'What have you been up to? It wasn't work, was it?'

He came and stood in the doorway.

Tricia grinned and giggled nervously knowing she had been caught out. 'Hello, Dad, you're home early.'

His mock anger disappeared and he smiled. 'Well, out with it, what have you been doin' and then you can help me feed the pigs.'

She went on to relate their adventures and the change in Stephen who had grown in stature away from the presence of his older brother.

'Oh, I nearly forgot, Dad. We bumped into Jamie the poacher and he asked if you wanted a salmon.'

'Not this week.'

'I'll see him when I return from the Hall on Monday. Come on, let's feed the pigs, I'm starvin'… Ha! Ha! I didn't mean it to sound like that.'

Cath laughed, and said, 'Knowing how you two eat it sounds right to me.'

Ted let out a huge belly laugh, and retorted, 'Come on, Tricia, we can get insulted by a better class out in the paddock.'

He ducked and ran for the door as Cath chased him with the ladle she was holding.

Half an hour later hungry after feeding the family pigs they returned.

'Wash your hands,' Cath scolded before she would serve the dinner, 'and if you're good there's gooseberry crumble for pudding.'

Tricia rolled her eyes, 'My favourite!'

She lay in bed that night reflecting on her surprise at the new demeanour of Stephen. "Schooling with him might not be such a bad thing after all."

~~~~~

CHAPTER 2

The following Monday morning Cath presented Tricia to Miss Hardcastle at the Hall and she immediately whisked her off to a carriage in the courtyard where Stephen was waiting. Cath had barely time to wave before the carriage wheeled away and down the drive on its way to Lunesdale. Twenty minutes later, it pulled up outside the local dressmakers.

The dressmaker measured Tricia and then discussed dress patterns designed to improve her wardrobe to be delivered to the Hall two days hence.

Shopping over, Miss Hardcastle took them to Mrs Howarth's Bakery famous for its meat pies and treated them to a gingerbread man, which they devoured on the journey back to the Hall.

The moment they arrived, they were whisked into the library. Miss Hardcastle called Tricia to her side, 'Patricia you have come here to work and as such, you can have Master Harry's desk and I want you to make full use of his exercise books. You can write I take it?'

'Yes, ma'am, but I don't know if it's up to scratch as we were writing on slates at the village school.'

'We will find out. For the rest of this morning we are going to do writing and spelling and this afternoon we move on to French and reading.'

'But ma'am, I don't know nowt about French but I can read.'

'That's why you're here, Patricia, and the word is nothing, not nowt. In here you will speak proper English, do you understand?'

'Yes, Ma'am!'

'Run along now. You will find paper, quill and pencils in the desk.'

—

Thus began Tricia's time as a companion to Stephen. Miss Hardcastle took to her immediately and lavished a lot of attention on her and she did many things not normally open to girls. She studied for five and half days a week with time taken for dinner at midday for the next two years and things were easier for the family with many unexpected benefits for Tricia.

Weather permitting, she was taken on field trips to study the wildlife and collect specimens for her biology lessons. She had lived all her life in the backwoods and marvelled at the way nature was intermingled with life in many ways. Miss Hardcastle took them into the town frequently to try out their mathematics while shopping and retrospectively, Stephen applied himself when he asked to be shown rudimentary domestic science skills but for Tricia, French and playing the pianoforte were her real passion and she took to them fervently.

—

A few months before Stephen was due to move on to Public School, Lord Henry died and his eldest son James took the title of Lord Kearsley and with it the responsibilities. He begrudgingly allowed Tricia to carry on with her studies knowing that when Stephen went away his obligations to his father's wishes would cease.

James made one major change as Lord of the Manor. He decided that he would use his wealth made from cotton, railways and canals, to entertain the upper classes and decreed that from now on the Estate would become less rural and the breeding of pheasants was now the priority to encourage shooting week-ends.

Ted, still had the snaring rights on the bottom field close to their cottage and frequently a pheasant would become trapped in one of his snares and it had become the custom to keep them but Lord James forbade the practice insisting that all birds, alive or dead, belonged to him. To enforce the issue he employed more gamekeepers and so it was, one evening while out checking his snares, Ted found a dead pheasant and unthinking, took it home.

The following morning Cath was frightened out of her wits. The backdoor of the cottage slammed open and the Bailiff from Lunesdale along with the gamekeeper forced their way in. They went directly to the larder and found the pheasant hanging there.

It was immediately confiscated. Ted was arrested and taken to the local jail and from there to the prison in Lancaster to await trial for theft and poaching.

The immediate cataclysmic result of Ted's demise was James Kearsley's insistence that he needed their tied cottage and he gave Cath and Tricia just three days to move out.

Cath suddenly felt old for her thirty-two years and looked at their future with a great deal of trepidation. She called Tricia into the kitchen and spoke to her gently.

'Tricia, sit down, there's a love.'

Tricia pulled up a chair to the kitchen table and sat opposite her mother.

'What is it, Mam?'

'Tricia! Your Dad's been sent away for a long, long time and we probably won't ever see him ever again.'

'Can't we go and visit him, Mam?'

'No, love, he's gone to the other side of the world and we've got to move out. His Lordship wants the cottage.'

Tricia jumped up, ran around the table to Cath's enveloping arms, and cried, huge sobs wracking her slight body.

Cath pulled her in tight and consoled her. 'There, there, dear, let it all out.'

After a few minutes, Tricia's tears subsided. She wiped her eyes on Cath's apron, and said softly, 'What do we do now Mam?'

Cath eased Tricia up from her lap and placed a hand on each of her shoulders. 'Tricia, love, we'll have to look for work. Tomorrow we go into Lunesdale and if there's nothing there we'll go to Lancaster and try the Mills.'

Tricia looked at her Mother wide-eyed, and said, 'I'll have to go to work too, Mam?'

'Yes, love. You're fourteen now and we need every penny. I gave Dad some of our savings and we have enough to carry us over for a couple of weeks, maybe. We'll call on my Cousin Lily and see if she can help.'

Lord Kearsley vented further distress on the family when he seized Tess, their pigs, and chickens and asserted his position to make sure that local employment was unavailable. Reluctantly, Cath spent the two shillings she made by selling some of their furniture, to hire a driver and cart to take them to Lancaster.

~~~~~

CHAPTER 3

1842

When they arrived in the human midden of the Lancaster slums Tricia eyed the rows of soot-blackened houses and tenements with alarm. The smell was overpowering. Cousin Lily and her husband Bert rented an end of terrace two up two down house in a row overhanging a tidal stream which was a fetid open sewer fed daily by fresh excrement from the household privies. You could see the putrid odour rising from the green slimy water when the tide came in.

Lily demanded two shillings a week rent in advance and Cath had little option but to agree to this blackmail.

A makeshift bed was made for Tricia on the floor in her Cousin Andy's room. He was eighteen and worked as a big-piecer in the Lune Cotton Mill with his father Bert who was a tackler. Andy had learned the rough ways and language of the adults while Jimmy aged eleven worked as a machine cleaner, the most dangerous job in the Mill. Then there was little Amy who was four.

Cath, it was decided would have to make a bed up every night using cushions on the landing and she was determined to get them out of there as soon as conditions would allow.

Cath slept fitfully on her makeshift bed and found that Andy and Bert were none too careful where they put their feet when they staggered home drunk.

On the first morning, a loud clattering on the window woke Tricia from her restless sleep and Andy crudely kicked her awake as he scrambled around in the dark looking for his clothes. She ignored his hand moving up and down her body outside the thin coverlet thinking maybe it was likely that he wasn't used to having a bed where his clothes usually lay.

Further sleep was impossible and being the newcomer she was

made to empty the piss-pot. The stains on the floor suggested he was not too careful where he did his ablutions after a night drinking and the smell of stale urine mixed with body odour made her nose curl.

The rest of that day Cath and Tricia explored the area looking for work in service or shop work. It paid less but was much more desirable than their other option. The Mill!

Their search for alternative accommodation was equally frustrating and as they trudged around they gazed in horror at the drains and sewers emptying their filthy contents into the tidal ditch. Built over it was a tier of doorless privies in the open road common to both men and women and they could hear bucket after bucket of filth splashing into it. Although extracted upstream the ditch was also the source of drinking water and was more akin to watery mud than muddy water.

With heavy hearts, they trudged home an early start in the Mill looming on Monday morning.

Monday came and the frantic banging on the window by the waker-upper dragged Tricia from her sleep. Once more Andy kicked her as he got out of bed. She didn't complain as she knew it was for the best.

Still tired with barely open eyes she tottered downstairs in her cotton nightie. She cringed in disgust as she caught the piss-pot on the doorjamb and splashed some down herself. Cath helped her wash under the one tap and rinsed her nightdress hoping it would dry by nightfall. The water was freezing and Tricia could not imagine what it must be like in the winter. Cath dug out a cotton dress suitable for work and a new smock.

For breakfast, she wolfed down two treacle water-papes and drank a mug of weak tea, but before she could put on her coat Lily stopped her and cut the frills from the wrists of the dress.

'You don't want you to snag up on one of those machines, do we,' she said.

Tricia threw the coat around her shoulders, pushed a muslin bonnet on her head and they rushed for the door. Their clogs were lined up by the door and Cath remembered to pick up their food bag. Dinnertime seemed a long way off and Cath wasn't sure what condition the food would be in. Andy and Uncle Bert assured them it would be all right and would supplement what they could buy at the Mill.

The weather was disgusting. There was a fine steady drizzle and it mixed with the smoke from hundreds of chimneys in clinging yellow smog. It turned their clothes black. The cloying sulphur smell mixed with the sewage and Tricia had great difficulty stopping herself from being sick.

The flickering street gaslights were dimmed to a dull amber glow and they had to trust young Jimmy who could barely walk let alone run as the damp weather was making his swollen knees and ankles hurt more than usual.

Cath and Tricia placed themselves on either side of Jimmy and with a hand under each elbow they helped him along. Cath observed quietly to herself, 'Eleven and crippled like an old man.'

It was a peculiar sensation running through the town. The rhythmical tapping of clogs on the cobbles carried them along and as they became closer to the Mill, the crowds of pale-faced workers grew until they were shoulder to shoulder in a dash to beat the deadline.

The Mill was two red brick, six-storey cathedrals with a myriad of grimy windows and a large chimney from the boiler-house poking up between them, which added more soot to the lung-searing mix. The weather was pushing the smoke down and they could taste the coke.

Cath and Tricia stood to one side at the Mill gate while the rest of the workforce clocked in. A sensation they couldn't account for was a solid regular thumping underfoot. On the stroke of six a.m. the thumping changed to a ground-shaking vibration and the gates swung shut. Stragglers, even those a few yards from the gate had their names taken.

The last worker disappeared into the factory and they plucked up the courage to knock on the Overseer's door. A large ruddy-faced man appeared wiping the remains of his breakfast from his face. 'Well...! What have we here,' he uttered through a faded red handkerchief.

He had long since given up trying to extend his jacket around his bulk and his neckcloth blended with the weather while hanging from his lapel was a pair of half-glasses held together with cotton binding. In ludicrous contrast, he had a gold hunter watch and chain stretched across his bulbous paunch.

Uncle Bert had said to mention his name and so it was when they introduced themselves they were expected. 'Old Bert Glover gives thee a good reference and you've got a start in the weaving shed. It's five and a half days a week starting at six in the morning until seven in the evening an' you'll get six-shillings and fourpence a week until you're up to speed and then Mom you'll get eight-shillings. The little 'un will get seven shillings. After a month if you're no good, you're out. Don't be late else it'll cost you a penny a minute.'

They nodded and he asked them to make their mark. They signed the book and he was surprised to find they could both write. 'Educated a bit then? I thought you were not from these parts?'

'We're from Lunesdale. My husband has been transported. We have to do something,' Cath said, 'and this seemed a likely place.'

'Quite right,' he replied, 'see what you can do. Follow me and I'll take you up to your shed. Have you got your piece?'

They had been forewarned about this new language and they nodded, at the same time subconsciously checking their mid-morning snack.

He continued, 'You get fifteen minutes for breakfast and an hour for dinner which the owner provides for a penny a day. It's only stew and tha'll not get any today if you haven't got a bowl. Mind on and bring one tomorrow.'

Bert, Andy and Jimmy worked in the Number 1 Mill but they followed their guide up to the fifth floor of Number 2 Mill. Tricia counted ninety-five steps before they entered the weaving hall through a swing door weighted to close behind them.

It was cool in there and the building shook. The noise was

terrible and numbed the senses. It was a non-stop clattering, rattling and clacking. Over the din you could hear the rhythmic slap, slap of the drive belt joints as they went around the driving wheels of each loom. Speech of any kind was impossible and she saw people mouthing silent words and using unfamiliar hand signals through the rising mist of cotton waste. It was only twenty-past six and already the heads of the workers were covered in a grey snow like down.

The hall covered a large area and weaving looms stretched in rows as far as the eye could see. The belts which came down from revolving shafts high up in the roof were a forest of writhing leather and coupled with the swirling mist of cotton dust it was impossible to see the opposite wall. There were high arched windows down both sides of the hall but the gas lamps remained lit and they had only walked a couple of steps into the place when Tricia sneezed.

They were introduced to the floor Supervisor, a grim, pasty-faced man of robust stature called Charlie Snape or 'The Snapper'. He wore a crumpled top hat as a sign of his authority which gave him a slightly incongruous appearance as he didn't wear a jacket but walked around with the sleeves of his off-white shirt rolled up and swinging a gnarled cane. He introduced them to an elderly woman called Gertie who was to be their mentor.

'Don't go easy on 'em, Gertie. I want 'em on the line quick.'

Gertie nodded and then Tricia giggled as Gertie pulled a face at his departing back.

They were put into a corner on two opposing single power looms and after storing their 'piece' and top coats, their initiation into the mystique of weaving began. It was strange learning from someone they couldn't hear but they found by elucidating every syllable and using hand signals they were able to follow Gertie's instructions.

At eight o'clock, the machines were switched off for twenty minutes while they had their breakfast of bread and dripping. At one-thirty, the machines were switched off again but this time for an hour. Gertie found them a can they could use and Tricia had to negotiate the stairs down to the kitchen level and pay tuppence for two portions of thick stew and then carry it back to the machine floor. The stew was surprisingly tasty if a little salty with plenty of meat and a dumpling floating on the top. Already tired, there was no let-up after the dinner break. A tackler came along and made the looms quicker and while they were waiting, Tricia watched how he stopped and re-started the machines with the leather clutch operated by a lever.

It was a slow walk home as her legs ached from the continuous standing at the loom and her clogs weighed a ton. They caught up with Jimmy at the gate and helped him. Some days, he told them, when Uncle Bert worked late, he had to crawl home. Andy refused to help him. 'You'll never get used to it if I keep helping yer,' he told him.

With extra income coming into the house, they were able to add cheese, tomatoes and butter for their bread to their supper. After a mug of weak tea, Tricia fell into her makeshift bed, dowsed the candle, and was asleep before the glow went from the wick.

Tricia dragged herself awake, her aching limbs tying her to the bed when her muzzy brain became aware of another sensation. A rough hand was moving over her body. It traversed from her buttocks slowly upwards before cupping one of her tiny pubescent breasts.

Her eyes opened wide in fear, and in the gloom, she lashed out at her unseen molester. Throwing the covers back, she screamed. 'Get off me! Go away! Mam!... Mam!...'

She was knocked to the floor by Andy who grabbed his clothes and pushed crudely through the door shoving Cath to one side as he did so.

Cath steadied herself and in the first light of dawn seeping through the grimy cloth hanging at the window, she found Tricia standing on her bed clutching her thin cover.

What is it, my pet? What's wrong? Have you been dreaming?'

'No, Mam. Andy was touching me. I heard the window rattle then I felt this hand moving over me.'

'Are you sure? He wasn't just looking for his clothes.'
No, Mam. It wasn't the same. He grabbed me here.'
She put a shaking hand over her breast.
'Oh, dear,' said Cath at the same time hugging Tricia.' I'll have a word with Lily but he's going to deny it. Come on, love, get yourself dressed. It's getting late.'

Tricia stumbled down the narrow stairs and into the living room. There was no sign of Andy who had dashed off without breakfast. She hurriedly washed her face under the tap. The water was cold but it refreshed her red-rimmed eyes and she calmed down as she ate her water-papes and drank her tea. She put her outdoor coat on and followed Cath and Jimmy out of the door clutching their dinner cans.

—

The rain had stopped and the jog through the town and over the canal bridge without the choking smog was less harrowing. Before she turned into the factory gates Tricia looked longingly at the countryside beyond and wished she was back in their cottage.

Gertie was waiting by the machines when they arrived and after a short time going over the procedure she plumped herself into a chair and left them to it only stirring when things went wrong. By dinnertime, Tricia was used to the routine but she wondered if her legs would carry her through the day.

That night Cath had to force Tricia to eat before she crawled upstairs to bed. Tricia rolled herself tightly into her bed-cover shaking inwardly at what the morning may bring but tiredness overcame fear and the candle had hardly become a wisp of smoke before she was asleep.

The week continued without further mishap. The looms were speeded up a little each day Tricia and Cath became inured to the noise and the shaking but went home tired beyond belief.

~~~~~

CHAPTER 4

Sunday brought welcome relief and despite Tricia's protestations, Cath insisted that Tricia attend the local Sunday school in the belief that any knowledge gained would be beneficial. She paid her penny and joined Jimmy and Amy in the nearby Chapel.

The class was thirty minutes old when Parson Pickup, a tall skinny man with stooped shoulders and reading glasses perched on the end of his nose queried her better quality clothes and her knowledge.

She quickly explained the family circumstances and from then on he put her in charge of the younger element while he attended to the others in the class.

At the end of lessons, he accompanied Tricia home and she giggled quietly most of the way as she tried to match his long stride. In his traditional Parsons apparel of black suit and knee-high gaiters, white shirt and statuary black neck-cloth, and a modern stove-pipe hat instead of the more familiar tri-corn, she imagined him as a gangly magpie. She was also impressed by the fact that he didn't seem to mind getting his shoes dirty in the refuse and mud in the road.

Looking up at him as they walked and chatted made her neck ache and she was glad when they reached Auntie Lily's house and she burst through the open front door shouting excitedly, 'Mam! Mam!... I've brought a visitor.'

Pickup removed his hat and had to stoop to enter the tiny hall where he waited. The intrusion caused great consternation to both Lily and Cath and they dashed around furtively tidying and hiding things in the fervent hope that their unforeseen guest would not be aware of their poverty.

Wiping her hands on her pinny, Cath stepped forward to meet the Parson as he waited patiently. She bobbed in a half curtsey, and said, 'Good day, Parson. What can we do for you? She hasn't been naughty, has she? I'll tan her backside if she has.'

Pickup nodded his head in reply to Cath's polite gesture, which was unusual in these deprived quarters. 'Elijah Pickup. Am I addressing Patricia's mother?'

'Why, yes… How silly of me. Mrs Catherine Cartwright.'

'Mrs Cartwright, I have come to ask a favour of you. I am impressed by Tricia's brightness. She is a gifted storyteller, and I would like to employ her at the Sunday school as an assistant. I will give her sixpence a week plus Sunday dinner. Does that sound reasonable?'

'Mr Pickup, I'm at a loss for words.'

She stood silently for a moment and then she smiled when she saw Tricia nodding her head out of Pickup's vision.

'There would be no difficulty whatsoever, Mr Pickup, but you do realize that owing to our straightened circumstances Tricia will still have to work during the week?'

'Yes, I understand and have no fear, I will not overwork her but it would be a shame to hide such a talent. I take it that I shall enjoy her company next Sunday?'

'Certainly, Mr Pickup.'

He turned to Tricia. 'I look forward to seeing you next Sunday, young lady. Be on time mind.'

He nodded to Cath and stooping low, turned and left.

They stood silent for a moment before Cath grabbed hold of Tricia and swung her around. 'Well done, Tricia. I'm proud of you. Come on, let's finish getting dinner ready.'

The now familiar daily routine continued. The five o'clock rattle on the windows followed by the cold wash. A hurried bite and a mug of weak tea before the clip-clop dash to the Mill.

The days were shorter now and they never saw daylight except at the weekend. They had been warned that the weaving hall was colder than the spinning shed and the autumn weather made sure that any heat rising through the floor was effectively cancelled out and they now worked with cold feet.

Their narrow-cloth looms were at full speed now and they

were told at the end of their third week they were fit to be transferred onto a broadloom the following week. Tricia had her doubts but Cath assured her that it would be all right.

Tricia looked forward to her Sundays. Her class grew larger as the word spread about her stories which she continued to both read and write. Pickup supplied writing paper and making full use of her meal breaks she was able to prepare in what little time she had to spare. She also fulfilled her new passion for poetry at every opportunity and the little food parcels Mrs Pickup gave her after every session were always welcome.

—

October became November and with it Andy's nineteenth birthday and he and Bert disappeared into the Alehouse immediately after work.

Cath and Tricia helped Lily around the house and after tea Tricia went to her room to read by candlelight.

It was her favourite Bronte book only now the pages were dog-eared with constant use. Cath found her asleep and removed the book from tired fingers, tucked her in and blew out the candle.

—

Tricia struggled but could not move. Her breathing was difficult. She tried to shout out but rough unshaven skin covered her mouth. She couldn't turn her head and she tried to scream again but only a muffled whimper escaped. She kicked out with her legs at the same time twisting from side to side but Andy's heavy body held her down.

'Shush, my baby,' he uttered in her ear. 'This is going to be our little secret. You say a word and I'll kill you.'

She felt his hand groping her and her scream when his fingers penetrated her was a barely audible grunt.

'A tight little virgin. Just what a man needs,' he leered.

He had pinned her down but had to shift his weight to lower his trousers. Tricia lashed out and in a desperate attempt to calm her he lifted his hand from her mouth. That was all she needed. Her screams could be heard up at the Mill.

Cath woke at the commotion and immediately realised her

daughter was in danger. In the murk, she found the broom she had used the night before and rushed into the bedroom, and struck out at the shadowy hulk thrashing around in the middle of the room.

Andy rolled away from the onslaught but Cath didn't relent. She kept on swinging and Andy in a desperate attempt to escape crawled to the door got to his feet and ran along the landing. In his haste he did not see Cath's bedding and tripped.

He staggered to the top of the stairs his arms waving wildly in a vain attempt to regain his balance. Cath caught up with him and she swung the broom at his head. Andy yelled in terror as he backed away into emptiness and tumbled down the stairs.

Awoken by the hullabaloo, Lily came out of her room and heard the sharp crack as Andy rolled over and over and landed in a heap at the bottom, his head lying at a crazy angle.

'What have you done?' shouted Lily, 'you've killed him.'

'Don't be stupid,' said Cath, 'He was raping Tricia and I chased him off.'

'That's what you say. You've never liked Andy and now you've done for him.'

Lily rushed down the stairs, took a quick look at her son, and rushed out of the front door shouting, 'Murder! Murder! Andy's been murdered.'

Cath stood petrified. She couldn't believe her ears. Her cousin was accusing her of murder. What was she to do? Her thoughts were disturbed by Tricia's sobbing and forgetting her own problems she turned and went to her daughter's aid.

Faces appeared at grimy windows and it was not long before people were gathering in the street as Lily pointed towards her house shouting,' Murder! Murder! She's murdered my Andy.'

The urgent clacking of Police rattles could be heard getting closer and a few minutes later two Peelers ran into the street.

'What's going on 'ere?' said the bigger of the two.

Lily ran across to them. 'It's murder.' She pointed again to her house. 'There's a woman in there an' she's murdered our Andy.'

'Whoa, there, misses. What do you mean—she murdered your Andy?'

They began walking towards the front door as Lily explained. 'She ran up behind him and hit him over the head with the broom handle and knocked him down the stairs.'

'Who did?'

'My cousin!'

'Show us.'

Lily led the two constables into the house and pointed to Andy lying at the bottom of the stairs.

'There, see. Now, do you believe me?'

'An' where's your cousin?'

They listened and wracking sobs could be heard coming from the back bedroom.

Lily pointed. 'She's up there with that whore of a daughter. She led him on, that's what.'

'Fred. You stay here with her while I have a look.'

'Right, oh, Bill. Be careful, she may still have that broom.'

'I don't think so. There's too much crying from up there.'

He stepped over the inert body, climbed the stairs and went along the landing into Tricia's bedroom where he found Cath in the dim glow of a candle on Andy's bed with Tricia sobbing in her lap.

Cath helped Tricia up and before he could speak, she said, 'What can I do for you, constable?'

'Your cousin says you knocked the lad down the stairs. Is that right?'

'No, Constable. He was raping my daughter, can't you see the blood on her nightie. I caught him and hit him with the broom. He ran away, tripped on my bedding and fell down the stairs.'

'You didn't hit him at the top of the stairs, then?'

'I may have done. It all happened so quickly.'

'Right, misses. I'm arresting you on a charge of suspected murder!'

'Who's going to look after, Tricia?'

'Your cousin will have to. Anyway, she's a big girl. Hurry up, or I'll drag you off as you are and it's cold in those cells.'

Tricia jumped between them. 'You can't take my Mam. It's a lie. She was helping me.'

'Now, now, Tricia, don't be alarmed. It will be all cleared up in the morning. You lie down and try to sleep. You need to be fresh to go to work. Come on, I'll tuck you in.'

Five minutes later Cath was dressed, and she followed the Constable down the stairs. Lily hung her head and turned away as her cousin was led out of the door and marched to the Police Station under the Town Hall.

Tricia lay sobbing as she listened to the horse-drawn Police van arrive to collect Andy's body and shortly afterwards the waker-upper came along the street blowing his horn and rattling windows.

Lily ignored Tricia that morning except to say, 'Watch your step you little whore and look elsewhere for your lodging. You ain't stopping 'ere. You, or your murdering mother.'

'What am I to do,' pleaded Tricia.

'I don't care. Just get you and your stuff out of 'ere.'

'Please, Auntie Lily, Why can't I stay here? I'll be good, honest. It wasn't my fault.'

'You led him on you little slut. He told me the first time you complained.'

'I didn't. I don't know what you're talking about. I woke up and he was on top of me fiddling.'

'You would say that now he's gone. No more nonsense. Get out!'

It was a cold morning and Tricia ran to work sobbing and pulling Jimmy behind her but already a plan was formulating in her head.

They clocked in with seconds to spare and as soon as she reached the weaving shed she ran weeping to Gertie.

Ignoring the shouts of Snapper to get working Gertie hugged Tricia to her. 'There, there, love. What's the matter?'

Between sobs, Tricia told Gertie the whole story and finished. 'But it wasn't my fault and I don't know what to do.'

'First of all, we have to get you sorted. Wait while I have a word with his nibs.'

Tricia waited as Gertie waddled painfully down the hall to

Snapper and watched as both of them silently conversed with arms waving and agitated gesturing. At last, Snapper banged his cane against his boot and waved her away. For the first time that day, Tricia smiled as Gertie came towards her grinning.

'Right, Tricia, love. You're working with me. Only today, mind. You'll have to fend for yourself tomorrow. Come on, let's get started.'

Tricia worked through the day in a daze and the hours seemed to drag. At last, it was time to go home.

She left Jimmy to fend for himself and ran back to Lily's but stopped short of the house when she saw their belongings piled up in the street. Seething with anger she burst through the front door and ran through to the kitchen and hands-on-hips demanded to know what was going on.

'Why's my stuff out there? You can't do that.'

Lily swung around. 'I can and I have. Get yourself and your rubbish and clear off or I'll call the Police and 'ave you done for trespassing.'

Tricia stood her ground but knew she could do nothing. 'Where do you expect me to go?'

'I don't know and I don't care. Piss off you little tramp.'

Deflated Tricia turned away and then turned back. 'I'm sorry Auntie Lily, truly. I'll go, but can you take our stuff off the street. I promise I'll pick it up as soon as I find somewhere to live. I have an idea who will take me.'

Hands-on hips, Lily said, 'Okay! You have until tomorrow night.'

Tricia's face softened. 'Thank you, Auntie Lily. I'll do my best.'

She made her way slowly out of the house trying to decide what course of action she should take when Lily followed her out and indignantly broke into her thoughts.

'Come on then. You don't think I'm going to put this stuff back on my own do you?'

'Oh, no, I'm sorry. I wasn't thinking.'

It took only a few minutes to put their meagre belongings in the hall. Tricia pulled a shawl around her shoulders and trudged through the cold November evening down the street to the Chapel.

—

Becky, the maid stooped to peer into Tricia's face. 'Hello, Patricia. What are you doing here?'

Tricia stood with her head hung low. She had been practising her speech but she was unable to speak, instead, a silent tear rolled down her cheeks.

Sensing something was wrong Becky reached out to Tricia. 'Come inside. I'll tell the misses.'

Mrs Pickup came shuffling down the hall. 'Who is it, Becky?'

'It's Patricia, Mrs Pickup, and she's crying.'

'Patricia! Whatever is the matter? Wipe your feet and come along into the drawing-room. Becky, have Cook make some chocolate.'

Tricia sobbed and said quietly. 'I'm sorry. I won't trouble you. I'll go.'

'Don't be silly, girl. Come along.'

Tricia followed Mrs Pickup into the drawing-room.

'Sit down Patricia.' She pointed to an armchair in front of the fireplace and gave Tricia a handkerchief. 'Now tell me all about it.'

Tricia related the facts to Mrs Pickup and finished. 'And now I need to find somewhere to live and I didn't know where else to go.'

'You finish your chocolate, Patricia, while I go and speak to my husband. I'm sure something will turn up.'

She left the room and Tricia sat nervously twiddling her handkerchief around her fingers. Five minutes stretched into ten and Tricia guessed they were having a deep discussion about her future and she was sure the longer it went on the worse it would be.

At last, the door opened and Mrs Pickup came in accompanied by her husband. Tricia stood up and Pickup stopped before her.

'Sit down, Patricia. After a long discussion, we have come to a solution to your problem. It won't be easy but it will be favourable to what awaits you out there. Here is the way of it. You will come and work for us in the kitchen and helping Becky in the mornings do the housework. In exchange, we will pay you four shillings a week plus food and lodging. You will share a room with Becky and eat with Cook and Becky. Is that clear?'

Tricia sat quietly for a few moments thinking about the offer and the alternatives and it didn't take her long to realize that she would be better off with the Pickup's than working in the Mill and paying rent in the slums.

'Well, Patricia, what do you think?'

Tricia stood. 'I wish I could tell me, Mam. I'm sorry. My mother. When can I start, sir?'

'You will make yourself comfortable with Becky tonight and tomorrow morning you may borrow the handcart and fetch your belongings, and then you start work immediately. Now run along and sort your arrangements with Becky, and remember, she and Cook are your seniors. Ah... I've just thought. Do you still want to work on Sundays?'

Tricia couldn't believe her ears. Did she want to work on Sundays? For the first time that evening, she smiled. 'Yes, sir, and I'll accept your offer. I'll try my hardest, sir.'

'Good, now run along and ask Cook for something to eat.'

Tricia started towards the door and then stopped.

'Yes, what is it, Patricia,' said Pickup rather abruptly.

She bit her lip unsure of herself before answering. 'Please, Mr Pickup, sir, can I take some warm clothes down to my Mam in the morning before I start work and I'll have to tell the Mill. I'll be quick, honest.'

'I see no reason why not. What do you think, Martha?'

'You may take all morning, Patricia, and call in on Cook before you go. I'm quite sure they won't have fed her very well down there, but you must be ready to work by one o'clock. Is that understood?'

'Yes, Mrs Pickup, Ma'am. I... I...'

'That will be all, Patricia. Go to Cook.'

Tricia enjoyed the substantial meal and Becky made arrangements for her new roommate. She was not happy to have her living space restricted but she knew Tricia and thought they would get along and she was also glad of the help.

Awake early the next morning the habit of dashing down to the Mill engrained in her she told the Mill supervisor of her circumstances and was surprised to receive the balance of both hers and Cath's wages after stoppages for the Mill store. Eleven shillings, but a lifeline.

Her next stop was Auntie Lily's who demanded a week's rent from her. After a bitter argument, Tricia conceded and loaded up the handcart. It took two journeys up to the vicarage. Their big trunk was one load on its own. She picked out the warmest clothes she could find and trekked down to the Bridewell at the Townhall.

Under the eyes of a watchful constable, she was able to give Cath the clothes and take away soiled ones at the same time she pressed the whole nine shillings into her mother's hand.

'No, Tricia. I have no use for it here. You take half as you need to look after yourself now.'

'I have a job, Mam. I'll keep four shillings.'

'Very well, love, but be careful with it and work hard.'

Tricia started crying. 'When will you be coming home?'

'I don't know, love. It is a serious charge your Auntie Lily's made.'

Tricia flung her arms around Cath and sobbed uncontrollably before the constable broke them up.

'Come along now, I've given you long enough.'

Tricia stepped back. 'Bye, Mam. I'll come as soon as I can, promise.'

'I know you will love, but you must look out for yourself now and do your best for Mr Pickup. He's the best chance you have right, and Tricia?'

'Yes, Mam?'

'Don't give yourself to a man before you marry.'

As Cath was led away, Tricia shouted, 'I promise, Mam!'

She walked slowly back to the vicarage not sure what that entailed and huge sobs wracked her body as she wondered if she would ever see her Mother or her Father again.

Tricia saw Cath several times over the next few weeks and noticed her mother was losing weight. She also took along some clean clothes, which Mrs Pickup had allowed her to wash, and she slipped her Mam two shillings on each occasion. It wasn't much but it would go a little way to supplementing her diet or go towards whatever the future held for her.

When the December Quarter Sessions came around Cath was called up before the Judge and Tricia who had been called as a witness by her Mother watched incredulously as Lily told damaging lies about her cousin.

As was the manner of the Court, neither Lily nor Cath had legal representation. Cath was in the dock while Lily stood on the witness stand and accused her. The jury slumped indolently on benches down one side while the red-nosed, the Rt. Hon. Judge Beakly, wearing an unwashed wig, tried to stay awake throughout the proceedings.

He leaned forward, lifted his pince-nez and peering through his cataracts, demanded. 'The nature of your accusation against the defendant is murder is it not?'

'Yes, M'lud.'

'That's a serious charge, Mrs Glover. You know the penalty for murder?'

'Yes, M'lud.'

'As I understand it, the defendant is your cousin?'

'Yes, M'lud, an' she murdered my son.'

'Quite! Be so kind as to give us the details.'

He slumped back and took a long draught from a flagon secreted under his bench.

'It was a Thursday night, Your Honour, and I was sound asleep when I was awoken by scuffling on the landing. Both my husband and me dashed to the door just in time to see her hit my Andy over the head with the broom handle and then push him deliberately down the stairs. We could tell that he was dead.'

'That's a lie,' shouted Cath above the hubbub.

'Quiet, Cartwright.' Beakly reprimanded, 'you'll get your turn shortly.'

'But, Your Honour, she's telling lies.'

'Maybe so, but meanwhile keep quiet or we'll be here all day.'

Cath lapsed into a sullen silence knowing that circumstantial evidence was mounting against her.

'Continue, Mrs Glover.'

'That's it, Your Honour. Like, I said, she pushed him down the stairs. My husband will vouch for that.' She looked at her husband. 'Won't you, Bert.'

He nodded.

'Are you calling the witness to the stand, Mrs Glover?'

'Yes, Your Honour.'

'Very well step down. Herbert Glover! Take the stand please.'

Bert unwillingly stepped forward and took his place.

Beakly leaned forward for a closer look. 'Right, sir, what have you to say for yourself?'

Bert hesitated. 'Err…'

'Get on with it man.'

'Err… Yes, sir. It was like the misses said, sir. We opened the door and saw her.' He pointed at Cath. 'Push our lad down the stairs after she hit him.'

Beakly coughed and dabbed at his mouth the telltale red smear of wine giving up his secret. 'Very well, you may step down—Mrs Cartwright! The evidence against you is quite damning. What have you to say for yourself?'

Cath stood upright and glared at her cousin before speaking. 'Your Honour, I did hit Andy with the broom, but only after I caught him raping my daughter.'

The hubbub rose to a crescendo as this new accusation was debated by the onlookers.

'Silence!' Beakly shouted above the noise. 'I can't hear what's being said and we want justice to be done.'

After a few moments, Cath continued. 'I slept, Your Honour, on a bed made up of cushions on the landing, there being nowhere else for me to go. When I awoke and heard scuffling and muffled screams coming from my daughter's room. She shared a room with her Cousins Andy and Jimmy, you understand. I got up and went into the room and in the gloom, I saw Andy on top of Patricia molesting her. I grabbed the broom which had been left there the night before and set about him.'

Beakly stirred and leant forward. 'One moment; when you say you saw Andy, how did you know it was him if it was dark?'

Cath thought for a moment. 'Err… I didn't at the time. It was just somebody attacking my daughter, but it turned out to be him.'

'I see. Carry on.'

'I just kept hitting him and he scrambled away and pushed past me onto the landing where he tripped on my bedding. I caught up with him and hit him once more and he tumbled away from me and fell down the stairs. I didn't push him deliberately, Your Honour. He tripped at the same time as I hit him in defence of my daughter.'

'He wasn't raping her,' shouted Lily. 'She led him on, the little slut. She did it once before. He told me.'

Beakly lowered his pince-nez and wiped his forehead with the back of his hand.

'Is this true, Mrs Cartwright?'

'No, sir. A couple of months ago he molested Patricia. She was asleep and his actions awoke her. I believe my daughter but what he told his mother after I reported it, I don't know.'

'She's nowt but a common whore,' bellowed Lily.

Beakly sighed. 'Mrs Glover. Control yourself. You've had your say. Let us move on. Mrs Cartwright, have you any witnesses.'

'Yes, Your Honour. I call my daughter, Patricia.'

Tricia, her knees knocking, pushed through the throng and onto the witness stand. She smiled at her mother but didn't feel happy at the prospect of speaking in front of the assembled rabble of onlookers.

Cath smiled back to reassure her. 'Patricia. I want you to tell the Judge what happened that night.'

Tricia turned to look at Beakly, who yawned. His regular imbibing having dulled his awareness. He waved his hand. 'Carry on girl. Be as quick as you can.'

'Err... It was like my Mam said, sir. I was fast asleep when I felt this weight on me. I tried to scream, but there was a rough hand over my mouth. I wriggled but his body held me down and then with his other hand he began pulling my nightie up. That's when I got my arms free to beat him. He took his hand from my mouth and I screamed and then my Mam came in and beat him.'

Beakly looked over his pince-nez. 'Very plausible young lady. Tell me. Are you a virgin?'

'What do you mean, sir?'

'Have you had sex with a man?'

'What's that, sir?'

'On the night in question did your assailant penetrate you?'

'What do you mean, sir?'

'Did he go inside you?'

'He stuck his finger in me down there, sir, and it hurt and I bled. Is that what you mean?'

'Just a finger; nothing else?'

'No, sir.'

'Hrr...umph...' Beakly sat back and thought for a few moments before he declared. 'Mrs Cartwright—it is clear from this young ladies evidence that she has no knowledge in the ways of a whore. However, Mrs Cartwright, you took a man's life. I believe there was no forethought in that deed; therefore, I am reducing the charge to manslaughter. Does the jury agree?'

The assorted men in the jury deliberated for a minute before the foreman announced. 'We agree with your decision, my Lord, and we recommend four years penal servitude.'

Beakly's response was immediate. 'Catherine Cartwright, you have been found guilty of manslaughter. Therefore, the decision of this court is that you will serve four years penal servitude. However, I am commuting that to transportation. You will be taken from here and incarcerated in the prison hulk in Liverpool Bay and from there taken to the colonies for a period of no less than seven years. Take her down.—Next case!'

Tricia was devastated. She turned just in time to see Cath hustled away. 'Mam! Mam!' she shouted.

Cath turned her head at her daughter's pleas and stood her ground long enough to shout over the crowd with tears in her eyes. 'I love you, Patricia. Work hard and stay with the Pickup's if you can. I'll be back. I promise!'

It had taken just eight minutes for Tricia's last anchor with normality to disappear down the steps onto oblivion.

Tricia stepped down from the witness box and walked steadfastly across to her Auntie Lily, and with a strength pulled out of nowhere, said with some determination, 'One day, I will get you.'

She turned away and with her head held high and shoulders back she walked from the court to an unknown future and the prospect of Christmas on her own.

She worked hard to take her mind off her plight but she was disturbed when she took her place in Church the Sunday following her court appearance. She was sure she heard the whispered words—slut, whore and murderer as she walked to her pew.

~~~~~

CHAPTER 5

Becky and Tricia became good friends and one evening curious about Tricia's writing every night before going to sleep Becky said, 'What are doing with all that scribbling, Tricia?'

'I'm writing a book.'

'What on earth does a fourteen-year-old know to be able to write a book?'

Tricia went on to explain about the short stories and poems she wrote for Mr Pickup on Sundays and now she was recording her life for a bigger, proper book one day.

'Oh, that would be interesting,' said Becky, 'I wish I could read and write. I had to go to work early as we had no money on the farm.'

'I'll teach you,' said Tricia. Here's some spare paper and a pencil. First, we'll do the ABC. You have to know your letters to get the sounds that help you read. Copy me. First, we do the capitals and then underneath we'll do the small letters.'

Little by little their friendship gelled. The extra work kept Tricia's mind occupied and time passed quickly but Tricia noticed that her class at Sunday school was getting smaller.

Christmas **1842** was a happy affair. The Pickups invited their staff to join them around the table for dinner after Church. At first, Tricia was quiet and subdued but her earlier misgivings dissipated as the day went on. If life continued like this, she thought, it wouldn't be too bad.

—

1843

Midway through January, the Rev. Pickup called Tricia into his study. 'Sit down, Tricia.'

Tricia cast her mind back trying to think about what she had done. As far as she could recollect she had done nothing but burn extra candles while writing.

'Tricia. I'm not sure how to say this.' Pickup paused for a moment before continuing. 'You have noticed that your Sunday school class is diminishing?'

'Yes, Mr Pickup. I don't know why. Maybe it's because it's winter or they have less money.'

'No, Tricia. It's something more serious. Someone is spreading a rumour that their children are being taught by a scheming teenage whore.' Pickup raised his hand as Tricia was about to butt in. 'I know what you are about to say and I don't believe in gossip either. However, I cannot let the School suffer. Therefore, Patricia, I must release you. You will continue working here in the house as usual.'

Tricia was stunned and sat quietly with the shadow of a tear hanging in the corner of her eye. The loss of the extra money, although not disastrous, was nevertheless a big blow. After a minute she spoke. 'I'm sorry to have caused you any trouble, Mr Pickup. There's no truth in it. Are you sure you want me to stay here in the house?'

'Yes, Patricia. I have talked it over with Mrs Pickup and we agree that you are a hard worker and should continue your employment here.'

'Thank you, sir. I'll try my best. I promised Mam.'

'Tricia. Becky tells me that you're teaching her to read and write. Is this true?'

Tricia realised that he must have questioned Becky about her behaviour during their investigations and she was annoyed but at the back of her mind she realised Becky had to protect her job.

'Yes, sir, and she's doing well but I need some children's books for her to read. My Bronte is too difficult at the moment.'

'Don't worry. She may borrow some of the books from the Sunday School and why don't you use some of your stories?'

'You have all the copies, sir.'

'Aah… Yes. I see. I'll bring them to you. Do you have enough paper?'

'A little more would help, sir.'

'Very well. Now run along and do your work.'

Tricia stood, bobbed, and left the room the diffident tear finally tumbling uncontrolled down her cheek. In her mind's eye, Tricia knew the source of the rumours but was unsure what to do about them.

Later that evening after writing up her journal she queried Becky about what had been said between her and their employer.

'I'm sorry, Tricia, I didn't mean to tell him anything, but he insisted. I only told him what we do here, about us reading and things. Then he asked if you went out at all or if you brought anyone here. You know, fella's.'

'What did you tell him?'

'Nothing, honest. You stay here, except for Sundays when you go to Church. We haven't got time for any hanky-panky, mores the pity.'

'Becky! What's hanky-panky?'

'You know. What you do with fella's.'

'No, I don't.'

'Tricia, they're all saying you are a whore, and you don't know what you do with fella's?'

'That's what I'm supposed to have done with Cousin Andy and I don't know what they're talking about.'

'Oh, dear… Now it's my turn to teach. It's part of growing up. Have you started your periods yet?'

'What are those?'

'You have been under a bush, haven't you?'

Becky went on to give Tricia the facts of life from a women's perspective and finished, '…and, Tricia, seeing' as how you didn't know anything about these things you can't be a whore like they say.'

'They said I was one of them in court Becky and I didn't know what they meant.'

'A whore is a woman that gives her body away.'

'They make money from it?'

Becky looked towards the ceiling and silently asked for guidance. 'Some women are poor and have to do it. When you're in love a man and a woman do like I just told you, but when a man does it to a woman against her will, it's called rape.'

'Have you had this sex, Becky?'

Becky paused and looked thoughtfully at Tricia before answering. 'A long time ago; don't tell anyone, mind.'

'Was it nice?'

'If you do it because you want to—yes, but if it's forced on you like your cousin was doing to you—no. That's enough, let's get some sleep.'

Tricia's mind was in a whirl and she found sleep difficult. Growing up sounded complicated and she decided she didn't want to.

Tricia's periods started the day before her fifteenth birthday which fell on Easter Saturday and on that day the rain which had been falling without enthusiasm ceased. The sun appeared from behind the clouds drying the leaves and cheering the birds and it turned into a bright spring day. For a treat, the Pickup's gave her the day off.

Becky had saved a little of her wages and bought Tricia a second-hand copy of Jane Austen's *'Emma'* and although she missed her Mam and Dad enormously, ignoring the dull ache in her lower stomach, Tricia felt better about life than she had done for a long while.

She asked Becky to cut her hair just below her shoulders and spent the rest of the day altering her clothes. She was not only growing upwards but outwards. Her only disappointment was having to purchase new footwear from her savings.

During the service on Easter Sunday, Tricia thought the congregation was less than usual but dismissed it as one of those things but she did think she heard the hint of a whisper when she walked to her seat.

A few days later, she was asked to go on an errand down to the local grocery store. It was an unusual request but Cook was late and needed something urgent. Tricia didn't mind, anything to break the routine.

She went into the shop and asked for a pound of butter, which the proprietor, Mr Morrison started to cut and wrap when Mrs Morrison came out from the back. She took one look at Tricia, and said sharply, 'What are you doing in 'ere? We don't serve whores—Get out!'

Tricia stuttered. 'Err… Aah… I… I…'

'Steady on, love,' said Mr Morrison, 'that's no way to speak to a young lass.'

'You get on with your work, Tim Morrison. That slut helped kill Mrs Glover's lad with her shenanigans.'

'Awe, that silly rumour, he was a drunken git anyhow.'

'That ain't a rumour. Mrs Glover told me herself.' She turned to Tricia. 'Are you still here? I told you to leave.'

Tricia left the shop crying and ran back to the vicarage. Cook was angry but after Tricia explained what had happened she calmed down and cuddled her with a few comforting words. 'There, there, Tricia. Never mind. There are some nasty folk about. I'll send Becky, but it's queer that rumour's come up again.'

What's that,' asked Tricia.

'Nothing, lass, come on; get on with your work.'

Tricia carried on with some misgiving and even a few kind words from Becky that night didn't allay her fears. She blew the candle out and wished that her Mam was there to help and eventually cried herself to sleep.

—

Tricia cried out and sat bolt upright in bed. Her movements awoke Becky who said rather angrily, 'Will you go to sleep, Tricia. We have to be at work in a couple of hours.'

'I'm sorry, Becky, but I dreamt I saw Mam at the end of the bed and she said—'Goodbye, Tricia. I love you and stick with the old one'—and then she disappeared. I'm worried about her.'

'It was only a dream, Tricia. She'll be alright, you see.'

'You're probably right. I'm sorry.'

'Okay, but go to sleep now, we have a busy day tomorrow.'

Tricia pulled the sheet over her head but sleep wouldn't come. Deep down she knew something was wrong.

—

What was noticeable over the next few weeks was the Sunday congregation getting smaller and smaller. What started as one or two empty seats became a surge until in the middle of May there were no more than a dozen attending and the Sunday school was down to eight.

This disturbed Tricia who had a funny feeling that all was not right in the vicarage. Four weeks after the incident at the grocers, the Reverend Pickup called Tricia into his study once more.

'Sit down, Patricia.'

A chair had already been prepared for her in front of his desk and Tricia feared the worst. She did as she was bid and fiddled with her fingers unable to look him in the eye.

'Patricia,' he continued, 'I get no pleasure from what I am about to say.'

Tricia looked up. 'What have I done, sir?'

'You have done nothing, Patricia. You're a good worker, polite and give me no reason to complain. However, I've been instructed by the Church Elders to dismiss you.'

'Why?'

'You may have noticed the congregation is getting smaller.'

Yes, sir.'

'It is because of a malicious rumour concerning you. It appears that a certain section of our female community are saying that the Church is now employing loose women and suggesting that there is impropriety between you and me, which we both know is untrue. However, I cannot stop lies and conjectures and it would appear that their word is stronger than that of the Lord but also because of decreasing numbers the Church cannot afford to operate. Under those circumstances I have no alternative but to let you go. I will give you an excellent reference and you have until the end of next week to find alternative lodgings.'

Tricia sat stunned, unable to speak. A lonely tear formed and a huge sob wracked her body. She stood, curtsied, left the room without looking back and went to her room and threw herself across her bed. Tears held back by her force of will were released and flowed in abundance.

Becky found her there an hour later. She sat beside her and put an arm around her. 'I'm sorry, Tricia. It won't be so bad. You'll soon find somewhere, you see.'

'But I loved it here, Becky, and I'll miss you. You were such a good friend. I'll miss everybody. You made up for my Mam and I didn't do any of those things they say.'

'I know. We all know, but people are so nasty and old Pickup had to do what he was told.'

'That's all very well, Becky, but what will I do?'

'You have ten days, Tricia. That's more than enough time to find somewhere. Cook says she knows a few houses looking for servants and the Misses gave me this.' She gave Tricia a slip of paper with a few names and addresses on it. 'She said that with their reference you should have no bother.'

Tricia's stopped crying and took the note off Becky. 'I'd better start looking then. Which one of these is best?'

Becky looked over her shoulder, pointed, and said. 'I've only heard of those two, the rest are strangers.'

'I can't go to that one, Becky.'

'Why not? It wouldn't be hard there. That's their townhouse and they don't stay there often.'

'It's James Kearsley. It's him who had my Dad for stealing and he would recognise me.'

'I see. Try the rest. This one's not so far away. Go this afternoon. Splash your face first.'

Refreshed, and wearing her best dress, which she had altered to suit her blossoming figure, Tricia presented herself at the first address on her list. It was a Mr and Mrs Goody who owned the local haberdashers in the main street. The parlour maid showed her in and after waiting a short time she was called upstairs.

When she entered the greeting was pleasant, 'Good morning, child. Please, take a seat.' Mrs Goody pointed to a chair set at an agreeable distance from the armchair she was sat in. She held up Tricia's introductory letter. 'You are interested in the position of under-maid and kitchen assistant?'

'Yes, ma'am.'

'You come with good references, but tell me, why did they dismiss you?'

'They were told to cut expenses by the Church, ma'am.'

'I see. The name Cartwright rings a bell. Please, excuse me one moment.'

She rose and left the room and Tricia wondered what could be wrong. Everything appeared to be going smoothly. After five minutes, Tricia became fidgety and wandered across the room to look at the books aligned neatly in a ceiling to floor bookcase. She was still there when Mrs Goody returned.

Startled at the sudden entrance of Mrs Goody Tricia stammered. 'Aah… Err… I'm sorry but…'

'Don't worry child, you have an interest in books?'

'Yes, ma'am, I love to read when I have the time.'

'You were educated then.'

'Yes, ma'am, I had schooling until I was eleven and then private tuition as a companion to Lord Kearsley's son for over two years.'

'I thought you spoke well.'

Mrs Goody frowned and appeared perplexed. She was reading Tricia's letter and alternately rubbing her chin while in deep thought. Tricia returned to her seat and waited while Mrs Goody made up her mind on whatever problem was bothering her until at last she thumped the letter into her lap and said in a tone which suggested she was reluctant, 'Miss Cartwright, it is with no great enthusiasm that I say this. Taking in the circumstances of our business and the rumours circulating about your character I am sorry, but I cannot in all conscience even though you are suitably qualified, employ you in this household.'

She stood and offered Tricia her letter. 'Take this child and I wish you well for the future. I suggest that you look further afield.'

Tricia held back the tear, which was forming, curtsied, and said, 'Thank you, Mrs Goody, ma'am, for seeing me. I apologise for wasting your time.' She turned and left the room.

Mrs Goody's stood speechless. Not only was she upset by

what she had done but she was being made to feel guilty by a fifteen-year-old.

Tricia trudged back to the vicarage and sat on her bed disconsolate where Becky found her half an hour later.

'Well, how did it go?'

'It didn't.'

Tricia related to her the circumstances of her interview including Mrs Goody's suggestion.

'Do you think I should, Becky, look further afield, that is?'

'You could try Carnforth. It's not too far an' I hear with all that railway building going on there is plenty of work.'

'I'll try one or two here first and then I'll make up my mind.'

'Good idea.'

Tricia sobbed herself to sleep that night but before she dozed off she felt a comforting hand on her shoulder and a quiet voice say—'I'm watching over you, take care, darling.'

Her next two enquiries were equally unsuccessful and for the same reason. Someone had been spreading wrongful rumours about her. She knew they could have come from only one source, which made her more determined to find ways of clearing her name, but how?

In desperation, she determined to go back to the Mill, but where to lodge? Reverend Pickup had obligingly told Tricia she could leave her larger belongings in the carriage store until she needed them, which made moving easier and so with only two days to go before she was required to leave Tricia waited outside the Mill for Gertie.

She did not have long to wait and with barely concealed eagerness she ran across to meet her and fell in beside her as she shuffled down the road.

Gertie greeted her warmly. 'Hello, love, what are you doing here? I heard you had a good job in the local vicarage.'

'I've come to ask a favour, Gertie. Someone is spreading bad things about me and I've lost my job because of it.'

'I've heard those rumours, Tricia, an' nobody who's worked

with you, believes them.'

'Gertie, I have to leave the vicarage tomorrow and I have nowhere to go. Can you help me?'

Gertie stopped and looked Tricia squarely in the face for a few moments before answering. 'Tricia, I don't have a smart place like the vicarage or what you was used to afor you came to these parts, but I would like some company and your rent would help a lot.'

'Oh, could I stay with you, Gertie?'

'I only have two rooms and you'll have to share with me. The rent will be one-shilling and sixpence a week, mind, so you'll have to get a job and I won't be running around after you.'

'You won't have to, Gertie. I'll run around for you, honest.'

'You'd better come and look at the place first before you make your mind up.'

'I'll come home with you now.'

She linked an arm through Gertie's and helped her hobble home on her arthritic joints.

Gertie apologised for their slow progress. 'I'm sorry, dear, but my hips are aching sommat terrible and my bunions are killing me.'

'No matter, Auntie Gertie, I can call you, Auntie? You feel more like an Auntie than Mam's cousin ever did.'

Gertie patted Tricia's hand. 'Yes, you can, love. I like it.'

They attracted many glances as they made their way slowly home, not least of all Tricia whose early pleasant attractiveness was turning into adult femininity.

Tricia's earlier enthusiasm began to wane as they made their way deeper into the slums and her heart sank even further when at last Gertie steered her into the courtyard of a tenement building. The forgotten stench of open sewers once more assailed her and the row of open privies down one side of the yard made her cringe. Someone had tried to give cubicles privacy by draping sacks across as a crude flimsy door. They ducked under lines of drab washing and into the rubbish-strewn stairwell.

'Not far to go, love. I live on the first floor.'

Gertie grabbed the rope, which had been rigged as a crude

banister and pulled herself up the narrow staircase. Tricia followed, and disregarding niceties, gave Gertie a lift by pushing her expansive bottom but she was surprised how easily Gertie negotiated stairs. Maybe going up ninety-five steps every day in the Mill had toned her muscles.

Gertie opened the door with an oversize two lever key and pushed open the door. 'There we are, love. It ain't a palace, but it's home.'

Tricia was surprised at how clean and tidy it was. The walls were a dull grey but Gertie had done her utmost to brighten the place up with a couple of rag carpets and a floral loose cover over a rickety easy chair. She had also placed a coloured cloth over the bucket, which was under the cold tap in a corner.

In the bedroom, Gertie had thrown a brightly coloured quilt over her truckle bed and her belongings were hidden behind a curtain suspended on a piece of rope.

'Have you got a bed, Tricia?'

'Not yet, but I'll get one by tomorrow, Aunt Gertie.'

'Good girl. When you get it, push mine a bit this way, and put yours alongside. You can put your boxes at the bottom and hang your clothes in with mine. Bring your own potty, mind.'

Tricia hugged Gertie, Thank you, Auntie. Mam had a good feeling about you.'

'I'm glad about that, young lady. Now help me get some dinner on.'

'You cooking a meal, Gertie?'

'Yes, love. You have to keep body and soul together. One pot of stew a day is not enough so I spend my money on lots of veggies. I have soup at night with a slice of bread. It helps soften the bread.'

Tricia lit a fire in the grate and they soon had a pot boiling.

Ninety minutes later she left for her last night at the vicarage and she promised Gertie she would bring some food with her. It should work out with two of them providing an income if she could get a job. She didn't like the idea but she would return to the Mill and ask for her old job back.

She had seen an old bed in the carriage house at the vicarage and Mrs Pickup sold it to her for a modest sum. Her bedding she bought in the local flea market and at the same time, she acquired new clogs, bought a mixture of vegetables and potatoes and some tea. She paid a lad idling around the tenement two pence to help her move in and by mid-afternoon, she was finished.

Her savings were diminished, 'But things won't be too bad,' she decided.

~~~~~

CHAPTER 6

Armed with her soup can and 'piece' she arrived at the Mill office at six o'clock sharp. The overseer didn't recognise her and she had to remind him of her earlier visit with her Mam.

'My you've changed. Some fella will be snapping you up in no time. How is your Mam anyway?'

Tricia's head dropped. 'I don't know. I haven't seen her since before Christmas. They took her off to Liverpool very quick after they sent her down.'

'Shame that, an' for a layabout like him. He deserved it, I reckon.'

Tricia hid her surprise. It was the first time anyone had said anything against him and in favour of her Mother. "There's hope yet," she thought.

'You can have your old job but you're grown up now so you'll be on eight shillings a week. Come, I'll take you up to Snapper.'

Tricia sneezed as she set foot on the top step and she was a little disturbed when she saw some of the women mouth something to their neighbour as she walked down the centre aisle. Familiar with the silent talk of the Mills she understood the words, 'There's that Cartwright slut.'

Snapper recognised her and left her with Gertie to get her up to speed and with the parting words, 'You'll be expected to keep up from now on as you're on full pay, understand?' He banged his cane on the end of the nearest machine and bellowed. 'Get to it. We're here to make cotton not stand around bloody talking!'

Tricia stored her belongings and watched as the tackler pulled the lever over to engage the drive belt with her machines. A quick initial snatch and they settled down to a rhythmic clack-clack as the belt joints passed over the drive wheel. From that moment she was too busy to worry about floor gossip.

Time passed quickly but she welcomed the breakfast break.

She flopped down beside Gertie quite out of breath. Five months away from the machines had made all the difference and her legs ached abominably. This worried her as tomorrow she would be operating alongside the old hands and expected to cope with four wide machines.

Dinner time brought another surprise. While she stood waiting in the queue to collect hers and Gertie's stew she saw Auntie Lily ahead of her. She hid behind the lady in front and was relieved when Lily appeared not to notice her.

She paid her two-pence and held her cans out for their ration of soup and frowned when she was given less than usual.

'Excuse me, but could you fill them up, please?'

'Get along with you, you little tramp. Whores ain't welcome here.'

Upstairs she showed Gertie their cans, and said, 'How long has Lily Glover worked here? They're giving us short measure because of her. And they're calling me names.'

'Are they now?' She filled Tricia's can from hers, and said, 'You eat that. I'll be back in a jiffy.'

'But you can't go down, Gertie. It's too hard for you.'

'A couple of flights of stairs hurt no one. Now you wait while I give 'em a piece of me mind.'

The machines had started before Gertie arrived back with a full can. She flopped back in her seat and took a few deep breaths before she spoke to Tricia. 'Don't worry lass they won't be bothering you again. If they do, I'll have me mate Snapper see to them.'

At the end of the day, they caught up with Jimmy as he was leaving.

'You go on, Aunt Gertie. I want to have a few words with my Cousin Jimmy over there.'

'Okay, lass, it won't take long to catch up.'

Tricia thought, "The way my legs feel I won't see you at all."

'Jimmy!'

He looked up startled, 'Hi, Tricia. What are you doin' here?'

'I'm working in the Mill again. Jimmy, why is your Mam working here?'

'She had to work 'cos we lost Andy's money, and yours.'

'Serves her right, who's looking after Amy?'

'That toothless old codger from across the street.'

'I see. Are you alright Jimmy?'

'Aye! My legs are killing me, but that's nowt. They always have.'

'I have to go, Jimmy. Take care.'

'And you, Tricia. I miss you.'

A tear tried to escape but she held it back as she hurried after Gertie.

There had been no rain for a couple of days and with no puddles to avoid, Gertie had made good time and was not far from their block when Tricia caught up with her.

Tricia got the fire going while Gertie prepared the soup and after their meal, Tricia wrote a few words in her diary before she read from her book to Gertie who fell asleep before the end of the first page. Tricia said a quiet prayer for her Mam and Dad and followed her.

She woke before the waker-upper rattled the windows and arrived at the Mill early the next morning to prepare for her first day as a full-time weaver. Two narrow-gauge machines were one thing but four full-size ones were a different prospect altogether.

Snapper showed her which machines were her responsibility and was relieved to see that she wasn't too far from Gertie's station. Six o'clock came and with a long drawn out groan, the leather drive belts took up the strain, gathered speed and the weaving shed rattled into life.

Immune to the noise the women responded, Tricia included, and she found that by watching the others she managed to get herself into a rhythm and as time progressed, she relaxed. She was too busy to notice what went on around her. As the new girl, the silent conversations between the operators didn't include her.

It was after the breakfast break that she felt something was wrong. Two machines having broken threads at the same time was not unusual but to have four go down with multiple threads was rare. In the first instance she took no notice and put it down to coincidence but when it happened again an hour later she had an awful feeling her machines were being sabotaged.

The Snapper came along while she was repairing the damage and cast his eye with obvious displeasure over the silent machines.

'What's going on here? If you can't manage you'll have to go. Come on, pull your finger out!'

'I'm trying my best, Snapper. It must be bad thread for all four to go like that.'

'No such thing in this Mill, lass, the others are coping.'

'I know, Mr Snape. I'll try harder. Honest!'

'Watch it. Much more of this an' you're out, understand.'

'Yes, sir,'

A few minutes work sorted out the problem and once more she settled down onto the rhythm. A little before the Dinner- break she detected a movement at the back of one of her machines and she quickly nipped through the access gap and grabbed one of the cleaning boys about to cut the threads from underneath.

'Got you, what do you think you're doing?'

'I'm sorry missy, but someone is paying' me to do it, honest.'

'Who?'

'Her over there with the blue turban.'

Tricia looked in the direction he was pointing and wasn't surprised to see it was Lily who was unaware that her little plan had come unstuck.

'Right, you little beggar. You say nothing about this but no more cutting or you won't be able to sit down for a week, okay?'

'Yes, missy, I won't say anything.'

'Good. Now get on with you.'

From that moment there was no trouble and the rest of the shift went smoothly. Snapper wandered past and the only sign he showed was a slight uplifting of his permanent scowl.

—

She talked her problem over with Gertie that night and the only action she could think of was to go at Lily face to face, but how?

Her opportunity came quicker than expected. Midway through the following morning she glanced over at Lily through the cotton mist and saw her leaning against her machines which had stopped.

She summoned the dozing Gertie and had her watch her charges while she crept between the rows of machines and came up behind the unsuspecting Lily. Tricia wasn't sure what she was going to do until a few yards away she realised the Lily was resting against the drive wheel talking to Snapper and the tackler who had been working on her broken machine.

Tricia lunged forward and pulled down the clutch lever of the damaged machine. The drive partially engaged and grabbed the sleeve of Lily's dress pulling her down towards the wheels and she screamed in terror. Just as Lily's arm became ensnared between the pulley and the belt, Tricia eased the pressure. Lily was trapped, and in obvious pain and blind panic overcame her when she saw Tricia holding the lever. Another yank and she could lose her arm or be pulled up to the ceiling only to be dropped onto the moving machinery and probably lose her life.

Snapper went to intervene and Tricia shouted, 'Stay back or I'll rip her arm off.'

He stopped and the commotion brought other onlookers. Machines were abandoned as word spread around. Above the clatter of the machine floor, Tricia yelled, 'Tell them the truth Auntie Lily, or I'll pull this lever and up you go.'

As if to emphasise her words she put a little pressure on the lever and a little more of Lily's arm was pulled into the vice-like grip of the belt and wheel.

Lily's screams became louder. 'What is it you want?'

'Tell them the truth about me and your Andy. Tell them it wasn't my fault. Hurry or I'll yank this lever all the way.'

In obvious pain, Lily shouted, 'It wasn't her fault.'

'Louder! Lily. We can't hear you.'

She pulled the lever enough to pinch Lily's arm a little more.

'Aagh… Okay. Stop it please. I'll tell everything.'

Tricia eased the pressure slightly. By now the whole shed had gathered around. They all knew of the injuries sustained when someone became trapped in a belt.

'I'm waiting,' said Tricia.

'It was my Andy's fault. He tried to rape her that morning. She's clean and no whore.'

'What about my, Mam,' screamed Tricia?

'I lied,' replied Lily, 'she did hit him but he tripped. It was his own fault. I would have done the same for my daughter.'

'Now tell Snapper about my machines.'

'It's right, Snapper. I paid a lad to sabotage her.'

Snapper stepped between them. 'Alright, Tricia, you can let go now. Come on everybody get back to work. The fun's over.'

Tricia released the lever and the tackler eased the drive wheel back to free Lily's arm. While everyone was milling around, Tricia went to Lily's side and whispered in her ear. 'Get yourself around the town and clear my name because if you don't I'll kill you the next time.'

Lily glanced at Tricia and stepped back as she saw the hate in her eyes. Such a transformation from the little girl she had known.

She nodded. 'I'll do that. I'm sorry, truly.'

'Sorry, doesn't bring Mam back.'

Tricia made her way over to her station with tears in her eyes and she muttered to herself, "Nothing will bring me Mam back—Nothing!"

Ten minutes later Snapper paused as he passed Tricia. 'That took some guts, lass, but watch out, you've made an enemy there.'

Tricia didn't stop working, but said over her shoulder, 'Thanks, Snapper, but I had to do something for people to find out the real truth.'

'You did that. Now get on with your work, I won't have any slackers on my watch.'

There was a hint of humour in his voice and Tricia had a little smile to herself.

The immediate effect of her actions came when she went down for her midday meal. Her can was filled to overflowing and the canteen lady pushed an extra chunk of bread into her apron pocket as a quiet way of saying, "Sorry."

Back at her machines, she shared her extra bread with Gertie and as the day wore on she became included in the silent conversations but they were mostly of the adult variety, which she, for the most part, didn't understand.

Six o'clock came and Tricia was surprised not to see Jimmy hanging around the factory gate. She shrugged and helped Gertie on the slow trudge home.

She lit the fire and while Gertie tidied up she soon had a pan of broth made from the weekend's leftover cooking. While they waited she broached Gertie about Snappers warning. 'What do you think, Gertie? Snapper said I should be on my guard but my Aunt appeared okay when we left.'

'I think he's right, child. She's a bad one that one and because of the humiliation, I shouldn't wonder if her hate doesn't smoulder. Saying is one thing but doing it is something else. Be watchful.'

When dinner was over and the washing up done, Gertie dozed in her battered rocking chair while Tricia wrote up her journal and added a little more to her latest children's story.

At nine o'clock she tumbled into bed and pondered over Snappers warning before tiredness overcame her.

~~~~~

CHAPTER 7

1845

The next eighteen months were without incident. Her prospects around the town had improved and in Church she was welcomed as one of the congregation. The Reverend Pickup asked her if she would return to the Sunday school as his assistant but her loyalty to Gertie and a stubborn reaction to what she considered hypocrisy made her decline the offer although the extra money and the offer of a square meal tempted her.

There had been a rumour around the factory for a while that things weren't going well in the cotton industry and one Monday morning there was heightened excitement as the story spread around the sheds that the owners were going to visit.

Until dinnertime, there had been no sign of them but as Tricia was about to enter the canteen she heard voices speaking French. She stopped and listened attracting some strange looks from the other women clamouring to get their meal. One of the girls stopped, and said, 'What are you doin', lass. Get thee dinner.'

Tricia held her hand to her ear, and uttered, 'Shush, I'm listening,' and she pointed into the canteen.

The girl paused for a moment and cocked an ear. 'It's double Dutch to me,' she said, 'how can thee understand that?'

'It's French and I learned it, see. Now get on while I listen some more.'

She stayed by the door for five minutes longer when she realised the voices were becoming closer. Hitching up her skirt she pretended to rush into the canteen as if she was late and bumped into Lord Kearsley and two guests. He gave her a queer look as she muttered her apologies with her head down and made her way to the counter.

As the canteen assistant took her can Tricia glanced towards the door and was glad to see Kearsley's back disappearing.

'You're late, lass, 'said the woman, 'where've you been?'

'I was listening to Kearsley talking to those gentlemen.'

'They speak a different language so we can't understand.'

'It's French and I learnt to speak it when I was little.'

'What did they say?'

'They're going to cut our wages and make us work an extra hour a day and they want to take the meat out of our dinner. Tell everyone who comes in and I'll spread the word on the floor.'

'Are you sure, lass? You're not making it up?'

'Did it sound something like. *'Nous allons réduire les salaires et retirer la viande de leur régime alimentaire.'*

'It sounds like sommat they said.'

'It's what I told you. They're going to cut our wages and food.'

'Good enough for me. Here's your pot, go and tell them upstairs.'

Tricia dashed upstairs narrowly avoiding Kearsley again as he came out of the spinning shed.

Breathlessly she ran across to Gertie and told her what she had heard. The old lady calmed her down and made her repeat it.

'Right, child, finish your dinner before it's too late while I spread the word around. They tried it once before and still they don't know us Lancaster people.'

An hour later the machines ground to a stop as the tacklers closed each one in turn and the word spread quickly that there was to be a mass meeting in the yard.

Gertie thrust Tricia's wrap at her, and said, 'Come on, lass, now we'll show 'em.'

Clutching their shawls and coats tight around them against a biting autumn wind the workers assembled in the yard. The earth-shattering vibrations of the machinery changed to the solid thump of idling steam engines when a vociferous young man with a bright red neck scarf and flat cap jumped onto a wagon and began to wave his cap shouting for quiet at the same time.

The babbling voices changed to an angry rumble as he began to speak.

'Fellow workers!' He pointed towards the offices. 'I've had

word that they're planning to cut our money. Are we having any?'

'NO!' came the angry response.

'Right then, but I'm not going to tell you. Tricia Cartwright is going to tell us what she heard direct from the horse's mouth. Tricia, where are you? Come on Tricia, don't be shy.'

Tricia cowered in horror. She didn't want this. How could they, it wasn't her fault.

'Tricia, Tricia,' chanted the crowd and someone behind her pushed her forward until she stood by the wagon. The young man looked down. 'Come on, love, there's nothing to fear. Give us your hand.'

He reached down, took her outstretched hand, and pulled her up onto the makeshift speaking platform.

'Okay, lass, don't be shy. Tell us what you heard, but hang on a sec.'

He turned to the crowd and waved his arms. 'Quiet, you rabble, let's hear what she has to say.'

He looked down at Tricia, and said, 'Amy from the canteen says you overheard Lord Kearsley speaking and you understood him as you speak French. Is that right?'

Tricia clung to his arm for support. 'Yes,' she said quietly.

'Someone in the front shouted. 'Speak up, we can't hear you.'

The lad gave her a nudge. 'Come on, lass, at the top of your voice.'

'I speak French,' shouted Tricia, 'and I heard every word they said.'

'And what was that,' said her mentor.

A warm feeling came over her. Tricia took a deep breath and she found hidden strength from somewhere and she shouted, 'They're planning to cut our money, take the meat from our mouths and make us work longer hours.'

There was an angry rumble from the crowd which changed to shouting and jeering.

Tricia waved her arms to quieten them. 'And that's not all. They're planning to put up prices in the Company store and make us pay more for our dinner and it was suggested that we should only be paid in Company tokens.'

This last remark turned the whole meeting from an angry crowd to a tumultuous revolt.

Their leader who was still holding Tricia's arm shouted. 'Are we having that—NO! Are we going to—STRIKE!—What do you say?'

There could only be one answer and he got it. 'STRIKE! STRIKE! STRIKE!' they chanted and en-masse they turned towards the gate and surged forward chanting as they did so.

Tricia tugged at the young man's sleeve. 'Yes, love?'

'What's a strike, mister?'

'How old are you, Tricia?'

'Seventeen.'

'Aye, you're a bit naive aren't you? First, let's get down from here and I'll tell you as we walk.'

He jumped down and Tricia sat on the edge and they both giggled as he grabbed her by the waist and swung her down.

'You're a good looking lass, sixteen you say?'

'Seventeen.'

'My name's Jack, Jack Young, it sounds better than mister. Besides I'm only a few years older than you.'

Tricia pulled her wrap tighter around herself and they walked side by side towards the gate while Jack explained their action.

'A strike, Tricia, is when all the workers in a factory all stop work and shut the place down over some grievance. You heard Kearsley say they are going to cut wages and other stuff and we don't like it so we walk out in protest.'

'Is that legal, Jack?'

'No, but it's the only weapon we have. I could go to gaol.'

As they were about to walk through the gate a voice called out. 'Hey, you two, hold it there.'

Tricia and Jack both turned towards the voice and saw Lord Kearsley and his Partners accompanied by Snapper approaching. They stopped and waited and Jack could feel Tricia quivering nervously beside him.

'Stick close, girl. You'll be okay.'

Kearsley stopped before them and immediately berated them for their action.

'You,' he said pointing with a shooting stick at Jack. 'I'll have you deported for this, and you young lady. You'll never work again in this town.'

Jack snatched his cap off and made to raise his hand palm outward when one of Kearsley's associates jumped forward with a pistol in his hand.

Jack took a pace back. 'Hold on,' he shouted, 'I mean only to talk. Lord Kearsley! You're planning to drop our wages, up our hours and the prices in the store and cut our food. What are we supposed to do?'

'Whoever told you this claptrap? It's a lie.' He pointed to the crowd lingering outside the gates. 'Get them back to work.'

'Lord Kearsley, sir. You were discussing it in the factory with your friends here.'

'How could you possibly know that?'

'Young Tricia here speaks French, sir. She overheard you.'

Kearsley looked at Tricia. 'Do I know you?'

'Patricia Cartwright, sir.'

Realisation dawned on Kearsley and he knew he had been rumbled. 'Hardcastle taught you well. Wait there the pair of you.'

He turned away and shepherded his visitors out of hearing. They talked for several minutes before Kearsley called Snapper over. After a few moments of nodding and talking Snapper returned to Tricia and Jack but before he spoke he removed his hat and scratched his head in deep thought. Finally coming to a decision he said, 'Get them back to work, Young. His lordship will take no action if you do that and he promises to keep everything as it is, but you've got to make up the lost time.'

'Okay, Snapper,' said Jack, 'but for how long?'

'I don't know, he didn't say and it's not for me to guess. Tricia, come with me.'

Jack touched Tricia on the arm. 'I work in Number 1, I'll see you around.'

Tricia nodded, 'I will look forward to it.'

Snapper went to put his arm around Tricia's shoulder but thought better of it as they walked across the yard towards the factory. 'Tricia, you were not to know, you're only a child and if I was you I'd be looking elsewhere for work as there's bound to be trouble after this. Stay on 'til you find something but be careful and don't go listening to other people's conversations. Got it?'

'Yes, Snapper, and I'll work hard, honest.'

'I know, lass.' He immediately changed his hat to that of an overseer. 'Now get up there on the shop floor. Go on!'

Tricia laughed and skipped away. Word spread quickly and two hours later the factory was back up to speed but they worked late into the night to make up for lost production.

Before they crawled into bed that night, with the prospect of only four hours sleep, Gertie said, 'Tricia, Snapper told me what went on today and you'd best heed his warning. This won't be the end of it mark my words. Here, take this and carry it every day.'

She gave Tricia a short, ivory-handled stiletto knife on a long twine lanyard.

'What do I need that for, Gertie?'

'It's what I carried when I was on the streets in case of trouble.' Tricia's eyes widened at the revelation, but she said nothing. 'In the morning,' continued Gertie, 'we'll put a slit in the seam of your skirt so you can put your hand through and this will be tied around your waist and dangling underneath. Now get to bed, it'll be morning soon enough.'

She fell asleep immediately with a different vision of Gertie.

~~~~~

CHAPTER 8

After a quick alteration to Tricia's skirt they plodded through darkened streets made worse by the soot-blackened autumnal drizzle. The wet cobbles reflected the dim candlelight coming through shielded windows and the street gas lamps gave out a dull yellow cone and they found their way by instinct. As they got nearer to the Mill more people joined them but Tricia was uneasy.

Some sixth sense told her she was being watched. She shuddered and looked around but could see nothing unusual only the familiar faces of other workers, who, like herself had covered their heads and were crouched down shuffling through the rain.

When they arrived at the Mill she told Gertie to go ahead and pretended to fiddle with her clogs while she took a few moments to look around. She dismissed the notion as she spotted nothing untoward and went into work.

The climb up the stairs made her breathless as she methodically counted each step, 'ninety-three, ninety-four, ninety-five...' She pushed open the door of the weaving shed and her fatigue left her as cheers from her work colleagues greeted her. As she walked to her station they crowded round and patted her on the back and said things like, 'Well done, lass,' or 'that was a grand thing tha did there, girl.'

A wayward tear ran down her cheek but the moment only lasted a little while as Snapper banging his cane against his leg chased them to their machines.

'Let's be havin' yer. Get to it now!'

His tone and his manner were not his usual brusque self, but as they turned away some lingered a moment, to say, 'Well done, lass,' and Gertie came up behind her and gave her a quick hug.

The tacklers slammed over the clutches and another long slog began which would only end when the clock had gone full circle and darkness had settled once more.

Two minutes after six the shed was rocking again to the

rhythmic slap of the drive belts and Snapper wandered past Tricia's work station. 'Well done, lass, but think on what I said,' and he was gone. Unknowingly she had protected his job as well as her co-workers.

During the breakfast break, the congratulations were no less enthusiastic but all enquiries about Jack Young drew a blank, which disturbed her, and it was not long before the incident and the measures mentioned by Lord Kearsley were forgotten as the daily grind of fighting for every living morsel carried on.

At going home time the rain had stopped and with Snappers warnings at the back of her mind she again had that uneasy feeling that she was being watched as they made their way home. Gertie dismissed it as Tricia's vivid imagination but to make sure she lagged behind but it was difficult to discern features under the poor street lighting and she saw nobody suspicious.

'Nay, lass, there were nowt there, you would have seen 'em. I shouldn't have said anything. Giving you that knife has got your head working overtime.'

'It's a funny feeling, all the same, Gertie.'

She slept fitfully that night as weird dreams flashed through her brain and the next morning she unwillingly clambered out of bed to get ready for work.

Mercifully, it was dry and Tricia buoyed by the reassurance of the knife banging against her leg felt relieved, and her feelings of apprehension disappeared as she got nearer to the Mill.

'Maybe, Gertie was right,' she thought.

—

When the evening hooter sounded an exhausted Tricia stumbled down the stairs eagerly looking forward to her bed but she was still mystified about the absence of Jimmy by the gate.

"I wonder what's happened," she said to no one in particular.

She was miles away with her thoughts when—'Boo!' Her body jerked involuntarily with fright. She turned to see who her tormentor was, and through her weariness, she forced a grin when she saw it was Jack Young.

She scolded him, 'What did you do that for? You near

frightened me to death,'

'Sorry, lass, just a bit of fun. I've been trying to catch you but you're hard to get hold of. Even with the old woman, you walk quickly.'

'Yes, Gertie fair scoots along especially going home.'

'Where is she tonight, Tricia? I can call you, Tricia?'

'Yes, you can, and Auntie Gertie will be along in a minute. Can I call you Jack?'

'Please do. Tricia, can I walk you home?'

At that moment, Gertie joined them. 'Hallo, hallo, what's going on here,' she said eying Jack up and down.

'Auntie Gertie, Jack wants to walk me home.'

'Oh, he does, does he? She wagged a finger at Jack. 'You may walk Tricia home young man but you will follow me and no hanky-panky.'

Jack did a mock bow and replied whimsically. 'There'll be no messing about, I promise, Auntie Gertie.'

She muttered, 'Cheeky bugger,' and turned away but not before Tricia saw her smile.

Jack and Tricia fell in behind her and Tricia blushed but enjoyed the thrill as Jack took her hand and slowed their pace until Gertie was some way ahead.

'Tell me, Tricia Cartwright; is Gertie really your Aunt?'

'No, we adopted each other when I became homeless, but not in a legal sense, and we share two rooms. It's not posh but it suits us and because there are two of us we eat pretty well. What about you?'

'I work in the spinning shed in №1 but I know all about you giving it to that Lily.'

Tricia flushed. 'Oh, that. It was nothing, but I had to do something to clear my name. Because of her, I was homeless.'

As they dawdled behind Gertie, Tricia told Jack about her adventures since they had arrived in Lancaster. 'And now you know as much as me, Jack Young. What about you?'

At that moment, they turned into the yard of the tenement. Jack stopped took his cap off and pulled Tricia back. Holding his cap across his chest, he said, 'I know you're tired, lass, but I want to know. Can I walk you home every night?'

Before she replied, Tricia looked across at Gertie who was waiting by the door. 'Go up, Auntie, I won't be a minute,' she called and then turned back to Jack. 'I don't mind but tomorrow you must tell me about yourself.'

He kissed her on the forehead. 'I'll be there, lass. You try getting rid of me, and with a loud, 'Wha-Hey!' he ran up the lane without glancing back.

—

Tricia awoke the next morning and the dreary process of getting up and going to work did not dampen her spirits, even the walls looked whiter she thought as she joined the others in the mad dash to beat the six o'clock deadline.

But nothing would make the clock go quicker and the day dragged interminably on. Not even the brighter mood of her compatriots lifted her and by the time the hooter signalling the end of work sent its deep-throated song through the Mill she was dancing in frustration.

She hurried down the stairs wishing people out of the way as she ran for the gate but her heightened emotional feelings were dashed when Jack wasn't there. Fiddling with her shawl she walked backwards and forward by the gate until Gertie joined her.

'What's up, lass, hast thou been let down?'

'I'm sure he'll come, Gertie. He's busy or something.'

'Don't waste your time they're all the same. Say one thing and mean another. Come along.'

'You go ahead, Gertie, I'll wait a little longer.'

'Mind on and come sooner than later. It's no good for a girl to be on her own at this time of day.'

'Just a couple of minutes, Gertie, I promise.'

'Okay, I'll get the supper on but be careful.'

Gertie shuffled away and Tricia's head drooped as she stared at her feet while her head whirled with excuses for Jack's absence. "Maybe he's working late," or, "he's forgotten," the list was endless. Stretching the promised two minutes as much as she dared she turned despondently for home dragging her feet and kicking out at pieces of rubbish or scattered mud in anger at the loss of another friend.

She was more than halfway when she heard running steps behind her and her mood changed and then she panicked mindful of Gertie's warning and immediately began to walk faster. As the steps came closer, her pace quickened further until she was almost running when a voice called out, 'Tricia, stop! It's me, Jack.'

Not believing her ears she slowed wishing it to be true when he called again, 'Tricia, love, it is me, honest.'

This time she recognised his voice. She stopped and turned, and in the evening light, she could see a lanky figure grasping his cap in his hand running pell-mell towards her. She pulled her shawl tight around her and ran towards him and when they met she was laughing with joy.

Jack teetered to a stop in front of her and threw his arms around her, uttering breathlessly, 'I'm right sorry, lass, some bugger hid my boots. I'll kill the blighter when I find him.'

Tricia clung tightly to him. 'I've got you now,' she said, 'I was so upset because I thought you'd forgotten or maybe didn't mean it.'

Jack could feel her shaking as he held her and he gently eased her back and kissed her forehead. 'I'll never forget thee, lass, not as long as I live.'

She looked into his eyes and she could see he meant it.

A strange feeling enveloped her, one she'd never felt before, and as if a magnet was pulling her she reached up to him. As their lips were about to join he hesitated and kissed her on the nose instead. Inside she felt deflated but then, he said, 'I think I love you, lass, but I'm not taking advantage because you're still young. Come on, I'll walk you home. I bet Aunt Gertie's going potty.'

He took her hand and they wandered slowly through the summer dusk to Tricia's place. They had only gone a small way when Tricia turned to Jack and said, 'Jack, you haven't told me where you live.'

'Have I not? I live up by St. Thomas's.'

'Jack, that's back out of town. What about your supper? You're already late.'

'I'll get the leftovers. It's okay.'

'No, it's not, you can share ours. Stay there I'll ask, Gertie.'

The decision had been made and Jack stood with his mouth open ready to reply when Tricia dashed into the block and up the stairs. Gertie was stooped over the pan on the fire when Tricia burst into the room.

'Auntie Gertie, can Jack stop for supper? Please, he has a long way to go.'

Gertie stood up and sternly placed a hand on each hip. Tricia's face dropped as she feared the worst but Gertie, seeing her pretence at anger had worked broke into a smile. 'Just this once, lass, but give us a minute to tidy up.'

Tricia sprang forward and hugged Gertie. 'Oh, thank you, Auntie, but I can't promise about the once. Err…, what was that?'

'What, love, I never heard nowt.'

'I thought I heard someone cry out.'

'It's probably those Milligan kids playing on the stairs.'

'Aye, you're probably right.'

She ran out of the door before Gertie could reply and down the stairs as quick as she could in the darkness and ran laughing out into the yard but stopped abruptly. Jack had disappeared.

'Jack, Jack, where are you? Don't mess about, you can stay.'

She wandered in and out of the drab washing hanging on the lines calling his name over and over without success and she wrinkled her nose as she did a quick peek into the latrines which revealed nothing.

'JACK!' she shouted as loud as she could. 'Stop messing, where are you?'

She stopped and a dejected tear rolled down her cheek when she noticed a small bundle lying on the floor under the washing. Her curiosity got the better of her and she walked across the yard and picked it up. She recognised it instantly as Jack's cap.

'That's odd,' she thought, 'he would never leave this behind.'

She searched around some more and noticed scuff marks in

the dried up dirt on the yard floor. Puzzled she followed them and in the street against a wall she found Jack's red neck scarf and further down the street she saw a boot. She ran over and picked it up and sobbing she dashed back to Gertie. In her haste, she pushed the door to their apartment hard and it crashed against the wall marking the plaster with the coat hook.

'Gertie, Gertie, I think something awful has happened.'

'What do you mean, Tricia, and where's, Jack?'

'That's what I mean, Gertie, he's gone missing but he's dropped his cap and neckcloth and I found his boot.' She showed Gertie the items. 'He would never go without these and there are marks in the yard, like there's been fighting.'

'I knew there'd be trouble. Me and Snapper were only talking about it yesterday. You keep that knife handy, girl, and don't go nowhere without me or someone you know.'

'Who can it be, Gertie?'

'I don't know, but you and Jack upset the bosses and they don't like people who lead the other workers like that. You'd best look somewhere else for work.'

'But, where?'

'You heard what Kearsley said. You will never get a job hereabouts. It will have to be out of town. Snapper will give you a reference. Try Preston, it's only ten hours or so on the packet boat down the canal. Let's have supper and get to bed, I'm knackered.'

―

Tired and depressed Tricia dragged herself out of bed and dourly toyed with her food, meagre though it was, until Gertie urged her to eat, and said, 'pull your finger out, lass, you've all day to go yet.'

'You're right as always, Auntie, but I don't know what to do.'

'You must first work your notice as you want all the money you can lay your hands on. I'll speak to Snapper.'

Tricia hugged Gertie, 'Thank you, Auntie; I don't know what I'd do without you.'

'Never mind that, come on, we're late.'

On Gertie's urging, Tricia ran on ahead and just scraped through the gate on time but her depression increased and she was sobbing by the time she completed the long climb up the stairs. Caught in two minds she decided not to mention Jack's disappearance and waited instead for Gertie to speak to Snapper but she hadn't seen Gertie since she had clocked on that morning.

At dinnertime, she forced herself to eat and halfway through Snapper called her over to a corner of the shed. Her thoughts were in a whirl as she imagined all sorts of things which may have happened but Snapper showed his humane side, when he said, 'Tricia, Gertie fell and bashed her head so I've sent her home but not before she told me what's happened and here's what you do. I have a cousin working in Horrocks Yellow Mill in Preston and I'll give thee a letter to take to him and don't worry, they use the same machines as here, but you'll have to do your notice which means working 'til Friday night. Now finish your dinner and get back to work and I'll see you later.'

'Oh, thanks, Snapper, and I won't let you down.'

'If tha does I'll come personally and spank yer. Now get on.'

Tricia laughed and hurried over to her machines feeling in a more hopeful frame of mind but now she had Gertie to worry about.

Six o'clock couldn't come quick enough and as she grabbed her things and made ready to dash for the stairs Snapper shoved a letter into her hand and walked away.

She stuffed it into her pocket and ran home thankful that the early October evenings still afforded her enough light for her to see her way along the cobbled streets. She ran into the yard and up the stairs calling Gertie's name and burst into the room only to fall headlong over the inert body of Gertie.

She screamed, as she crawled over to Gertie and shook her shoulder. 'Gertie, Gertie, wake up, wake up, please.'

Tricia sobbed when she got no response and more in hope than anything else she shook Gertie again. 'Come on, Auntie, wake up, please,' but the stiffness in Gertie's body and her pallor told her the worst. Tricia sat back with a jerk and rested her head against the wall. 'Oh, dear, what do I do now?'

Then she heard a shout and a clatter from the stairs and

jumped to her feet. 'Mrs Milligan will know,' she said to herself. She ran from the room and up the stairs all the while calling, 'Mrs Milligan! Mrs Milligan!'

A gaunt woman with the pasty pallor of a life hidden from the sunlight in the Mills came to the door of her flat wiping her hands on a cloth. 'What is it, whose shouting my name?'

Mrs Milligan looked old and worn but Tricia knew she was only twenty-six. Life in the Mill and three children had ravaged her. 'Oh, it's you, Tricia, what's the matter?'

'Can you come, Mrs Milligan, it's Gertie. I think she's dead and I don't know what to do.'

'Wait a moment while I take the pan off the fire.'

Moments later, she joined Tricia and they made their way into Gertie's flat. Mrs Milligan touched Gertie's neck and stood back. You're right, lass, she's dead. You'll have to call the Peelers. I'll get our Willy to fetch them. What happened?'

'I don't know, my boss at the Mill said she'd had a fall and banged her head and he sent her home and I've just got back.'

'Right, lass, don't move her and wait here while Willy goes for the Peelers. Would you like a cup of tea? It's only weak, mind.'

'Oh, thanks, Mrs Milligan but I'll pass the time doing it for myself to take my mind off it.'

'Okay, but if you want anything let me know.'

'Okay, I'll do that.'

Mrs Milligan laid her hand on Tricia's shoulder and gave her a gentle squeeze. 'I'm sorry, lass, she was a lovely lady. Can you manage on your own?'

'I think so. I was moving on soon anyway but I was going to take Gertie with me.'

'Leaving, aye? Anywhere nice?'

'I was looking at…' Tricia shivered. Alarm bells were ringing, and she said, 'I hadn't made my mind up but Gertie said Scotland would be nice.'

'I've heard it's cold up there. Never mind, take care. I'll go and get Willy.'

Mrs Milligan turned away and left Tricia to her own devices

and it was some time before the Police arrived. A Sergeant followed by a Constable arrived breathless at Tricia's door and when Tricia opened the door, they saw the body of Gertie.

'My, my, what's happened here?' he said as he felt for the notepad in his uniform pocket.

Biting her lip Tricia recited the days' events leading up to finding Gertie and when she had finished the Sergeant walked around the prostrate figure a few times and bent over and looked closer when out of the blue, he said, 'She's had a bang on the head. You didn't hit her did you?'

Tricia was flabbergasted. 'Wha..., what do you mean?'

'Did you argue over food or money and hit her?'

'No... No, I told you, she fell at work and banged her head. Ask my boss, Snapper.'

'Oh, Snapper, I know him. Are you sure now?'

'Yes, mister, I told you.'

'Okay, that'll do. Cover her up and we'll put her over by the wall until the mortuary boys get here.'

Tricia took a blanket off Gertie's bed and the two policemen gently lifted the body over to the wall and with a consoling pat on her shoulder they left Tricia to contemplate her next move.

Two catastrophes in two days were too much and Tricia sat on the end of her bed and cried when suddenly something snapped inside her. She stood up, dried her tears, and set about making her supper and while it was cooking she began to collect her things and pack them. With the kidnapping of Jack, sitting idle in Lancaster was not on the cards as she felt it wouldn't be long before they came for her. It was unfortunate but she would have to leave without her pay.

After supper, the mortuary men came and took Gertie away and Tricia paid them one pound ten shillings to look after her and then on an intuition she began guiltily to search through Gertie's things and in her mattress found her hidden hoard.

'My, my, the wily old devil,' she said to herself, 'Loose change and two gold sovereigns that makes eight pounds and thirteen shillings.'

What was left after paying the bill for Gertie added to her own meagre savings came to over ten pounds and that night she said a silent prayer for Gertie and her Mam. The rest of the evening was spent packing as much of Gertie's useful effects with her own belongings and that done she decided her first move in the morning would be to buy a handcart.

~~~~~

CHAPTER 9

October 1845

Tricia arose early but without the rush to get to the Mill, she was able to take her time and plan her day. She didn't indulge but had her usual breakfast before wrapping up against the bad weather. Her first stop was the flea market behind the Lune Iron Works.

She saw what she wanted immediately and she picked up the handle and swung it side to side a few times before kicking each wheel. The rims were new and the woodwork in good fettle but she rubbed her chin and hummed and haahed until the stallholder became fed up, and said, 'Well, are you having it or what?'

She tilted her head slightly and looked at him. He was an elderly man with a few days growth of beard who looked kindly enough. 'It looks good. How much?'

'One guinea'

'Too much, five shillings'

'Nah! You're kidding. The wheels are worth more than that.'

She shook her head and made to walk away when he took hold of her arm and stopped her. 'I'm sorry; miss, but I need the cash. How about seventeen and sixpence?'

She looked at him and his eyes were pleading, and she said, 'Six shillings.'

'Oh! Miss, you are hard. How's about fifteen? It's got a lock and bar as well.'

He showed her how it fitted through the front wheels.

'That's more than I get in a week.' She rubbed her chin and was about to speak, when he said, 'Thirteen bob, miss.'

She smiled. 'I'll take eight.'

'Done!' he said, 'and you're getting a bargain.'

They shook hands and she pulled a little canvas bag from her pocket and counted out the money. 'There we are. sir. Tell me, how long are you here for?'

He swung an arm pointing to a circle of household items around him. 'Until I sell these, miss, or one o'clock.'

She pointed. 'Is that a canvas cover for the cart?'

'Yes, miss.'

'I'll give you sixpence for it and another sixpence if you look after them until I get back.'

'How long will that be?'

'I'm going to the packet boat and then I'll be straight back'

'Okay, miss, but the packet boat has finished.'

'Are you sure?'

'You best check but be as quick as you can'

She gave him the extra shilling and started the long walk up to the canal pleased that this walk was not the drag to the Mill. Although she had been living there for several years she had never paid any attention to her surroundings but as she walked quickly through the urban district along North Road towards the town centre she was able to see Lancaster for the country town it really was.

At the Horseshoe junction, which she passed every day on the way to work, she crossed over into the narrow gorge which was Penny Street and she saw the open space in reality for the first time. Before it had been head down helping or shielding Jimmy or wearily with eyes half shut struggling home after a twelve-hour shift. In Penny Street, she saw shops and tradesmen's outlets dotted amongst the houses and children with their mothers out for the daily shop.

She pushed on up to Penny Street bridge over the canal and into the Packet Boat lodge where she was met by a jovial well-built man whose waistcoat was stretching its buttonholes to the limit. Tricia giggled as she imagined what would happen if he didn't wear a fob watch and chain across his middle but maybe the wide leather belt with a huge brass buckle was helping.

He smiled, and said, 'What can we do for you, miss?'

'I want to go on the packet boat to Preston.'

'I'm sorry, missy, but the packet is finished. The Canal Company run trains now.'

'Oh, dear, what can I do?'

'When do you want to go, missy?'

'Tomorrow and I have a handcart'

'Cross over the road and down to your left and you can catch the train in the station there.'

'Is it cheap?'

'Two shillings and sixpence.'

'And the cart?'

'That would be another shilling.'

He saw her face drop as she turned away and he called her, 'One minute, missy, if you don't mind slumming it a little you can travel on one of the limestone barges.'

'How does it work?'

'They like to make a bit extra on the side above what the contractor pays so you gives the bargee two shillings, missy, and you get food and your own bunk.'

'How long does it take?'

'Two days, you stop overnight in Garstang.'

'Okay, mister, I'll do it.'

'Your name, missy?'

'Tricia Cartwright.'

'Be here at seven in the morning and you are lucky as a lot of bargees are drunken bastards. They are a nice family who likes the Church and have a boat with a front cabin. Just leave a tanner on the end there as you leave.'

'And my cart?'

'Bring it along and be on time, mind.'

Tricia skipped to the door and as she left she shouted

cheerfully, 'Thank you. See you tomorrow,' and tossed a sixpence towards him.

She alternated between running and walking and arrived out of breath at the flea market just as he was closing down.

'By, golly, miss, you cut it close,' he said.

'It's not one o'clock yet.'

'You're right, missy, but I sold all my stuff.'

'I would have been quicker but I had to fiddle a trip on a barge. It's all done now and thanks for keeping them for me.'

'Thank you, miss, for buying them. I'll get me a noggin on the way home. Oh…! I greased the wheel hubs for you so it should run okay and left a spare bit of canvas in there for you.'

'Thank you! What's your name again?'

'Mr Bobbins'

'Mr Bobbins, how would you like more stuff to sell.'

'I would love it. Have you got any?'

She gave him the address, and said, 'Get yourself there this afternoon and you can have anything I don't want, okay?'

'Do you want paying for it?'

'Give me what you like when you've seen it.'

'Okay, see you later, Miss.'

She grasped the 'T' handle of the cart and was surprised at how easy it moved. "I'll manage this no problem," she said to herself and with a quick wave was on her way.

Back at the lodgings, she stowed the cart under the stairs and locked it. She spent the rest of the day packing and cooking and setting it out ready for loading the next day. She couldn't load the cart until morning in case stuff was stolen.

At three o'clock Bobbins arrived with a horse and cart and after an hour they had cleared the flat of everything including both beds and he slipped her two shillings as he left, and with a squeeze of her hand, he said, 'You take care, miss, and good luck for the future.'

In the evening, the cooked food had cooled and she poured it into four pickling jars and sealed the lids ready for loading. She estimated she had enough food to last her four days and content with her day's work she sat on her bedding and fashioned the spare bit of canvas into a cloak before she slept exhausted by her efforts.

She awoke with the call of the 'waker-upper' and not knowing when the next meal was going to be she ate as much as she could for breakfast and began the many trips up and down stairs loading the cart.

A little after six she was ready and she had a last look around before she dropped the keys on the floor and closed the door behind her with a tear in her eye.

The weather had relented and the morning was dry and with a little spring in her step mixed with a little sadness, she made her way to the Penny Street dock. The clerk was waiting for her and walked with her along the canal bank to a low wide beam barge and introduced her to a hard-looking wiry man with a straggly beard who was tidying up a rope on the bow.

'This here's Miss Cartwright, the young lady I told you about, Tom.' He turned to Tricia. 'That there's Tom Devlin. Have you got the cash, miss?'

Tricia fumbled in her moneybag before she stepped over to Tom with her hand out. 'Here you are, Mr Devlin, two shillings.'

He touched the peak of his cap. 'Yes, Miss Cartwright.' Tricia was surprised by the soft welcome burr of his voice which was opposite to his appearance. 'Welcome aboard. Hold on a minute and I'll get you some help with that there cart.'

'Call me, Tricia, Mr Devlin, please'

'Okay, missy.' He turned towards the stern of the boat some sixty feet away, and bellowed, 'BILLY! Get your arse out here!'

The head of a fair-haired young lad appeared above the cabin roof. 'What is it, Dad?'

'Get along here, lad, and help with this young ladies cart.'

'Coming!'

He clambered out of the cabin and ran along the narrow plank walk on the top of the cargo cover to the bow. Tom turned the cart until it was end on to the barge, and said to him. 'Chuck that rope down, Billy.'

Billy obliged and Tom tied it around the handle, and said, 'Pull it towards you, Billy.' He looked at the Dock clerk, 'Grab the other side, matey and we'll have this on in no time.'

Between them, they lifted the cart and Billy pulled it across the forward deck of the barge behind the 'proven tub' which had the horse feed in and when it was placed securely, Tom said, 'Tie it down by the wheels, Billy, and then Miss Tricia can get her stuff out.'

When it was all done Tom helped Tricia up the small gangplank set up as temporally access to the bow and she saw a red-painted wooden wall with a narrow folding door and sliding hatch which pushed back over the roof of the small front cabin.

Tom pointed to them. 'Don't worry, missy, you push the hatch away from you and then pull the bolt at the top and the door will slide open There's a bolt inside as well if you want to stay private. There's plenty of room, and that's your place. There's a little stove in there and plenty of bedding. My wife, Edie, cooks and we'll bring food to you when it's ready. In you go!'

Tricia was a little unsure but felt she had no option and approached the door and pushed the hatch. It slid easily as did the door. It was not the tiny hole she was expecting but big enough for a large person to squeeze through.

Her nose crinkled at the body odour inside but the cabin itself was cosy with two bunks in a recessed bed space, a small stove with some logs and coal alongside, a folding table and a chair and a well worn but clean rag rug covered most of the red lead-painted floor. There were panel lockers one of which was big enough to hang some clothes and a bench seat with hinged lids and the light from the two tiny portholes was adequate. She climbed out again and when her head appeared, Tom said, 'Well, Miss Tricia how is it?'

'That will do just fine, Mr Devlin.'

'Miss Tricia, when you come out mind the tow rope which is fastened to the post in front of you.'

She saw the post with a long stout rope attached stretched across the canal to the right bank and Billy coming from the canal stables in between two powerful Clydesdale horses followed by a smooth-haired black cat. She watched as he hitched the horses one behind the other to the barge and when he had finished he clambered onto the front one and without further ado with a kick of his heels, he shouted, 'Walk on!'

As the horses dug in and heaved, Tom unhitched the rear painter and jumped aboard while Edie steered the barge over to the right of the canal. The momentum of the boat gradually picked up and after a minute they were able to progress with little effort. Her journey had begun but she was curious about the hunting horn dangling across Billy's back and the cat which had jumped on the back of the second horse.

Alongside the doorway for her bunk were three vertical steps and as the weather overnight had turned milder than it had been all summer she climbed up and sat on the roof. As they began to move Tricia glanced towards the rear of the boat and saw Edie in the stern who waved to her. She then she pushed the hefty tiller bar over to starboard and eased the barge into the centre of the canal while Tom was busy tidying up ropes and things and then she found out about Billy's horn as they approached the Penny Street bridge and he blew two long blasts.

As they moved under the bridge her first instinct was to duck but there was plenty of room and she sat back and began to enjoy the ride. A couple of minutes later they passed the L&PJR train station and she saw her first railway steam engine. It was an ugly thing belching thick black smoke and she wondered what the fuss was about.

She much preferred the leisurely pace of the barge as they took a south-westerly route out of town. They passed Springfield Hall and the canal turned to a southerly direction and out into the countryside alongside Alderliffe Hall.

Tricia leaned back on her hands and took a deep breath as already the air was fresher and the smell of the Mills was left behind. "I could get used to this," she said to herself. She looked over her shoulder at the sound of Edie calling. She was holding a mug in the air and asking Tricia if she wanted some tea. Tricia waved back and nodded but now she had a dilemma. The twelve-inch wide plank walk which held the canvas cover over the cargo. First she had a job to do. She slid down onto the deck and ducked inside her cabin and one at a time she grabbed the horsehair mattresses off the bunk beds and pushed them out of the door.

She clambered out, spread one on the front decking, and pushed the other onto the roof and then she pulled herself up onto the roof and feeling a little bit wobbly she took her first steps along the cabin roof and onto the beam walk. The canal was smooth and the width of the barge kept it steady. Her first steps were tentative but she gradually gained confidence and by the time she reached the middle she perked up and was nearly skipping by the time she had reached the end where she clung onto the water barrel for safety. She lowered herself down and stood alongside Edie.

'Well done young, missy, you should work on the barges. You're a natural. Would you like some tea?'

'Yes, please Mrs Devlin, but no sugar.'

'Okay, missy, you hold this tiller and I'll fetch it.'

'But?'

'Don't worry, missy, look at the front and keep it in the middle and if it wanders you only need to move it a little to bring it back. You pull it gently toward you to go left and push it away to go right. I won't be two ticks.' She didn't wait for an answer but stooped down into the cabin and left Tricia nervously holding the long tiller shaft.

The cabin was only a couple of feet high being built down into the barge and Tricia could see over it. The canal was on a long curve to the left and she had to have her wits about her as she remembered Edie's instructions but after her first jerky pull on the tiller she got the hang of it and corrected the error without dragging the horses into the water. Tom who was doing something at the front of the barge stood up and saw who was steering and gave her the thumbs up as Edie appeared with her tea and took the tiller back.

'You did okay, lass. I felt the jerk but you got it back.'

'Thank you, Mrs Devlin. I'm enjoying this.'

'It's not always calm like this. When the bad weather comes you still have to do it and it's no fun standing here I can tell you, and you still has to walk with the horses. We only get time off when they're loading or unloading or we don't get paid, which ain't much.'

Tricia considered the last remark and noted that their clothing although workmanlike was clean, and the barge was well painted with many fancy buckets and flowerpots, before she replied, 'I'm used to hard work. I've done it all my life.'

'What were you doin' before?'

'I was in the Mill.'

'That's hard work.'

'You're right but they're trying to cut the pay and up the hours, that's why I'm moving.'

'You're going' to Preston?

'Yes.'

'They have the same problem you know?'

'There was more to it than that, Mrs Devlin, the bosses were after me. They already got my friend, Jack.'

'I'm old enough to be your mother, Tricia, but you can call me, Edie. What's with your friend?'

'I'm going to call you Auntie Edie. It's more respectable.'

'You speak well. Tricia. How come you were in the Mills and you wear a bonnet as the rich kids do.'

'I had good schooling and my Dad, said, "Whatever your plight always take pride in your appearance," but Mam and I were left on our own so we had to work and Mam has since passed away.'

'I'm sorry. Tricia. What about your friend?'

'I overheard the bosses in the Mill planning to up our hours and we had a meeting Jack was the leader and he called me up to tell the other workers what I had heard and they voted for a strike. The bosses blamed me and Jack and set out to get us.'

'And, Jack?'

'He was waiting outside the house for me and I heard a scuffle but when I got there he had gone.'

Just then they heard the blast of Billy's horn. Tricia looked up and there was a low bridge with a barge coming the other way.

'Okay, Tricia, I am going to be busy. We'll talk later.'

Tricia put her mug down and clambered onto the roof and as she began walking along the narrow plank, Edie called out. 'Mind the bridge, lass.'

The other barge was coming through the bridge and it was then she realised that Edie had not looked at her when they talked but had been looking forward the whole time, and she said to herself, 'Lesson learned, Tricia. Thanks, Auntie Edie.'

She walked to the halfway point and sat down with her legs dangling on the tarpaulin cargo cover and watched the two boats manoeuvre.

The other barge was a single horse boat. The horse was pulled up and moved to the inside of the towpath and the barge eased over to the opposite bank and because the barges don't have brakes the barge master wound the towrope around a strapping post to stop their horse being pulled into the canal. As the barge slowed to a stop he unwound the rope and it dipped below the surface.

Billy keeping their rope tight guided the horses close to the edge of the canal while Edie edged the barge closer to the towpath which was the right bank and the cat jumped down and leapt onto the barge and up onto the plank walk and sat beside Tricia. She tickled it behind the ear and he purred as they watched the manoeuvres.

The horses stepped over the other towrope and continued unhindered along the canal and under the bridge while Tom who was walking the towpath behind Billy kept a watchful eye on the ropes as they crossed. When they were clear the other horse continued its daily grind as they got underway.

While this was going on the two crews passed the time of day, and Tom said 'Thank you,' for the courtesy shown.

Tricia also waved and when they had completed the exercise, she thought, "That was clever, how do they decide who goes first?"

She stood up and made her way forward and turned the mattresses over and then sorted through her cart and retrieved her notebook and sketch pad and leaned back against the cabin door and began writing and drawing with Lucky sleeping beside her.

She hadn't been scribbling long when the barge edged to the bank and Tom jumped onto the towpath and caught up with Billy on the horse. Billy slid down and gave his Dad the horn and Tricia laughed as he shot through a hole in the hedge bordering the canal bank. She guessed what he was doing and made a note on her pad.

Billy caught up with them a little while later and clambered back on board and with a bacon butty in one hand and a mug of tea in the other he walked along the boardwalk and joined Tricia at the front.

'Hello, Billy, having a break?'

'Yes, Miss, we swap over every so often but Dad likes to walk. He says it keeps him thin.'

Tricia looked a Tom walking beside the lead horse and had a little giggle. 'He must eat a lot then, Billy?'

'Yes, Miss, we do okay now there's only three of us.'

'Don't call me Miss, Billy. Tricia will do. I'm only a few years older than you. Was there more of you then?'

'Yes, mi…, Tricia, I have two brothers but they don't like the barges so they work on the farm near our cottage just north of Lancaster and that's why we have your cabin spare.'

'I'm glad about that, I am loving this.'

Billy looked down at her sketchbook and pad. 'You can write, Tricia?'

'Yes, Billy, can you?'

'No, and is that a picture of Lucky?'

'Yes, I couldn't resist as he posed alongside me.' She gave Lucky a little push and his green eyes glared at her before he shuffled a little way across the deck. Tricia patted the deck beside her. 'Sit down, Billy, I'll show you.'

'Ooh,..! I can't!'

'Yes, you can. It's easy. Come on.'

He sat down, and Tricia after turning over her work gave him the writing paper and she used the sketchpad. She held up her pencil. 'Right, Billy, the first thing we do is hold your pencil or your pen like this.'

He fiddled a bit and finally got it right. 'Now, Billy, we do the alphabet first. Copy me. The first letter is a capital 'A'.'

He tried and his actions were slow and wobbly. 'No, Billy, don't press hard. Have a practice at the bottom. First press softly and then a bit harder until you find the right pressure.'

He did three strokes, and Tricia said, 'Stop, that's it. Okay, do letter 'A' again but soft.'

He did it and Tricia said, 'Well done. Now we do a little 'a'.

When she was satisfied they worked their way slowly through the alphabet and they had just done the letter 'Z' when Edie shouted. 'Billy! Get back here now.'

'Got to go, Tricia, It's my turn on the tiller.'

'We'll do more later, Billy.' She tore the page out, and said, 'Take that to your Mam.'

He grabbed it off her and athletically jumped onto the top of the cabin and ran to the back of the barge waving his bit of paper. 'Mam! Mam! look what I did,' he shouted as he ran.

Edie took the paper off him and read it before she ruffled his hair. 'Oh..., well done,' she said, 'did Tricia teach you that?'

'Yes, Mam, she's clever and she did a picture of Lucky.'

Edie looked forward and gave Tricia a wave and then she said to Billy. 'Right, lad, back to work, grab the tiller.'

They swapped places and Edie disappeared into the cabin only to appear later with some shopping bags just as Tom blew the horn. Tricia looked up and saw they were approaching a bridge and on the other side, there was a building. She was wondering what it was when Edie called her. She looked to the back of the barge and Edie waved and held up the bags and hollered, 'Shopping! Are you coming?'

Tricia nodded and checking where the bridge was she climbed onto the cabin roof and hurried to the rear.

'Hello, Tricia,' said Edie, 'we have to jump off. Can you manage that?''

Tricia had watched them all morning jumping on and off and thought she could manage. 'I think so,' she said, 'you go first.' In the back of her mind was the thought that getting back on was something else.

The canal through the bridge was narrower, Tom slowed the horses down, Billy steered the barge into the side and the rubbing slowed it down. Edie jumped and ran forward a few steps. Tricia balanced on the side, hitched her skirt up, took a deep breath and tried to emulate Edie. When she landed she stumbled and staggered forward but stopped in time. 'That was fun,' she laughed, 'I'll have to practice more though.'

Edie gathered a one-gallon urn and a large metal jug and a sack off the side of the barge and then hurried over to Tricia, 'Are you okay, Tricia?'

'Yes, Auntie Edie, I'm enjoying this trip more and more. What are we doing?'

Edie pointed to the building by the bridge. 'This is a farm shop where we top up our food supplies. Can you carry the urn for me?'

Tricia picked up the urn and together at the side of the bridge they turned down some sandstone steps through the hedge and followed a path around to the front of the premises and joined a pathway coming down from the nearby gravel roadway that went over the bridge. Tricia heard a scuffling noise behind her and looked back to see Lucky following them. She smiled. "I wonder what he's up to," she thought.

The outside of the building was covered in items necessary for the day to day upkeep of barges from ropes to metal baths and tubs and long poles and fancy patterned buckets. Either side of the door were boxes of every type of fruit and vegetable seasonably available in quantities unseen in the middle of Lancaster.

The shopkeeper met them at the door and greeted them. 'Hello, Edie. That was a quick turnaround. Have you brought that little thief with you?'

'Yes, he's enjoying your dogs' lunch around the back.'

Tricia followed Edie around the shop and helped with the bags but her only purchase was a pint of vinegar.

'Why are you buying that, Tricia?' said Edie.

Tricia thought it was unfair to tell her that it was a precaution against bedbugs so she replied, 'It was something my Mam taught me. Wipe the surfaces in the room with vinegar and it will smell like spring.'

'Oh, that's nice, I've never heard of that.' She turned to the shopkeeper and ordered some vinegar and to finish her shopping she filled up the jug with ale and the urn with milk.

'Come on, Tricia, we've got a good walk to catch up with the boat.'

They shared the load between them and Edie was grateful for Tricia's help as she would have to carry everything herself normally and they set off at a brisk walk and they had only gone a little way when Lucky ran past them. He darted into the long grass but returned empty-handed.

The barge was out of sight and while they were walking, Tricia asked Edie, 'Where did you find Lucky?'

'He found us, Tricia. We were parked up overnight in Preston a couple of years ago and when we went for the horses in the stable he was all snuggled up with them and he's been with us or rather the horses ever since. He sleeps in the stable with them and spends most of the time riding on them. He does go walkabout in Preston sometimes but he's always back in the morning.'

It took then half an hour to catch up with the barge by which time Tricia's arms were aching and she still had to get back on board but she needn't have worried as they had reached a bridge and the barge had stopped to let them catch up and while they did this they allowed another barge through.

The barge was tied to a strapping post and Billy on the top with a long pole with a forked end was holding the towrope of the other boat up in the air, and was walking along the narrow plank walk guiding it over their barge. At the stern, Tom took the pole and held it up for the last few feet until it had cleared and as he unhooked it he waved to the other crew who acknowledged their help.

Billy jumped off and uncoiled the painter holding the barge and ran to the horses that were waiting patiently stuffing their faces from a feedbag. He jumped on the front one and as he did so, the horses started heaving without a command from him.

While all this was happening Tricia and Edie had clambered back on board and stowed the new stores and when they had finished, Edie said, 'I think we deserve a cup of tea, don't you, Tricia?'

Tricia who was flopped on the bench around the stern, said, 'Yes, please.'

Edie looked a Tom who was on the tiller. 'What about you?'

'Tha knows me, lass, give us the jug.'

Edie already knew the reply, bent down, picked up the jug by the cabin door, and passed it to him before she moved inside the cabin. With one hand he flipped up the lid and began drinking. After two huge gulps, he put the jug down, wiped his mouth with the back of his hand, and smiled at Tricia. 'That was good, It gets better every time from that place.'

'How often do you stop there, Mr Devlin?'

'About once a week, it depends on how long it takes to get new loads.'

Edie popped her head out and passed a mug of tea to Tricia. 'He's a regular, just like Lucky. They even have a spare jug in case we forget ours.'

Tricia had a little giggle, before she said, 'Mr Devlin?'

'Yes, lass?'

'Can I ride on the other horse?'

'Can you ride?'

'Yes.'

'Okay, finish your tea.'

'What are the horse's names?'

'The front one is Queenie and the second one is her son Prince.'

'Where's Prince's dad?'

'That's Albert, he's on our smallholding up by Lancaster and we hire him out for breeding. We do alright because of that and with the likes of you but some bargees struggle.'

'Why's that, Mr Devlin?'

'You needs a good business head otherwise the contractors

fiddle you. Edie's the brains and she keeps them in line. I think they're scared of her, a bit like me. Have you finished?'

Tricia lied, and said, 'Yes.'

'Come on then, I'll give you a lift up. Are you okay with a skirt?'

'Yes, I can do side saddle.'

'Ooh, posh, aye? Did you hear that, Edie? She reads, writes and does side-saddle. I knew you were smart when I saw you.'

Edie took the tiller and edged the barge to the side and Tom jumped first and held his hand out but Tricia was feeling confident and she dangled her right foot over the side and when she judged it was right she jumped and ran forward with the boat.

'Nice one, lass,' shouted Tom, 'you're a natural.'

They hurried forward to the horses and slowed when they were slightly in front of Prince. 'Right, lass, keep walking the same speed as Princey Boy and I'll lift you on. Are you ready?'

'Yes, Mr Devlin, I love horses.'

'Okay, here we go. One, two, three!'

He grabbed her around the waist and with one big heave lifted her onto Princes back. She shuffled around to get the best position while Tom untangled a cotton rope bridle and gave it to her. 'Don't use it, missy, It's just something to hold.'

'Thank you, Mr Devlin, and I can talk to Billy from here.'

'Watch out for the bridges as you'll have to duck your head but Billy's horn will warn you. Take care now.'

He went back to take over the tiller and although it had been a long time since she had been on a horse she soon settled to the slow steady rhythm and was glad she had opted for the barge.

She had only been on Prince for a couple of minutes when she felt a gentle thump behind her and as she looked around Lucky squiggled his way past her and settled down with his back legs on the horse and his front legs and head on her lap.

Billy looked around, and said, 'He's taken to you.'

'Why's that, Billy, doesn't he mix with the family?'

'He does but he prefers the company of the horses.'

After half an hour of swapping small talk with Billy, she heard the banging of a tin plate and when she looked behind her and saw Edie calling her for dinner.

Billy shouted to her. 'Can you manage, Tricia?'

There were no bridges ahead so Billy jumped down and came back to Tricia, pushed Lucky away and held her as she slid down. 'Thanks, Billy, when do you get your dinner?'

'Mam brings it and I eats it on the go.'

'Billy! If you're going to learn to read and write you must speak nicely also. It is not "I eats it on the go" it is "I eat it on the go." Got it?'

'Thanks, Tricia, I eats it anyway.'

Tricia looked to the sky and shook her head. 'There's no helping this child.'

She waited while Tom eased the barge towards the bank and then he let go of the tiller, stretched out a hand, and urged Tricia to take hold, and then he said, 'When I give the word—Jump.'

She took his hand and trotted alongside the barge, and he said, 'Ready?'

'Yes.'

'JUMP!'

As she jumped, he pulled and with a little bit of a scrabble she landed on the narrow decking down the side of the cabin and grabbed the handrail with her free hand.

She took a deep breath and laughed. 'Wow! That was iffy.'

'You did well, lass, they usually fall in.'

She eased herself backwards and jumped down into the cockpit and because it was a nice day she sat on the bench and Edie gave her a nice bowl of Lancashire hot pot with dumplings. Edie sat with her and Tom ate his with an arm hooked over the tiller.

When she had finished she sat back, placed her bowl in her lap, and said, 'That was lovely, Aunt Edie.'

'Would you like some more Tricia?'

'Have you got enough?'

'Yes, love, we have. Give me your bowl.'

'What about, Billy?'

'He'll get his in a minute. I want him to sit with you and can you teach him more?'

'I'd love to, Aunt Edie. Have you got a slate anywhere?'

'You eat your stew, Tricia, I'm sure we have.'

She nipped into the cabin and returned moments later with another bowl full.

'Get that down you while I find that slate'

Tricia had a little titter to herself as she could hear Edie muttering as she dragged things about in the tiny living quarters in the cabin but eventually she popped her head out waving a school slate.

'Found it,' she cried. She gave Tricia the slate, 'And here's some chalk. Take as long as you like.'

'Thank you, Auntie Edie, I'll do my best.'

She put the bowl down on the bench and with the slate in one hand did the balancing act to her cabin. While she was waiting for Billy to join her she took the mattresses inside but she left the vinegar wash until she had finished with Billy's lessons. It was not long before Billy joined her with his bowl of stew and sat with his back against the cabin.

'Right, Billy, while you're eating I want you to read what you did earlier. Your ABC's'

'Do I have to?'

'Yes, that's the only way.'

He muttered something unintelligible, pulled the scraps of paper from his pocket, laid them alongside his legs, and studied while he ate. After a few minutes, he was finished and put his bowl down

'Right, Billy, pick up that slate and when I read a letter out you write it down and then show it to me. Got that?'

'Yes, miss.'

They both laughed, and Tricia said, 'The letter D.'

Tricia continued her lessons for the next couple of hours only stopping when Billy had to relieve Edie while she made mugs of tea for everyone and had a toilet break. After the tea break she moved onto simple arithmetic and was impressed how quickly Billy picked it up but it all had to stop when they reached the

Garstang Basin as he had to help with the mooring and unhitch the horses and lead them to the canal stables where he settled them in and filled their feed bags.

Tricia volunteered to help and led Prince with Lucky on his back and she was a little worried when she thought Prince appeared to be limping.

They spent an hour currying the horses before Billy called, 'Enough, time to get back for our nosh.'

As they left, she heard Prince snorting and she looked over the door and saw him pawing the ground with his left hoof. She shrugged as she thought maybe he was just moving the straw to where he wanted it.

While they walked back to the barge, Tricia said, 'Billy? Did you ever go to school?'

'No. I would have to stay overnight or sommat and Mam and Dad couldn't afford it. I sometimes went for a few hours but they didn't bother with us boat kids as it was sometimes weeks before we went back and I'm too old now.'

'You're never too old, Billy. I'll leave you one of my books and you keep trying?'

'I have a Bible but that's too hard.'

'You're good at counting, how come?'

'Mum taught me sums because we have to check we don't get cheated by the contractors.'

'Aah! That's why. For a minute I thought you were clever.'

She gave him a push on the shoulder and ran on laughing.

'Aye!' he shouted, 'that's not fair,' as he chased after her.

Back at the barge, tea wasn't ready so Tricia spent time cleaning the surfaces in her cabin with vinegar. As she finished she heard Edie calling her and with a spring in her step she did the balancing act along the top of the barge to join them.

While they sat around eating bread and dripping followed by an apple with a mug of tea, Tom said, 'You're getting a bit cocky coming over there, lass, you be careful because it's a big drop and especially bumpy on the landside.'

'Thank you, Mr Devlin, I will and thank you for the lovely

trip. I am enjoying this. It reminds me of when I was tiny and living in the country. I wish my Dad could see me.'

'Where is your Dad, Tricia?'

'Australia, I hope.'

'Oh! What happened?'

'They said it was poaching.'

'And your Mum, Tricia,' piped in Edie.

'Mam died soon after we moved to Lancaster. I've been on my own since.'

'Oh, that's sad. What are you going to do in Preston?'

'Go back in the Mills. My old boss gave me the name of a friend of his who could help me.'

'Best of luck, young lady,' said Tom, 'we have to pack up and get to bed because we have an early start tomorrow.'

Tricia stood up. 'Thank you again, I'll see you in the morning.'

She scrambled onto the cabin roof and this time made her way carefully forward to her cabin. Inside she lit a candle and read her favourite book before lying down on the bottom bunk and pulled the covers over her. It was then she felt a gentle thump on the end of the bunk and a furry black body curled up alongside her.

She smiled to herself. She was lucky to get such a nice family, a lovely boat ride and now she had a cat. She snuggled down and closed her eyes feeling happier than she had for a long time.

—

Tricia slept well and when she finally awoke and rubbed the sleep from her eyes Lucky had gone but she was surprised that the barge wasn't moving. 'I wonder what's wrong,' she mumbled to herself, 'they said it was an early start.'

She straightened her dress, brushed her hair, and tied it in a ponytail before she ventured out and peeking over the top of the cabin she looked to the rear of the barge. She saw Edie bobbing about in the rear cabin space and climbing up onto the walkway she went to the rear and caught Edie by surprise.

'Morning, Aunt Edie, how are we?'

Edie looked up, and uttered, 'Ooh! You made me jump, Tricia. I'm okay, and you?'

'Very good, Aunt Edie, I slept very well. Why are we waiting and where are Mr Devlin and Billy?'

'They are in the stable. We are having trouble with Prince. Do you want some breakfast I have some toasted cob ready?'

'Yes, please, I'll eat it on my way to the stables.'

'What can you do there, Tricia?'

'I know a bit about horses, maybe I can help.'

Edie disappeared into the cabin to reappear moments later with a large slice of toasted cob. 'There you are, Tricia, and that's my homemade blackberry jam on it.'

'Tricia folded it into a sandwich, and said, 'Thank you,' before she jumped down onto the towpath and as she hurried towards the stable she began crunching on her toast. She took the last bite as she turned into the stable yard and she heard raised voices.

'I've got to, Billy, that bloody horse is no good to us and we have to get going.'

'But you can't, Dad. Just leave him here and we'll get him on the way back.'

'You know we can't, Billy, we can't afford it. He's gotta go.'

'DAD! Don't.'

Tricia burst in only to see Tom with a raised pistol pointing at Prince. 'Don't do that, Mr Devlin, what's the matter with him?'

'Mind your own business girl,' shouted Tom, 'He's gotta go.'

'Mr Devlin, I know horses what's wrong?'

'He's done something to his leg and won't let us near him.'

'Mr Devlin,' said Tricia appealingly, 'let me talk to him. Just five minutes.'

Tom lowered the pistol and looked at her, screwed his face up like he was about to explode and then shook his head. 'Bloody women,' he cursed, 'Okay, five minutes and then he's had it.'

Tricia stepped forward and gently opened the stable door and squeezed herself in. She paused long enough to pluck a handful of feed from the manger on the wall and walked across to Prince slowly holding her hand out and stopped two paces from him.

'Hello, Prince,' she said, just above a whisper, 'what's the matter? Talk to me.'

Prince snuffled and stared at her warily. She edged forward. 'Come to me, Prince, let me see.'

He snorted again and shook his head. 'Come on,' she said, 'you want to don't you. Come on.'

She moved closer until she could reach him but all she did was blow into his face. He calmed down and looked at her and she took a breath and carried on blowing gently at his nose. She stepped closer while she blew until his nose was almost touching her. She kept blowing and held the feed towards his mouth.

He looked at her and gave a gentle shake of his head before he nibbled at the feed. 'That's a good boy. Now let me look at you. It was the left front wasn't it?'

Tom and Billy couldn't believe what they were seeing. A slip of a girl talking to a horse. She rubbed his nose and blew again before she turned so that her left shoulder was under his neck and then she ran a hand down the front of his leg to the fetlock and as she did so Prince lifted his foot. She stooped down and looked at the base of his hoof and she saw straight away what the problem was.

She looked over towards Tom, and said, 'Have you got a spike?'

'Yes,' he replied.

'Bring it here, but slowly.'

She tilted her head and blew once more at Prince's nose and whispered gentle words as Tom approached from the rear so that Prince could not see him but he did sense him and snorted.

Tricia stroked him with her free hand, and whispered, 'It's alright boy.'

Tom leaned forward, and said quietly, 'What is it, lass?'

'Look in his hoof. It's a thorn or something wedged in the back of his foot above the shoe.'

Tom leaned closer and saw the object. 'It's a broken horseshoe nail picked up off the towpath.'

With the spike, he gently eased it out. Prince sensed that they were helping and stood quiet, until finally, Tom said, 'It's out now.'

'Ease back, Mr Devlin, and I'll check all around.'

Tom looked at this girl telling him what to do but he did as he was asked and one at a time first on the left side and then walking around at the front of Prince she checked his right hooves and when she was satisfied she stood in front of Prince and blew into his nose again. 'Are we friends,' she said.

He nuzzled his nose into her shoulder, and she said, 'Come on, you've got a job to do.'

She started walking towards the stable door and Prince followed. At the door, she stopped. 'He's yours, Billy. Give him his nosebag I doubt he's eaten much overnight.'

Billy looped the bridle over Prince's head and hooked up the nosebag and with Tricia on one side and Billy on the other followed by Tom with Queenie they walked back towards the barge. They had only gone a few yards when Lucky came out of nowhere and jumped onto Prince's back and feeling better all round Prince perked up and strode purposely to his daily task.

Tricia had a little smile to herself as it was the first time she had done it and had never believed that the trick taught her by the Ostler in Kearsley Hall would work. While Billy was left to hitch the horses up, Tricia and Tom walked the little way to the barge when Tom put his arm across her shoulder and gave her a little hug.

'Thanks for that, young lady, you saved us a lot of money.'

'It was nothing but would you have shot Prince?'

'I didn't want to but we can't afford to stable him or a vet and we need to deliver on time otherwise we lose money and new horses are expensive plus it would have made Queenie's work harder and she's getting on a bit now.'

'Oh! It's all down to business?'

'Yes, lass, it is. By the way, where did you learn that?'

'At the Hall where Mam and Dad worked. I used to go into the stables and the Ostler showed me.'

'Thanks again, lass. Come on; jump on, we've got to get going.'

He took her arm, helped her on, and then set about untying the barge and in two minutes they were on their way. The sky overhead was looking grey but Tricia chose to sit at the front by her cabin with a mug of tea when a smooth black figure leapt across the gap between boat and land and scrambled up and snuggled into her lap.

Billy urged the horses to go quicker and Tom was cursing the number of boats going the other way as they tried to make up lost time while Tricia spent her time between riding and walking and continuing her lessons with Billy and the day passed quickly.

They slowed a little for Edie and Tricia to jump off at a little hamlet called Borrowdale where they dropped off a pile of washing with the local laundry lady. They didn't hang around but on the way back to the canal Edie pointed out a three-storied cottage with shutters on the windows. 'See that, Tricia, that's a church school where some of the bargee kids go. I wish I could send Billy but they won't take him now.'

'He would have to stay overnight wouldn't he, Aunt Edie?'

'They have to sleep rough and have no food until their barge comes back the other way.'

Tricia remained silent but mentally thought it was unfair but they had to hurry and she concentrated on their fast walking. Tricia noticed that Edie's skirts were shorter so she had turned up the hem of her dress and pinned it in place. She found it much easier to get on and off the barge and climb onto Prince and somewhat out of breath they caught up half an hour later but there was no let-up for Edie as she set about making dinner.

Edie served up dinner to Tricia and was putting out Tom's when their journey came to an abrupt halt. They were in the process of passing another barge when the master of the other barge made a fudge of securing his towrope. The rope didn't droop to the bottom of the canal and instead wrapped around the front of their barge. The other barge dragged to a sudden stop and swung across the canal, their horse was pulled into the canal, and the rear of the barge became wedged on a hidden mud bank.

Tom exploded and the air became blue as the legality of the birth of the other barge master was called into question. Edie tactfully returned Tom's dinner to the pot as quickly as he blew up he calmed down and set about retrieving the situation.

First, the rescue of the horse and above all get the nose feed bag off as this could fill with water and drown the horse. While that was being done, Billy unhitched Queenie and Prince and led them to the front of the other barge. Using the tow rope of the other barge which had been pulled clear, Billy hitched up Queenie and Prince and with the help of Tom and the other bargee who were using long poles set about pulling the barge off the mud bank. After much pulling, pushing and tugging they turned it lengthways so that it was facing the right direction and lashed to some strapping poles. Queenie and Prince with heads stuck in feeding bags waited patiently to carry on with their daily task.

The whole operation had taken a long time and made an early arrival in Preston impossible and with Billy eating his dinner on the go and Tom eating his with a foul look on his face they continued silently on their way.

The delay had caused a queue and the manoeuvres passing other barges further slowed their efforts and the mood did not get any better as the early grey clouds now bundled together and it started raining but Tom allowed Billy to go with Tricia into her cabin and do some more reading and Lucky joined them and it was late evening as the light was beginning to fade when they arrived at the Preston coal wharf

They stopped at the discharge Dock by Canal Street and they unloaded Tricia's cart and Tom took her by the shoulder and walked with her to the Coal Wharf and around to the bottom of Wharf Street and the Dock exit.

'Where are you going, Tricia?'

'King Street by the Yellow Mill.'

'Go up Wharf Street and turn left into Lune Street and then right at the top. Someone will tell you which way from there. Best of luck, gal, but a Mill is not for you.'

'Thank you, Mr Devlin, I will try to move on from there.'

It was dark now and with her collar up to shield her from the drizzle, she took the handle and began walking up to the Wharf Street exit and Preston.

—

The lamplighters were out early that evening but the few lamps that were lit were only a pale cone in the murky weather and at the junction with Lune Street and Friargate, she paused to look around undecided which way to go. Tom had said ask someone but there was no one and after a minutes deliberation to keep the rain and wind behind her she chose to go right.

She had only gone a little way when she came to the narrow Chapel passageway and she pushed her cart into it and took shelter for a few moments from the weather. She had only been there a few seconds when she visibly jumped with shock as a man's voice from further down the passage, said, 'Hey, Lass! What are ya doin' in this weather?'

'Oh...! I'm looking for King Street.'

'You new here?'

'Yes.'

'Okay, gal, I'll show you, I'm going that way. Come on, the rain's eased.'

A dark body pushed itself off the wall and walked towards her. She felt a little scared but in the dark he looked presentable in working man's apparel of long hairy sideboards with a squashed peak cap and a worn suit and waistcoat and a scruffy necktie. His trousers were unpressed and scuffed with ties around his lower leg. His boots had seen better days also.

'Here, let me pull your cart.'

He took the handle off her and wheeled it out onto the street. She wasn't sure but lost in a strange town, she followed. He slowed and let her catch up, and he said, 'You going to work in the Mill then?'

'Yes!'

'Do they know your coming?'

She hesitated. 'Err... No. It was a last-minute thing.'

She felt like she had said enough and she fell silent as they reached the Market Place. They went down the side of the Town Hall and left into Church Street.

'Not far,' he said, 'in daylight you can see the Mill from here.'

They crossed the muddy main street opposite a run-down

church and a hundred yards later they turned into an alleyway called 'Waters' which opened out into Leeming Street

The rain came down heavier and after fifty yards he put his hand on her shoulder and guided her into a narrow street with characteristic two up / two down workers terraced houses.

'Where are we?' she said, as they stopped by a narrow passageway between two houses.

He pointed to the house on the right. 'I live there,' he said,' we'll shelter from the rain as it's a good walk to King Street from here. Would you like a mug of tea?'

The weather was bad and after a moment of deliberation, she said, 'Yes.'

He pushed her cart down the passage and through a wooden gate. 'It'll be okay, that's my yard,' he said.

When they stepped up to the front door he rested a hand on her shoulder as he unlocked it. He pushed it open and guided her in with a firm hand in the middle of her back and kept on pressing as he pushed the door behind him and in his haste overlooked checking it was closed.

She was faced with a dull darkened room with a large table and chairs in the middle opposite a built-in fireplace with an attached oven and a sink with a draining board full of unwashed utensils.

She suddenly had her doubts, but too late. He took hold of her raincoat from behind and pulled it off her and threw it down and with a huge shove he sent her tumbling forward facedown onto the table.

He pushed a chair out of the way and holding her down with one hand he ripped open the fly flap on his trousers before he pulled up the hem of her dress and underskirt and crudely pushed his hand in and groped her. As he manoeuvred between her legs and thrust forward to penetrate her. Lucky, who had snuck in through the open door, flew up from the floor and onto his neck and snarling wildly buried his claws into his cheek and left a deep scratch.

With a loud shout the perp stood up and reaching for Lucky

dragged him off and hurled him against the wall. Tricia rolled over and reached into the slit in her dress and felt the reassuring feel of the knife but she was still doubtful about using it. Her attacker turned to face her and punched her in the face pushing her backwards onto the table. Ignoring the blood gushing from her nose and holding her by the throat he made ready to molest her from the front. He heaved her skirt up and threw himself forward onto her. Unbeknown to him her knife had tilted up and as he landed on her he let out an ear-piercing shriek and rolled away holding his left thigh with blood spurting from his femoral artery. His weight had pinioned him onto the blade.

Tricia jumped up dragging the knife away by the lanyard as she did so and ignoring the crying heap rolling around the floor she grabbed her coat and ran for the door oblivious of the increasing pool of blood seeping through his trousers.

She ran into the alley and flicked up the catch on the gate. Throwing her coat over the cart she staggered sobbing back into the street undecided which way to turn. Still uncertain, while looking from left to right shivering in the cold she heard a plaintive, 'Meow!'

It was Lucky and trusting to instinct she turned in his direction and ran as quick as the cobbles and the cart would allow. Keeping in the shadows Lucky kept pace with her and at the junction with Church Street he ran across her to the left. She followed and by the Church he led her across the street but they didn't go the way they had come. Lucky took her down Fishergate and Lune Street and into the Coal Wharf from the opposite direction.

Checking around every corner he led her through to the stables. He jumped up onto the third stable door and Tricia looked in she saw Prince. She slid the bolt over and dragged her cart inside and locked the door. Exhausted and crying, she flopped to the straw-covered floor.

She felt a soft nose nuzzle into her and repeatedly give her a gentle push until she was under the manger in deep warm straw. There he left her sobbing until she fell into a disturbed sleep.

Tom was in the hold of the barge helping the dock labourers shovel limestone into the large bucket-like containers ready to be hoisted dockside when he heard Billy shouting, 'DAD! DAD! Help!'

He stopped working and listened and, Yes! It was Billy still shouting as he was running. 'DAD! DAD! Come quick, it's Tricia.'

He threw his shovel to one side and scrambled up the ladder to the dockside and saw Billy running towards him waving. 'DAD! DAD! It's Tricia, she's hurt. Come quick.'

Tom ran to meet him and when they met Billy was gasping for breath. 'What is it, Billy, lad?'

'It's Tricia; she's hurt and lying in the stable. She has blood on her.'

'Okay, lad, lead the way.'

Together they ran back to the stable and when Tom stepped into the stable he saw a bundle of clothes under the manger with Prince standing over it and Lucky wrapped around her head. Tom stopped and patted his thigh, and said quietly, 'Come, Prince.'

Prince stood watching thoughtfully before lowering his head and snuffing around Tricia. He moved away and Tom crossed over to the bundle and when he got close he could see, protected by Lucky, Tricia in a fitful sleep with blood on her face and smears down the front of her clothes.

He knelt beside her and rolled her over. She groaned and cringed away.

'It's alright, lass, you're safe. It's Uncle Tom. Come now let's look at you.'

She rolled onto her side and looked up and Tom could see the bruised cheek and the smear of dried blood coming from her nose. He looked at her body and could see the smear of blood from her waist and down the front of her dress.

He called Billy forward. 'Billy lad, help me get her outside and then you shut the stable and run on with her cart and tell your Mum to get our bedroom cleared. I'll be right behind you.'

'Come on, Tricia, stand up. I'll help you.'

He put an arm around her shoulders and helped her sit up and holding onto Tom, Tricia pulled herself up. As she stood she wobbled and Tom didn't wait. He scooped her up and started walking with his precious package back to the barge.

He had only gone a short way when Billy passed him pulling Tricia's cart.

The barge was half empty and it stood higher on the quay so he had to get Edie and Billy to help Tricia onto the barge and then Edie encouraged her down into their bed cabin.

'What happened to her, Tom,' said Edie.

'I don't know. Get her undressed and changed and with a mug of tea and some toast, she may be able to tell us. I've got to get back to work.'

As he turned away he whispered to Edie before he climbed out of the cabin and saw Billy waiting. 'Leave the cart there, Billy, and get back to the horses.'

'Okay, Dad, is she alright?'

'I think so. She took a bit of a battering and is frightened but she'll be okay.'

'Oh, good, can she stay with us? I like her.'

'We'll see. Now get on with ya!'

Billy ran off back to the stables and Tom jumped down into the hold and got stuck in again while telling the dockworkers what had happened.

Edie made Tricia comfortable and went to get a bowl of warm water and when she returned she began to clean her up. She sat Tricia on the side of the bed and helped her off with her dress and then she saw blood on her underskirt.

'What happened, Tricia, you're not hurt are you?'

Tricia wiped away a tear, and said, 'No, only my face and I hurt across my hips.'

'But where does this blood come from, Tricia?'

'This man was trying to rape me and he fell on my knife.'

'You have a knife?'

Tricia pulled the knife from under her and showed Edie. 'It was given to me by my Auntie Gertie when I was being chased once before. I have a slit in the seam of my dress and when this man jumped on me I reached for it but I didn't use it. He fell on it and it stuck in his thigh. It's a secret, don't tell anyone.'

She took Tricia by the shoulders and looked her in the eye, and smiled. 'I won't, Tricia, but what a good idea, I wish I'd thought of that.'

Edie finished cleaning Tricia up and when she was all done, she said, 'Have you got clean clothes, Tricia?'

'Yes, Aunt Edie, in my cart.'

'Right, lass, you lie down for a bit and I'll go and fetch them.'

Tricia lay down and Edie threw a blanket over her. 'Try and sleep, Tricia.'

Edie made sure Tricia was comfy and left. After she had collected Tricia's clean clothes she made a mug of tea and went back to join her.

Tricia wasn't asleep and she sat up and drank a few sips of tea, 'Oh, that's the best mug of tea I've had in a long time. I feel better already except for my achy face.'

Edie put her mug down, and said, with deep concern. 'Tricia? This man, did he penetrate you?'

Tricia shook her head. 'No, but he hurt me trying until Lucky saved me.'

'Lucky saved you. How do you mean?'

Tricia told Edie all about it... 'And when I got out of the house he showed me the way back to the stables.'

'My, my, he has taken to you and speak of the devil.'

Lucky jumped down the steps into the cabin and joined Tricia on the bed. She stroked him and tickled him behind the ear, and he purred. 'Thank you, Lucky,' she said.

'Have you finished your tea, Tricia?'

'Yes, Aunt Edie.'

'Okay, come over here and I'll tidy your hair, or would you rather lie down?'

'I'm feeling alright. My cuppa and Lucky and you, Aunt Edie, make me feel better.'

Tricia slid off the bed and stood in the middle of the cabin while Edie brushed her hair and left it in a long ponytail down her back. When she had finished, she said, 'Where's your bonnet, Tricia?'

'I didn't stop to look, Aunt Edie, I just ran. I grabbed my coat because it was by my feet. I have another bonnet in my cart.'

'Oh, good, but I like your hair the way it is.'

'Aunt Edie, we'll leave it off today. Can I have another mug of tea and then I'm going to get ready and go to find my job.'

'You are not going anywhere young lady. You can have some tea and then go and rest and Tom wants to speak to you when we have dinner.'

Tricia picked up her tea and Edie took her down to their bed cabin. When Tricia was ready she left and closed the cabin door.

It was one o'clock when the barge was finally empty and Tom heaved himself on board and into the small deck area at the stern. Edie welcomed him with a jug of ale and after a couple of huge swigs, he said to Edie, 'Fetch Tricia and we'll talk while you get the dinner.'

Edie obliged and a couple of minutes later Tricia appeared and Tom stood up. 'Come here lass and let's look at ya.' Tricia stopped in front of him and he had a close look at her face before he said, 'That doesn't look too bad. A bit bloodshot in your eye but that will go in a week or so. Sit down, lass. I want to ask you something.'

He sat on the bench and left a space for Tricia who sat down alongside him. 'Yes, Uncle Tom what is it?'

'Tricia! I want you to join us because we like you. I won't charge you anything but you must teach Billy and we'll feed you for free, okay? You'll be safe on this barge.'

'Oh… err…'

'What's the matter, don't you like it?'

'Yes, I do, but can I think about it?'

'Yes, lass, you do what you think is right.'

Tricia's mind was in a fuzz but flashes of eight shillings a week less rent and food and twelve hours slaving shot through her head and seconds later as Edie came out with bowls of hot-pot, she said. 'When do I start, Uncle Tom?'

'You're part of the family now, Tricia, and I like that uncle bit. I fixed it for the crane to lift your cart onboard and you can make yourself comfy upfront. That's your classroom as well. We load up with coal this afternoon and when we leave in the morning, Billy is all yours. Let's have dinner.'

'Does, Billy know, Uncle Tom?'

'Not yet.' He looked around, 'Where is he, Mum?'

'I sent him to the market for some eggs.'

Tricia pointed up the dock, 'There he is and he's in a hurry.'

'Probably hungry, he always is,' said Edie.

Edie stood up on the bench and waved to Billy, and shouted, 'Stop running, Billy, mind those eggs.'

Billy slowed to a trot and arrived at the barge out of breath and it was a few moments before he could climb the ladder into the cockpit and when he did he blurted out, 'Wow! It's buzzing in the market. They say there's been a murder or sommat up by the Yellow Mill.'

'Okay, Billy,' said Tom, 'get your breath and tell us.'

'A man's been stabbed and bled to death and the police are asking all the cab drivers if they had a fare up there as wheels were heard clattering over the cobbles late last evening.'

Edie went down into the cabin and called Tom to follow and close the door behind him. Once inside she told Tom, Tricia's story and they talked for a few minutes before they went outside to finish their dinner. When he sat down before he started eating, Tom said to, Tricia. 'After dinner, you and Edie go to your cabin and get it set up and then you rest out of sight until we're tied up over the other side of the canal.' He turned to Billy. 'And you lad will keep your mouth shut. You've seen and heard nothing. Understand!'

Billy nodded, 'Yes, Dad.'

'Good, let's finish our dinner.'

———

It took the dockside steam crane three minutes to load Tricia's cart and with Prince pulling and the help of the two labourers with long quant poles the barge was eased into the coal loading wharf.

Loading the coal was quick as the side of the rail coal truck was unpinned and the truck tilted and with long rakes, the coal was pulled into the barge. After each truck, the barge was moved a few feet forward or back and the coal raked to keep the barge level and in two hours the job was done.

The barge was punted from the dock and across the canal where Billy was waiting with the horses. Once hitched up, instead of laying up for the night a few hundred yards from the Coal Wharf they kept going, Fifteen minutes into their journey Tom sent Billy to fetch Tricia if she was feeling alright and she joined them for a cuppa and a black pudding sandwich five minutes later.

As she climbed down into the cockpit, Tom said, 'Aye, lass, that's a right shiner there. We're going all the way to Kendal so you'll have time to lose the bruises.'

'Thank you, Uncle Tom.'

'Okay, lass, just make sure you feel okay before you get started with Billy.'

'Auntie Edie,' said Tricia, 'will we be stopping at Garstang?'

Edie nodded, 'Yes, Tricia, why?'

'I want some material to make a new dress. I can patch up the damaged one for everyday wear but I would like to make a new one and keep my best one for... you know... best.'

'Can you do dressmaking, Tricia?'

'Yes, my Mam taught me. I think she knew something was going to happen and she made sure I could look after myself by teaching me to knit and dressmaking and cooking.'

Tom looked at Tricia and shook his head, before he said, 'How old are you, Tricia?'

'Seventeen, Uncle Tom.'

'My, my, you sound a lot older than that, young lady.'

'Tricia!' said Edie, 'Lancaster would be better choice.'

'I can't go out in Lancaster in case someone sees me.'

'What's that all about,' said Tom.

'I'll tell you later, Tom, but that's why she was going to Preston.'

'Huh! I wondered why you were going to that shit hole.'

They finally tied up a couple of miles out in the North End

Basin by Bostocks Farm and there being no stables Billy let the horses loose in a small paddock with a couple of make do wooden shelters. Lucky stayed with the barge and settled into Tricia's cabin as if she had never been away.

—

Tricia got up early the next morning and wrapped up against the October weather she went with Billy to get the horses and when they got to the field they were in the far corner.

Prince looked up and after moments indecision started walking towards them followed by Queenie. 'That's unusual, Tricia, they don't normally do that. I have to fetch them.'

'Prince and I had a chat a couple of days ago, Billy, and the way he watched over me the other night I think he got my smell.'

The horses joined them and Prince went straight to her and after a quick sniff he stood quietly while she fitted the harness. Billy did the same to Queenie and they led them back to the barge and hooked them up ready for a long day's work.

Back at the barge, Billy ran over to Tom and excitedly told him what the horses had done and when he had calmed down, Tom said, 'Okay, son, grab your sandwich and get us on our way and when me and Mum are ready you can go and do some more learning with Tricia.'

Billy scooped his sandwich off the plate that Edie was holding and ran forward and climbed onto Queenie. He looked back and Tom gave him the thumbs up and with little persuasion, the horses leaned into their harness and they were on their way back up the canal towards Kendal loaded with coal for the Gas Works.

Tricia was sat on the roof of the main cabin with her legs dangling inside the cockpit enjoying her egg sandwich and a mug of tea when Tom, said to her, 'How are you feeling' this morning, lass?'

'A little bit tired, Uncle Tom. I didn't sleep well last night. I had a lot of nasty dreams.'

'Aye, you'll be like that for a while but it goes. Do you feel up to a bit of teaching today?'

'Oh, yes, Billy's a good pupil and picks up things quickly.'

'Okay, lass, give us a few minutes and then you can start, and if things go well we'll be in Garstang with time to spare for shopping.'

'Oh, good, I have to get some more paper.'

'I'll get the paper for you, lass.'

'It's okay, Uncle Tom, I need some for my drawing and my short stories.'

He shrugged and made himself busy coiling ropes and other things to keep his barge ship shape. Tricia went forward to her cabin and tidied up her teaching space. She had to do it properly now as they were looking after her and she spent a few minutes trying to remember how Miss Hardcastle had taught her.

She has hardly had time to decide what she was going to do when there was a knock on the cabin door and when she looked up, she saw Billy peering in.

'Come in Billy and make yourself comfortable on my bunk. There's your slate and we're going to carry on with your reading and writing this morning and after dinner, it's arithmetic and times tables.

The morning began quietly with Billy only being called upon to help a few times but two hours into the journey Tricia felt faint.

'Billy,' she said, 'I'm not well. Go and help with the barge and I'll call you when I feel better.'

'Okay, Tricia, can I get you anything like a mug of tea?'

'No, Billy, I'm going to lie down for a bit.'

Billy put his slate and his paperwork on the top bunk and climbed out of the cabin.

'Give us a shout if you want anything, Tricia.'

'I will.'

He had no sooner left than she felt dizzy again and rolled onto her bunk and she cried as terrible reminders of that night tumbled through her brain. After a while, she fell into a troubled sleep and didn't hear Edie pop her head in to check on her.

It was three hours later when she felt well enough to tidy herself up and venture out and her head had only just appeared above the cabin roof when Edie called her and waved her to come to the rear. She acknowledged and climbed up onto the cabin roof but the thought of walking along the plank walk was daunting in her condition.

She stood for a moment wondering what to do next when clenching her fists and gritting her teeth, she said aloud, 'Sod it!' and took her first step forward.

She made it and was welcomed by Edie with a mug of tea.

'Here, lass, get that down you and then you can have some dinner.'

'Dinner!' said, Tricia, 'have I been asleep that long?'

'Yes, and I have some news for you.'

'What's that, Aunt Edie?'

'Do you remember that little school I showed you in Borrowdale on the way down?'

'Yes.'

'Well. I was talking to the lady who does the laundry and she told me they are short of a teacher for the new starters so I stopped and asked at the school and mentioned you and they want to see you when we come back next week. Is that okay?'

'Oh, I don't know.'

'What's the matter, Tricia? I've seen the way you teach, Billy. I'm sure you can do it and didn't you mention you had helped in a Sunday school when you were younger?'

'Yes, I did and I have references.'

'I don't think you have much to worry about. Now come on get some food down you.'

—

Although the weather had changed for the worse they made good time to Garstang. After tea, Edie went with Tricia into the village and their first stop was Smith's Marine Store with its vast array of goods from the simplest candle to fancy buckets and everything that a barge would need.

'They have lot's of stuff here, Auntie Edie,' said Tricia, 'but some of it is used.'

'That's good for us, Tricia. When barge people get short of money they sell their stuff here and we can buy it. There's new stuff also but second hand is cheaper. Go up to the top there and he's got some material and sometimes a dress or two.'

Tricia wiggled her way through the narrow passage between shelves and came upon the clothes rack and after a few minutes searching she found a skirt which could be altered and somebody had traded in their Sunday dress which Tricia thought with a little tweaking would fit her nicely and she included a new apron also. She knew it was shrinking her savings pot but thought it was worthwhile with the prospect of a job.

She joined Edie who had topped up her candle store and she was holding a newish waistcoat.

'Who's that for, Auntie Edie?'

'Tom, he's been driving me mad with that worn-out thing of his. I swear it's older than me.'

Tricia laughed as she could envisage the clash that was going to commence when they got back to the barge as she remembered the battles her Mam and Dad used to have. She wiped away a tear as she remembered her Dad's favourite neckerchief which was wafer thin by the time her Mam wrestled it off him.

The next stop was the book store where ignoring the peculiar looks at her battered features she topped up her chalk and watercolours and a good bundle of paper. With a little haggling and a bit of flirting she wangled some cotton drawing paper and feeling quite pleased with herself they made their way back to the barge.

'That's a good bundle you've got there, Tricia,' said Edie, 'will you need all that if you take that job?'

'I think so, Aunt Edie because I like to write my little stories and then do the paintings in them. I have a lot in my cart.'

'My, my, you do everything.'

'I had a good teacher for a couple of years until Dad left us. That's why I would like to help other children like Billy.'

'Oh, he's hopeless at drawing, Tricia.'

'I haven't got the time to teach him that but his arithmetic, reading and writing come first and he's doing pretty well.'

'Thank you, Tricia. I want him to leave the barges.'

'Keep him out of the Mills they're horrible.'

'He said he wants to join the Merchant Navy.'

'This will do him good.'

When they arrived back at the barge Tricia prepared to make her way to her cabin when Edie, said, 'No hanging around chatting tonight, Tricia, come and get a mug of tea and a slice of bread and dripping and then I'm going straight to bed.'

'Give me two minutes, Aunt Edie. I'll just put my stuff away.'

As she made her way along the plank walk Tricia thought it must be the extra work without Billy that was making Edie and Tom tired and admired the sacrifice they were making for him.

Later, when Tricia's tormented dreams wouldn't let her sleep she felt a comfortable pressure at the back of her knees. She stretched a hand out and gave Lucky a few strokes behind the ear and feeling at ease with her feline protector she fell asleep.

The following day was Sunday and there was a cold north-westerly wind blowing and Tricia was glad of the small stove which heated her cabin. Because it was Sunday she wore her new apron with a long hand-knitted woollen scarf crisscrossed over her chest and pinned at the back and with her canvas coat on she went out early and helped Billy with the horses.

When they were hooked up she expected Billy to get them on their way but instead, she was surprised to be called to the cockpit where Tom was waiting with a bible and with heads bowed they listened as he read aloud from it and then said a few prayers and at the end together they said, 'Amen!'

Tom lowered the bible, and said, 'Thank you, Tricia, for joining us. We'll get on our way now.'

Billy jumped off the stern and went to the horses who were munching on their first bag of feed and with a signal from Tom who unhitched the quayside painters, he got them on their way. Tricia joined Edie and had a bowl of porridge and a boiled egg for breakfast and went to her cabin ready for another day's tutorage with Billy.

He joined her half an hour later and she asked him about the little prayer meeting.

'We do it every Sunday, Miss Tricia, but if it's raining we squeeze up in the cabin. When we're docked in Preston or Kendal we go to Church there. We could go in Lancaster but Dad doesn't like the church there, he said they're too up themselves.'

'Okay, Billy, we're going to practice your writing this morning and later we will do spelling and reading.'

There was more traffic going south and Billy got called away quite a lot. Edie and Tricia hopped off at the Farm Shop but catching up with the barge was harder as they were walking into the wind and showery rain. They made Lancaster by seven o'clock and tied up on the left bank in a wider part of the canal opposite the White Cross Mill not far from the stables and they settled down to a late supper.

It had been a long day and Tricia left them while Tom was finishing his jug of ale and as she climbed down into the cabin Lucky slid past her and curled up on her bunk waiting for her. He didn't have long to wait and Tricia went to sleep quickly but she was disturbed a few times during the night by vivid dreams.

―

The next morning feeling refreshed after a cold wash she poked her head out and saw activity at the rear and glad that the weather had improved although it was still cold she joined Tom and family in the cockpit for their breakfast of porridge, boiled egg and bread with the statutory mug of tea.

Breakfast over Tom stood up and, said to Tricia, 'I'm sorry, lass, but I have to take Billy from you today, Mum is not well so you're free to do what you want.'

'I'll help Aunt Edie. I cannot sit around doing nothing.'

'Thanks, lass, see what you can do.'

'I'll help Billy with the horses, and Aunt Edie, you take it easy until I get back. I know, boil some water and I'll wash up.'

Billy waited until she had jumped back on board before he released the horses into their daily grind while Tom took over the steering. He unhitched the mooring ropes leaving the one at the rear until last and leapt back on board and guided to barge to the middle of the canal.

Tricia went down into the cabin and was amazed by how pristine it was and she told Edie off for starting the washing up. Tricia took over and asked Edie what was the matter. 'Oh, it's nothing, Tricia, it's the first day of my rag week and I'm always bad. I'll be a lot better tomorrow. How do you manage?'

'I think I'm lucky, Aunt Edie. I feel off colour but able to carry on just like my Mam.'

'Aye, we're all different. Men are lucky, I think they should have babies as well then they would know what pain is.'

'Is it bad, Aunt Edie, I mean having babies? My Mam said I was a hanger-on.'

Edie went to pick up a tea towel and Tricia stopped her and when she sat down, she continued, 'I've seen many births up and down the canal as we help each other, Tricia, and some mothers give birth like shelling peas and others can take many hours. You sound like one of them who didn't want to come into the world. There is pain when you're pushing the baby out which I cannot describe but when the baby's born you forget all about it as you're focussed on the new life in your arms.'

'Thank you for that insight, Auntie Edie, I feel a little easier about it now.' She stepped back and wiped her hands. 'Right, that's the dishes done, what do we do now?'

'I usually prepare dinner, Tricia, and I can do that.'

'No, Aunt Edie, you can lie down and I'll do dinner and I tell you what. I can pay my way a little as in my cart I have some preserved food which I made just in case. Let's mix them with what you have and we'll have a feast today. What do you say?'

'Are you sure, Tricia, you don't have to?'

'Put your feet up, Aunt Edie and I'll be back in a few minutes.'

Tricia climbed up the narrow steps and up onto the roof and checking for bridges she made her way to her cart. After a little digging around she collected the preserving jars and with both arms full made her way back to the main cabin looking forward to showing off her skills drilled into her by a caring mother.

She poured the contents of all four jars into Edie's large pan and added to her urban mix carrots, turnip and greens, which she had not eaten for nearly four years, plus a better grade of stewing steak all bought from the canal side farm shop. Satisfied she could not improve it anymore she left her hot-pot simmering and put a kettle on for mid-morning tea. She had to admit to herself that getting back to the rural diet was the best thing to happen to her since they had been forced to leave Lunesdale.

As the kettle boiled, they arrived at Tewitfield locks and had their morning mug while waiting for a barge to exit the bottom lock. Edie, although still feeling rough had to manage the tiller while Billy and Tom handled the ropes and the lock gates and the long process of negotiating the eight locks began with barges passing in between each lock and the whole process just to travel half a mile took over two hours before they could once more proceed without hindrance.

Tricia felt guilty while they were working hard so in between nipping to check her hot-pot she retreated to her cabin and did some alterations on her new possessions. After much soul searching she repaired the knife hole in her old skirt and packed it away thinking it may come in useful should she be reduced to working in the Mills again.

While it had been tea at the bottom of the locks it was hot-pot and dumplings at the top and both Billy and Tom had second helpings and it was dark by the time they tied up in the Gas Works Basin in Kendal and no time was wasted. As soon as supper was over it was into bed.

Tricia was anxious about going to bed as her nightmares over the previous few days had given her little peace but she persisted and with the calming influence of Lucky, she slept.

—

Her body clock was used to early rising but Tricia was surprised to be woken up by loud shouting and lots of mechanical banging and she felt the barge tilt and shake. She quickly got up and by candlelight she splashed her face and got dressed before poking her head out of the hatch. It was dusk and she could see two steam cranes dragging coal out of the barge and piling it high on the dock. She could see Tom standing on the edge of the hold and leaning on the rear cabin overseeing the operation but getting to the back of the barge was going to be difficult as the boardwalk and canvas cover had been dismantled.

Wrapping herself up in her scarf and canvas coat she rammed her bonnet onto her head and clambered out onto the deck but when she went to jump down onto the dock she took a hasty step back. So much coal had been unloaded from the barge it was now two foot higher.

She knew there were planks in the storage bin but too heavy for her to manage so through the shadows she waved to Tom and it was three minutes before he saw her through the murky October dawn.

He waved back and called Billy to go and help her and between them they manhandled a plank across to the dock and then began the game of dodgem as they manoeuvred between the cranes whose drivers were so intent on their job wayward bodies on the canal bank were a hindrance to be ignored.

Laughing they got to the rear where Edie greeted her with a mug of tea and five minutes later called her down into the cabin out of the coal dust to have mashed boiled egg mixed with butter and black pepper with homemade bread soldiers. While eating her breakfast Tricia looked at Edie and saw she was more like her old self.

The unloading never stopped and two hours later with the help of Tom and Billy the last few tons of coal were finally swept up and the barge towed down the dock to allow the next one in.

Tom and Billy cleaned the inside of the hold while Edie and Tricia did the cabins. When the last of the coal dust had gone they grabbed a quick mug of tea and the journey up to the limestone loading dock began.

It was a well-run operation. While they had been unloading a barge had been loading limestone and it passed them at the entrance. Immediately they had tied up after making sure the cabin doors were tightly shut loading began and Tricia realised why these bargees were called the black and whites as the whole of the barge became covered in white lime instead of coal dust.

There was little rest for the horses as by two o'clock fifty tons of limestone had been loaded, the barge turned around and they were on their way back to Preston and Edie served up dinner.

While they were eating, Tricia said to Edie,' You're not stopping overnight?'

'No love,' said Edie, 'we want to get as far as we can and then we can stop at Borrowdale instead of Garstang while you look at that job and then if you're staying we'll unload your cart.'

'Ooh... Auntie Edie, you shouldn't do that, I feel terrible.'

'Don't, love, you have done a lot for Billy and that's how we pay you. Now finish your dinner and then you can work with Billy for a little while until we get to the locks.'

'What about my face, Aunt Edie, will I be alright for my interview?'

'It's a little bit yellow with a bit of blue near your eye but you'll be okay. I told them you slipped jumping onto the barge and that's why you couldn't go then. It's a common enough accident.'

It was going dark when they tied up above the top lock. While Billy led the horses to a stable once used by the passenger Packet boats Tom lashed the barge to mooring posts and was more than pleased to be first in the queue for the morning rush.

Immediately after supper, they bedded down for the night ready for an early start and Tricia made Edie promise to get her up so she could help Billy.

Dawn was peeping over the horizon when Tom woke them and they got dressed and out on the job to avoid someone jumping the queue. Tricia went with Billy for the horses and in ten minutes they were hitched up and ready to go.

Tom couldn't wait and had the forward painter unhitched and the rear one loose and ready in his hand and as soon as Billy waived his arm he unhooked it and threw it aboard and jumped on after it and they were off into the top lock. Tricia looked back up the canal and as Edie had predicted competition was fierce and another barge was trying to sneak up on them.

They had breakfast while the lock was emptying and going down was quicker than the journey up and they were out and on their way in an hour and a half and Tom was pleased.

Once they had manoeuvred through the queue of barges waiting to go up the locks the journey south went smooth and even in the inclement weather they made good time and stopped overnight four miles south of Lancaster. This new routine unsettled the horses who once again were tethered in a field. They were not distressed but unhappy not to be berthed in a warm stable with bags of feed.

Up early but without the need to rush they made Borrowdale by late afternoon. Tricia and Edie went to the store and on the way back stopped at the School House where they were met by the Reverend Isaiah Bishop who invited them into his office.

'Good evening, ladies,' said the Vicar, 'how can I help?'

'Good evening, Reverend,' said Edie, 'I called in to see you five days ago after hearing you required a new teacher and I told you about this young lady who is travelling with us.'

'Oh, yes, I remember you said she'd had an accident and couldn't come.' He looked at Tricia, and said, 'And what's your name young lady?'

Tricia did a half curtsey, before she replied, 'Patricia Cartwright, sir.'

'Miss Cartwright, I'm very sorry…' Tricia mentally slumped fearing the worst. '…but I'm busy preparing my sermon for Sunday. Can you call tomorrow morning, at say, nine o'clock?'

Tricia didn't hesitate and answered enthusiastically, 'Yes, sir, and I will be on time.'

'Good, I have to do the Sunday service at ten.'

He showed them out and it was then that Tricia said to Edie, 'Is that alright? I forgot you need to move on.'

'Don't worry, love, we're ready for it.'

They had a relaxing supper and a long natter while Tom enjoyed a couple of pots of ale before retiring.

Tricia could not sleep because of all the questions she was anticipating but the gentle purring of Lucky curled up alongside her calmed her nerves and morning couldn't come soon enough.

—

Tom did their Sunday service and wearing her best Sunday clothes with a bonnet and lace-up boots and carrying her portfolio, Tricia, treading carefully trying to keep her boots clean walked the short distance to the school and taking a deep breath ventured into the open front entrance into the hallway.

On the left was a narrow room with many hooks on the walls and next door was a classroom with small desks for the infants and opposite was a larger classroom. She was peering through the glass panels of the door when the Reverend Isaiah Bishop spotted her. He stopped what he was doing and he came out to see her.

'Good morning, Miss Cartwright, how are you this morning?'

'Good morning, Reverend Bishop, I am well, sir.'

'Come with me and I will get the housekeeper to make some tea. You drink tea?'

'Yes, sir.'

They went to the last door on the right of the hallway and into the small but efficient office lined with books and other paraphernalia and a large desk with a seat on either side.

He pulled a seat out for her and when she was settled he went around the desk and sat opposite in the most comfy office chair she had ever seen. He picked up a Chinese basket gong and shook it and a few moments later a tidy elderly woman dressed in black with a white bonnet and apron appeared. 'Yes, Mr Isaiah?'

'Mrs Cheetham, meet Patricia.' She nodded Tricia's way, 'can you make us tea, please?'

'Right away, Mr Isaiah,' she looked at Tricia, and said, 'best of luck, Missy,' and backed out of the room.

'Now, Miss Cartwright, tell me about yourself. First of all, how is your face, it is still looking a little yellow?'

'I can barely feel it, sir. I was lucky I only gave it a glancing blow as I fell. I don't think I will be jumping on moving barges again.'

'You work on the barges, Miss Cartwright?'

'No, sir, I was travelling with them from Lancaster to Preston because they were cheaper and they took my cart at no extra cost.'

'You are going to Preston?'

'If I am not successful today, sir, but initially I gave their son Billy lessons in Maths and English and when we got to Preston they asked me to stay on and teach Billy some more. They are a lovely family and I had enjoyed the trip, so I said, 'Yes,' and while travelling north Mrs Devlin heard about this vacancy and here I am.'

'Why were you going to Preston in the first place?'

Tricia knew she had to tell a little white lie and did so without any guilt. 'After the death of my father I was left to look after my ailing mother for a couple of years and now she has left this mortal coil I am free to pursue my ambition which was to become a Governess or a teacher and I was advised that there may be more positions available in the Preston area.'

'Oh, I see. How old are you, Miss Cartwright?'

'Seventeen, sir, and I have references.'

'Let me see them. Tell me, Miss Cartwright, your hands are rough like you have been doing manual work.'

Tricia pulled the references from her portfolio and as she handed them over, she said, 'The top one is from my tutor when I had private tuition when employed by Lord Kearsley as a companion to his grandson. My hands, Mr Bishop, are because when I had to look after my mother I took on some manual labour when available.'

Bishop studied the documents carefully and then went through them again.' Mmm…' he said, 'you speak French and it says here you are college worthy at Maths and English. How do you find the circumference of a circle, Miss Cartwright?'

'Pi times diameter, sir.'

'And the area of a circle?'

With a hint of annoyance in her voice, she replied, 'Pi times R squared.'

'And what do you call an angle greater than 180°?'

She held her breath to stop herself sighing, and replied, 'Reflex.'

'Last but not least, what is a triangle with unequal sides?'

Tricia had to think for a moment as she visioned each triangle in her mind before she answered, 'Scalene but if it has two equal sides it is called an isosceles triangle.'

Bishop glanced at her over his glasses but said nothing instead he read her second reference again and while he was doing so, he said, 'What made you take up French?'

'It was part of the curriculum of the grandson and I loved it and took extra homework.'

He put her references down, and said, 'French was never my forte but what are you reading now?'

"*Pride and Prejudice'* by Jane Austen. I like her books and I am minded to buy her book called *'Emma'* which I have heard is very good.'

'Besides reading do you have any other hobbies?'

'I learned to play the pianoforté and sing while I was studying at Kearsley Hall and when I had any free time I used to sneak into the library and play the pianoforté but it is a long time since I did either.'

'Miss Cartwright. Why have you chosen to teach infants?'

'I enjoyed my teaching experience in the Lancaster Church School when I was younger...' she patted her portfolio, '...and I write my own children's stories and do the artwork when I can.'

'If I offer you the job how soon can you start?'

'Immediately, sir, that is after I have found somewhere to live and settled in.'

'Good. You have accommodation upstairs over the school and you will be paid fifteen shillings and sixpence a week. You start at nine in the morning until midday and two p.m. through 'til five o'clock, Monday to Friday and two hours after church on Sunday. We are a Church of England and a charity school and all children have to pay a penny a day to attend except Sunday. Sometimes we make an exception. In the interests of the children, we have a service every morning. We do get some Catholic children. Do not try to convert them. There will be a deduction from your income towards Mrs Cheetham's salary who is your housekeeper come lady's maid and some for the cook. You will have to pay for your heating and your meals. I might add that getting coal is sometimes difficult and a little expensive. Is that satisfactory?'

The thought that she would be employing servants was a little disturbing but she was hardly able to contain herself at the income she would receive which was far more than she had dreamed of, and she said conservatively, 'By all means, Mr Bishop, sir.'

'Good, when can you move in?'

'Today, Mr Devlin is unloading my cart as we speak.'

'He's pretty confident of your success and they must think a lot of you to stop their barge.'

'They are a wonderful family and adopted me and they have worked extremely hard over the last few days to get me here early and I cannot thank them enough. I was not taking any income from them, only food, and they saw it as a way of paying me… Oh!… I might be able to help with the coal.'

'How's that?'

'Mr Devlin carries coal north frequently and is always looking for extra income.'

'Thank you, Miss Cartwright, welcome to Borrowdale in the Parish of Longbottom. It has been nice meeting you. May your stay with us be agreeable? Here is your key. Your accommodation is through that door at the end as is the kitchen. Mrs Cheetham will show you around when you move in.'

—

Disappointed that he hadn't asked to see her artwork she could hardly contain herself. She was a teacher now and therefore a lady so dancing or skipping were a no, no, but she did walk a little quicker so that Tom and Edie could get on their way.

When she reached the canal, she crossed over the bridge and the broad smile as she ran down the slope towards them told them all they wanted to know.

Edie was the first to speak. 'You got the job, young miss?'

'Yes, Auntie Edie and they want me to start tomorrow.

'Well done, young Trish,' said Tom, 'we packed all your things and unloaded your cart because I knew you would. Billy will help you up the slope.'

She hugged Edie and then took Tom's hand in both of hers,

and said, 'Thank you both for all you have done. I shall miss you. You must stop by now and then, in fact, Uncle Tom, I have an offer you cannot resist.'

'What's that, young lady?'

'I have to buy my own coal so how would you like to get me three hundredweight every time you travel north. That will be more than enough for me and the rest can go to the school as it operates on charitable donations.'

Tom looked at Edie and they both shrugged and nodded. 'That will be the day after tomorrow, lass and then every time we pass north.'

'How much, Uncle Tom, you must make a little profit.'

'I'll charge you the canal trade price and that is fourpence a hundredweight bag and you can order as much as want.'

'Oh, lovely, make that four hundredweight and I will give you my cart to carry it in. Billy can help me up to the school now and bring the cart back. The chase after you will serve him well if he joins the Merchant Navy.'

It was hugs all round and Tricia waited until they were underway before she started the short walk to the school and a new life.

~~~~~

PART 2

A NEW BEGINNING

CHAPTER 10

Mrs Cheetham was waiting for them and in no time at all they had emptied the cart and Billy made to run back to the barge when Tricia stopped him. 'Take my cart, Billy...' She handed him a book, '...and take this dictionary to help with your reading.'

'Don't you want these, Miss Tricia?'

'No, Billy, and I promised the cart to your Dad so that you can bring our coal up to the school. You will have to run harder now to catch up. Take care and I'll see you on Tuesday.'

'Thank you, Miss Tricia.'

While Mrs Cheetham helped her unpack she showed her around the apartment which was to be her new home. Her bedroom was a nice size with wardrobes and bed linen supplied and big enough for two people. Tricia was happy to see the washbowl and jug were the same Royal Doulton pattern as the family keepsake chamber pot she had rescued when Auntie Lily kicked her out. It was only a potty but a link with her lost family.

Next door was a parlour connecting to a living room and hidden in one corner a dumb waiter disguised as a cupboard which allowed food to be transferred up from the kitchen and dirty dishes back down and all the rooms had a fireplace.

There was another room on the landing which Agnes did not show her, but merely said, 'This is a spare room which we use for stowing things. The cooking and washing, Miss Cartwright, is done downstairs and the latrines are outdoors.'

'What about water, Mrs Cheetham?'

'The best, miss, it comes from an underground spring and there is a pump in the kitchen and all waste is fed by a local beck into the canal.'

'Into the canal, but some barge people use the canal water for drinking.'

'Was that the people you were with?'

'No, they had a water tank which they filled at every stop.'

Mrs Cheetham scooped up Tricia's small pile of washing and at the same time, said, 'Sensible they were. Now let's get some lunch before the afternoon Sunday school begins.'

'Mrs Cheetham, before we go can I ask you one thing?'

'Yes, miss, what is it?'

'Can you call me Tricia when we are alone?'

Mrs Cheetham, visibly relaxed, smiled, and said, 'Of course, dear, and you shall call me Agnes or even Aggie. I feel better already—I must get lunch now, missy and we have dinner in the evening.'

—

It was two o'clock and she was moving things around into positions she liked and then moving them back again when she heard the laughter and chatter of the children as they arrived for the afternoon session of Sunday school. On a whim, she tidied herself up and coiled her hair into a large bun before sorting through her portfolio and retrieving one of her early stories. She waited for ten minutes before venturing downstairs and taking a deep breath eased the door open and slipped into the room.

The Rev. Isaiah Bishop was alerted by the children as they all looked towards the door. He waved her forward and at the same time, said, 'Miss Cartwright, come in, come in.'

A feeling of calm swept over her and she felt a gentle nudge in her back as a familiar voice whispered, "This is your time, work hard and all will be right."

Suddenly she felt at home in the company of young children and she stepped forward with a smile on her face, and mentally said, "Thank you, Mam."

Bishop turned to face the class and in a commanding but gentle manner, said, 'Please stand.' The whole class did as they were bid and Bishop continued, 'Children, I want you to meet, Miss Cartwright. She is our new teacher and will start officially on Monday and will be doing Sunday classes from now on.' He turned to Tricia, 'Miss Cartwright, this is our Sunday class made up of all ages. Have you anything you would like to say to them?'

She held up her booklet, and said, 'I would like to read them a short story if I may, Mister Bishop.'

'Is it a well known one? Miss Cartwright.'

'No, sir, it is one I wrote some time ago about 'Henrietta' the matriarch of the farmyard.'

Bishop stepped down from the lectern and called Tricia forward. 'Carry on, Miss Cartwright, the floor is all yours.'

She chose not to stand on the lectern but instead stood in front of it with the children around her. 'Good afternoon, children'

'Good afternoon, Miss Cartwright,' they answered in unison.

She held up the booklet upon which was a painting of a Hen sitting on a nest with an egg peeking out from under her. 'Boys and girls this is Henrietta and I am going to tell you a story about her. She is the oldest mother hen in the farmyard. Are you ready?'

'Yes, Miss.'

She opened the booklet, took a deep breath and began reading…

"Once upon a time on a chilly February morning, Henrietta didn't feel like laying eggs. All through the night, the wind had been howling and when she poked her head out of the door she saw the dreaded snow lying all around…"

When she reached the end of the story she lowered the booklet and someone at the rear began clapping and soon the whole class was doing it and Bishop joined in and a high pitched child's voice shouted, 'More!'

When the clapping stopped with a huge smile on her face, Tricia said, 'If you are all good I will read another one next week. Now you must finish your lessons.'

Bishop thanked her and she left the room glowing inside ready for her new direction in life but a big priority was a trip to Garstang the following Saturday to increase her wardrobe. Not only would it give her more options but also meant Mrs Cheetham would have to wash, dry and iron them less often. As she turned to go up the stairs a soft furry object rubbed up against her ankle. She looked down and it was Lucky. 'Come and see our new home, Lucky, that is if you're staying.'

She mounted the stairs and Lucky bounded up alongside her.

After dinner that evening with Lucky curled on her lap she spent a few hours studying her old school books and trying her hardest to remember how Miss Hardcastle had gone about teaching her and Stephen. Reading stories was one thing but this was a whole new scene and she didn't want to fluff it on her first day.

Before she went to bed she rubbed goose grease into her hands in an attempt to soften them.

—

The night passed swiftly. She had no sooner closed her eyes than Agnes was knocking on her door. 'Miss Cartwright, time to get up. Can I come in?'

Tricia rolled over, rubbed her eyes, and said sleepily, 'Yes, Agnes.'

Agnes entered holding a candle in front of her and a fluffy black ball shot past her. She crossed the room and lit the candle on the dressing table.

'Missy, was that a cat I just saw?'

'Yes, Agnes, that was Lucky. He's adopted me and will be staying. He's house trained and eats nearly everything we do except onions and if you could feed him and leave him some water I would be grateful.'

'I like cats, Missy and I will see to him later.' She opened the curtains which was a disappointment as in the gloom all that was visible were rain clouds.

'Right, Missy, up you get and we'll have you spick and span in no time. We must impress this morning.'

Tricia yawned, 'Do I have to, Agnes, can I have another ten minutes?'

'No, Missy, not today.'

While Tricia threw the covers off and swung out of bed Agnes filled the bowl and Tricia plunged her face into the cold water. She stood up and took the towel from Agnes and wiped herself. 'Ah! That's better. I can see now.'

'Coldwater, Missy? I have hot water ready if you want it.'

'Cold water is fine, Agnes, it is what I have used all my life but I do like a hot tub at night.'

Agnes helped her get dressed and then did her hair. She did a simple chignon worn at the nape of the neck with three twists dangling down over each ear. She looked in the mirror and she liked it. 'Oh, Agnes, you have done a wonderful job.'

'You look like a proper lady now, Missy.'

'Thank you, Agnes,—Agnes?'

'Yes, Missy.'

'Agnes, you keep calling me, Missy. Why?'

'Calling you, Tricia, makes me feel uncomfortable. I find Missy is a good middle of the road means of addressing you. It is both friendly, and courteous. Do you mind?'

'No, Agnes, but I will not call you, Aggie.'

'Right, Missy, let's get breakfast or you will be late and that would not do. Boiled eggs and buttered toast soldiers I think you said. I'll bring them up shortly and I expect a certain cat is starving.'

Tricia was about to say she would join her downstairs and then thought better of it. She had moved up in the world and this was a new life she must get used to. She spun around in front of the mirror and decided she was not sure about her blouse and she quickly changed it for a white one with black edging like railway lines on either side of the buttons which were also black and had a high frill collar with black edging and it matched her grey skirt. It had been one of her Mam's favourite Sunday outfits and another keepsake she had managed to hang on to. Satisfied, she went through to the living room for her breakfast which Agnes was laying out on the mahogany dining table and the warmth from the fire made her new lodgings feel cosy.

'There you are, Missy, and Lucky has gone walkabout.'

'He does, Agnes. He'll be back.'

At eight forty-five, she went down to her classroom and laid things out ready and while she stood taking it all in the Rev. Isaiah Bishop entered. 'Good morning, Miss Cartwright, are you well this morning?'

'Yes, Mr Bishop, and looking forward to my first day. Do we

have a curriculum or is it down to me?'

'Now that we have the babies as I call them separate I will leave that to you but we stick to the basics like times tables and the alphabet with writing and reading. I'm sure you know the routine.'

Thank you, Mr Bishop. I must ask, as the autumn chill is in the air can we light the fires? I have arranged for a coal delivery tomorrow?'

'But Miss Cartwright, I don't think we have the funds this week.'

'It is sixpence per hundredweight and four hundredweight is being delivered and I will pay. Two hundredweight for me and the rest is for the school. It will be every fortnight, is that okay?'

'I… err… Miss Cartwright, I cannot express myself. That is less than fifty per cent of what we usually pay and such charity. How on earth did you manage that?'

'My secret, Mr Bishop, but you could tip the young lad that will deliver it.'

'Miss Cartwright, I have a feeling that things are looking up for you already. I will get the handyman to light them, the children will be pleased. It's nine o'clock, time to let the little terrors in. We have Assembly in the big room and then the babies will come in here.'

'I'm ready, sir.'

—

Assembly lasted fifteen minutes and when it was over, Bishop said, 'Babies! That is the five to seven-year-olds, you go now with, Miss Cartwright. The rest stay here with me.'

There was lots of shuffling around but they sorted themselves out and Tricia counted eleven going into her classroom, She followed them in and they all stood by their desks and as she closed the door behind her, they said in unity, 'Good morning, Miss Cartwright.'

'Good morning, children. Now I want you to all sit in the front rows. Sort yourselves out.'

When they had settled down she noticed one boy struggling to sit behind one of the small desks. She pointed to him, and said,

'What's your name, young man?'

'Isaac, miss.'

'Isaac, how old are you?'

'I'm seven, miss, nearly eight.'

'When are you eight, Isaac?'

'Two weeks, miss.'

'Isaac, come with me. You others sit still and quiet and wait.'

She remembered the silent warning her teacher used when she was an infant and she reached under the lectern and took out a slim flexible cane and hooked it over the front before she signalled Isaac to follow her.

They crossed the hall and after a gentle tap on the door, she led Isaac into the senior classroom. Bishop stepped down from the lectern, and said, 'What is it, Miss Cartwright?'

'This is Isaac, Mr Bishop. He's eight in two weeks and I think ready for the senior class.'

'You are probably right, Miss Cartwright—Isaac! Find yourself a desk. Quickly!'

Isaac scurried across the room and jumped into an empty desk by the window.

'Is everything to your expectations, Miss Cartwright?' said Bishop, '

'It is early days, Mr Bishop.'

She left the room and was surprised at the quietness as she stepped into her classroom and they all stood up as she walked in. 'Sit down, please, children.' She picked up a piece of chalk and stood in front of the blackboard and pointed to a young boy at the back. 'Now, starting from there give me your names and age.'

They did as they were bid and in no time she had a means of identifying the six girls and four boys in her class.

She put down the chalk and took a sheaf of papers that she had prepared and proceeded to hand them out. 'Now, children, we are going to have a little exam.' She could see the eyes of her class open wider in surprise, and continued, 'Don't worry, this is not important. Write your name on the bottom and do as much as you can and that will tell me how much you have learned already. You have five minutes starting now.'

She could see the reflection of the large station clock in the hall so was able to judge the time but she made her mind up. She needed to purchase a watch. The trip to Garstang was getting needy very quickly. While she waited she wrote the two times table on the blackboard without the answers and glancing at the clock, she said, 'Times up, children. One row at a time, bring your papers to me, please.'

They brought their results to her and in return, she gave them a blank sheet of paper. 'On these I want you to put the answers to the two times table while I check your results.'

She sorted through the results and made a small diagram and waited a few more minutes until they had all stopped writing. 'Now children we are going to move around again. I want Philip, a scruffy rundown child with worn-out shoes, dirty undersized clothes and untidy dull hair, Carol, Nancy and Delia to sit together over here on my right and you others over here on my left. Go!'

They shuffled around and when they were settled, she said, 'I want you all to help me move the empty desks over to the back wall so that we have two separate groups.'

When they were all sat down once more she noticed that the three girls sat separate from Philip. She knew why but said nothing as her plan would still work but she was determined that Philip's problem would be looked into. She turned to the blackboard and wrote the answers to the times' table on it, and said, 'Now children tick off your answers.'

'How many got ten?'

Six hands shot up including, Philip.

'Nine!'

Three hands went up leaving the baby of the group, Nancy. Tricia went over to Nancy and looked at her paper and much as she expected she only had five. 'Well done, Nancy.'

She went back to the front of the class, 'Now children, using your slates we are going to have a little arithmetic game. I will call out the sums and you will write down the answers, some are hard and some easy so that everyone gets a chance. Ready?'

'Yes, miss,' they answered collectively. 'Question one. What is three plus two?'

They all scribbled away and when they had finished, she said, 'Who got five?'

All but Nancy's hand shot up and Tricia saw that Philip was the quickest. 'Well done. This one is for you, Nancy. Two plus one.'

Nancy looked pleased and when she had finished she waved her hand. 'What did you get, Nancy?'

'Three, miss.'

'Good, I knew you could do it. Next…'

And the game went on covering the four major sections of basic Maths and she made a note that Philip had over eighty per cent. Through the rest of the morning she covered the alphabet, writing and spelling and in the open area she had created some childhood games 'Ring a Ring o' Roses' being a favourite, with a little paper creativity making paper boats. On the stroke of twelve, she said, 'Dinner time, children. See you at two o'clock and don't be late.'

They stood up together, and said, 'Thank you, Miss Cartwright,' and filed out. As Philip was going past her she stopped him. He looked thin and had dark rings below his eyes. 'Philip, have you eaten today.'

'No, miss.'

'Have you got any lunch?'

'No, miss.'

'Where do you live?'

'Me, and me Mam have a shack behind the Bulls Head pub.'

'Does your Mam, work?'

'She takes in washing, miss.'

'Philip, come with me.'

'Yes, miss.'

She opened the door and allowed Philip to go first at the same moment as The Rev. Bishop was leaving the other classroom. 'Hello, Philip, what have you been up to?'

'Nothing, sir.'

'I asked him to stay, Mr Bishop.'

'Oh, and why is that, Miss Cartwright?'

'I am taking him to Mrs Cheetham for a meal and get him cleaned up. I will pay the extra of course.'

'No need, Miss Cartwright, and if you speak to Mrs Cheetham she will show you a collection of old clothes donated by some parents as their children grew out of them.'

'That would be good, Mr Bishop.'

Bishop stood to one side and let her and Philip through and as she took him down the corridor past the office and into the kitchen area she noticed he was walking awkwardly. 'Why are you walking like that, Philip?'

'My shoes are too small, Miss.'

Mrs Cheetham was preparing Tricia's lunch. She pointed at Philip, and said, 'What's he doing here?'

'I've spoken with Mr Bishop and I want you to clean him up and give him a good dinner. Have you any white vinegar?'

'No, Miss Cartwright, but I have plenty of the ordinary vinegar. Is it for his hair?'

'Yes, and Mr Bishop says we have some second-hand clothes and some boots if we have any.'

'I'll feed him first, Miss Cartwright and then clean him up. You go upstairs Miss and I'll bring your lunch.'

Tricia turned to face Philip, and said, 'You behave young man and do what Mrs Cheetham tells you. Now sit there at the table and wait.'

Philip was flushed with embarrassment and was looking down to the floor, when he muttered, 'Yes, Miss.'

Tricia lowered herself so that she was looking directly into his eyes and she lifted his chin with her finger. 'Now, Philip, you are a clever boy and you must not be shy or feel bad about it. I know what it's like to be in your position. Eat as much as you can and I'll see you in class when Mrs Cheetham is finished. She stood up and left him to it and went to her room.

—

Philip returned to the classroom full of foreboding at what might happen. He stood outside the door and he could hear laughter and singing and taking a deep breath he opened the door and stepped inside. The laughter stopped and there was a gasp of astonishment at what they saw. There was a smartly dressed clean boy with trimmed hair, a white shirt, a smart jacket and matching breeches a little too large for him but that was good as he would grow into them, and a pair of boots a size too big with stuffed toes.

Tricia smiled. Mrs Cheetham had done a good job. She called Philip over to join the group and the older girls approached him and began touching his new clothes.

'That's not Philip Chadwick,' said Carol.

Nancy walked around him and sniffed. 'Definitely not.'

Delia said with a smile, 'Are you a new boy?'

Philip was speechless. Delia poked him. 'What's the matter, can't you speak?'

Tricia intervened. 'Alright girls, you have had your fun. This is the new Philip, and I want you to help him. Now, what were we doing?'

The games went on for another twenty minutes before Tricia called a halt and they returned to their desks and this time the older girls called Philip to sit closer. Tricia was pleased and hoped the transformation could continue.

For the rest of the afternoon, she gave them a talk on the wildlife all around them including many flowers and birds and for the last fifteen minutes she read them one of her many stories.

At five o'clock, she called time and they put their stuff into their desks, stood up, and said, 'Thank you, Miss Cartwright.'

'You are welcome. Remember, nine o'clock tomorrow.'

'Yes, Miss.'

As they left the room Tricia stopped Philip. 'Here is a note for your mother, Philip.'

'It's no good, miss, Mam can't read.'

Tricia deliberated for a moment and then said, 'I will walk home with you, I want to speak with your Mam. Wait here while I tell Mrs Cheetham and get my cloak.'

—

The autumn weather was kind to them as they followed the road alongside the canal. As they approached the pub, Tricia could see not a shed but a solidly built wooden shack. Philip opened the door and stepped inside and his mother looked up from her ironing, and said, 'What the hell is that you're wearing?' and then she saw Tricia.

'Mam,' said, Philip, 'this is Miss Cartwright my teacher'

'Oh...Oh…' stuttered Mrs Chadwick as she did a clumsy half bow while wiping her hands on her discoloured apron. 'I'm sorry; I was not expecting you, Miss.'

'Mrs Chadwick, it is my fault and I will not keep you as I can see you are busy.

She looked around and made a note of the workspace with a large copper boiling tub, rinsing tubs and a huge manual mangle. By the open door of the boiler, flat irons were being heated and there were clothes in various stages of laundering spread around. At the other end of the room was another door leading into the tiny living area.

'Mrs Chadwick, this is the new Philip, he is very bright in fact top of the class and I want him to stay that way. These clothes are his school clothes only. I will teach him and give him dinner every day but in return, you must look after him. What is for his tea?'

'Dripping butty, Miss.'

'Good, give him the same for breakfast. Use your soapy laundry water to bathe him and wash his hair. Have you coal for the winter?'

'No, Miss, it's too expensive.'

'I will arrange it. What do you normally pay?'

'One shilling a hundredweight.'

'My, my, that is expensive. I will charge you sixpence per hundredweight. Philip can return with me this evening and use the school barrow to bring some to get started. How much do you normally use?'

'I use the boiler every day so about two hundredweight a week.'

'I will get you two bags tomorrow.'

'Thank you, Miss, but I can't pay you.'

'No need. You will do my laundry and get Philip some working clothes, but it must be good and I know you work hard but smarten yourself up while you're doing it.'

Her eyes widened and she was about to shout something uncomplimentary when she had a sudden change of mind while looking at this stern authoritative young woman in front of her. 'I... Err... I'm sorry... I will do my best.'

'Thank you, Mrs Chadwick, remember what I said, Philip must attend Sunday school.' She put an arm around Philip's shoulder, and said, 'Philip, put your old clothes on and come up to the school. Mrs Cheetham will be waiting for you.'

'Yes, Miss Cartwright.'

Philips mother chipped in, 'Thank you, Miss, what little I save on coal will help me pay for Philip's schooling.'

When she got back to the school Tricia told Agnes of the new arrangement with the coal supply. '... and I'm farming my laundry out to Mrs Chadwick in exchange for the coal.'

'I've heard she does a fair job. She's had a hard time since they sent her husband packing.'

'What do you mean?'

'He was deported.'

'How sad, I have sympathy for them, it happens far too frequently.' She didn't expand on that, but added, 'I'll have a hot tub after dinner tonight, Agnes.'

Morning assembly over, Tricia took Nancy's hand and led her over to the older group. 'Now girls, and Philip, I want you to help, Nancy. Do your own work and show Nancy if she gets it wrong.'

Delia moved over on her seat and let Nancy sit alongside her. 'Thank you, Delia.' She clapped her hands and all eyes were upon her. Today children, we are going to start with your favourite subject. Arithmetic!'

She laughed when she heard the stifled groans. She turned to the blackboard where she had written the three times table without the totals. 'Using our slates write this down.'

When they had all finished, she said, 'After me, chant... One three is three, two threes are six...' and so on right to the end. When they had finished she wiped the board and continued, 'On your slates write the answers.'

The morning continued with a mixture of subjects and games until midday. Tricia called time and the children filed out of the classroom and she stopped Philip. 'Yes, Miss, have I done something?'

'No, Philip,' she gave him a folded note with money inside, 'I want you to do something for me. After dinner I want you to go to the canal basin and wait for the barge called *'Walnut'* and give this to Mr Devlin and then come straight back here.'

'Yes, Miss.'

'Good boy, there will be tuppence for you when you get back.'

'Thank you, Miss.'

'Make sure and eat all your dinner first.'

Philip ran off to the kitchen and she went upstairs to her rooms where Agnes had her lunch laid out.

—

When Philip arrived at the canal basin the '*Walnut*' was already there and Billy was just leaving on his delivery trek and Tom was about to cast off the forward tie rope.

Philip ran past Billy and over the bridge and called out, 'MR DEVLIN!'

Tom stopped what he was doing and waited for Philip. 'Whoa, lad, take it easy. What is it?'

Philip was panting for breath with one hand on his knee and the other holding up Tricia's note. 'Miss ... Miss err...'

'Take a deep breath, lad,' said Tom.

Philip took more than one breath and gradually regained his posture and held the note forward. 'Mr Devlin, Miss Cartwright said to give you this.'

Tom took the note off him and called Edie who pooped her head out of the cabin before she walked along the top of the barge to the front, and said, 'What is it? Can't I cook the dinner in peace now?'

Tom held out the note and the money. 'Here, read that and take the cash.'

Edie studied the note, counted the cash, and said to Tom, 'She wants six bags not four and she's sent the money.'

'Oh, bugger!' said Tom as he saw that Billy was off the canal and two hundred yards away with his heavy load. He shoved a hand in his pocket and withdrew a penny and held it out to Philip. 'Here, lad, run after young Billy and tell him to come back here.'

Philip had a huge grin on his face at the thought of more cash and without reply grabbed the penny and started running after Billy just as Edie began remonstrating with Tom. 'You can't put more on that cart. It's too heavy for Billy now. He won't manage six.'

'We'll have to hang on. I'll help him. What's that girl doing, starting her own business?'

'I wouldn't put it past her,' laughed Edie.

'It's a good job it's only six she wants as we have no more bags.' said Tom, 'and we'll tie up on the canal side tonight instead of in the Garstang basin. That way we might get a good run through in the morning.

At that moment Billy came back through the gate into the basin with young Philip behind him. Philip, aware of what Tricia had told him, as soon as they were by the barge he turned and legged it as quick as his little lungs would let him.

With the wheels on the cart almost bending with the strain Tom and Billy arrived at the school and were guided around to the back by the handyman and had unloaded four bags when Tricia appeared.

'Hello,' she said, 'I did not expect to see you, Mr Devlin.'

'I wasn't expecting to be here but a certain young lady demanded coal and here I is.'

'I cannot thank you enough, Mr Devlin, you're so kind. I see you're down to your last two bags. Could you deliver them to Mrs Chadwick? She lives in a shack behind the Bulls Head pub across the road from the canal. I'll get young Philip to show you.'

'Billy can do that and I'll leg it back to the barge. Same order in a fortnight?'

'Yes, please, Mr Devlin. Give my love to Auntie Edie and you take care also. Oh! Mr Devlin, on your way back to Preston can you send Billy to the school and I will tell him what we need. Is that alright?'

Tom knuckled his forehead, 'Yes, Miss Cartwright...' Tricia blushed and laughed, as he continued, '...I have to call you Miss. You has an important job.'

She smiled at him and he nodded as she turned away to hide her blushes. 'I'll go and get Philip,' she said, and hurried indoors.

In the classroom, she called Philip forward and pressed twopence into his hand. 'Give that to the young man who is taking coal to your Mum's and you show him the way and then come back here. Don't rush. She rubbed the top of his head, 'Good lad, off you go.'

When they arrived at Philip's home he rushed inside shouting, 'Mam! Mam! We have loads of coal. Billy says where do you want it?'

Mrs Chadwick wiped her hands on her apron and followed Philip outside and was surprised to see Billy waiting with two bags of coal. 'Oh, dear, two bags, I can't pay young man.'

'That's alright, it's all paid for and Miss Tricia says to leave it here. Where do you want it?'

Mrs Chadwick pointed across the yard. 'In that shed over there, please.'

'Okay, Mrs, and we'll be back in two weeks.'

'Thank you.' She took Philip by the shoulder and led him inside. 'Change your clothes and you can help me.'

'I can't, Mam. Miss said to go back even if it's just for an hour.'

She was about to remonstrate with him when she recalled her conversation with Tricia and reaching into a cupboard she gave him a biscuit. 'Eat that on your way back.' She put both arms around him and hugged him, 'and you learn as much as you can.'

When Philip got outside Billy had already left and was legging it across the road to a gap in the canal border ready for the long haul to Kendal.

After school had finished Tricia had her dinner and spent an hour planning the mornings' lessons before lounging in the luxury of a hot tub happy with the way the day had gone. Feeling cosy and warm she went to bed early and was joined by Lucky.

On Thursday they had an increase in numbers. An eight-year-old girl and her younger brother. Tricia introduced the boy to the class and did what she had done with Nancy using the older children as helpers. The boy's sister joined the seniors.

At lunchtime, she asked Agnes if she would accompany her to Garstang on Saturday.

'Of course, Missy,' she said, 'that is part of my duty. It would not do for a young lady to be without an escort.'

'Oh, thank you, Agnes. What is the best way to get there?'

'One is the stagecoach, Missy, but you can't rely on its timing and the other is a walk up the road to the rail station.'

'How far is that?'

'It's only a quarter-mile after the canal bridge.'

'I've never been on a train so that is what we will do.'

'Fingers crossed, Missy, the weather stays fine.'

After school had finished Tricia was tidying the classroom and writing up the next day's arithmetic problems on the blackboard when Bishop came into the room.

She stopped with the chalk poised. 'Hello, Mister Bishop, can I help you?'

'Miss Cartwright, I have been instructed by my wife to invite you to dinner on Saturday evening. Can you do that?'

'Oh!'

'What's the matter? Is there a problem Miss Cartwright?'

'Oh, no, Mr Bishop, it is just that on Saturday I am going shopping with Mrs Cheetham, and I am not sure when I will return. I don't know the train timetables.'

'Miss Cartwright, I would not be a gentleman if I did not help. My carriage will be at your service on Saturday at nine o'clock sharp and there is no need to worry because it is only a family affair and Mrs Bishop loves showing off her entertaining skills.'

'Will not your family need your carriage, Mr Bishop?'

'I will have great pleasure riding my new stallion and my wife will be too busy making arrangements for the evening and my children have their own.' He turned to leave and stopped. 'One more thing, Miss Cartwright, I have been informed by one of my parishioners that we will have three more pupils on Monday. One for you and two for me but there is a strange request. Can you get them cheap coal to help pay for them? I can't think why but the school appears to have a new magnetism.'

He left before she could reply and Tricia couldn't wait to tell Agnes the news and when she did Agnes got into a bit of a flap. 'Oh, dear, what am I going to do?'

'What is the worry, Agnes?'

'I have to get your best evening wear ready.'

'In that case, Agnes, you will have to help me buy something easy to wear but modern. At dinner tonight you can check my table manners. I am a bit rusty.'

'Missy, I think you must reconsider where you shop. Preston would give you a wider variety and the market would help me with next week's menu for cook.'

'How far is it, Agnes?'

'Further than Garstang.'

After a moment's hesitation when her last experience of Preston flashed through her mind, she said, 'Preston it is. Should we inform, Mister Bishop?'

'No, Missy, the coachman will take you wherever you want.'

'Agnes—tell me more about the Bishops. I must be ready for Saturday evening.'

'Mr Isaiah Bishop, Missy, is the younger brother of Lord Abraham Bishop, the owner of Bishop's Mill in Preston, one of forty such Mills in the town. They both benefited from their fathers Will but Abraham got the business and title. The Rev. Mr Isaiah Bishop has a son Clifford, who is a lawyer, and two daughters, Hilda and Constance, both married.'

'Mr Isaiah's wife?'

'That is Lady Eleanor, who has an income of her own so they

are quite comfortable but they tend to keep themselves to themselves.'

After dinner, Tricia went over her plans for the following day and corrected the homework she had given her 'gang' as she called them and at nine o'clock she went to bed and read for half an hour before snuggling down with Lucky curled up behind her knees.

It was three o'clock in the morning when she turned uneasily in her sleep with the feeling that something had invaded her dreams. A thin distant rhythm that was not yet a tramp but a steady insistent something that drums into your senses and then it turned into a cold hard clatter the unmistakable click-clack of clogs over cobbles. Their shawls over their heads faceless beings crowded down the never-ending street.

The rain gave the slate roofs of the terraced houses a polished appearance and they glistened in the early dawn. The toneless clack—clack—clack became faster and faster and echoed off the walls like horses hooves racing on the stone cobbles, and then, over the deafening cacophony the unmistakeable blast of the six o'clock siren.

Tricia's scream blended with that of the ghostly crowd and she sat bolt upright shaking with anxiety. Holding her head in her hands and leaning forward onto her knees, she wept.

After a couple of minutes she wiped the sweat off her brow and laid back and the comforting movement of Lucky as he wrapped himself across the top of her head calmed her. She reached above her and gently stroked behind his ear and the soothing massage of his tongue across her forehead eased her into an uneasy sleep.

The following morning over breakfast she told Agnes of her dream but wanting to keep that undesirable part of her past a secret, she said, 'It is weird, I can't remember a thing only a constant drumming and waking up with a scream and Lucky's tenderness.'

'I can never remember my dreams either, Missy,' replied Agnes, 'and I certainly don't recognise faces.'

The rest of Friday was without incident. Her new scholar blended in and being Friday after the lunchtime break they did drawing, played more games and listened intently to the latest adventure of 'Henrietta.' She wasn't sure that Bishop would approve but she thought play was an important part of learning.

~~~~~

CHAPTER 11

The coachman bowed slightly and greeted her as he held the door open and offered her his free hand. 'Good morning, Miss Cartwright. My name is Brown and I am at your service for the rest of the day. You are well?'

'Yes, Mr Brown, and I see the weather favours us today.'

'Yes, Miss, and with a southerly breeze it should stay fine.'

He helped her in and then turned to Agnes, and with a large grin, said, 'and you Mrs Cheetham? How are you?'

'No better for seeing you, you clown, and we are going to Preston,' she responded, but the lightness of her tone told Tricia that theirs was a good relationship.

When they were sat comfortably opposite each other he folded the step and as he closed the door, he said, 'Enjoy the trip it should be a little over an hour and a half.'

While he was climbing into his seat Agnes helped Tricia pull a rug over her knees and she said, 'We're in good hands, Missy, but you must only call him by his surname. No, Mister. That is the protocol. He is your servant.'

"Oh, dear," thought Tricia, "I have so much to learn."

—

The Saturday morning carriage traffic into town was quite heavy but Brown deftly manoeuvred his way into Fishergate and stopped on the corner at the junction with the Market Square. He helped Agnes out and then held a hand out to Tricia. 'Allow me. Miss Cartwright.'

She took his hand and he helped her down and when they were ready Agnes stopped him. 'Where will you be, Brown?'

'Out at the Mill.'

'How will we reach you?'

He pointed up the Market. 'Wait in *'Katies Parlour'* and I will pick you up at three o'clock.'

'And if we need you earlier?'

'It is only a short ride out to the Mill and I will be waiting.'

'Thank you, Brown, you may go.'

There was a hint of banter in their manner and Tricia smiled while she listened. After he had driven off, Agnes said, 'This way, Missy, we will go to the *'Elegance'* couturier first.'

'I want to go to a Bank, Agnes,' said Tricia.

'Do *'Elegance'* first and then the bank. This will give them time for alterations.'

'*Elegance'*, Agnes?'

'Don't worry, Missy, they have pre-owned stock and it is a good mixture of upper and lower class. Mr Bishop's wife and daughters love it and with your tall graceful bearing you should have no problem.' She lowered her voice. 'And remember, do not pay cash.'

Tricia had never thought of her figure before being more preoccupied with her working attire but she felt excited at the prospect of going upmarket but the money issue came as a surprise. It would be a new experience for her, but with her salary plus her savings, she could afford it. "I wish Mam was here," she said mentally, as they walked up the Market Place. Agnes insisted on walking on the outside but with the dry weather, there was little likelihood of horse muck being sprayed on them.

They stopped outside and like all shops, the front was narrow with two multi-paned bay windows with highly polished wooden frames and a recessed door but if the outside was anything to go by then it promised good material inside.

Tricia made to reach for the door handle but before she could press on it the door was opened by a smartly dressed teenage girl. 'Welcome, ma'am.' She stepped to one side holding the door until both Tricia and Agnes were inside and she then closed the door behind them. 'What can we do for you today, ma'am?'

Agnes stepped forward. 'Excuse me, young lady; we would like to speak with the proprietor, please.'

'Certainly, ma'am, wait one moment.'

She went down the shop and spoke to a smart middle-aged lady who stopped what she was doing and walked towards them. Agnes stepped forward to meet her and words were exchanged before they both approached, Tricia.

'Good morning, Miss Cartwright, I am, Mrs Rose, and I am advised you have a special engagement and this is your first shopping trip alone. Come with me.' She turned to Agnes. 'Please take a seat, I will look after your mistress.'

She stood to one side and held an arm out to guide Tricia through and she then followed her down the shop. They went through some curtains into a wide dressing room.

'Take a seat, Miss Cartwright, and tell me your wishes for this your first spree. The freedom, it's something I remember with such happiness.'

Tricia explained the situation that had been suddenly thrust upon her.

'Oh, dear, you need it tonight. I can usually do it at twenty-four-hour notice,' She paused, and thought for a moment before she snapped her fingers, and said, 'I think I have just the attire you need. I won't keep you long but I need to have it retrieved from upstairs.'

She left the dressing room and spoke to an assistant who went up a staircase hidden behind curtains only to return two minutes later carrying a dress of the period complete with petticoats wrapped in a soft cloth. Mrs Rose took it from her and returned to Tricia.

'Here we are, Miss Cartwright. This was ordered by a young lady about your build a little while ago but she was unable to collect it.'

She helped Tricia undress and change into the chosen outfit complete with a corset. When she was ready, Mrs Rose uncovered a mirror, and said, 'What do you think? It is the best wool-silk blend and will hold its shape. It is very much in vogue and we have a pelerine to match and if you so desire, a shoe store so that you can complete your outfit.'

Not used to this type of spending Tricia felt a little alarmed as she slowly spun but she was willing to invest in her future. The dress was beautiful. It was a mixture of printed and dyed fabric with vertical stripes of blue flowers on a golden bronze background and she did not dare to ask the price. She decided to stick it out and purchase it.

'I love it, Mrs Rose and I will take it but it is a little too long.'

'If you can give us a couple of hours, Miss Cartwright, I will make a hem-saver which will give it a longer life and shorten it. Can you do that?'

'By all means, Mrs Rose, and I will add some shoes but can you measure and make me three work dresses with a plain tailored bodice of blue, brown and grey, please.'

'Most certainly but grey is a little dull and with your complexion and deep black hair I would suggest maybe a floral pink as an alternative.'

'Under normal circumstances, yes, Mrs Rose, but I want to look a little stern but smart.'

'I understand.' She spent a few minutes measuring Tricia and then helped her back into her day clothes. 'Your evening dress will be ready in a couple of hours and your work outfits by mid-week. I will send them to you along with the invoice. Where shall I send them?'

'Bishop School House in Borrowdale.'

'Ah... Is this where you dine tonight? With Lady Bishop who is a customer of ours.

'Yes.'

'Have no fear. Although she dresses well she has no airs or graces. Now, Miss Cartwright, I will hand you over to one of my assistants and she will take you to our shoe department.'

She held the curtain open and allowed Tricia through. She joined, Agnes, and moments later an assistant came to them and led her through to the rear of the premises and racks of shoes. Mrs Rose had given the assistant the pelerine to assist in the choice of evening shoe which did not take long and as a precaution she bought a pair of overshoes.

As the assistant was walking away Tricia stopped her. 'Yes, Ma'am?'

'I would like a new white lace collar and cap for my maid added to the bundle, please.'

'I will see to it immediately.'

'Thank you.'

As they left the shop, Agnes said, 'Oh, Missy, you shouldn't have.'

Tricia stopped and turned to face her. 'Agnes, you are teaching me a lot and I have to repay you. Come now, I need to go to the bank first and then buy a watch.'

Agnes led Tricia back to Fishergate and into Church Street where they entered the Preston Bank. After half an hour during which Tricia had set up her account they returned to the Market and, Agnes, said, 'I know the very place to buy your watch, Missy, and being a pawn shop you can get a decent one cheap and you can pay cash.'

In the Market Place, Agnes bought some supplies to be collected later and then onto the pawnbroker and in the bay window, there was a fine collection of jewellery and watches and many other things left by the needy people of Preston.

As Agnes closed the door behind them, the proprietor said, 'Good morning, ladies,' he checked his watch. 'No, it is afternoon. My name is Goldsmith. What can I do for you?'

'Good afternoon,' said Tricia, smiling and her eyes twinkling at the enjoyment and freedom of her new lifestyle, 'I would like to purchase a reliable pin on watch, please, for use in my classroom so it need not be too posh if you get my meaning.'

He ducked below the counter and pulled out a tray of various models of watch. 'Here, miss, are a collection of sterling silver ladies watches.'

Tricia looked through them and at the prices, and said, 'Have you nothing a little less fancy. I only need it for work.'

'One moment, miss, I think I know what you need.'

He went into the back of the shop and returned a moment later with a watch wrapped in paper. He laid it on the counter to reveal a British Sterling ladies pocket watch with fire gilt works by William Williams of Wales, with a plain white dial, Roman numerals and silver case with hallmarks for London, 1836, maker's mark BN complete with a broach pin fastener.

He looked at her mesmerised by her eyes and her smile. He took a deep breath. 'This has only become available recently and I was considering keeping it for my wife. However, business comes first. What do you think?'

'It is silver, have you not got anything in stainless steel?'

'Don't worry, miss, I don't get much business for ladies watches and I will let you have it at a very reasonable price.'

Tricia picked it up and held it against her left shoulder and looked into a mirror and she liked it. 'How much, Mr Goldsmith?'

Goldsmith glanced at Agnes before he wrote a figure on the wrapping paper and slid it over to Tricia who took the pencil off him and wrote something below his figure. He looked at her, and said, 'you drive a hard bargain, miss,' and wrote something else. Tricia considered it and crossed out his figure and put her own in its place. Goldsmith held his hand out. 'That's a deal, miss. Now can I get you something else?'

'No thank you.'

As Goldsmith wrapped it up Tricia turned away from Agnes and counted out the cash from her bag and covertly handed it over to him. 'Thank you, Mr Goldsmith that will be all today. I am sure we will do business again.'

She held her bag open and he dropped it in, 'You are welcome back anytime, miss.'

He watched her leave the shop and scratched his head. 'How did I get manoeuvred into that,' he said to himself, 'you're getting senile, that was cheaper than a stainless job.'

Outside Tricia, said, 'We have time to spare Agnes, let me treat you to a spot of lunch. Where is the best place?'

'If you don't mind slumming it a little, Missy, the best lunches are in the public house at the top of the Square. It's good honest food and all the stallholders use it.'

'Lead me to it, Agnes.'

Agnes opened the door and stood to one side as a blast of body odour mixed with tobacco smoke wafted over them and introduced them to wild chatter and laughter as the hard-working Mill workers released their frustrations with humour and ale.

A fresh-faced buxom girl with a nipped-in waist whose charms were almost overflowing the neckline of her blouse approached them. 'Why, hello, Agnes, who do we have here?'

'Nancy, this is my sisters' daughter, Tricia,' Tricia looked at Agnes and shook her head with a mixture of shock and surprise, 'and we've come to sample your cuisine.'

'If it's food your wanting, follow me.'

There were cubicles around the walls of the Inn divided by a high pinewood settle and she led them through the ever-moving clientele to one in the corner.

She stood by the end of the table in such a way allowing Tricia to slide in one side and Agnes the other. 'We haven't got a menu, miss,' she said to Tricia, 'but Agnes knows what's available. Would you like a drink?'

Agnes replied, 'I'll have a half glass of mild ale and Tricia will have a glass of lemon juice, please.'

'Will do. I'll be back in a minute.'

Nancy left and Tricia, said, 'What do they have, Agnes?'

'You are eating tonight so I suggest a light meal. How about a tray of mutton with bread and cheese and a little salad chucked on.'

'I like the sound of that. My Dad liked mutton sandwiches.'

Nancy brought the drinks, and said, What'll it be, Agnes?'

Agnes gave her their order and they sat back. A public house was a new experience for Tricia and she was surprised by the rough but good atmosphere. Agnes saw her looking around, and said, 'Take it all in, Missy, you will see both sides of the coin today and what you see now for all their poor living conditions is the happiest. P's and Q's are not the first things on their mind.'

Lunch arrived and they ate in silence and when they were finished Tricia reached for her bag and Agnes stopped her. 'This is on me, Missy.'

'Oh, Agnes, you mustn't.'

'This is my level, Missy, outside you are in charge.' She threw some coins on the table and stood up. 'Now, let's go.'

They made their way out to the street and, Agnes said, 'What now, Missy?'

'I need a bookshop, Agnes.'

Agnes pointed across the Market Place. 'Over there, two shops up from '*Elegance*'.'

In the bookshop, she found her choice *'Emma'* and next to it was '*Sense and Sensibility* by the same author. Although trying to read between work and her writing was difficult she bought both of them hoping that the more she became experienced things might get easier. On the way to the counter she added the latest Johnson dictionary to replace her old one.

Back in the Market Place once more Agnes enquired if they had any further retail therapy and after a moment's thought, Tricia, said, 'No, Agnes, we can go home now.'

'Right, Missy, let's catch a hack out to the Mill.'

'A good idea, Agnes, I have spent too much already.'

On the corner of Fishergate, they hailed a cab which whisked them out to the Mill and disturbed Brown in the middle of his nap. 'Wake up, Brown,' shouted Agnes, 'time to go you lazy so and so.'

He sat up and rubbed his eyes, and said, 'My pleasure, Mrs Cheetham.'

'We have to call at *'Elegance'* and the market on the way, Brown.'

He helped them in and made sure that they were comfortable before he set off for the town centre where he retrieved Tricia's shopping leaving a promissory note in exchange and the box of supplies from the market stall. Making their way out of town was quicker and the journey home fifteen minutes shorter.

Brown helped them out and unloaded their shopping, and said, 'Miss Cartwright, I will return at seven-thirty sharp.'

'Thank you, Brown,' she replied, 'that was a pleasant ride.'

'My pleasure, Ma'am.'

~~~~~

CHAPTER 12

Bishops Mill House was a mile and a half from the school and screened from the road by the trees on the long drive. The house was a large sandstone structure that breathed a mixture of hospitality and elegance. It wasn't a vicarage nor was it a country manor.

It had taken a little over ten minutes to get there and they were greeted at the door by the butler, Innes, who assisted Tricia down from the carriage. She was glad that she had persuaded Agnes to forgo fashion tradition and leave out the whalebone busk from her corset as she was able to bend more easily when alighting and her option of an outmoded bonnet enabled her to see at a wider angle. Once she was down on level ground the butler helped Agnes although he was not obliged to, while Tricia was shown into the house and across the entrance hall to a side room by the housekeeper. Agnes joined her and helped her off with her cloak and bonnet and put on her pelerine. A quick check of her hair and she was all set.

'If you don't mind me saying, Missy, you look beautiful and you should capture the hearts of all the gentlemen tonight.'

Tricia took a deep breath and nodded. 'Thank you, Agnes; I don't know what I would have done without you.'

'Stay there, Missy, and I will call the butler and he will take you up to the drawing-room. Mind and don't drink too much,' she scolded with a smile.

She popped out of the room only to return moments later with Innes the butler, who said, 'Please follow me, Miss Cartwright.'

Tricia crossed her fingers and waved them behind her back to Agnes who nodded and smiled as Tricia left the room. They stopped at the drawing room door and, Innes, knocked before opening it. He took one pace inside and announced in a dignified manner, 'Miss Patricia Cartwright,' and stepped aside to let her enter.

Tricia saw the family assembled on sofas in front of the huge fireplace with the men standing behind as she tentatively walked forward into the room with all eyes upon her.

The Rev. Isaiah Bishop detached himself and came over to her. 'Welcome, Miss Cartwright.' He held an arm out in a curled fashion not to embrace her but to guide her forward into the inner circle of the party and they stopped before his wife. 'Miss Cartwright, meet my wife, Lady Eleanor.'

'Good evening, Miss Cartwright, and welcome to our home.'

Forewarned by Agnes, Tricia fulfilled the protocol of politeness to the lady of the house and curtsied, before replying, 'Good evening, Lady Eleanor, it is lovely to be here.'

Bishop continued to introduce her to the family, which consisted of his two daughters and their husbands, and then his only son, Clifford. He reached out and took her hand and kissed it. 'Welcome, Miss Cartwright, my father was indeed a little circumspect with his portrayal of you.' With a slight bow, he smiled and continued, 'and I believe I must stay alert as you have a shrewd intelligence which befits your position.'

Patricia liked him. She curtsied and smiled in return. 'It is my pleasure, Mr Clifford, may we both stay alert although I may abuse my position and burst into Mathematical propositions.'

Bishop remained silent slightly bemused and Tricia did not see the raised eyebrows of the women at this jovial reaction on a first meeting.

'So long as that does not include economics, Miss Cartwright,' was Clifford's cheery reply.

Bishop was about to interrupt the conversation when Innes chose this moment to enter and announce, 'DINNER IS SERVED!'

Dinner was a happy affair and Tricia was thankful that she had been seated at the lower end of the table next to the younger daughter and her husband. She was able to divert the conversation away from her upbringing and concentrate on local affairs and the school but she could feel the eyes of Clifford watching her and the odd time she glanced down the table towards him he smiled and wiggled his fingers in a mock wave. She could feel the colour rising in her cheeks and pretended to take a drink while concentrating on her food and the conversation around her. Much to her surprise, she discovered Agnes was right. Although they had five courses the total quantity was no more than your average daily meal.

After dinner the gentlemen remained to enjoy their cigars and brandy while the ladies retired to the drawing-room where they sat around Tricia and admired her dress and Lady Eleanor was quick to sit back and say, 'I told you, ladies, the best shop in town is *'Elegance'*. They are so adept and quick. You say they did this for you in a few hours, Miss Tricia?'

'Yes, My Lady. I needed something more in keeping with the times and my previous one had become damaged in my holiday jaunt on the canal.'

'They did well for you, Miss Tricia, but please call me, Mrs Bishop. That title is a throwback to my family and has already been subverted by the grandchildren of my siblings. Tell me more about this canal trip.'

Tricia had to think quickly but she was prepared for such an event and with a touch of panache, replied, 'It was a last-minute thing. I decided on the advice of a friend that there would be more opportunities in the Preston area. Instead of the hustle and bustle of a train journey, I met this lovely family on a barge and at a modest price they agreed to bring me to Preston. I had my own cabin and they included food, so I said, "Yes," and enjoyed a nice two-day cruise. On the journey, I began teaching their son and when we reached Preston they asked me if I would continue teaching him. I had enjoyed the trip up to that point and I agreed. They didn't pay me but supplied all my needs for the two weeks it took and it was two days into the trip when during a stopover at Borrowdale I heard about the vacancy at your husbands' school. I completed my promise to finish teaching the boy and the rest as they say is history.'

'This boy, where is he now. Is he at the school?'

'No, Mrs Bishop, although intelligent he was beyond school leaving age and he has designs on joining the Merchant Navy.'

'Oh, we wish him well and my husband speaks well of you. I believe the pupil number has increased already?'

'Yes, Mrs Bishop, but I cannot put that down to my presence.'

'You are too modest girl.' She sat back and flipped her fan across her face a couple of times, before saying, 'Now ladies, shall we enjoy another glass of that lovely wine?'

Without waiting for an answer, she stood up and pulled a disguised embroidered rope hanging down the side of the chimneybreast and before she was properly settled the butler knocked on the door and entered.

'You rang, my lady?'

'Yes, Innes, bring us some of that lovely Rosé wine, please.'

Innes bowed and backed out of the room and Mrs Bishop continued, 'Now, ladies, let us have some entertainment. Miss Tricia—my husband tells me amongst your accomplishments you can play the piano.'

'Err! Yes... a little, but it is a long time since I sat behind a keyboard.'

'Never mind, dearie, I am sure you underestimate yourself.'

Eager for Tricia to show her talent the pianoforté was unlocked and Mrs Bishop and her daughters prepared to be both charmed and entertained. At first, Tricia faltered and stopped to take a breath and then her inner dogged self took over.

She manoeuvred the stool and pulled herself upright and with a look of determination on her face she started afresh. She sang very well and went through the wide range of songs she had learned while schooling at Kearsley Hall and then she added a few she had learned from the unseen choir in the Mill who over the noise of the machines and while walking to and from work lifted the spirits of their fellow workmates.

Midway through her performance the men on hearing the charming entertainment had entered the room quietly and stood just inside the door and then joined the ladies in enthusiastically applauding her as she finished and turned to face them. Clifford in particular was vociferous in his admiration and shouted, 'More!'

Tricia stood up and smiling broadly bowed slightly, and said,

'I am sorry, ladies and gentlemen I have exhausted my repertoire but I have enjoyed it immensely. Thank you.'

'Miss Cartwright, it is us who should be thanking you. That was most pleasurable. I had a suspicion of a hidden talent there. I could sense it in your demeanour but we cannot finish there. Who's next? Clifford! It is time for you to show off. Miss Cartwright, he is the most sort after tenor in the whole of Lancashire and church services would not be the same without him.'

Clifford stepped forward and acknowledged his mother, and enquired, 'And who is going to accompany me on the instrument? Miss Tricia, you can play, can you read music?'

'Oh, no,' said, Tricia, 'I could not possibly. It is so many years since I studied and most of my early learning I did by ear and classical music is beyond my forte.'

'Mother,' said, Clifford, 'It is down to you to show your talent.'

'Very well,' she replied, 'but Miss Cartwright you must join me at the stool. I feel that your talent lies dormant and needs stirring.'

The piano stool was too narrow so another was brought in for Tricia to sit alongside Mrs Bishop and when it was all set Lady Eleanor began playing and on the correct note, Clifford joined in singing in a most sonorous voice. Tricia looked up at him and was immediately smitten. Good looks, a sense of humour and talent that tweaked her feelings, and he is a lawyer. This was more than she had bargained for and she busied herself following the music and turning the pages.

He finished two songs and then called Tricia to join him. 'Miss Cartwright, please give me the pleasure of singing with you?'

She looked up at him and tilted her head slightly, before replying, 'Yes, Master Clifford, but it must be something I know.'

'Of course, Miss Cartwright, which is your favourite?'

She gave him a title and waited while Mrs Bishop played the introduction and together they did a duet. When they finished their performance, it was well applauded and the Rev. Bishop was most vocal with his admiration. His son's talent he knew about but Tricia had climbed the ladder in his estimation and was a real benefit to the school.

Tricia was encouraged to have more wine but she took heed of Agnes's warning and declined and all too soon the evening ended. In the hallway as Agnes was helping her with her cloak Clifford approached, and said quietly, 'Miss Cartwright, it would give me great pleasure to escort you home. May I?'

Tricia was taken aback and she could feel the colour rising in her cheeks and looked to Agnes for guidance and the slight nod of her head was enough. Tricia replied with forthrightness that even she did not know from whence it came, 'Most certainly, Master Clifford, you can entertain both myself and my escort Agnes here.'

He laughed and bowed sweeping his top hat across his knees. 'It will be my pleasure, Miss Cartwright.'

He stood alongside her and held an arm out and unhesitatingly she hooked her arm in his and they went out to the carriage with Agnes, who was smiling secretly to herself, two paces behind. She had seen this all before.

The journey home was short and in that time, Clifford said to Tricia, 'Miss Cartwright, would it be in order if I asked if I may visit one evening?'

'Master Clifford, you may visit at your leisure but I must warn you that my dwelling is far from the comforts of Bishop Mill House and I am very busy most evenings preparing the lessons for my pupils so you must give me fair warning. I will of course have my chaperone present and I apologise beforehand for the lack of a pianoforté.'

The carriage entered the short drive up to the school entrance and stopped. Clifford was quick to alight and held his hand out to Tricia, which she gratefully accepted. 'Thank you, Master Clifford. You have the job.'

He laughed uproariously and kissed her hand. 'Thank you, Miss Cartwright, for a wonderful evening.'

She humorously did a half curtsey and hitching up her skirts went indoors closely followed by Agnes. As the doors closed behind them they heard the carriage drive off and Tricia couldn't stop herself from hugging Agnes. 'Oh! Agnes, what happened there?'

'I don't know, Missy, but methinks you've got yourself an admirer.'

As they climbed the stairs, she said, 'You are right, Agnes, we had good repartee from the moment we were introduced. I like him.'

―

Her two hours in Sunday school were busy. She read a parable from the Bible with a discussion afterwards and for a break she read one of her stories before doing half an hour of arithmetic followed by spelling and reading. To finish the day, she said a small prayer and then followed the children out onto the forecourt where she noted a group of three mothers.

They shooed their children away and one of them called out, 'Miss Cartwright!'

Tricia paused and looked across. 'Yes, ladies, what can I do for you?'

They approached her and one who appeared to be the leader, said, 'Miss Cartwright, we are told you can get cheap coal. Is that right?'

'I do have an outlet, yes, but it is limited.'

'Well. Miss, if you can get us coal as you do for Mrs Chadwick we can send our children to the proper school instead of just the free Sunday school.'

'Ladies, I cannot promise, but I will try. My supply is not due for another eight or nine days and then you will have to buy enough for two weeks at a time. Can you do that?'

They looked at each other and words were exchanged, before the leader, said, 'We will manage, Miss Cartwright. Can we send our children tomorrow?'

Now Tricia had a problem. Should she say, 'Yes,' and risk the wrath of Bishop, or say no and deny the children schooling?

She looked at the three ladies and could see the pleading look in their eyes as they sort to improve the chances of their children.

In an instant, she made her mind up. 'I am putting my job on the line, but, "Yes," you can, ladies. Mind and make a note and you can pay us back a little at a time. You know; give six payments every week instead of five until you have caught up. How does that sound?'

One lady made to hug her instead she stopped and did a little bob, 'Thank you, Miss. They said you was good.'

'I shall look forward to seeing them.' She picked a piece of paper and a pencil from her bag. 'Write down their names and ages, please.'

They looked at each other and shrugged but Tricia anticipated their reply. 'Do not worry, ladies, read them out to me.' She wrote the names down and thrust the paper into her bag. 'I must go now, ladies, and don't forget. Tell me on Monday how much coal you need.'

That night while reading her book with the aid of two candles she paused and looked at Lucky curled up by her feet. 'Lucky, I think I am in deep trouble with this coal thing.'

He tilted his head to one side and looked at her as if to say, 'A barge full!'

—

She was in the classroom early on Monday morning in anticipation of Bishop arriving and when he poked his head around the door he gave her a welcoming, 'Good Morning, Miss Cartwright, I trust you are well?'

She stopped what she was doing and with an anxious smile, she replied, 'Good morning, Mr Bishop. Yes, I am well. Could you spare me a moment, please?'

He stepped inside. 'Yes, of course, what is the trouble?'

She made her way around the desks and approached him. 'Mr. Bishop, I may have made a mistake yesterday by allowing three ladies to send their children to school this morning.'

'That is alright, Miss, the more the merrier.'

'They cannot pay immediately but I gave permission on the understanding they pay an extra penny a week.'

'Oh, I see. Is there a reason for this? I know, do not tell me.

You have promised them cheap coal?'

'Err... Yes. That was the deal.'

'Can you manage all this coal?'

'I may have reached my limit.'

'Miss Cartwright...' Tricia's heart stopped for a moment until he continued, '... They are welcome as are any others who may want cheap coal but on one condition. If they miss paying the deal is off. I do not aspire to increase my wealth, Miss. I want only to educate as many children as I can so that they may have a brighter future. As for coal, do not allow it to interfere with our schooling.'

'I will do my best, Mr Bishop. The coal thing is something I did not anticipate.'

He took out his watch. 'It is time, Miss. Let them in.'

Back in the classroom she prepared to do the register when two new girls put their hands up, holding pieces of paper. Tricia knew what they were and collected them when three more of her usual pupils held up pieces of paper. Her heart sank but she collected them and carried on with the day's lessons.

In her living room during the noon break, she checked the pieces of paper and as she expected it was more orders for coal. She groaned and leaned forward on her elbows holding her forehead in her hand wondering what to do and wishing she had never mentioned coal in the first instance. What was she to do?

Agnes entered with her lunch and saw Tricia shaking her head in dismay, and said, 'What is, Missy?' as she laid the plates on the table.

'This coal promise I made has got out of hand. Surely the price issue is not that bad?'

'You, Missy, are only charging fifty per cent of the price charged by the dealer around here. He charges the poor the same as the class. You are going to get a lot more, believe me.'

'Oh, dear, what can I do?'

'I'm glad I'm not in your shoes, Missy. You have to speak to your suppliers.'

'Billy, who does the deliveries, is coming tomorrow. I just hope he can persuade his Dad to drop off more which may be difficult as they scrape it off the Keswick load and say nothing but twenty-six bags is too much I think.'

'Fingers crossed, Missy. Come on, eat your lunch now.'

After lunch, she had more surprises as two more pupils from the senior class gave her orders for coal taking the total to thirty-two bags. That was more than a ton and a half and she didn't think it possible. Mentally, she said to herself, "Come early, Mr Devlin, you need to speak to your other bargees."

The afternoon went well and she was relieved when four o'clock came. Standing by the door watching the children leave she was looking forward to a cup of tea when she heard a loud shout. 'Aye! You! Miss! I want to talk to you.'

She looked across the circular turnaround to see an overweight stumpy man with a misshapen top hat and the ubiquitous gold watch chain, brandishing a large stick climb from a four-horse curricle, a sign of his wealth, and stride towards her.

She was a little frightened at first and then she felt the adrenalin rising inside her and she pulled herself up to her full five foot six inches and waited for the blustering untidy mess to approach. Two paces away he stopped and pointed his stick. 'You're pinching my customers?'

She didn't flinch nor answer immediately. Instead, she looked him up and down a few times and then directly into his eyes, and said, 'And who might you be you untidy bad-mannered whatever it is you are?'

He opened his mouth to speak, and only blustered, 'I… err… I … I am George Catchpole.'

'Do I know you?'

'Err… I'm the coal man around here and you're pinching my customers.'

'So you are responsible for the poor freezing during the winter. Lower your prices and things could be different.' Something clicked in her brain, and she continued, 'Mr Catchpole? You are able to deliver over a wide area are you not?'

Somewhat confused, he shook his head, before he replied, 'Yes, what's that got to do with it?'

'Mr Catchpole, if I supply the coal cheaper than you pay for it maybe we can work together on this so long as the poorer people in our society benefit.'

Catchpole visibly relaxed and lowered his stick to a more restful position intrigued by this attractive business head before him and he lowered his tone and spoke in a more formal manner, 'I am sorry, Miss, how do I address you?'

'Miss Cartwright. Miss Patricia Cartwright.'

'Miss Cartwright, are you suggesting that you supply the coal and I deliver it.'

'Yes, we join forces and sell it at a maximum of seven pence per hundredweight for the poor. That is a penny-halfpenny each per bag. For the people that can afford it, you charge what you want so long as I get my penny-halfpenny and I will know if you are cheating because the people that bring my coal will tell me how much they deliver, and I can do the maths, is that clear?'

'Understood, Miss.'

'Good. The coal will be dropped off at the canal basin. The next delivery will be on Thursday. A young man called, Billy who we will employ at four shillings a week, will keep a tally and fingers crossed business will pick up. Shall we call it a deal?'

'Yes, Miss, and I apologise for my earlier behaviour.' He stepped forward and held out his hand. 'This is unusual, let us shake on it.'

Tricia held out her hand and he shook it rather shyly. 'That's a deal, Miss.'

'Accepted, how many customers do you have Mr Catchpole?'

'A lot, Miss, I can get through twenty-five tons a month as I have customers in Garstang.'

'At your original price, I am surprised. Do you need that much coal now?'

'It would be a great help, Miss.'

'I will speak to my suppliers. Have you a yard near the canal and space in Garstang. It would make it cheaper to drop it off instead of dragging it there in a cart?'

He pondered momentarily, before he replied, 'Yes, up the high road by the rail yard and in the canal basin in Garstang.'

'It will take some organising, Mr Catchpole, but this week, do my delivery from the basin here and I will try for the extra twenty-five tons. Give me your contact details, you know where I am.'

He dug out a card from his waistcoat pocket and handed it over, 'Here you are, Miss. We should have tea sometime.'

'I am sure we will, Mr Catchpole, and I look forward to a good business together. We may have to buy a barge, who knows.'

Catchpole raised his hat, bowed and returned to his curricle just as a fashionable Brougham entered the short gravel drive. As Catchpole wheeled toward the exit the Brougham pulled up in his place. Tricia's face lit up and her heart began to beat faster in anticipation as the athletic figure of Clifford Bishop swung the door open and jumped out with the boundless enthusiasm of a lovesick calf.

He stopped and with his right leg stretched forward he did an exaggerated sweep of his hat across his body, and bowed, as he said, 'Good evening, Miss Cartwright, I trust you are well?'

The brightness in the eyes of both of them conveyed a message that needed no clarification. She laughed and held her hand out as she too did an exaggerated bob, and replied, 'Good evening to you, Master Clifford, I am quite well thank you …,' she looked around, and lowered voice, '…and all the more happy for seeing you.'

He took her hand and kissed it before he nodded his head down the drive, 'And who was that, I pray? Not another suitor.'

'That is my new business partner, Mr Catchpole.'

'That slimy character? What would you be doing with him?'

'Let us go inside, Master Bishop, and I will tell you more.'

He turned to his coachman and signalled him to stand down just as the Rev. Bishop rode around the side of the building. He touched his hat in acknowledgement and carried on down the drive.

Clifford followed Tricia through the school and upstairs into her parlour. 'Welcome to my humble abode, Master Bishop.'

'Humble it may be, Miss Cartwright, but I admire your choice of furnishings.'

She did a half curtsey, 'Thank you, Master Bishop, but I must give due homage to my lady's maid who does such wonderful work looking after me. Will you join me in afternoon tea?'

'I most certainly will, Miss Cartwright.'

Tricia went over to the fireplace and reached for a hidden braided strap and gave it a gentle pull before taking her seat on the sofa. Clifford chose to sit in an armchair and as they settled there was a knock on the door and Agnes stepped into the room. 'Yes, Miss, you rang?'

'Yes, Agnes, could you bring afternoon tea for two, please?'

Agnes nodded, 'Yes, Miss,' and backed out of the room taking note of Tricia's nod toward the rocking chair in the corner. She nodded in confirmation and closed the door.

As it closed, Clifford said, 'Soo..., you managed to capture Mrs Cheetham. She is a good honest worker.'

'You know her?'

'Yes, she brought me up as a child before I went to school, and then, in order to keep her, Father transferred her to the school.'

'I am glad he did that.'

There was a gentle tap on the door and Agnes entered pushing a trolley and conversation stopped while she laid out the afternoon tea on the coffee table. When she had finished she stepped back, and said, 'Will there be anything else, ma'am?'

'Do we have any red wine available, Agnes?'

'Yes, ma'am, do you want me to bring it?'

'No, Agnes, but put a bottle in cold water in case.' She smiled at Agnes, and added, 'I do like it cool.'

'Yes, ma'am, enjoy your tea.'

Agnes eased herself from the room and Tricia hitched herself forward and prepared to pour the tea and when that was done and they had each selected a sandwich from the trolley they sat back and Clifford, said, 'Tell me about, Catchpole.'

Ignoring the silent figure of Agnes creeping into the room and sitting in the rocking chair with her knitting, Tricia took a bite from her sandwich and watched as a black furry figure snuck in and curled himself around Agnes's feet.

She then replied, 'He was charging too much for coal and many families I have found could not pay for schooling for their children and coal, and coal won, so I found a cheaper method of delivery to which he objected.'

'And now he is your partner?'

'Yes. I can supply it and he is going to deliver it and at twenty-five tons plus a month that puts at least three pounds-two shillings into my bank per month.'

'How did you seal this deal?'

'With a good old handshake as is the custom.'

'The custom amongst men and he will ignore it at some time in the future. Mark my word.'

'Oh, dear, what shall I do?'

'Miss Cartwright, as your legal advisor I will draw up documents and he will sign and make it all above-board.'

'I can't afford a lawyer, Master Bishop.'

He put his cup down, and said, 'Miss Cartwright, If you deliver a glass of good red wine and join me and the family at dinner tomorrow night I think that will cover any expenses that may arise.'

Tricia turned towards Agnes who had anticipated the request and was already on her way to retrieve the said bottle of wine cooling in the kitchen. Two minutes later she returned with the bottle and two glasses and set them down.

'Thank you, Agnes, will you join us?'

She shook her head, and said, 'No, ma'am,' before returning to her knitting.

Clifford did the honours and then raised his glass. 'Here's to your business, Miss Cartwright, what shall we call it?'

'Catchcart.'

They stood opposite each other both of them smitten; an unseen message in their eyes, and for the first time, Tricia felt a strange heart-warming tingling sensation passing through her body. After a moment's hesitation, they clinked glasses and drank.

'My, my, you have good taste, Miss Cartwright.'

Tricia smiled and deigned to tell him that it was Agnes who

had chosen it. 'Thank you, Master Clifford; I will make sure that our supply is well-tended too for future visits. Now I have a bigger problem.'

'What's that?'

'I have to get to my supplier and see if the new arrangements can work.'

'Where is he, this supplier?'

'He should be in Garstang overnight. His son was due to contact me tomorrow but that is too late now.'

'Miss Cartwright, let us take a journey to Garstang. It will be slower now it is getting dark but the high road is not too bad.'

'Oh, can we?'

'Yes.'

Clifford looked over to Agnes. 'Don't worry, Mrs Cheetham, I will look after this precious jewel. We should be back by eleven all being well.'

'Do not wait up for me, Agnes.'

They quickly dressed and hurried out to the waiting carriage and they were soon on their way at a steady trot. The recent dry spell had smoothed out most of the grooves in the road and they made good time to the Garstang canal basin and a quick search unveiled the *'Walnut'* and Tom was sitting on the rear bench with his feet up smoking and drinking his beer.

He looked up with a surprised look on his face when he heard Tricia's voice, saying. 'Hello, Uncle Tom, can we disturb you for a few moments?'

'Oh... Err... Yes.' He stood up. 'What are you doing here, Miss Cartwright?'

'Uncle Tom, how formal. Can we join you on the barge as I have business to discuss with you?'

'Most certainly, Miss.'

He held a hand out and helped her negotiate the narrow gangplank and the steps down into the rear well of the barge and Clifford nimbly jumped down behind her.

'Uncle Tom,' she said, let me introduce Mister Bishop, my lawyer. Do not worry he is here to help both of us.'

Tom held his hand out and Clifford without a second thought accepted it. 'Good evening, Mr Devlin.'

They sat down on the bench seat in a semi-circle and Tricia didn't waste any time. 'Uncle Tom, I want twenty-six hundredweight this week and twenty-five tons as soon as possible after that and every month from thereon. Can you arrange that?'

Tom took his hat off and scratched his head before saying. 'Did you just say, twenty-five tons, Miss? So you want twenty-six tons and six hundredweight this month?'

'Yes. I need the small order quickly.'

'My, my, you are in business, aren't you?' He turned towards Clifford. 'I always knew she had it in her.' He faced Tricia again. 'How about fifty tons on Thursday?'

'We cannot afford two months payment.'

'Pay me when you get it and then I can do that every two months.'

Clifford broke into the conversation with a cough. 'Mr Devlin?'

'Yes, sir,' said, Tom.

'Mr Devlin!—Miss Cartwright has a business called Catchcart. I will draw up a contract on that basis which you will have to sign along with Miss Cartwright and her partner. Will you be able to fit that in with your current contract?'

'Yes, it is only a two-day job from Preston.'

'Very well, Mr Devlin, consider it done. I will deliver the contract to you by tomorrow evening—Miss Cartwright, are you happy with that?'

Tricia nodded. 'I am always happy with what, Uncle Tom does—Uncle Tom, I will have the money for the small order for you on Thursday and then I will arrange to get the rest as soon as possible or would you accept a promissory note.'

'A note from you, Miss, will do fine.'

Edie who had been listening from inside the cabin slid the door open and chipped in. 'Good evening Miss Tricia and good evening to your companion who hasn't taken his eyes off you all evening.' She looked directly at Clifford. 'Will you join my husband with a jug of ale, sir? I promise it's the best.'

The class distinction of the occasion disturbed him and he was caught in two minds but then he noticed how at ease Tricia was. To cover himself he took out his half-Hunter watch and looked at the time, before he replied, 'It is nine o'clock but if Miss Cartwright is happy then—Yes!—I would love to.'

'You're welcome, Mr…?'

'Bishop, ma'am.'

She turned to Tom. 'Give me your jug, you great lump.'

He laughed at her and handed it over and Clifford had a quiet smile to himself. He was beginning to like this family.

Edie went to go into the cabin when Tricia, said, 'Where is, Billy, Auntie Edie?'

'He's down the front reading your book. He says nobody else is having that cabin in case you come back.'

Clifford glanced at Tricia and realised then that it was more than a business connection and wanted to know more, before Tricia added, 'I have a job for him. Will that be alright with you pair?'

'Doing what, Miss?'

'As my shipping agent. He will make a note of what is landed plus what is delivered and helping around the school but coal comes first. He will be paid four shillings a week plus food and lessons when I can do them.'

Before Tom could open his mouth Edie jumped in, 'When does he start, Miss?'

'When he returns on Thursday.'

'We will have his stuff ready. He has somewhere to stay?'

'I will have it ready by the time he gets there.'

'He's yours, Missy. I want him off the canal.'

'Thank you, Auntie Edie. We must go now. Take care.'

Edie stepped forward and gave her a motherly hug, 'Best of luck with the new business,' she whispered, while Tom touched his cap as they left the barge and made their way to the Brougham.

The first ten minutes of the journey were in silence before Clifford spoke. 'What is your relationship with these people, Miss Cartwright?'

She didn't answer immediately but glanced sideways at him. He was looking ahead, not angrily nor happy but fixated on his thoughts and after a few moments she replied in a manner much against her inner feelings. 'Mr Bishop, if it is wealth or class you require for my approbation then I am sorry to disappoint. They are my adoptive family who sometimes work in excess of eighty hours a week and these working-class people put themselves out for me when I was in distress. They took me under their wing. I did not give nor did they ask for anything in return other than lessons for their son to improve his basic Maths and English although Jane Austen would be too much for him I gave him my copy of a Johnson dictionary to help. When Mrs Devlin went to the village shop en-voyage she heard of the vacancy at the school and delayed the barge while she arranged my interview which I explained to your Father.'

'What was your distress?'

'Is this another interview?'

'I am merely interested in someone I could see in my future.'

Taken aback somewhat by his reply she paused and took a deep breath before she answered. 'I hired a cabin from them for a leisurely journey from Lancaster to Preston which was originally planned as two days and during the trip, I began teaching young Billy when I had an accident. I was badly hurt and they looked after me at no charge other than to teach Billy, which I did.'

'This accident? What happened?'

'I tried to copy young Billy jumping back on the barge and I tripped smashing my face against the bulwark. Have we finished with the interrogation,' she added rather sternly.

He jerked his head around to face her, lifted his hat and scratched his head, before he said, with a look of penitence on his face. 'Miss Cartwright, I apologise profusely for my behaviour. It was uncalled for and I had no right to question your integrity. My father is a classless man. He believes in the soul of a person although he does concede that knowledge of the middle class does help but I saw from your performance on Saturday evening that you are well versed in our foibles.'

'I had a two and a half year intensive preparation in the etiquette of the upper classes from the Governess of the young boy for whom I was chosen as a companion. She was more intent on improving my status than that of the young man but she did warn me to avoid the real upper class, the ones who I was obliged to serve etc…, as much as possible as they are in a world of their own. She was particularly abusive of the men of whom she said that their brains come no higher than their thighs.'

He laughed, and said, 'Miss Cartwright, I hope I can rise above that…' they had a momentary giggle between themselves at the innuendo, '…but please, do accept my sincerest apology for my behaviour.'

'I do, Master Bishop, and in the future, you also must accept me for what I am. I got here through sheer hard work and I promise I will not abuse your position to improve my situation but carry on steadfastly in my own manner.'

'From what my Father says and what I have seen, you will go a long way.'

'I have, Master Bishop, two ambitions in life and that is to find my father and secondly to improve the education of today's working-class children and in Borrowdale School, I have the perfect situation, however, I do have to make sure of my own circumstances first.'

Their conversation had eaten away at the time and before Clifford could reply they wheeled into the school drive and pulled up by the door. Brown jumped down and opened the door for Tricia.

'Thank you, Brown, a most enjoyable ride.'

Brown knuckled his brow, and said, 'Thank you, Ma'am.'

Clifford clambered out and they took a few steps to the door.' Can I show you to your residence, Miss Cartwright?'

'No thank you, Master Bishop, Agnes will be waiting.'

She held her hand out and with the same exaggerated bowing gesture; he kissed it and said, 'Good night, Miss, I will send Brown at seven tomorrow evening.'

'I have no doubt, Master Bishop that your horses have the

road here already ingrained into their brain—Good night.'

He waited until she closed the door before he jumped back smiling into the carriage and disappeared into the night just as the first drops of rain began to fall.

~~~~~

CHAPTER 13

An hour after the contract had been signed by Tom Devlin with an 'X' and countersigned by Edie, Clifford dismounted from his horse outside the residence of George Catchpole. He opened the gate and strode up the footpath through a garden showing the fading plants of autumn to be met at the door by the head butler.

'Good evening, sir, how may I help you?'

Clifford presented his card. 'Tell your master I would like to speak with him on an urgent business matter.'

The servant glanced at the card, and said, 'By all means, sir, please step inside and would you like your mount taken to the stables?'

'No thank you, this will not take long.'

The butler stood to one side and allowed Clifford into the entrance hall. He took his hat and cloak and placed them over the back of a chair before he crossed the hall and knocked on a door before entering. Moments later he came out. 'Mister Catchpole will see you now, sir.'

He held the door open and then closed it behind Clifford.

Catchpole stood up and walked forward to meet him with his hand out. 'Good evening, Mister Bishop, we meet again.'

'Good evening, Mister Catchpole.'

'What can I do for you, Mister Bishop? Sorry! Please take a seat.'

Catchpole stood to one side to let Clifford through to an armchair before he settled into what was his chair with its drink laden side table. Before he sat down Clifford handed Catchpole two documents.

'What's this, may I ask, sir?'

'That, sir, is a business contract between you and one Miss Cartwright.'

'But we shook hands on the deal just last night and there was no mention of a contract.'

'Miss Cartwright, sir, is a naive young lady with little knowledge of the skulduggery involved in handshakes. This contract makes your partnership legal and I believe more beneficial to you than her. A few legal responsibilities have been added in addition to what you agreed. Please read it.'

Catchpole took a swig of his pre-dinner port and rammed a pair of mangled pince-nez onto his nose. His head moved along each line as he struggled to take in the legal jargon before, in frustration, he slammed the documents down into his lap,

'What does this mean,' he demanded.

Clifford leaned forward and looked directly into Catchpole's eyes. 'It means, sir, that should Miss Cartwright come to any harm both legally or physically, death by duel would be an easy option. Do I make myself clear?'

Catchpole's cheeks became redder as he strove to control his anger but he was in a corner and the business was too good to miss. He let out a long sigh and reached for a quill and ink on the side table on the other side of his chair.

'Where do I sign?'

Clifford reached over and pointed. 'Here, below that of Miss Cartwright on both pages.'

Catchpoles signed and blotted dry both contracts. Clifford took one and rolled it, and said, 'Thank you, Catchpole, you had better get yourself prepared as your partner has organised the first fifty tons for delivery tomorrow shared between Borrowdale and Garstang, and make sure you treat young William Devlin with respect. He is her representative.'

'Did you just say—fifty tons?'

'I certainly did, Catchpole. This lady does not hang about. I hope you have the means to unload it.'

—

Dinner that night was a less formal affair with the Rev. Isaiah, Lady Eleanor and Clifford present. Later, after the men had enjoyed their after-dinner brandy and the ladies their coffee, Lady Eleanor persuaded Tricia to entertain them once more on the pianoforte but Clifford stepped in after two songs and relieved her and they spent the next hour or so playing *quadrille* until once again Clifford called a halt.

'We must stop now,' he said, 'Miss Cartwright has a busy day ahead of her of which her latest interest will play a part I have no doubt.'

'Yes, Miss Cartwright,' said Lady Eleanor, 'I hear you have taken over the coal business here.'

Tricia coloured slightly as she answered, 'Not quite. I am only trying to make life a little easier for the poorer people amongst us and cheap price coal allows them to send a child or even two to school which is my aim.'

'Very admirable, my dear, Isaiah says you are also subsidising the school coal.'

'I have like the other clients reduced the bill. I had to keep warm after all.'

'I wish you every success. Come, let us go.'

Lady Eleanor walked with Tricia to the door where Brown was waiting with the coach. At the door, she took Tricia's hand. 'It has once more been a wonderful evening with your company, Miss Cartwright,' she lowered her voice, 'Clifford is quite smitten so I have no doubt we will be seeing more of you.' She raised her voice, 'Take care now, Miss Cartwright.'

Brown helped her up into the carriage and Clifford joined her for the short drive home where upon arrival they did their humorous exaggerated "goodbye's" their previous day's vexatious exchange forgotten.

The following day Tricia was disturbed during her lunch break by Billy. Agnes showed him into her apartment at Tricia's request but before Agnes left, she said to Billy, 'Have you eaten today?'

'I had a dripping and fish butty early on, Miss Tricia.'

Tricia looked across to Agnes stood just inside the door and said, 'Agnes, when we have finished could you fix young Billy up with something. We won't be long and I will pay later.'

She backed out of the room and closed the door behind her as Tricia spoke to, Billy. 'Now young man, what can I do for you?'

'Dad sent me to tell you that he's unloading your extras and twenty-five ton at the Borrowdale basin now and then he will be moving on to Garstang.'

'Oh, jolly good. Is Mr Catchpole there?'

'Yes, and he's got two men loading up his cart to take your orders out.'

'And what are you going to do, Billy?'

'Go with Dad to Garstang and then jump off here on the way back to Preston.'

'Bring a mattress and your things with you and you can stay here in the spare room and when you are not working you can improve your education. You will have to pay for your food and help the odd job man around the school and in the kitchen when you are not keeping account of the coal. Got that?'

'Yes, Miss Tricia.'

'Alright, Billy, go to Agnes and she will give you something to eat and then hurry back to the barge and we will see you tomorrow.'

Billy knuckled his brow and ran out of the room while Tricia carried on with her lunch at the same time planning her afternoon lessons happy that her new business income was soon to be in her Bank. Although her mind was distracted from schooling she wondered how much she would need to follow her father's trail across the world.

At two o'clock when the school assembled for the afternoon session it came as no surprise when two more children gave her notes asking for coal but she suspected they were already customers of Catchpole and it would not be a problem.

~~~~~

CHAPTER 14

The next couple of months went smoothly with an increase in school numbers and a corresponding increase in customers interspersed with chaperoned visits for afternoon tea with Clifford and twice a week invitations to dinner at Bishops Mill House. Saturday shopping trips into Preston kept her busy as she strove to improve her wardrobe in line with her new status and it was on one of these expeditions in the second week of December that a surprise awaited her when she called into the Preston Coal Dock to visit Auntie Edie and Tom.

As the carriage approached the dockside stood by the barge were two well-dressed businessmen talking to Tom. Brown pulled the carriage to a stop and she told Agnes to remain seated as Brown helped her down. Tom approached. 'Welcome, Miss Cartwright.'

Tricia was slightly taken aback by the polite reception more used to a friendly one, when Tom continued, 'Come and meet these two gentlemen, they wish to discuss a business proposition with your company.'

He led her over to them, and said, 'Gentlemen, allow me to introduce my employer, Miss Cartwright.'

Throughout the shock of the introduction, she managed to retain a firm profile, as she said, 'Good afternoon, gentlemen, what can I do for you?'

The leading man took off his hat, did a half bow, and was visibly confused to be confronted by this young female opposition to his ego before he spoke. 'Good afternoon, Miss Cartwright, I am Mr Stephenson and this is my compatriot, Mr Coolidge.' Coolidge did the gentlemanly bow but stood back as Stephenson continued, 'We represent the Lancaster & Preston Junction Railway and we would like to talk over a business deal concerning the supply of coal.'

'Without my partner and lawyer present, gentlemen, I cannot discuss my business but you could outline the issue and I will arrange a meeting as soon as possible. Shall we go into town and find a more comfortable environment?'

'Most certainly, Miss Cartwright, do you have anywhere in mind?'

'Yes, *Katie's Parlour.*'

'I know it. We will see you there shortly, Miss Cartwright.'

Tricia wheeled away back towards the carriage but as she did so she winked at Tom, and said in a most officious manner, 'Brown! Take us to '*Katie's*.'

Brown kept a straight face. He knew underneath she was play-acting as he helped her into the carriage and soon had them on their way. After working his way through the busy Saturday crowds they pulled up outside '*Katie's*'. Brown helped her and Agnes down and she said to him, 'This should not take long, Brown. Keep warm.'

He knuckled his hat and opened the door for them before he clambered back up to his seat and edged forward a few yards from the café front. Inside she was met by the owner Katherine who showed her to a table and placed Agnes on her own on the other side of the room. She returned to Tricia just as Stephenson and Coolidge entered. 'These are the gentlemen I am waiting for, Miss Katherine, can you give us afternoon tea and whatever Agnes my maid requires and sent a mug of tea and a beef sandwich to my coachman, please.'

'Yes, madam, will the gentleman be requiring anything stronger?'

'Not in my presence, what they do in their own time is up to them.'

Katherine smiled, and said, 'I wish more ladies were like you. It will not be long, madam.'

Stephenson and Coolidge stood waiting patiently until Tricia was ready and she invited them to sit and fully expecting to hear opposition to her business she went straight in with, 'Thank you for waiting, now what was it you wanted to discuss.'

Stephenson liked her straightforward attitude, and said, 'We are led to believe that your company supply coal.'

'Yes, I do or should I say, my business partner and I do.'

'At a reasonable price?'

'My customers think so, yes.'

'Miss Cartwright, I think we can help each other.'

'In what way? You said you represent the Rail Company.'

'Yes, and we also work together with the canal company and if we can use the canal to convey our coal to the Garstang & Catteral Station this would not only be cheaper than rail transportation but would also free up the line for more passenger transport. The added business would help you also.'

'I see. You want me to carry your coal to Garstang. Can you give me any idea how much and what price would you be expecting?'

A waitress arrived with the afternoon tea and laid it out and poured the tea while Coolidge retrieved a small notepad from his pocket and handed it to Stephenson who opened it and placed the page in front of Tricia. She read it, not once, but twice just to make sure she had read it correctly before she looked up.

'What do you think, Miss Cartwright?'

'I am not impressed, Mr Stephenson.'

She took a pencil from her bag, wrote a figure on the pad, and slid it over the table for Stephenson. He looked at it and showed Coolidge who wrote another figure and Stephenson gave it back to Tricia.

She checked it, shook her head, scribbled another figure, and pushed it back. Coolidge didn't wait but reached for the pad, glanced at it and wrote something else and he pushed it towards Tricia.

She looked and did a mental calculation before writing another number and handing it back. 'That is my last offer, gentlemen. If you do not accept it then any deal is off.'

'My, my, Miss Cartwright, you do drive a hard bargain. Give me a moment to talk to my partner. They stood up and walked over by the door facing away from her but she could hear it was a foreign language. Two minutes later, they came back and after taking a sip of his tea, Stephenson said, 'Very well, Miss Cartwright, we accept your offer. Can you set it up by the New

Year? Oh! I must add that there are plans for a sideline from Garstang out to the coast which will boost your business maybe in a couple of years.'

'I will do my best to get this underway, Mr Stephenson. My lawyer will be in touch. Have you a card and can you sign that note and give it to me, please?'

He looked at the savvy young woman in front of him doing things that he had only previously come across from his own genre but said nothing. He tore the page from the pad and signed it and gave it to her. 'My pleasure, Miss Cartwright, it has been a delight doing business with you.'

She signed it, before replying. '*Cela a été un plaisir pour moi aussi, messieurs.*'

Stephenson sat back sharply and looked at her with wide eyes realising his planned secrecy had been in vain. Who was this multi-lingual young lady still old enough to be his daughter?

They stood up and Tricia held out her hand. Stephenson took it, bowed, and gave it a quick peck. 'I look forward to meeting again. Miss Cartwright.'

Coolidge touched his hat and they left. Tricia was not sure they were happy but inside she was as her bank balance was most definitely boosted but where was she going to get all those barges? She sat down and did a quick calculation on the back of the page and satisfied, she called for the bill and paid it plus a tip.

Outside Brown held the door open while she and Agnes climbed in and as she sat down, she said, 'Brown! Get us to the docks as quick as you can. I need to see Mr Devlin.'

'Yes, ma'am, hold tight.'

As the carriage pulled up Tricia had the door open and twisting slightly sideways nimbly climbed down and ran over to the stern of the barge. As she edged over the narrow gangplank the cabin door slid open and Tom stuck his head out checking on the noise. 'Hello. Missy, what're you doin' here?'

'Uncle Tom, I have to talk to you about some business. Can I come in?'

'Why yes.' He stood to one side and let her in and she sat on the bench seat along the side of the cabin while Tom returned to his comfy seat at the rear. 'Now, Miss, what is it you have to tell me?'

She held up the piece of notepaper. 'I have here a contract deal to supply coal to the L&P Junction Rail Company at Garstang Catteral and I need lots of barges. Can you help me?'

'I dunno,' he said, 'how much and at what price?'

She quoted the quantity and the price after deducting fifteen per cent 'That price is more than you get from the Gas Company and also more than you get for my local delivery. Interested?'

'Yes, but I can't deliver all that.'

'Can you sub-contract it? That is, hire your friends and pay them less than you get from me so that you make a profit on every ton delivered. This does not include Catchpole; your contract is with me. I will get my lawyer to write up contracts for you to give out but this must all be done by New Years Day.'

'That sounds good. It is only a two-day job which they can fit in between the Gas Company or maybe I can get some just to do that.'

'What about your two sons? Can you not fit them up with a barge just to run back and forth? Billy has his hands full already and he is swatting for the Merchant Navy.'

'Missy, I will find something, this is too good to miss.'

'I have to go now Uncle Tom. I will have those documents with you as soon as I can but you must continue with my local contract, it is after all for a good cause.'

'I'll cover that one myself and hire the others to cover the rail one.'

'Thank you, Uncle Tom.' She turned to Edie who had been sat quietly in the corner. 'And thank you, Auntie Edie, for being so patient. I wish you all the best.'

She went out on deck where Tom helped her onto the plank and Brown was ready to assist her into the carriage and in the blink of an eye had them on their way home. It would be tight as they were running late but Tricia had every faith in Brown.

—

When the men joined the ladies after their ubiquitous brandy Tricia approached Clifford and took his arm and led him to the end of the room before she asked if she may have a quiet word with him. He nodded and they chose to sit by a card table that was not in use.

Clifford fearing the worst, said, 'What is it, Miss Tricia?'

Tricia opened her evening bag, withdrew the note, and gave it to Clifford. 'That is a temporary contract with the L&P Rail Company to supply coal to their Garstang depot. Could you draw up proper contracts and I want you also to represent and prepare contracts between my Uncle Tom and his sub-contractors of which there will be quite a few.'

Clifford looked at the tonnage figures and the negotiated prices, before he said, 'When did you do this?'

'This afternoon in Preston.'

'Are you telling me you negotiated a business deal while you were out shopping?'

'Yes, whilst having a cup of tea. It was all over quite quickly and I do not think they were too happy at the result.'

'Hmm... I see you spoke to Stephenson. I know him. He will not have enjoyed dealing with a woman and you have made a good result.'

'I have discussed this with my Uncle Tom already and he is all for it and probably recruiting as we speak.'

'And what are you paying him?' She lowered her voice and told him. '…and you have deducted fifteen per cent for your cut, Miss?'

She nodded. 'And it is my company, not, Catchcart.'

He folded the note and put it into his pocket. 'I will keep that and deal with your contracts on Monday. What do I call your company?'

She deliberated for a moment before replying, 'I want to stay incognito, any ideas?'

'How about, 'Bishop Canal Coal Company or BCCC?'

'Bishop?'

He leaned forward, and said quietly, 'Would you like to be a Bishop?'

She sat back with a jerk and looked at him with surprised eyes.

'Did you just propose, Master Bishop?'

He smiled and reached across and touched her hand. 'In a manner of speaking, Yes. Do you desire I go on my knee?'

She laughed aloud and immediately covered her mouth concerned by the audience at the other end of the room and looked at him her eyes conveying her delight. 'No, but you may grovel at some later date.'

'Do I take it that was a, Yes?'

She put a finger over her mouth and with her head tilted looked at him as if deliberating. 'Hmmm... that calls for a decent glass of wine while I think about it.'

'You tease,' he said, and called for Innes.

The wine was duly delivered and they both stood but before either could speak Lady Eleanor approached them and because Tricia had been in their company so often lately her address was less formal. 'Clifford and the charming Miss Tricia, may I ask what you are up to?'

Tricia curtsied, 'My Lady, your son has just proposed.'

Lady Eleanor opened her mouth to speak and then closed it again but after a moment's deliberation, she said, 'And pray, what was your reply, Miss Tricia?'

'Give me a moment.' She turned to Clifford and raised her glass. He did the same and as their glasses clinked, she said, 'Yes!'

Lady Eleanor clapped and called for her two daughters and their husbands to join them and urged The Rev. Isaiah to order some champagne.

'Why champagne,' he said, 'is not your ordinary wine sufficient?'

'Isaiah! Tricia and Clifford have just become engaged. Let us celebrate.'

'Champagne it is,' replied Bishop, and he pulled the chord by the fireplace and as Innes pushed his head around the door he immediately gave him the instruction to deliver it *'poste haste'*.

The rest of the evening was enlivened by the occasion and Tricia sang joyful songs and played the pianoforte and in the confined space dancing was also a must.

All too soon midnight was upon them and the celebrations came to a close and after many hugs and kisses, Tricia and Clifford made the journey back to the school sitting closer than on the previous formal occasions. Outside the school Clifford reached across and pulled Tricia towards him and they kissed.

She pushed him away gently, as she said breathlessly, 'Goodnight, Master Bishop, I look forward to our closer liaison.'

'Goodnight and sleep well, Miss Cartwright.'

Tricia opened the door and Brown helped her down aware that the relationship had progressed.

~~~~

CHAPTER 15

Tricia was on her way to Church when she saw Billy and stopped him.

'Yes, Miss Tricia, what is it?'

'Billy, what is your Dad doing today?'

'He's dropping off your local stuff which is where I'm going now before going on to the Garstang Basin, Miss.'

'He returns to Preston tomorrow?'

'Yes, Miss, after he's loaded some local farmers cargo.'

'Oh, good, tell him to wait for Mr Bishop who will have a contract for him and some paperwork to give to his sub-contractors. I will tell Mr Bishop he will be there.'

'Will do. I've got to rush now, Miss. Dad will be at the Basin already.'

'You run along, Billy, and take care.'

After Church, she had a quick lunch and then did her two-hour stint in the school before entertaining Clifford with afternoon tea and it was after their tea that things became a little fraught between them as she explained to him that under no circumstances were her business deals part of their relationship.

'I wish to break away from tradition, Clifford, insofar that any money's I make stay separate from yours. I have sweated blood and tears to get where I am, and I am not going to let that go nor will I stop working. I am not going to sit around all day twiddling my thumbs or going out on unnecessary visits.'

'But you will only be too glad acquiring the standard of living that goes with our prospective marriage.'

'That I grant you will be a bonus and I will never under any circumstance let you down in that respect, Clifford, however, I will give up my salary from the school but I will carry on teaching voluntary. That school for underprivileged children is my priority. I will provide towards our family outgoings but the actual business and income remain mine.'

'But…'

'No, buts, Clifford, I will never change my mind under any circumstance and I want that arrangement kept a secret between us. I will never tell anyone or make a laughing stock of you.'

He stood up and began walking up and down the room rubbing his chin in deep thought. After a few minutes, he stopped by the door and looked at her. 'Miss Cartwright, I am sorry but I cannot accept your terms. It will be the traditional method or not at all. Our engagement is off. Good evening to you.'

He reached for the doorknob, as Tricia said. 'I would sooner stay single than throw away everything I have worked for, and by the way, Master Bishop, do not forget the contracts and charge the exorbitant fee to me and forward my details to Companies House. It will be BCCC of course and I will pay you as soon as is possible.'

He stood momentarily mesmerised by this woman who knew about company registration which was only a recent necessity and unable to get the final word he gritted his teeth to stop himself shouting out in anger frustrated by this model of female stubbornness. Instead, he swung the door open and slammed it behind him as he dashed for the stairs.

Two minutes later, Agnes on hearing the disturbance rushed in and saw Tricia standing in front of the fire with the glint of a tear in her eye. 'What is it, Missy, what has he done?'

Tricia hurried over to Agnes and hugged her, 'Oh, Agnes, you have just witnessed the shortest engagement in history all because I insisted on my financial independence and I refused to stop working.'

Agnes patted Tricia's back. 'There, there, dearie, you have done what I would never have had the nerve to do. We have to stand up to them. It will come about one day and you may as well start now.'

Tricia stepped back and held Agnes at arm's length. 'Oh, Agnes, thank you. Please, do not tell anyone, not the money side of it anyway. Did you know about my new business?'

'Yes, Missy, I was there when you started it.'

'How silly of me.—Agnes, please bring two glasses of red wine.'

'Two, Missy?'

'Yes, you can help me celebrate.'

'What about dinner, Missy?'

'I will forgo that tonight, Agnes, we will have supper instead. Nothing fancy, mind.'

'Make yourself comfy, Missy, I will be only a few minutes.'

Agnes left the room while Tricia made space available on the sofa nearest the fire alongside her and true to her word Agnes returned with two glasses of wine and set them down on the low fancy table in front of them.

Tricia patted the sofa beside her. 'Sit here, Agnes.'

'Oh, Missy, should I?'

'Yes, you are my guest tonight, Agnes, so you will have a comfy seat in my presence.'

When she was settled they picked up their glasses, and Tricia, said, 'To BCCC and the future, Agnes.'

They raised their glasses and took a sip. 'My, my, Agnes, that wine is beautiful. Did I buy that?'

'No, Missy, I must confess, Mr Bishop left it.'

Tricia laughed, 'Serves him right. Now, Agnes, how do you feel these days, are you well?'

'Yes, Missy, although I think the stairs are getting steeper by the day.'

'Is that all, Agnes, are you telling me everything. What about doing two jobs? Does that not affect you?'

'Yes, Missy, some days I am too tired.'

'Very well, Agnes, come the New Year I want you to be my lady's maid and companion and I want to hire a housemaid to take over your other duties. Do you know anyone reliable?'

'Yes, Missy, my friend in the Mill House told me of such a young lady that may suit your needs.'

'Good! Get in touch with her and set up an interview. I am going to promote our scullery maid to cooks assistant so I need a new scullery maid

'There is a kitchen hand at the Mill House also who wants to move.'

'Get her, but she must learn cookery skills as part of her job and I will instruct Cook to do so.'

'I'm sure she will, but where will they live, are you going to get a bigger place?'

'I like it here. Billy can go back on the barge. He says he is going to Liverpool in the New Year to join one of those new steamships. The kitchen girl can go into his room. The housemaid can take up the empty room in the attic opposite you. Is that alright?'

'Yes, Missy, it will give me someone to talk to.'

'That's settled, and, Agnes, because you have been a Mother figure to me I will be giving you a wage increase when my new business starts. No argument, I have made my mind up.'

Agnes stood up and straightened her dress and pinafore when, Tricia, said, 'What are you doing, Agnes?'

'I am going to get supper, Missy, which is my job, but may I ask one thing?'

'Yes, Agnes, what is that?'

'You don't appear upset by the loss of your fiancée.'

'Inside I am Agnes, I do love him but I will not give up all my hard work to add to his five thousand a year. I know it is not the done thing but I would rather stay single than give it up.'

'Very good, Missy, he will be back.'

'Do you think so?'

Agnes nodded as she backed out of the room.

—

Monday started with an increase in pupils and customers to her local coal and she noted that the distance the children walked to school was increasing as the news spread about the cheaper fuel. It reminded her of her early school days when she had to walk two and a half miles to the local charity school in Lunesdale.

Later, after the children had left for the midday break, Rev Bishop entered the classroom. She stopped what she was doing and with a half bob, enquired, 'Mr. Bishop, what can I do for you?'

'Miss Cartwright, Lady Eleanor sends her condolences for the dissolving of your engagement to our son but she hopes that you will still grace our table with your company.'

'Mister Bishop, how could I possibly refuse but would things not be a little icy in the circumstances?'

'I know he is angry and both I and Lady Eleanor wish that you both can be reconciled but we have some extra guests this weekend to distract him from his mood.'

'Mister Bishop, I cannot possibly discuss the issue, but—Yes, I will be only too happy to accept your invitation.'

'Good, she will be pleased as she loves your entertainment and the sterling work you are doing here and as of today your salary will be wholly commensurate with your position.'

'Oh, thank you, Mister Bishop, I only hope I can live up to your expectations.'

'You will, Miss Cartwright, you have matured beyond your years in the short time you have been with us. May the rest of your day go peacefully?'

'Thank you, Mister Bishop.'

He nodded his acknowledgement and left and it came as no surprise when Clifford's clerk arrived on horseback with the new contracts for BCCC with L&P Junction Rail and the sub-contract between her and Tom.

When she had finished signing she inquired of the clerk, 'How is Master Bishop this day?'

'Not well, Miss, he is walking around muttering to himself and being quite bossy which is not him and any attempt to enquire is met by an angry stare and foul language and he's delivering these later. I hope he's bucked up by the time I get back. Did you want to send a message, Miss?'

'No, I have no wish to interfere with his thoughts today.'

He nodded and touched the peak of his hat as he left the room and she retired to her dining room to finish her lunch.

The rest of the day passed without incident and while Agnes was serving dinner that evening, she said to, Tricia, 'I sent a note to your potential housemaid and kitchen girl and they both accept.'

'But I have not interviewed them, Agnes. How do I know if they suit me? Are they right for the job?'

'Oh, Missy, I know I shouldn't but the maid is my niece and the kitchen help is my sister's granddaughter and they better behave themselves.'

'Agnes, how could you, you naughty…' she searched for the correct term, and said, '…lady. Tell them they are starting New Years Day but for your pain, you will get the rooms ready and make sure they have the correct attire. Oh! Tell them I will pay one penny per day more than they get now and they can say they left for the money.'

Agnes bowed, and said, 'Yes, Madam.' She backed out of the room with a smile on her face.

Tricia stood transfixed looking at the door shaking her head, 'I wonder how many more relatives she has?'

—

Tricia was settling down with a book after dinner when there was a knock on the door and Agnes came in.

'Yes, Agnes, what is it?'

'Young Billy is here with a gentleman to see you. Shall I let them in?'

'Yes, Agnes.'

Agnes disappeared only to return two minutes later. After a gentle knock she opened the door and standing to one side, she announced, 'Mr Thomas Devlin and Billy, ma'am.'

Tricia tried to hide her disappointment when she heard Tom's name, she was hoping for Clifford.

As they came into the room, she smiled as she greeted them. 'Why, hello, Uncle Tom, what can I do for you so late at night?'

'It's about that new contractor, Miss,' he said formerly.

'Oh, please take a seat, Uncle Tom,' she said gesturing towards the sofa, 'and you Billy sit over there by that table. I cannot offer you beer, Uncle Tom but we may have some whisky.'

'No thank you, Miss, we won't keep you.'

He sat down and Tricia sat opposite. 'Now Uncle Tom, what is it?'

'We had two visitors today, miss. Them two fella's you spoke to, and they asked if we could deliver some coal before the contract started.'

'What did you say?'

'I said I would have to speak with you first as you're the boss.'

'Thank you, Uncle Tom. If I said, yes, could you manage it? I mean, it is not too soon?'

'Yes, Miss. I have six barges already signed up and I'm sure we could slip a few early loads in.'

'Very well, Uncle Tom, if you can manage it.' She turned to face Billy. 'Billy, come here.'

He crossed the room and stood by the end of the sofa. 'Yes, Miss?'

'Billy, stay with your Dad, and make sure you get signatures and receipts for any cargoes for the Rail people and get them to me.'

'Yes, Miss.'

'When do you go away, Billy?'

'Next week, Miss, so I can do that.'

'I thought it was New Year.'

'It was but I am an indentured apprentice with the British and North American Royal Mail Steam-Packet Company and they have moved me to a new ship and so I have to go.'

'That's good, now sit there with your Dad.' He sat down and she continued, 'Uncle Tom, you have a system with the Keswick Gas Company. Use a similar tally system to them. What are you going to do? Full time or a bit of each?'

'My other sons are joining me and have got themselves two barges and we are going to do it full time to Garstang and use my colleagues for the rest.'

'Are they happy with that?'

'Yes, Miss, they're looking forward to the extra cash.'

'Will the Gas contract be affected?'

'No, Miss, the deliveries may be a little slower but the cargos are guaranteed both ways so the lads don't mind doing it.'

'Thanks for telling me, Uncle Tom, the crafty so and so's were trying for some cheap stuff before the New Year. Was there anything else?'

Tom and Billy both stood up. 'No, Miss, that is all.'

She took Tom's hand. 'Uncle Tom, I am always glad to see you. Give my love to Auntie Edie.'

'Yes, Miss, and you can get ready for bed now.'

'Uncle Tom, I am grown up now.'

'Aye, and you is looking well. Take care.'

Agnes showed them out of the room and enquired if Tricia would like a drink or something.

'Yes please, Agnes, can I have a cup of warm milk and then we will call it a day.'

'I'll bring it right away, Missy.'

It was on the following Saturday when she next saw Uncle Tom while on her weekly shopping trip to Preston and her eyes opened in amazement when she saw the total receipts. "Oh, my, what is it going to be like when we start full time," she said to herself. She had never imagined an income this large. A quick calculation and she reckoned she would be earning five hundred pounds a year if not more and they said they were looking to expand.

She stopped for a moment as a daring idea slipped into her head. "What if she bought the coal directly from the mine?" and then she remembered something her Dad used to say. "Never overthink things it usually ends in disappointment." With that in mind, she dismissed the idea.

—

Having been accepted into the family she now visited alone and it was in nervous anticipation that she shivered as she stepped down from the carriage but she had to smile as Brown was his usual cheerful self as he did an exaggerated bow.

'Thank you, Brown. A most pleasant ride. I expect nothing less.'

He touched his hat. 'Thank you, Miss Cartwright, enjoy your evening.' He watched as she walked up the steps to the main door and he nodded as he said to himself. "I like her."

Inside, Innes took her coat and gave it to the housemaid before he led her to the drawing-room. He knocked on the door, opened it, and stood to one side as he announced in a mild but official manner. 'Miss Patricia Cartwright!'

The Rev. Isaiah Bishop got up from 'his' chair and walked across to meet her. 'Welcome, Miss Cartwright, please allow me to present my new guests.'

He led her across the room and she swapped pleasantries with Lady Eleanor before he introduced her first to his elder brother Lord Abraham and his French wife, Felicity. He bowed, and said, 'A pleasure, Miss Cartwright, my brother has been extolling your virtues quite liberally.' She curtsied and lowered her head slightly. 'I hope I can live up to his values, sir.'

'I am sure you will, Miss Cartwright.'

Next in line was a large gentleman of medium height. 'Mr Trueman,' said Isaiah, 'it gives me great pleasure to present Miss Tricia Cartwright.' He stepped aside and showed her forward. 'Miss Cartwright—Mr Trueman.' She curtsied and he bowed, 'Mr Trueman is a member of my Chapel and a subscriber to the school.'

'Good evening Miss Cartwright, it is a pleasure to meet you. He has done nothing but sing your praises all day.'

Tricia could feel herself colouring up and Bishop sensing this took her arm and brought her across to a tall thin gentleman whose erectness disguised his age but who looked familiar. 'Miss Cartwright—Mr Harwood. He is also a subscriber.'

Harwood bowed and took her outstretched hand and kissed the fingertip as she did a half curtsey. 'Miss Cartwright, a pleasure to meet you, but tell me, have we not met before?'

'Err... I do not think so Mr Harwood. I have a fair memory for faces and I do not recall meeting you.'

His next words astounded her. '*N'était-ce pas un moulin à Lancaster?*'

(Didn't we meet in Lancaster?)

Although taken aback slightly she was quick to respond in a stern manner, '*Monsieur, c'est de mauvaises manières de parler*

dans une langue étrangère. Veuillez montrer votre respect.'
(As a guest it is bad manners to speak in a foreign tongue. Please show some respect.)

He straightened up sharply and stared at her with disbelief before looking at Bishop and saying, 'I beg your pardon, Mister Bishop, I do apologise for my blunder. Such an oversight on my behalf.'

'Apology accepted, Mister Harwood but I do admire those with the ability to express themselves multi-culturally.' As they moved forward to meet Clifford who was next in line he leaned towards Harwood, and whispered, 'Do not mess with her, Harwood. She is highly intelligent and will have your guts for garters.'

Harwood showed no reaction and was sure his first thoughts were correct but, "Could this handsome young lady be the same one who was a skivvy in a Mill?"

Tricia stopped in front of Clifford, smiled, did a half curtsey while holding her hand out. 'Good evening, Master Bishop, how are we?'

He smiled back at her as he shook his head and took her hand. 'You are incorrigible, Miss Cartwright.' He kissed the tips of her fingers. 'I am well, Thank you, and I look forward to your entertainment later.'

She acknowledged the husbands of the two girls before joining the ladies on the long sofa. She had only been there a matter of minutes swapping pleasantries when the booming voice of Innes called out, 'DINNER IS SERVED!'

Lady Eleanor had been tactful in her table settings and Tricia was sat next to her opposite Clifford and there was no denying that all through the meal although she tried at first to avoid it the two swapped glances and by the third course they were exchanging pleasantries and comfortably mixed with the general conversation.

Dinner over the men stayed put to enjoy their brandy and no doubt discuss the ladies while the ladies retired to the drawing-room for coffee or wine or both.

During the conversations and laughter, Lady Eleanor leaned

over to Tricia, and said, 'What was that exchange with Harwood all about? It looked quite serious.'

'Oh, it was nothing. He had me confused with someone else.'

'But it sounded quite stern and in French which you speak wonderfully well.'

'I had a good teacher and I also told him off for using a foreign tongue whilst here as a guest.'

'Ah! That explains his disturbed appearance. You are strict, Miss Tricia. Are you like that with your children?'

Tricia laughed, and said, 'I wish. I am far too lenient with them but they work hard and I do not mind.'

Lady Eleanor laughed and tapped her on the knee. 'And you sell them coal?'

'Yes, if it gets them into school.'

Eleanor became serious. 'Tricia, try and make it up with Clifford. He has been sulking all week.'

'I think he has softened somewhat already, Lady Eleanor, we shall see.'

The men joined the ladies in the drawing-room and Lady Eleanor stood up to greet them, and said, 'Let us play some games for an hour before we have light entertainment.'

There was a rumble amongst the men and Clifford stepped forward. 'No Mother, our guests are here for one thing and that is to hear Miss Tricia play and sing of course.'

To hear him use her name was a delight, but she went a little coy at the request to entertain so early. With a little encouragement from Lady Eleanor and the other ladies she accepted and went over to the pianoforté but before she started she called Clifford over and asked if he would join her in the first song and with suppressed eagerness he readily accepted and the evening's entertainment began.

She had been playing and singing for almost an hour when her repertoire was exhausted and the rest of the evening was spent playing cards. Just before one o'clock, Isaiah called a halt and while they were preparing to leave Harwood approached Tricia who was a little apprehensive but bravely faced him as he spoke.

'Miss Cartwright, thank you for the evening's entertainment, you were most excellent and I understand Mister Isaiah's enthusiasm for you and I must add, your French is admirable.'

'And thank you, Mister Harwood. It makes my practising worthwhile to hear that…' and tongue in cheek, she added, '… and my French comes from my mother's Huguenot ancestors.'

He was about to turn away when he stopped. 'One other thing, Miss Cartwright, I beg your forgiveness for my rudeness earlier but you look very similar to a young lady I met under different circumstances in Lancaster.'

'All is forgiven, Mister Harwood, these mistakes are easy to make but is she not lucky to look like me. I wish the best for her.'

'Thank you again, Miss Cartwright.' He stepped back and bowed and she gracefully curtsied in return and he went on his way to collect his cloak and hat.

Clifford joined her. 'What did he want? He was not being rude again, was he?'

'No, Clifford dearest, quite the opposite.'

He looked down at her and smiled at the familiarity of her reply before he led her across the room and into the Hall where Innes and the housekeeper were waiting patiently their sleep time getting ever and ever shorter.

Brown as ever bowed deeply to his favourite guest and touched his hat when she pressed a coin into his hand.

'Thank you, Brown, a most excellent ride.'

Clifford climbed down and assisted her up the steps into the entrance Hall and onwards up the stairs. Outside her door, he took her by the shoulders to face him and went down on one knee. Taking her hand, he said, 'Miss Tricia Cartwright, may we call a truce and will you accept…' He held up a ring with a heart-shaped ruby surrounded by diamonds, '…this ring and be my wife. I have no interest in your possessions, only you. I love you!'

Lost for words she pulled off her glove and held her hand out, before saying, 'It gives me the greatest pleasure, Master Clifford, to say—Yes!'

He kissed her hand and slipped the ring on her finger before he stood up and held her by the shoulders once more. He pulled her forward and kissed her gently on the nose before she reached out, pulled him down and kissed him on the mouth.

After a minute, they separated, both breathing heavily. They smiled at each other and simultaneously pressed forward the pair of them wrapped up in an amorous bubble that only stopped when there was a polite cough from the bottom of the stairs.

They separated and looked at each other through love glazed eyes. 'Oh, Clifford,' whispered Tricia, 'when can we marry?'

They both laughed, and he replied, 'Christmas is to close, methinks February.'

She stretched up and kissed him. 'I look forward to it. Now go or Brown will fall asleep.'

She turned the key and opened the door as he went down the stairs and gave her a blown hand kiss. Inside she closed the door and flopped back against it. Her mind was in a whirl, was this real; the love of her life had returned and re-established their engagement. She looked at the ring and even in the dim light it shone and if she had been out in the open she would have been skipping and singing in happiness instead she kissed the ring stripped off her cloak and waltzed into the parlour where Agnes had left a light supper for her with a glass of milk.

Before she climbed into bed she knelt and said a prayer for her Mam who she knew would be pleased for her. Shooing Lucky to one side she got into bed and clutching a pillow to her breast she fell into sweet dreams.

The next morning as she breezed into the dining room, Agnes greeted her, 'Good morning, Missy, I see the engagement is back on.'

'Oh, Agnes, is it that obvious?'

'Yes, Missy, one should not dally at the door when canoodling and Brown needs to get that cough seen to.'

'Oh, Agnes, I am sorry. Did we wake you?'

'No, Missy, I never sleep until you come home. Your Mam

would never forgive me.'

Tricia ran across the room and cuddled her. 'Oh, thank you, Agnes, you are so kind and I promise you when I move to my new home with Clifford you are coming with me. Mam would give me nightmares if I didn't.' She stepped back and held up her hand to show her the ring. 'And this is what he gave me last night. It is beautiful is it not?'

'My, my, you lucky lady, that is beautiful. Now, Missy; rings aside sit down at the table while I get your breakfast.'

Tricia laughed and curtsied. 'Yes, Miss.—There is one thing, Agnes. In February when we marry I will be moving to new premises. I will be taking you, your niece and great-niece, with me but we will need new staff for the school so check your relatives.'

When she attended Church, Clifford met her and they walked down the aisle with her hand resting on his as he led her down to the family pews. Members of the congregation saw this and knew the significance and there was delicate hand clapping as she sat.

They parted immediately after the service and she went for a light lunch as the school and the welfare of the children was her first commitment. Clifford joined her for afternoon tea and throughout when not eating or drinking they held hands.

When it was all cleared away and Agnes retired they snuggled closer on the sofa but she steadfastly refused to submit to nature the final promise to her Mam uppermost in her mind.

—

The final days leading up to Christmas were a mixture of work and good news. The Rail Company demanded more coal increasing her income although she had to be canny with her spending as contract companies were notorious for their late payments. One person who did however pay on time was Catchpole who declared it was his policy to start the New Year with a clean slate. This allowed her to slip Billy a couple of sovereigns on the day he left and to splash out a little on her wardrobe as a visit to Lord Abraham Bishops residence on the outskirts of Preston was on the cards for Christmas Day which this year fell on a Thursday.

—

It was while shopping on the Saturday morning before Christmas with Agnes that she noticed something unusual. While perusing the stalls in the local market she spotted a colourful children's booklet on the rag and bone stall. She thought nothing of it at first until she saw the title *'Henrietta'* and the picture of a hen. "It cannot be so," she said to herself, "I have not published my book yet."

She did not hesitate. 'Agnes, I want to look at something on this stall.'

She picked the booklet up and the stallholder, said, 'Yes, Miss, can I help?'

'Yes, I wish to purchase it. How much?'

'It's tuppence, Miss. It's very popular. I have sold a few over the months and if you look in the Lancaster Gazette and the Preston Chronicle they're in there as a series once a month.'

'Have you any more of these booklets?'

He rummaged in a box under the stall and produced a battered copy. 'Here's another. It's different and a bit bashed. I'll let it go for a penny.'

She did not show her feelings but inside she was seething. These were her books or rather a published version of the stories she had left with the Rev. Elijah Pickup. 'I'll take both of them.

She paid him and gave the booklets to Agnes to put in her bag and after a moments deliberation, she decided that a cup of tea and a scone in *'Katies Parlour'* was the answer to her annoyance.

'Come, Agnes, it is a pot of tea and a scone for us.'

'Yes, Missy, I could do with a drink.'

Later, in the Tea Room doorway while pondering what to do next she decided that she had had enough of shopping so they hired a hack and went to look for Brown who they knew would be waiting out at the Mill.

After dinner that evening whilst walking outside in the gardens with Clifford he stopped and holding her hand, he said, 'Tricia, my love, I had a word with your Uncle Tom yesterday and he told me you have a way with horses. Is that so?'

'Oh! Clifford, I do not know how to answer. I cannot boost

my own ego, but, yes, I do have a little experience.'

'You can ride?'

'Why, yes.'

'Can we go for a ride tomorrow while this mild weather persists?'

'Clifford, I would love to but I do not have a horse and it will be too dark after school.'

'I have arranged with Father to do school tomorrow and I have the horses and he did warn me that we are not married.'

She silently thanked Agnes for advising her to get the appropriate outfit for such an occasion, before she replied, 'Oh, thank you, Clifford, I will look forward to it.'

The following day after saying, 'Goodbye,' to the family she hurried back from the Church so she could change in readiness for Clifford's arrival and when he did she was both delighted and taken aback by what she saw. As she stepped from the rear door of the school into the stable yard he was stood between two horses one of which was a sixteen hands chestnut thoroughbred mare with a white diamond on her forehead and four white socks beautifully groomed.

She presumed that was Clifford's horse and not the steadfast workmanlike fifteen hands black horse he held in his left hand.

'Oh, Clifford, such beautiful animals.'

She walked towards the black horse and, he said, 'No, Tricia,' he gently pulled the mare forward. 'This is yours. It is my present to you.'

'Oh! Clifford, you shouldn't but she is such a beautiful creature has she got a name?'

'No. I thought you may like to do that.'

She stood in front of it and reached forward to touch her and the mare raised her head and snorted. 'Be careful, Tricia,' said Clifford, 'she is young and feisty. A bit like you.'

Tricia laughed. 'Give me a moment, Clifford; I want to talk to her.'

She held her hands by her side as she stood in front of the horse looking into its eyes and she gently blew into her nose. She paused and then blew again this time raising her hands into view and whispering. Still gently blowing and speaking she reached upward and softly stroked the horse down the diamond. The horse lowered her head and Tricia took hold of her left ear and softly stroked it as she curled her hand around it and gave it a gentle pull.

'There, there, baby,' she said, 'we are friends and I am going to call you, *Caterina* after my Mam. Can I ride you now?'

She took the reins off Clifford and led the horse over to the mounting stand talking softly to the horse all the time. The school handyman held the reins while she climbed up the steps and slipping her left foot into the stirrup sat on the saddle hooking her right leg over the side saddle pommel. She said, 'Thank you,' to the handyman and he stepped to one side and leaning forward Tricia whispered into the horses left ear and gave it a gentle tug at the same time squeezing her leg into its side and without a murmur it stepped forward and with Tricia's guidance walked calmly out of the yard.

Clifford followed, wondering "Is there no end to this woman's talent?"

They had been riding around the quiet country lanes for about fifteen minutes when Tricia said out of the blue, 'Clifford! What do I do if someone has been stealing my work?'

'In what manner, Tricia?'

'I found two booklets yesterday that were stories I wrote when I was fourteen. I still write them and read them out to my class.'

'Can you prove it?'

'Yes, Clifford, I keep copies of all my work plus the drawings that go with it.'

'I remember Father mentioned you wrote children's stories. You must show me and if I think we have a chance I will start legal proceedings. It may take a while.'

'I will show you when we get home over a pot of tea.'

A few minutes later Clifford guided them into a tree-lined driveway which led them up to a three-story ivy-covered country house with well-kept gardens and large grounds. A hundred yards short of the front entrance, he stopped and said. 'Well, Miss

Cartwright, what do you think?'

'It is lovely, Clifford. Why are we looking at it, are we visiting?'

'No, dearest, it is for sale and I would like to buy it as our new home.'

Tricia was lost for words. "A pedigree horse, and now this?" She never imagined she would ever be in this position. It only seemed like yesterday that she was working all hours in a steam ridden Mill.

Feeling quite humble, she enquired, 'Clifford, I don't know what to say. It is beautiful, and not too far from the school. Can we look further?'

'No, my dearest, the owners are not home, I will arrange a visit early in the New Year.'

'Thank you, Clifford. Let us go home now, I am feeling a little light-headed,' but already she was planning how she could benefit the school from her good fortune.'

―

Clifford put his cup down and dabbed his mouth with a napkin as he sat back on the sofa. 'Now, Miss Cartwright, show me this literary work of yours.'

'One moment, dearest, I will retrieve them.'

She left the room at the same time as Agnes came in to clear away the tea trays only to return moments later carrying her portfolio and she sat down beside him. First, she handed him the books she had found on the market stall and after he had looked through them he put them to one side and she opened her portfolio proper and let the whole work tumble across the low table and choosing carefully the work that matched that in the books she gave them to him.

He read them and checked them against the books and after he had done this a few times, he sat back. 'Tricia, you need to show me no more. This is most definitely copyright infringement. Thankfully you wrote the dates on your work and they are worn enough to be genuine. You must give them to me and I will begin proceedings but first I must approach the publisher.'

'The stallholder said these stories are published in the Lancaster and Preston newspapers.'

'In that case, I will approach the Courts and get an Order to freeze publication while we investigate. This may take a little while, dearest, but I will try my best. Then we go to Lancaster and sue your, Mr Pickup.'

'Oh, thank you, Clifford; if we are successful I will publish all my stories.'

'A complete book will be too expensive for ordinary people, Tricia, you will have to do a booklet monthly and the newspapers and then maybe libraries will buy the book. That's how it is done and think of a name. The public likes to see male authors.'

'This one is going to stay female, Clifford, although maybe a little shorter.'

'I thought you might.'

'And you must let me pay for your services.'

'I won't need that, Tricia. I add it onto the offenders' bill.' He helped her put her work back into the portfolio, before he said, 'Tricia! It is time for me to go. I will take these and *Caterina* with me. Our stable lad can look out for her.'

They stood up and they cuddled up together and kissed before they breathlessly parted. He scooped up his hat and they walked together down to the yard and as he mounted his horse, Tricia said, 'Clifford, tell your stable lad if he rides her, to gently pull or roll her left ear and she will be good.'

He leaned forward from the saddle and hooked an arm under hers and pulled her up and they kissed again. 'Goodbye, dearest, I look forward until tomorrow.'

—

On Wednesday evening she wished the last of her pupils a 'Happy Christmas' and told them not to miss Church School on the following Sunday and quickly hurried upstairs to help Agnes pack her bags for the three-night stay with the Bishops but Agnes as always was very efficient and had it all done. She did not check it as she knew it would be perfect and every item accounted for.

'Oh, Agnes, you are so good. What would I do without you?

Have you done your bags yet?'

'Yes, Missy—would you like some tea before we get prepared?'

'I would love some, Agnes. Can I help you with the bags?'

'No, Missy. That is not the way. The handyman will be here shortly to take them and he will also look after Lucky.'

Feeling a little foolish, Tricia sat on the sofa saying to herself mentally, "I will never get used to this."

Agnes duly obliged with a pot of tea and some sandwiches and Tricia sat there thinking how three months had changed her life. It wasn't long before Agnes called her to get ready.

Brown arrived at six-thirty and strapped the bags onto the platform at the rear before he helped Tricia and Agnes into the carriage and then he had the struggle pushing Cook up onto the seat alongside him for the drive to the Bishop residence.

Brown was his usual bubbly self as he helped her down from the carriage and she replied with an equally exaggerated reply as she slipped him a coin. 'Do not spend it all at once,' she said surreptitiously.

'I shan't, madam, enjoy your stay.'

'Thank you, Brown, you may help the ladies now.'

With a large grin on his face, he bowed extravagantly as she was welcomed by the Head Housemaid and he moved quickly to help Agnes and Cook.

Upstairs she was shown into a spacious room by the footman carrying the bags and regardless of the mild winter weather there was a welcoming fire glowing. "One of Catchpole's upmarket customers," she said to herself with a smile as she stood by quite the biggest four-poster bed she had ever seen and she was quite sure that Lady Eleanor had advised on all the feminine extras as the dressing table was loaded with goodies.

Agnes set about unpacking while Tricia availed herself of the bath that had been made ready. Feeling fully refreshed and the labours of the day washed away Agnes helped her get prepared for the evening's celebrations.

The dinner and the evening entertainment were quiet affairs

and Tricia excused herself from the expected pianoforté accomplishments on the grounds of tiredness after a hard day's work at the school and Clifford and his two sisters did their bit followed by an hour of card games and Tricia was glad to crawl into bed just after midnight.

She had a good night's sleep and was awakened early by Agnes in time to have breakfast. It was an unusual breakfast routine for her. She had to choose from many dishes that were laid out on a long sideboard in warm trays while drinks were brought to the table by one of the footmen.

She was halfway through her breakfast when Clifford joined her. He stood behind her and leaning forward he kissed her on the cheek and wished her a 'Merry Christmas' before choosing his breakfast and sitting opposite and like a lovesick child he never took his eyes from her. She felt a little embarrassed but his sisters and their husbands came to the rescue when they joined them. Christmas greetings were exchanged and mild conversation filled the room for half an hour before they retired to get ready for the morning Church service.

Rev Isaiah Bishop welcomed everyone as they entered the Church and likewise when they left after a grinding two-hour service which was longer than the usual Sunday service but he had a more pressing message to get across and he was able to join them for lunch where everyone swapped gifts.

Clifford surprised Tricia when he called for Innes to bring in a package. Innes duly obliged and lay before Tricia a beautiful handmade saddle decorated with the finest detail and she surprised him with a pair of riding boots. They hugged and kissed oblivious of the clapping around them.

Innes entered the room once more carrying a large polished mahogany box and gave it to Lady Eleanor who immediately called Tricia over.

Tricia did a half curtsey. 'Yes, my Lady?'

Lady Eleanor lifted the box and presented it to Tricia. 'I hear you do a lot of writing Miss Tricia so this modest writing slope is for you.'

'I cannot thank you enough, My Lady, and I assure you I shall make good use of it.'

'I want a signed copy of your next book, Miss Tricia.'

'My work is mainly for children but I have a plan for a more mature one.'

'Best of luck, dear. Let me see now, who is next.'

Tricia curtsied once more and rejoined Clifford on the other side of the room and explored the interior of her latest acquisition.

Presents exchanged and lunch over they dispersed for a rest before they prepared to get ready for the trip to Bishops Mill Manor the family residence outside Preston where Lord Abraham and his family lived.

Tricia stepped back from the mirror and twirled. 'What do you think, Agnes? Will I pass scrutiny tonight?'

What she wore was an understated, off the shoulder white gown. Not elaborate or flashy, but simple feminine nicely restrained fashion, which was her appeal. The décolletage was low enough to show her birthmark central at the top of her cleavage and it gave her an air of virginal simplicity.

'I wish I was young again, missy, I would love a dress like that and you will be the subject of scrutiny all evening possibly for the wrong reasons. Where did you get the idea?'

'I was going through the catalogues of dresses in *'Elegance'* when I saw this picture of who I believe is an opera singer. I had no hesitation and Mrs Rose was happy to make something outside of the strict unromantic boundaries that are set at the moment but I kept it a secret from you and she also did away with that restricting busk which pierces your stomach every time you breath'

'I could not agree more, Missy. I'm glad I don't have to dress up with you lot. Now let's do your hair.'

The white silk material of her dress highlighted her abundant shiny black hair which was tied back with a simple bow of the same material and left to hang down between her shoulders.

'There you are, Missy, I think you may be setting a trend tonight although the daughters of Lord Abrahams are a bit stuffy.'

'Agnes, are there no male heirs except Clifford in the Bishop family.'

'They did try, Missy, but were unsuccessful.'

There was a tap on the door, and Agnes called out, 'Come in, all is proper.'

One of the housemaids popped her head around the door, and said, 'They're preparing to leave, Miss.'

'Thank you,' said Tricia, 'we will be down directly.'

The door closed and they scrambled around making sure they had all the artefacts necessary for the evening's frolics.

The lady's maids and luggage were sent ahead while Tricia travelled with Lady Eleanor and her two daughters their voluminous skirts filling the coach like four deflated balloons. Clifford went with his Father and the two husbands. The distance to Bishops Mill Manor was not far but they had to negotiate narrow country lanes which in December, even allowing for the mild conditions were a coach driver's nightmare but they made it in reasonable time to be welcomed by the household staff already prepared for the surge of visitors.

The ladies were shown into an ante-room where they dispensed with the outdoor garments and tidied up their dresses before joining their partners in the hall and waited until it was their turn to be introduced to the rest of the guests by the stentorian voice of the butler.

'MASTER CLIFFORD BISHOP and MISS PATRICIA CARTWRIGHT!'

They stepped across the threshold into the large entertainment hall. There were more chairs than were necessary to ensure that no one had to give up a seat and the number of guests was low and mainly family as many of the upper class had defected to London for the winter season.

They were met by Lord Abraham of Longbottom and his wife Lady Felicity, who was of French descent and enjoyed Tricia's company who gave her the freedom to speak her own tongue.

Abraham greeted Clifford, 'Greetings Master Clifford, what a pleasure to meet you and your fiancée, Miss Patricia.' As he spoke he turned to Tricia, took her hand as she curtsied and kissed her fingers. 'My pleasure, Miss Patricia, I hope we have the pleasure of your fine voice later.'

She looked him in the eye quite openly, and smiled, as she said, 'I will try my best, milord.'

Tricia moved across to Lady Felicity and curtsied. 'Lady Felicity.'

'Miss Cartwright, how wonderful to see you and I do love your dress. You must tell me about it later. Do enjoy your evening.'

'Thank you, M'lady; I shall look forward to it.'

The protocol finished she caught up with Clifford and they mingled with the other guests while drinking champagne.

She was not a fan of champagne. She thought it too sweet although the food in front of you demanded the correct wine etiquette. It was not long before the voice of the butler demanded their presence in the dining room and they duly sat at the long table for the lengthy process of eating many courses with the correct wine. Being a special occasion time was not of the essence and it was almost two hours before everyone threw themselves back with ingestion exhaustion.

The ladies retired to the lounge for drinks of their choice while the men stayed to indulge in the obligatory brandy.

Tricia felt privileged to be accepted into this society so quickly. She preferred the less indulgent life of a schoolteacher but one should not complain at good fortune.

She was of course the centre of attention amongst the ladies who were desirous of knowing about her diversion from the current mode of evening dress. They all loved it but so many questions were asked. Where did she get it? How did she find out about it and most of all, did removing the busk make her more available to the opposite sex and even her hair was the subject of conversation.

It was a little overwhelming but she told them she loved the freedom and she felt more feminine and her fiancé approved of it as he thought that she was more approachable and he felt relaxed and able to talk more freely about everyday things rather than the observed protocol that current fashions dictated.

Tricia was relieved when the men entered the room and a string trio started playing. The men joined the ladies and Clifford was the first to offer his hand and take Tricia onto the floor. Her dancing like that of her music came back to her quickly and soon they were accompanied on the floor by the others and so the festivities went on late into the night. It was well after midnight when Lady Felicity requested Tricia to sing for them but she declined, saying she was too exhausted and Clifford also turned down the request and half an hour later the partying ended.

The first ten minutes of the drive home were a chatty affair each of them reminiscing over the evenings' events but eventually they fell quiet and taking into account the roughness of the highway they dozed until rudely shocked awake when the carriage jerked as the left front wheel collapsed tilting sideways dragging the horses down with it.

Brown was thrown off his seat and crashed to the ground before rolling into a ditch while Hilda and Constance were catapulted forward into Tricia and Lady Eleanor before falling in a tangled heap against the side of the carriage as it skidded to a halt.

At first, there was silence before the first groans and the calamitous noise of the horses trying to get to their feet. Tricia was lucky as she had been sat on the right and fell sideways onto Lady Eleanor while at the same time she was able to shield herself from the tumbling Constance with her muffle and she finished on top of the heap.

Protected by their voluminous dresses and crinolines it was difficult to untangle themselves when suddenly the top door was pulled open and Clifford assisted by the other men hung into the carriage and started to pull Tricia up and out of the carriage followed by the other three. None of them were seriously injured just shaken but it was a few minutes before Lady Eleanor, said, 'Where's Brown?'

The men looked at each other and shrugged before Clifford sprung into action. He dashed back to the men's carriage and retrieved a lantern and with the others began searching along the hedgerow and the ditch. It was not long before they found him bundled up unconscious at the bottom of the ditch with his left arm at a peculiar angle. Fortunately, the mild winter was holding and the ditch was dry and with little effort, they pulled him onto the edge of the highway. The pushing and pulling had stirred him awake and he lay groaning hold his left arm and shoulder. Isaiah called on the other two drivers to lift him gently into the men's carriage and lay him on the floor. He then told the ladies to also go into the men's carriage, 'And try not to smother Brown with your dresses, ladies,' he said.

His little joke relieved the tension somewhat and there was a little titter as the lady's maids helped them into the carriage.

Clifford poked his head through the door. 'You will have to be patient, ladies,' he said, 'but it will take us a little time to pull the carriage to the side,' and while looking at Tricia, he said, 'are you all in one piece?'

They nodded and he left them to it as he returned to help move the broken down carriage. The four horses although frightened and skittish were not seriously affected and were able with a little encouragement to drag the wreck off the highway before they were unhitched. With the luggage transferred the broken down vehicle was abandoned and the two fit carriage drivers were instructed to get the horses back home the best way they could while Clifford drove the ladies and Isaiah drove the other one with the four maids and the two husbands crammed together.

It was after three o'clock when they finally arrived home and the ladies went immediately to their rooms. Agnes helped Tricia undress and get ready for bed and when she was about to leave Tricia stopped her. 'Agnes,' she said, 'I do not want to see you before midday tomorrow but please check on Brown.'

'Yes, Missy.'

She nodded her head and backed out of the room.

Tricia pulled the bedclothes around her and snuggled down.

—

At ten o'clock, there was a gentle knock on the door and Agnes crept in and through sleepy eyes Tricia greeted her. 'Morning, Agnes, I told you to rest.'

'I have, Missy, and I have brought you some breakfast.'

Tricia struggled into a sitting position and stretched just as Agnes slid a tray across but she stopped her removing the lid from the dish instead she had a cup of tea which revived her before she had a peek under it. Agnes had brought her favourite two boiled eggs and toasted soldiers and she got stuck in hungrily.

As Agnes went to clear away the tray, Tricia, said, 'What of Brown, Agnes, do you know?'

'Oh, yes, Missy, the Doctor said it was a dislocated shoulder and with the help of the other staff he pulled it back into position. The noise from Brown was terrible but as soon as it clicked in he calmed down. He's resting now and the Doctor said he would be alright in a few days.'

'Oh, good, I thought we would lose him. He doesn't know it but he's coming with us when I get married.'

'That will cause a rumble, Missy. Mister Isaiah is not happy losing two of his staff.'

'He should have no trouble replacing them. With the dilemma in the Mills just now there will be plenty of volunteers.'

'It's the continuance, Missy, you have to train them.'

'Am I not lucky? You will not have to do that, will you?'

'No, Missy—I think you should get up now, Missy, Master Clifford wishes to go riding at half-past eleven.'

'I have not brought my riding outfit, Agnes.'

'Don't worry, I was sent to fetch it earlier.'

'By whom?'

'Master Clifford.'

Tricia shook her head. 'Men! He only wants to wear his boots.'

She scrambled out of bed and with Agnes's help she was ready and waiting for Clifford. She didn't have long to wait until there was a knock on the door and the housemaid poked her head around, and said, 'Master Clifford awaits your presence, ma'am.'

'Thank you,' said, Tricia, 'tell him I will be two minutes.'

'Yes. ma'am.'

She did a quick twirl in front of Agnes who was pleased with the result and she made her way downstairs where Clifford in his brand new boots was waiting.

'Good morning Miss Tricia, I take it you slept well after last night's debacle?'

'I certainly did, Master Clifford, and I hear that Brown is recovering.'

'He is.' He held out his arm and she curled her arm into his and they walked across the Hall and out to the carriage turnaround where the groom was waiting with the horses and a set of steps for Tricia to mount *Caterina* complete with the new saddle.

They had only been riding for ten minutes when Tricia, said, 'Thank you for this beautiful saddle, Clifford, it is most comfortable almost like it had been made just for me.'

'It was.'

'How did you do that?'

'Trade secrets, Miss Tricia, but Mrs Cheetham had a lot to do with it. Probably the same way you did the boots?'

'Yes, your footman was very helpful and the cobbler already had your old measurements anyway.'

'There are no secrets anymore but the horse is as comes supplied by nature.'

'And very nice too as is the weather which is outdoing itself after that dreadful wet summer.'

'Yes, it is quite unexpected but is giving the land time to dry out. It will not last though.'

The chit chat went on as they made their way home but Tricia insisted they go by their future home. They paused only for a few minutes and the house was visible from the road now that winter had cleared the leaves from the trees.

'I do love it, Clifford. Have we got it?'

'Yes. I did not wait to show you, dear, I bought it immediately to stop other competitors.'

'Oh, Clifford, I don't mind. Have you any plans?'

'I am thinking a reasonable proportion for arable farming and the rest for stock. What do you think?'

'I insist on some chickens. They have such a lovely personality and I love fresh eggs for breakfast.'

'Not roasted then?'

'Most certainly not.'

They laughed together and went on their way. The groundsman had spotted them and the house was alerted to their imminent arrival and the groom, the second butler and Agnes were waiting for them.

The groom offered to help her down but she athletically jumped to the ground lifted her riding skirt and joined Agnes who went with her into the house while Clifford stopped to talk to the groom about the horses only for them to meet up again over a light lunch later.

It being Saint Stephens Day there was a Church service and Lady Eleanor had insisted on a short service after the brain-searing lecture that Isaiah had given them on Christmas Day and the evening was very much like their usual Saturday.

Tricia accepted the invitation to stay over on Saturday and with the mild weather persisting, another ride was taken only this time they were joined by Isaiah and the two husbands, Constance and Hilda having opted for a lazy day.

Clifford had sent his valet earlier with a message to the current owners and got permission to ride around the land associated with their prospective purchase. The layout was similar to what Clifford had intended but it would require more manpower to bring it up to the standard he was planning. Farm labourers were in demand as the majority of men had gone into the towns for the higher wages in the Mills and were demanding better wages to stay put, but with the latest unrest, Clifford was sure he could manage.

They stayed out for two hours and after a late lunch Tricia opted to go home insisting that she must prepare for Sunday School the next day. She also declined Clifford's offer to escort her but she did dally with him a little longer by going for a walk in the gardens while her belongings were being stored on the carriage.

Brown drove them but he was assisted by a junior coachman

as he was still too weak to lift the heavy bags but it didn't stop the light-hearted banter when they arrived. He opened the door and with his usual exuberant bow and he held out his hand to help Tricia down.

'Thank you Brown, a most excellent ride. I see you kept your seat.'

'Yes, ma'am, and most comfortable it was too.'

'Brown, seriously, are you feeling better?'

He nodded. 'Yes, Miss, a little sore but I have to keep the pennies rolling in.'

She understood and slipped him something from her hand. 'You take care, Brown, I have need of you in the future,' she nodded towards the junior coachman helping Agnes and cook, 'you had better train him well.'

Brown could only reply, 'Thank you, Miss.'

Lucky was sat on the doorstep and gave her a long angry stare for leaving him for such a long time but as they were climbing the stairs Lucky shot past them and was quietly mewing and rubbing himself on the doorpost happy to see his mistress. 'Hello, young man,' she said, 'happy to see you too.'

She opened the door and followed Lucky in to find a warm glowing fire welcoming them. She wondered who had brought the message of her homecoming and she said to Agnes, 'How did they know we were coming home, Agnes?'

'Master Clifford dispatched one of the stable lads as soon as you expressed the desire to return, Missy.'

'Oh, they do a lot those boys.'

'He didn't mind, Missy, he was riding *Caterina.* Would you like some tea?'

'A small sandwich and a hot tub, and tell cook, Agnes, I don't want dinner only a light supper.'

'Yes, Missy, tea won't be long.'

—

New Year's Eve arrived and as Tricia relaxed with a cup of hot chocolate the mantel clock chimed midnight. As the last chime faded Agnes entered the room followed by Mary the new housemaid, Cook and her new assistant Bella and last but not least, the handyman, Reilly. Tricia stood as they lined up before her and one at a time they bobbed and exchanged small gifts. At the end of the line Reilly did a half bow and knuckled his forehead and gave her a lump of coal.

'Thank you, Reilly, and thank you for looking after Lucky.'

'No problem, ma'am, but he insisted on sleeping here.'

As soon as Reilly received his gift he took the lump of coal from her and put it on the fire.

She had given them money in small leather pouches and when the ritual was over, she said, 'Thank you all, you have been so kind. A Happy New Year to you all and may this year be a good one for you.'

They answered simultaneously, 'Happy New Year to you, Miss Cartwright and thank you.'

They all acknowledged her and left the room. Tricia stood dumbstruck with a tear in her eye in wonderment at how her life had changed. She pinched herself to make sure she wasn't dreaming. All she had to do now was wait for a dark-haired man to visit and then she could go to bed.

Her wish was granted when Clifford arrived. Agnes showed him in and he dashed across and hugged Tricia and kissed her to which she responded eagerly before he presented her with a gift parcel consisting of a black bun, shortbread, coal, salt and a small cask of whisky.

'Oh, thank you, Clifford.' She bent down and plucked a wrapped gift from the table and gave it to him. 'A Happy and fortuitous New Year to you, my love.'

'It makes me happy, my love, to know I am getting married this year,' he replied, 'shall we partake of some of that whisky?'

'Yes, darling, we shall.'

She pulled the tapestry ribbon by the fire and Agnes popped her head around the door.

'Yes, Miss?'

'Agnes, dear, could you bring us two whisky glasses, please, and some water, and where is Mary?'

'I told her to take the rest of the night off, Miss.'

'Very well, Agnes, as long as you don't mind.'

Agnes retired from the room only to return two minutes later with the glasses and a jug of water. She left them on the table and as she was leaving Tricia, said, 'That will be all, Agnes. I shan't bother you further.'

'Thank you, Miss.'

Clifford poured a finger of whisky into each glass and topped Tricia's with water and they stood in front of the fire and clinked glasses.

'Cheers,' they said, simultaneously and took a drink before putting their glasses down and going into a clinch. As they fell sideways onto the sofa Tricia whispered, 'May it be a long and happy one, Clifford, darling. I can't wait.'

After a few minutes before her senses let her give in to natures call she pushed him away.

'I can't, Clifford, I owe it to my, Mam.'

He hugged her and kissed her on the nose. 'I understand, my sweet, and I admire you for it.' They parted and straightened themselves out before Clifford picked up his hat and gave her one last hug. 'Goodnight, my love, I look forward to seeing you later in the day.'

She watched as he let himself out and blew her a kiss as he closed the door. She took a deep breath both overjoyed and mystified at the turn of events when she heard a familiar voice whisper, "This is your year, lots of love, Mam."

Tricia spun around but she was alone and a sudden realisation that there was school this day awakened her to reality. She blew out the candles and retired to bed to snatch a few hours sleep.

~~~~~

CHAPTER 16

1846

The Banns for her proposed marriage had been posted at the local Church, her class size had increased to nineteen and the school in total was thirty-nine and her income from the local coal orders had correspondingly increased. That was not her main concern on New Year's Day as she introduced her new pupils and arranged them so that the older ones were mixed with the new younger ones.

The Rev Isaiah Bishop was also pleased that more children were able to attend as this was his aim in this fierce industrial climate to educate as many children as possible to attain better positions in life.

In between Christmas and New Year L& NW Rail had pressed her for more business as passenger numbers had increased which enhanced her BCCC income and Tom Devlin told her that providing the increased deliveries was no problem as the bargees were queuing up for the extra work. There were, however, complaints from the Gasworks in Kendal about the decrease of deliveries and Tom had arranged a meeting on the following Saturday for a meeting between Tricia and the management of the works.

Tricia had to forgo a proposed visit to the house that Clifford was buying for them and Brown was now fit and able to drive the carriage to Preston and dropped her and Agnes outside Katie's which Tricia had insisted on instead of the more forbidding business halls or banks which would have suited the Gas Works representatives.

Inside Tricia spoke with Katy and a table was set up in a quiet corner but still visible to the room and having ordered tea for her and Agnes and a bacon sandwich and a mug of tea for Brown they sat back and waited.

They did not have long to wait before two well-dressed and overfed men entered and were shown over to the table. Tricia stood up, held her hand out and welcomed them.

'Good morning, gentlemen, Miss Cartwright of BCCC. I see the weather was kind to you.'

They seemed hesitant at first until the swarthy one of the two stepped forward and bowing took her hand. 'Good morning Miss Cartwright. I am Douglas James and my associate is Nathaniel Burley.' Burley stepped forward and bowed while shaking her hand, and said formally, 'Miss Cartwright, we chose to travel down yesterday, and yes, the weather was indeed kind as it has been all winter.'

Tricia said, 'Please take a seat, gentlemen.' She waved the waitress over and said to them, 'Order what you like, gentlemen and then we will get down to business.'

As soon as their order was delivered and they had partaken of a drink and a biscuit Tricia went straight to the point. 'Now, gentlemen, explain to me your problem.'

James was caught with a biscuit halfway to his mouth and he fumbled unable to decide whether to eat it or put it down. He opted to put it down and wiped his mouth before replying, 'Our deliveries have become less and our stockpile is shrinking and upon investigation we find that you have taken over most of the barges for your business. This cannot go on.'

'Why do you think the bargees prefer me to you, Mr James?'

He paused trying to think of a reply, before he said, 'A shorter turnaround and therefore more profitable.'

'Mr James, it could not be anything to do with what you pay them?'

At this point, Burley spoke rather aggressively. 'Miss Cartwright, we pay them enough and in my opinion too much.'

'Ah, Mr Burley, you have a voice.' She reached into her bag and drew out a small pad and a pencil. She tore out the first page and pushed it over to them. 'Now, gentlemen,' she pointed to one column, 'This is what I pay my barges,' she moved across to the other column, 'and this is what you pay and considering the journey time is eight days longer it is a pittance. Now turn the page over and this is my offer to you.'

They did as they were bid and studied it. 'That is what LN&W rail pay me plus extra for the work time involved. A halfpenny per day per hundredweight. That is my offer to you'

Burley grabbed the paper and studied it more closely through his *pince-nez* before he slammed it down on the table attracting attention from around the room. 'That is outrageous,' he said aloud, 'we can't possibly pay that.'

Tricia gave herself a little fan with her pad, before she replied, 'You prefer to close your business, Mr Burley? Why not review your profit margin? You look like you can afford it.'

James signalled Burley to lean closer and started to talk to him softly but before he had completed more than a few words, Tricia interrupted. 'Speak English, gentlemen, not only is it rude but I am fully *compos mentis* with the French language.'

They stopped and both looked at her disbelieving what they had just heard before James spoke. 'I apologise profusely, Miss Cartwright, but are these figures truly what the rail company pay?'

She nodded. 'Yes, and may I add that if you turn down my offer I will advise my manager to stop all journeys to Kendal but if you accept it I will guarantee a minimum of four barges per day. That should keep you running and top up your stock albeit not as quickly as before. Maybe I can fix it to be more in the first couple of weeks.'

'Miss Cartwright, please allow us to talk this over privately. We will go outside if you don't mind.'

'Feel free, gentlemen, I will order more tea in your absence.'

Burley and James stood and bowed slightly before they left the establishment while Tricia called the waitress over and ordered more tea. That done she turned to Agnes who had remained quiet the whole time. 'What do you think of that, Agnes?'

'Missy, I wish I had your guts but you did tell a few whoppers, can you do that, I mean stop all the barges going there?'

'No, but they don't know that. I will have some work to do if they agree to my terms.'

They sat back and enjoyed a cream scone with their tea and it was some ten minutes later that the men returned and nodding acknowledgement sat down.

'Would you like some more tea, gentlemen?' said Tricia reaching for the teapot.

'Yes, please,' said James, 'wetting my palate is what I need right now.' Burley nodded sourly.

They sat for a few minutes also enjoying a cream scone before, Tricia said, 'Well, gentlemen, what is your desire?'

Burley slid the page over to Tricia. 'Miss Cartwright, we grudgingly accept your terms but can you get us topped up as quickly as you say?'

'I will try my best.' She reached once more into her bag and withdrew what looked like a legal document furled and tied with a blue ribbon. She undid the ribbon and unfurled three papers and slid them over the table. 'This gentlemen, is our contract. Read it and sign it.' She signalled Katy who had been waiting. Katy nodded and reached under the counter and brought over a quill, an inkpot and blotter and put them on the table.

Tricia touched her arm, and said, 'Thank you, Miss Kate.'

Burley and James signed all three copies and Tricia did the same when she called Katy again and gave her the quill. 'Please sign at the bottom, Miss Katy.'

Katy complied and went back to her work while Tricia blotted Katy's signature. 'Thank you, gentlemen, as you are aware this contract starts a week on Monday. I will see to it that you are supplied this week under the same rules.'

'Thank you, Miss Cartwright, 'said, James, 'please allow us to pay for the refreshments.'

'That is alright, Mr James, I arranged the meeting here therefore it is my privilege. Do not forget your copy.'

Burley rolled up the contract and they both stood and this time shook hands firmly although Burley was quick to withdraw his hand, and bowing, they said, 'A pleasure, Miss Cartwright.'

James said, 'That was the quickest negotiation I have ever done. Goodbye, Miss Cartwright.'

They both nodded their acknowledgement and left.

When they had gone, Tricia said to Agnes, 'A satisfactory

morning, Agnes but now I have work to do. I reckon I need to buy some barges. I will settle with Katy and then it's down to the docks to tell Uncle Tom.'

'Hello, Uncle Tom, kind of you to see me at such short notice but I have a problem to discuss. It is a good problem.'

'Yes, Miss Tricia, what is it. I'm sure we can fix it.'

She gave Tom a copy of the contract. 'That, Uncle Tom is the new contract I have taken on with the Kendal Gas Company. Get Auntie Edie to read it to you but it says I have to provide at least four barges per day to Kendal if not more at the same rate as we get from the rail company plus extra for the time it takes. Is it possible?'

Tom took a piece of chalk from his pocket and started doing a calculation on the bench beside him. After a couple of minutes, he stopped, and said, 'Yes, Miss, we can do that but it's tight. One slip and we are in trouble.'

'So we need more barges?'

'Yes.'

'How many?'

'Five would be enough.'

'Uncle Tom, you are now my manager. I want you to organise it. You and your boys plus whoever you need do just Garstang. Everyone else signs a contract and they do a Kendal plus one Garstang. They are free to carry on with the limestone so they will get a lift on their income and whatever sideline you can pick up. You do farm stuff from Garstang, don't you?'

'Yes, Miss, and if we do it that way we need only three barges.'

'Could you get the crew for them?'

'Yes, Miss, there are many barge families with grown-up children who would do the job and you could get me a dumb barge, Miss.'

'What is that?'

'It's a barge with no cabin which we tow. It's half size and two horses can manage easily. There's one lying idle in Garstang.'

'Buy it, Uncle Tom, I will sort out the finance with you later.'

'Yes, Miss, I will do that tomorrow when we go up there.'

'Very good, I will go to the colliery office and negotiate with them for extra coal delivery. I should be able to reduce the price because of the extra demand.'

'The Colliery office, Miss, is up by the dock gates. They operate the rail line from here to the colliery that's why they have an office here and I'm sure you will get a good deal as they are pleased with the amount we carry now and the limestone people will be happy as they are moaning about the loss of cargo.'

Tricia sat for a moment rubbing her chin, before she said, 'Uncle Tom, are you happy with the money you get from the limestone people?'

'Yes, Miss, it makes the trip worthwhile.'

'Very well, we will leave it. There is one thing I insist on, Uncle Tom. All the barges doing my contract must have BCCC in large gold letters somewhere on their barge.'

'I think, Miss, for the extra money they won't mind.'

'Keep me posted on your progress, Uncle Tom. Oh! Crikey, I almost forgot. Get some extra deliveries to Kendal this week if you can, I promised.'

'You are a hard master, Miss Tricia, but I'll organise that.'

She stood up. 'I have to go. Agnes will be freezing in that coach. Take care and give my love to Auntie Edie.'

Tom knuckled his forehead. 'It's nice doing business with you, Miss, and all of my friends think so too.'

On the way home, she told Agnes what had happened and they had a little laugh when they discussed what Clifford would think of it and the extra work he was going to have to do.

―

Clifford surprised her that evening when he turned up in his two-horse curricle instead of Brown but it did allow her to mention to him the details of the deal she had struck.

He couldn't believe what he was hearing, and asked again, 'You did what? Made a deal with Kendal Gas in just an hour this morning?'

'Yes, Clifford, darling, and very civil it was too.'

'Aha! Now you want me to finalise the contracts and print more for Tom to give out to his sub-contractors?'

'If you could, dear, but I did get a witnessed signed contract this time. You know those contracts I had you make up for me.'

'Miss Cartwright, you are something. Are there enough barges?'

'No, that is something else. I need three but I will buy four. Can you come with me to the barge builders and oversee my purchases. Buying coal is one thing, but Barges?'

He looked to the heavens, and said to himself, "What next?"

Isaiah allowed her a morning off to negotiate with the Colliery. They lowered their price by three per cent for bulk buying which she passed on to her local Catchcart customers but not Catchpole's upper-class buyers or the Rail and Gas people. A week later she was able to buy three second-hand barges and one new one plus Tom's blind barge and put the new contract into action proper with the newer crews that Tom had organised.

The unusually mild winter conditions of **1845-46** continued and extra deliveries were made to Kendal as promised. Two weeks after the contract had been signed, on the Friday night after dinner, she sat back with a glass of wine for a little celebration as she estimated her income from coal was now in the area of one-thousand pounds per annum plus her school salary.

She looked to the heavens, and said, "Thank you, Mam."

Her free time for the next four weeks was taken up working and organising with Clifford on the furnishings for the Bishop New House and hiring new staff for the school with frequent trips to '*Elegance.*' The expertise of Mrs Rose was needed to make her wedding outfit which in the winter was a little more demanding but eventually her day came around.

The School was closed on Wednesday the eighteenth of February the date set for the wedding. She would have liked it on St. Valentine's Day but superstition following the rhyme…

> *Monday for wealth,*
> *Tuesday for health,*
> *Wednesday the best day of all.*
> *Thursday for crosses*
> *Friday for losses,*
> *Saturday no luck at all.*

…persuaded her to take the following Wednesday.

—

Agnes, Mary and Cook who had taken up residence in the New House arrived early to prepare Tricia for her big day. Agnes entered her room followed by Mary who was carrying a tray with her favourite breakfast and a pot of tea. Tricia sat up and Agnes straightened the pillows so she could sit comfortably and Mary placed the tray in front of her and poured a cup of tea she went to take the cover off the breakfast but Tricia stopped her.

'Not yet, Mary, I will finish my tea first.'

'Yes, Missy.' She had adopted the easy-going term that Agnes used and Tricia preferred. 'But we don't have a lot of time this morning.'

'Don't worry, Mary, I will be on my best behaviour and be as quick as I can.'

Tricia finished her tea and ate her breakfast while Agnes and Mary busied themselves preparing Tricia's bath and laying her clothes out. Agnes, because of her new position as Lady's maid did not have to do the general jobs but being Agnes she mucked in with Mary and as long as they were happy, so was Tricia.

Her morning ablutions over, they stood her on a cushioned platform in the middle of the room and began dressing her literally from the inside out. When they had all the undergarments on they sat her at the dressing table and Agnes began doing her hair.

She did not break too much with protocol and she had three ringlets on either side of her head but she did not like the chignon, preferring that for work only, instead, she had the remaining hair tied with a wide pale blue silk ribbon in an abundant ponytail hanging loosely between her shoulders.

Next came the dress. She had chosen blue for the same reason she had chosen Wednesday. It was superstition…

> *Married in white, you will have chosen all right.*
> *Married in grey, you will go far away.*
> *Married in black, you will wish yourself back.*
> *Married in red, you'll wish yourself dead.*
> *Married in blue, you will always be true.*
> *Married in pearl, you'll live in a whirl.*
> *Married in green, ashamed to be seen,*
> *Married in yellow, ashamed of the fellow.*
> *Married in brown, you'll live out of town.*
> *Married in pink, your spirits will sink.*

… she compromised with pale blue which also completed another superstition … *Something borrowed, something blue, something old, something new…*

Her dress was shot silk which twinkled with every change of light, her shoes and dress were new, she used an *old* underskirt of her mothers and Lady Eleanor had loaned her a diamond tiara for her headdress. The crispness of silk was ideal for shaping the long, narrow bodice to Tricia's slim contours without the aid of the busk and other bony restrictions, and it lent itself to the shaping of the voluminous skirt and the subdued beauty of shot silks were considered especially appropriate for the time.

She spun in front of the long mirror and loved what she saw and then to cover another superstition…

It is unlucky for a bride to look in a mirror before she went down the aisle. To avoid bad luck some small article was put on the bride after she took her final look in the mirror.

… Agnes helped her put on a silk bonnet at the same time there was a sharp rattling on the door. It was the stable lad who had come to report that Master Clifford had arrived at the Church. They did not rush as brides were allowed to be late. They helped Tricia put on a warm coat made to match her dress and a harmonizing muffle to keep her hands warm.

Tricia eased herself down the stairs where Brown was waiting with an open carriage dressed in his new dark green uniform ready for the short drive to the Church.

He bowed deeply, and said, 'If I may be allowed to say so, Miss, you look wonderful.'

She gave him a huge smile, and replied, 'You may say so, Brown, and green suits you also.'

'My pleasure, ma'am.'

He helped her into the carriage and Agnes followed and with a blanket over them they set off for the two-minute ride to the Church.

At the Church, Brown helped her down from the carriage and Agnes came around to check everything was perfect. As they went through the lychgate the bells began ringing and they walked through the churchyard and into the tower entrance and were shown into a lobby where Agnes helped her take off her coat and bonnet and put on a flimsy veil held in place by the tiara. The coldness of the Church could be felt and Tricia was glad of the warm underclothes she had put on.

When Agnes was satisfied Tricia stepped through the door and into the nave where she was met by Lord Abraham who had agreed to stand in for her missing father. She placed an arm on his and spread apart by her voluminous skirt they passed down the aisle in slow ceremonial style as the organ played.

The Rev Isaiah Bishop was on form and his rhetoric went on for half an hour and although there were braziers tactfully placed around the Church the cold was winning and everyone including Tricia was glad when the ceremony ended. Hand in hand, Mrs Tricia Bishop walked up the aisle with Mister Clifford Bishop acknowledging the congratulations from the frozen guests. At the door, Agnes was waiting and she helped Tricia with her coat and watched with a tear in her eye as she walked arm in arm with Clifford down to the lychgate and into the carriage.

As they pulled away from the Church an old boot was hurled after them dispelling another myth and they continued on their way to Bishops Mill House where the reception was being held.

The carriages had been lined up on Church Lane in order of

seniority and people couldn't wait to get aboard under a warm blanket and dash off to a stimulating drink and the welcoming fires of the house.

Greeting them in the entrance hall was Clifford already warmed up with a quick brandy, and Tricia. There were congratulations all round and an exchange of kisses amongst the ladies. When the last of the family and guests had gone through Clifford and Tricia joined them in a celebratory champagne drink before they filed into the dining room. They were sat at the head of the table where the speeches and raised glasses appeared to go on forever before they settled down to a sumptuous ten-course meal.

It was late afternoon before they were able to retire until the evening entertainment began and after they had undressed and changed into more comfortable attire Tricia and Clifford were left on their own. He came around the room to where she was sitting by the dressing table. She stood up and they held hands' looking into each other's eyes neither of them wishing to make the first move. It seemed like ten minutes but was only one before he swooped, picked her up, and carried her over to the bed. He laid her down gently and she willingly held up her open arms for him to sink onto her for the first time uninhibited by protocol.

She was disappointed the first time they came together as she felt him shrink and leave her as her body was crying out for more. When the excitement and the adrenalin from their first coming together left him his body returned to life and she felt the firmness of him deep inside and her senses responded until simultaneously they reached the heavens and they both lay huddled their breath coming in short gasps and their hearts pounding against each other's chest.

Together they fell asleep until a sharp knock on the door woke them and Clifford retired to his room through an adjoining door where poker-faced Carr his valet was in attendance.

Agnes, aware of natural behaviour, waited for a few minutes before she entered with Mary to prepare Tricia for the evening's entertainment. It was frivolous, musical and filled with laughter until ten o'clock when the music stopped and everyone gathered around to wish Tricia and Clifford well for the future and to send them off to the beginning of a new adventure.

Brown stopped the carriage by the steps leading up to the entrance and he reached down and pulled a lever which opened the door on Tricia's side but he didn't get down. Instead, Clifford came around and helped her down onto the step where he swept her up and carried her up the front steps to the house entrance where Archer their new butler and Agnes, promoted to house-keeper, were waiting.

Clifford carried her over the threshold of their new house and into the entrance hall. He lowered her down and she reached up and kissed him. 'Thank you, Clifford; it was such a wonderful day.'

He gave her a squeeze, and said, 'A celebratory drink, Mrs Bishop?'

With a huge smile, she replied, 'Most certainly, Mr Bishop, but nothing less than champagne.'

Clifford passed on the request to Carr who helped him with his coat, hat and gloves while Agnes helped Tricia before they went through into the living room and a roaring fire.

Two minutes later Archer arrived, poured their champagne and left. They touched glasses, and Clifford, said, 'Mrs Bishop.'

Tricia, simultaneously said, 'Mr Bishop'

Tricia sat on the sofa nearest the fire and Clifford relaxed into his favourite chair, which he had brought from the Mill House. Very little was spoken as Tricia was still in a daze at how quickly life had changed, while Clifford was soaking in the beauty before him relishing the fact that he was also master of his own household, but his mother had warned him that however tactile she may be she also had a strong nature..

Tricia put her glass down, and said to Clifford, 'I am going to retire now, my love. It has been a long day and I have work tomorrow.'

'I will join you; I too must fill my obligations. I have a trip to Lancaster to see about your booklets.'

'Oh, you didn't say. Is it important, do you need me?'

'No, my love, it is early days but hopefully, he may make it easy and be forgiving in his nature, after all, he is a padre.'

They both laughed as Tricia reached for the tapestry cord hanging down the side of the chimney breast. Archer entered and Clifford told him that Tricia was retiring but he would like another brandy. Archer left the room to pass on the message to Mary who, after the short training with Agnes, had been promoted to Lady's maid.

They parted with a kiss and a hug and Tricia left and went upstairs to her dressing room where Mary was waiting. She helped Tricia change into her night-time attire and with a cup of hot chocolate went through to the master bedroom which was laid out ready for her. She drank her chocolate, blew out the last candle and snuggled down and a few moments later she was glad to feel a soft bundle settle down by her knees.

It was sometime later when she felt the solid figure of Clifford slide in behind her and loop an arm over her. He kissed her on the back of the neck and like a pair of spoons they settled into a dreamy sleep with a pair of jealous green eyes peering through the darkness from the armchair.

The following morning while having her breakfast, Tricia wondered if she would ever get used to the new routine. They woke up together and let mother nature take its course before Clifford retired to his rooms and left Tricia to wander dreamily into her dressing room where Mary was waiting with a hot tub prepared and her clothes laid out ready for the day's teaching.

It was a blissful feeling and one she never dreamt she would see but one she was determined would last until her final goal was reached and to make her day even better the happy face of Brown was waiting with the carriage to take her to the school.

~~~~~

CHAPTER 17

The cold but dry winter continued and the first signs of spring were beginning to show when in the second week of March the weather gods decided that enough was enough. A major winter storm raged across the country bringing high winds, snowstorms and hail stones big enough to damage glass awnings over shop entrances and this was the way of things for the rest of March when on April 1st bad news reached them from Preston. Lord Abraham Bishop had been killed when his curricle was blown over during a storm as he was going into the Mill.

Some say he was a fool for travelling under those conditions especially as curricles were light and prone to tipping over but the news was devastating and arrangements were quickly made to travel down to Bishops Mill Manor.

Upstairs, Tricia had a problem but Agnes assured her that '*Elegance*' would have a black outfit ready for the funeral. 'They have your sizes already and with a message sent by you, Mrs Rose will have one ready overnight, Missy.'

'That is short notice Agnes, can she do it?'

'Yes, Missy, that is her job. When we drop you off get Brown to take the message into town and all will be ready for you the next day.'

Half an hour later a stable lad from Bishops Mill House arrived telling Tricia that the school would be closed until further notice, Tricia was quick to react. She gave the lad a list of all pupils and slipped him a guinea to go round and tell as many of them as he could.

He knuckled his brow, and said, 'Yes, Ma'am, thank you.'

A guinea was two months wages and he would do anything for the person who gave him that.

An hour later they were ready. Agnes travelled in the carriage, and Mary, wrapped up against the weather, rode with Carr in a two-horse curricle driven by the second coachman.

Brown, aware of the strength of the wind drove cautiously both to keep the horses calm as the wind gusts disturbed them and the slower you travelled there was less resistance and Clifford remained silent throughout the trip distressed at the loss of his grandfather and worried for Tricia who had told him that morning she was pregnant.

The funeral was held on Saturday and was well attended by other Mill owners and when the Wake was over and they had all departed only the immediate family was left along with Lord Bishop's lawyer who was enjoying the moment sat behind the enormous mahogany desk with an expectant audience in what had been Abrahams study.

He held up a manuscript and addressed them. 'Ladies and gentlemen, this will not take long. It is straight to the point.—№ 1. Lord Isaiah, along with the title Lord of Longbottom you inherit the Mill, the Manor and the London house in Eaton Square along with my wealth on the understanding you pay an annual allowance to Lady Felicity and make arrangements for her accommodation. Were this not the case you shall forfeit all which will be passed on to your son Clifford.

№ 2. The current liability which you, Isaiah, receive from the estate, will be passed on to your son Clifford. That is, Bishop Mill House plus £5000 per annum.' The lawyer threw himself back in the chair. 'That is it, ladies and gentlemen, less my fee of course.

The family stood for a moment taking it all in before Isaiah, spoke. 'Let us retire to the drawing-room and partake of a drink before we discuss the whys and wherefores, which I don't think are too difficult.'

In the drawing-room, they raised their glasses, and said a quiet, "thank you" to Abraham before Isaiah, standing with his back to the fire, spoke. 'My Family, you are my family now, this is what I suggest we do. I will of course be moving here into the Manor while you Clifford will be moving to the House. In that case, I see no reason why Lady Felicity should not move into New House, your property, Clifford. Does that make sense?'

Lady Felicity raised a hand, and said, 'Lord Isaiah, I would much prefer to stay here in the annexe. It is the right size for me and near to the town.'

Isaiah looked across at Lady Eleanor for help, and she said, 'I see no difficulty there, Isaiah; it would be good company for me.'

Isaiah looked across at his son who was sat on the arm of Tricia's armchair. 'Clifford, help me out. What would you like to do? First let me add, that you,' pointing at Tricia, 'Mrs Bishop will be taking over the school.'

Tricia's hand went to her breast, as she said, 'Oh, I wasn't expecting that.'

Clifford was also taken aback, and he said, 'Father, let me have a word with my wife.'

'By all means.'

He leaned forward and said to Tricia quietly. 'What do you want to do with our house?'

She whispered back, 'We have spent so much getting it the way we, sorry, I like it. I want to stay there.'

Clifford gave her a gentle nudge on the shoulder and laughed before he spoke. 'Father, we wish to stay in New House.'

'Bishops Mill House is part of the estate. What do you suggest?'

Tricia raised her hand. 'Lord Isaiah, can we not sell it and use the money for the benefit of the school. The class sizes are bigger and we need an extension and therefore more staff.'

There was silence while Clifford and Isaiah looked at each other, before Isaiah spoke. 'Clifford, my son. Where did you find this entrepreneur? What a dammed good idea. It solves our little problem and is exactly what I wished in my early days. It will boost our family image although that is not my intention.'

Clifford put an arm around Tricia's shoulder and squeezed her. 'I agree with that wholeheartedly. Let us drink to that and then retire for dinner.'

Bishops Mill House was sold and building work began on the school while Tricia because of her condition became headteacher and hired two more teachers to oversee the children. The class sizes increased and consequently so did her income until, one day George Catchpole had a heart attack and subsequently died.

Tricia did not trust Catchpole's sons so she shrewdly, with Clifford's help, bought their share and retired Uncle Tom from the barges and put him in charge of the Catchcart business while his sons watched over the BCCC contracts. So long as she had her fair income from the business she allowed Tom to keep Catchpole's income but changed the company's name to Cartwright & Devlin. Ltd.

It continued to be a good year and on the 5th November to the sound of fireworks Edwina Clifford Bishop was born just two weeks before the new extension to the school was finished. When the new school opened Tricia was well enough to continue as headteacher and three more mature teachers were hired. She hired Nanny Peters to care for Edwina but Tricia insisted that she should feed her and had a nursery built upstairs in her old quarters while she used the office downstairs and just loved Isaiah's posh chair which she had inherited.

Lord Isaiah meanwhile used his inheritance wisely and invested in improving the living conditions of his employees in the streets around the Mill and taking advantage of the credit boom in the mid-1840s farmed out a lot of work to home weavers which helped the local economy.

Clifford won her copyright case and she received a modest lump sum and was able to publish her children's stories in local newspapers and obtained a publishing contract for the book with a national publisher and she insisted on writing as Cartwright and it was released in time for Christmas.

—

In the May of **1847** when Edwina nicknamed Teddy was six months old, Lord Isaiah after a short illness died of typhoid fever leaving the title Lord of Longbottom and the Bishop estate to Clifford the only male heir. There was no option but to move the family home to the Manor while Lady Felicity and Lady Eleanor opted to move jointly into the New House.

Tricia abdicated her position as headteacher but remained in charge of all things financial and while some of the household staff had moved between the Manor and New House she retired Agnes who would remain her companion but moved her into a small cottage on the Manor estate. Mary was promoted to housekeeper and the head housemaid, Jill, became her lady's maid.

It was while discussing the moves that Agnes reminded her of Bella in the kitchen and after a short conversation with Cook she made her the cook's assistant and hired a local girl to replace her on the understanding that she also must be taught to cook. Brown was the Head coachman and therefore did the bidding of Clifford and the second coachman, Oriss, looked after Tricia's modest demands.

Things had regained some form of normality by July and one Tuesday morning when Tricia was enjoying her favourite breakfast there was a light tap on the door and Archer entered with a silver platter. He held it out to Tricia. 'A message, M'lady, with a letter attached has just arrived.'

Tricia reached out and took them from the tray. 'Thank you, Archer,' she gave it a brief once over and continued, 'this is addressed to his Lordship, Archer.'

'Yes. M'lady and he said to give it to you. Something to do with, BCCC.'

'I see—is the messenger still here?'

'Yes, M'lady.'

'Very well, Archer, give him some refreshment and I will attend to this immediately.'

'Yes, M'lady.'

He backed away from the table and left the room and inquisitively Tricia unfolded the message and read it once more while she finished her breakfast and was surprised to see it was from Uncle Tom and in it he referred to the attached letter which had been delivered to his sons in Preston dock early that morning. She pushed her plate back and while the footman was filling her coffee cup she began reading the letter and saw to her surprise it was addressed to – Lord Bishop of BCCC from the L&P Rail Company. It was demanding a meeting in Lancaster at the earliest possible moment and was signed by three directors the name of one of whom made her shake her head and check again. She had seen correctly. It was Lord James Kearsley.

"Fancy meeting him again. He must have shares in the company."

The footman was clearing the dishes away and she instructed him to send Archer as soon as he could. She got up from the table and made her way into the drawing room followed by Archer.

'Yes, M'lady, what can I do for you?'

'Archer, give the messenger the requisite tip and send him on his way but tell him also to thank Mr Devlin and that I will be coming to see him today.'

'Yes, M'lady, will that be all?'

'I am going to my study now, Archer, and I will call when I have fashioned an appropriate reply to this letter and I want it posted without delay.'

Archer nodded and after taking a step back turned and left the room and Tricia now spoke to Jill who had entered the room.

'Jill, has his Lordship departed?'

'Yes, Missy,' she also had adopted the familiar term which Tricia preferred, 'he left about half an hour ago. Trouble at Mill, as they say locally.'

'Oh, there's always trouble at the Mill. Tell Nanny I will be busy all day and to look after Edwina. I will be working in my study for a while and then I am going to ride across and see Mr Devlin at his business. Could you pass the message on to the stables, please, and I will need my lightest riding clothes as it promises to be a hot day today and tell Agnes I will not require her today but I will need her to escort me later this week.'

'Will you need lunch, Missy?'

'Probably not, but I will have some tea and a scone whilst I am changing. Oh! There is one more thing, Jill, have you seen Lucky? He's been missing for two days now.'

'No, Missy, we have looked for him but no one has seen him since he had his food on Sunday. We think he's fed up with moving and has gone back to the New House.'

'Hmm! You could be right but I think I know what he's up to, Jill. I had a funny dream last night.'

'Do you believe in dreams, Missy?'

'Yes, Jill, they are life's messenger.'

'What do you think has happened to him?'

'Lucky came to me in a time of great need and now he thinks I am safe he has gone to help someone else. I shall miss him.'

Jill left to prepare everything while Tricia made her way to her study and set about writing a reply to the rather stuffy letter she had received or rather had inadvertently been sent to Clifford.

She decided not to correct their mistake and replied in such a manner it sounded like Clifford. She also admonished them for demanding a meeting in Lancaster and pointed out that it was their problem and they should come to Preston and meet at the Bishop lawyers premises on Thursday or Friday and signed it merely as P. Bishop. BCCC.

Half an hour later she sent for Archer and gave him the letter before retiring to get changed for her ride to Uncle Tom's.

She pulled '*Caterina*' up alongside the steps outside the Devlin's modest cottage in Borrowdale not far from the school and Tom came out to greet her. He took the reins and she eased herself off the saddle and down the steps and Tom took his cap off, bowed slightly, and said, 'Good morning, Lady Bishop, what can I do for you?'

She laughed, and replied, 'Oh, stop it, Uncle Tom, but a nice cup of tea would go down well.'

He looped the reins around the rail a few times and followed her into the house where Tricia was hugging Edie who, knowing Tricia, had already put the kettle on and five minutes later she was sat on the sofa in the living room and Tom was in his favourite chair.

'What can I do for you, Lady Tricia?' he said with a smile.

'Uncle Tom, have we a problem with our coal deliveries?'

'No, lass, it's running like clockwork.'

'Have you any idea why the rail company want a meeting?'

'I can't say but it could be something to do with that new company who have built a line out to the coast from Catteral. They spoke to one of our bargees on the coal round as he thought the proposed charges by L&P were steep.'

'Could we manage more deliveries? The canal is busy now.'

'It is only a single line company that runs down to the coast to carry fish and farm produce so I don't think they will need much. Another four blind barges would I think do it.'

She deliberated for a moment before, she said, 'Where can I meet them, I mean now, today.'

'They have a yard and office on the quay at Catteral. They are better placed to receive coal than L&P.'

'Can you come with me now, Uncle Tom, that is, if you have a horse?'

'Yes, Lady Tricia, I'm coming with you. Give me ten minutes to saddle up. I might struggle to keep up with that racehorse of yours, though.'

'Don't worry, she's likes a gentle lollop, and thank you, I won't involve you but it looks better.'

The road was dusty and grooved because of the dry weather but they made good time and an hour later they pulled up outside the office of the new rail company. Tom dismounted and helped Tricia down and as they tied the horses up a smartly dressed man showing the excesses of business class living came out of the office to meet them.

He addressed Tom, 'Good afternoon, I'm Mr Merryweather, what can I do for you?'

Tom swung an arm in Tricia's direction and with great pride, said, 'Mr Merryweather, let me introduce Lady Patricia Bishop the owner of the Bishop Canal Coal Company or BCCC. I believe you wish to discuss deliveries?'

Merryweather blushed and turned to Tricia, who held her hand out and he bowed. 'My apologies, M'lady but I do indeed wish to discuss terms. Would you like to come into my office?'

'Yes, indeed Mr Merryweather,' and she added with a smile,

'and may I say that your name suits the current conditions.'

He bowed and guided her towards the door and as they stepped over the threshold, he said, 'I apologise for the state of my premises, M'lady, but we are busy men.'

'I understand, Mr Merryweather, and I am here on business.'

'Would you like to sit in my office chair, M'lady?'

'No, I am quite happy sitting on an ordinary chair, thank you.'

Merryweather went to his office chair and she and Tom sat opposite on plain wooden chairs.

'Now, Mr Merryweather, what do you have in mind?'

He quickly outlined the operation of the small company, and ended, '...And I think we will need around seventy tons a day to start with or maybe more in the harvest season. We will only have three engines operating,'

'That is not a problem, Mr Merryweather. I will offer you the same terms as the L&P Company. That is...' she gave him an outline of the contract, '...does that sound fair?'

'Yes M'lady, but I heard a rumble that the L&P are not happy with your fees and are looking to reduce them.'

'Thank you for that, Mr Merryweather. I am meeting with them later this week. Meanwhile, I shall have the contract drawn up and ready for you to sign by the end of the week. Give me your details and we will be up and running whenever you are ready.'

He pushed a card over the desk and wrote some more on a sheet of vclum before folding it and pushing it across the desk.

He stood up and held his hand out. 'That's a deal, Lady Bishop.'

She shook his hand and nodded towards Tom. 'I have a witness, Mr Merryweather and my number one trouble-shooter, Mr Tom Devlin.'

The two men nodded to each other and once outside helped Tricia mount *Caterina.* As she was about to ride off, she said, 'Nice doing business, Mr Merryweather.'

A little way down the road she spoke to Tom. 'That was a nice piece of information he gave out there. I now know what I'm facing.'

Friday morning on the stroke of ten dressed in her best finery her hair done in a business-like chignon topped with a miniature trilby style hat and feather. She dismounted from the carriage and she and Agnes entered the Bishop Solicitors Office. Inside, the Chief Clerk was waiting. 'Good morning, Lady Bishop, your guests are waiting in the Master's office.'

'Thank you, Roberts, Are Messrs Colston and Richards in this morning?'

'No, M'lady, they are both out doing other business.'

'That is alright, Roberts, I only asked out of interest. I shall need the services of the scribe this morning. Is he available?'

'Yes, M'lady, we have been pre-warned of your requirements and we have coffee brewing ready for your call.'

'You have a seat in there for my companion?'

'Yes, M'lady.'

'Good, let's go and upset my clients.'

Roberts took them through a side door and down a corridor and stopped outside a large mahogany bound door. He looked at Tricia and she nodded before he knocked on the door and went in leaving the door ajar.

'Good morning, gentlemen, may I introduce Lady Patricia Bishop.' He stood to one side, and said, 'Lord Kearsley and Mr Bletchley, M'lady.'

Kearsley and Bletchley both stood as she entered and walked across the room smiling with her hand outstretched. 'Good morning, gentlemen, I trust you had a good journey here?'

Kearsley had a puzzled look on his face but bowed and reached for her hand as did Bletchley. When the introductions were over Tricia walked around the mahogany desk and sat in a large leather chair. 'Please be seated, gentlemen.'

They both sat while Agnes sat in a corner behind Tricia and the scribe by a small table in the corner at the far end of the room.

'Now, gentlemen, what is it you wish to see me about?'

Kearsley still looking a little perplexed rubbed his chin before he spoke. 'I thought we had arranged a meeting with the owner of

BCCC, Lord Bishop.'

'Lord Kearsley, it may come as a surprise but I am the owner of BCCC. Lord Bishop is my husband and legal representative. Now! What was it that is so urgent?'

Kearsley coughed into his fist and looked across at Bletchley before he came straight to the point. 'In these hard times Lady Bishop, we think that the price we pay you for our coal is too high.'

'These hard times, you said, Lord Kearsley. You own a Mill do you not? Am I not correct in saying that the cotton and wool industry has never done better and you pay more to L&P Rail to transport coal to your Mill than I charge the Rail Company for theirs. Now I know the Rail Company is struggling and you have franchised it to the Canal Company but surely you should be looking at luring customers in by lowering your price. Alternatively, I could deliver coal to your Mill at my customary price or better still I have an agreement with the colliery who own the private rail line to my dock in Preston which I could expand and transport my coal to your Mill on your railway at my price. If an agreement is not reached then coal deliveries to L&P stop as of today which will please Kendal Gas as they will be able to build up their stocks now that the use of gas is spreading. I believe they have an interest in Lancaster. What think you, gentlemen?'

Kearsley and Bletchley sat for a moment slightly taken aback at the *force majeure* facing them. This was not what they were expecting and certainly not from a woman and it was a good minute before Kearsley spoke. 'Lady Bishop, will you allow us a few minutes to ourselves.'

'Most certainly gentlemen, would you like some refreshment? Let me know when you are ready.'

They both nodded in acceptance and Bletchley relaxed in his chair glad of a break from the decision he was going to have to make. They all stood and the men bowed as Tricia left the room. As the scribe closed the door behind them Tricia looked at Agnes, and said, 'I don't believe I said that, Agnes.'

They were shown into a waiting lounge and it was a few minutes later when coffee, sweetmeats and scones arrived and

Tricia, who was still shaking with nervous anticipation at what may come next had to use two hands to lift her cup but two sips of the caffeine fix settled her down.

'Well, Agnes, what do you think?'

'Is all that you say truthful, Missy?'

'I hope so, Agnes, but I must admit I am not sure about the Gas.'

Half an hour later the scribe came in and told them that Kearsley and Bletchley were ready, and he added, 'There was quite a lot of shouting going on. I don't think they had time to drink coffee.'

Tricia and her little party went back to the office and the men stood as she entered and nodded in acknowledgement and waited until she sat down.

'I hope you enjoyed your refreshment, gentlemen. Did you reach a decision?'

A troubled Kearsley stood up and walked behind his chair and while resting one hand on the back and glancing at a note he had in the other, he said, 'Lady Bishop, after a heated discussion we would like to suggest the following. Can you deliver to our railhead in Preston?'

'I can arrange that, it would make it cheaper than Catteral.'

'At what price?'

Tricia scribbled something on a notepad and tore the page off and Kearsley stepped forward to take it. He glanced at it and wrote something on it and gave it back.

Tricia read it and shook her head. 'No, Lord Kearsley, I cannot. That is less than what I pay the colliery. What I gave you is the price I charge my other customers before I add on the transport charge. Everyone gets treated equally. Your Mill will benefit as will your Rail Company. What the Mill pays L&P is your affair but as I see it there is a marginal profit increase for both.'

He nodded. She knew her business. 'What about you, Lady Bishop? Will not you be losing?'

'That is my affair.' She didn't tell him about the halfpenny increase she had put onto his deliveries to the L&P railhead which would neutralise the loss at Catteral and with the new contract she had just signed with Merryweather plus extra going to Kendal there was nothing in it plus Uncle Tom was looking at local deliveries to the Preston Mill workers.

Kearsley called Bletchley over to the side of the room and they exchanged words. They had only spoken for less than a minute when Tricia butted in. 'Gentlemen, speak English, please, I am *au fait* with the French language and a woman I may be, but don't patronise me.'

Agnes who was sat quietly behind Tricia was almost scratching her head while wondering, "Where does she get this from?"

Kearsley looked at her with a mixture of surprise and loathing but they continued their conversation in English in a low voice and exchanging ideas by passing a notebook between them. After ten minutes Tricia was getting both bored and annoyed and she started tapping her fan on the desk which appeared to send a message and with a final nod between them they returned to their seats and Kearsley was the first to speak. 'My apologies Lady Bishop but these are delicate things we discuss. However, we have come to the conclusion that you are offering us not the best but a reasonable deal but explain one thing. How are you getting our coal from your dock to our station yard?'

Tongue in cheek, she said, 'I have a franchise deal with the colliery and they have already looked at this possibility and laid an extension towards your yard. It will only take a short while to complete without any expense on your behalf. If you would care to partake of more refreshment I will have my lawyer make out the contract for you to sign, alternatively, if you are in a hurry, sign the bottom of the scribes pages and I will have the contracts delivered at a later date.'

'We will sign the papers, your Ladyship.'

The writer laid the pages out on the desk and both Kearsley and Bletchley signed and Tricia followed suit. She then called over Agnes and the scribe to sign as witnesses.

'Thank you, Lord Kearsley. May we do business again? I hear

that the Carlisle and Lancaster line has made a bid to join you.'

'That is early days, Lady Bishop.'

She held her hand out and Kearsley took it, and said, 'Lady Bishop, have we crossed paths before. I seem to recall meeting with someone who looked very much like you.'

'Indeed we have, Lord Kearsley. My father was Edward Cartwright.'

She curtsied and as he bent to kiss her fingers his face clouded over and the anger was visible in his eyes as he recalled the name. He dropped her hand and holding back the vitriol that was about to spew from his mouth he stormed from the room.

Bletchley apologised, followed him and continued apologising as Kearsley slammed doors behind him ignoring offers by the office staff to assist him as he barged from the premises cursing loudly.

Tricia followed him into the office and smiled as the staff stood bemused at such behaviour when the senior attorney present, said to Tricia. 'Did something go wrong, M'lady?'

'Only his past behaviour. It leaves a lot to be desired.' She turned to the scribe who was behind her, and she said, 'Can you get those contracts drawn up and bring them to me in *'Katies Parlour'* where I am going for lunch. I want three copies and I shall want them delivered to Lancaster.'

'Yes, M'lady.'

He hurried over to his desk while one of the clerks helped Tricia with her cloak and she scooped up her skirt and with Agnes in tow went out to her carriage feeling happy inside.

—

The following Tuesday Clifford joined her for breakfast and he threw a note across the table to her. 'This has just been delivered from my office and it concerns you.'

'I've been waiting for this,' she said.

'You haven't read it yet.'

'It comes from Lancaster is my guess and Kearsley wants to deny our contract.'

She opened the note and it was from the senior attorney saying precisely those words with the addition that Kearsley had refused to sign the contract. She passed it over the table to Clifford who read it, and said. 'What are you going to do about it?'

'Clifford! We have a signed and witnessed pre-contract document, is he not obliged?'

'Yes, but it will take a lot of litigation and expense to push it through.'

'Leave it with me, Clifford, I think I have the answer.'

'What do you intend?'

'I am going to stop deliveries to L&P instantly.'

'How does that help, Tricia, my love? You are contracted to supply them. You have nothing to lose by continuing as you are and if this Kearsley wants to cut his nose off to spite his face that is his problem. He may come round sometime in the future.'

Tricia looked at the note and then back at Clifford undecided. Her head was saying cut Kearsley and L&P off now and her heart was listening to Clifford. Taking a deep breath she calmed down, and said, 'Should I just forget this new contract and continue with the current one?'

'Yes, if as you mentioned last week Kearsley is paying more to his own rail company for delivery than what he would be paying you let him get on with it. He's just being stubborn.'

'Clifford, you're right. I'm glad you're my lawyer.'

'Do I have a choice?'

She threw a napkin at him and laughed as she walked around the table and kissed him on the cheek. 'Take care, my love.'

When she reached the door she turned back to face Clifford, and said, 'How much do you pay for coal at the Mill?'

'Too much.'

She walked back to him and drew a figure in the sauce on his plate. 'More than that?'

He sat back and looked up at her before replying, 'You can do it at that price?'

'Yes, and it will be delivered the same as it is now only you will pay me and not the Colliery. Do you have a contract with the colliery?'

'No, we order it and they deliver.'

'That makes it easier.'

'I must go, Tricia, my love, may we discuss this at dinner tonight?'

She leaned forward and kissed him on the nose. 'Yes, love,' she said with a huge smile. She ran a finger from his forehead down his nose and across his lips, 'you can talk to me anytime but you may have to use the persuasion of a primal source to get the answers.'

She left the dining room buzzing inside and went to her study where she sat at her desk and wrote a message to Uncle Tom advising him that things would stay as they are and then she wrote a letter to the board of Wigan Colliery seeking an early meeting.

She called for Archer and gave him the messages, and said, 'Archer! Give these to the stable lad and tell him he can take '*Caterina*' for a morning gallop. Also tell him if Mr Devlin, wants his message taken to Preston Dock he must do so.'

Archer bowed and left the office leaving Tricia contemplating her actions.

―

The colliery always looking to boost their business replied quickly and a meeting was set up at the Bishop Solicitors office for the following Monday while things continued as normal for BCCC on the canal. Tricia was surprised as she expected some backlash other than Kearsley's initial childish behaviour. She concluded that his co-directors may have had a calming influence on him, especially where the current costs to L&P were concerned. She hoped he would see sense and smother his pride.

Tricia loved getting dressed in her best finery. She felt that having attained her position that she should present herself in the manner her parents would expect. Their policy was never to lower your standards. Even if your shoes were worn out you always cleaned them and clothes were always repaired and neat at the beginning of the day no matter what.

With Agnes in attendance she presented herself in the office. Having worked with these gentlemen for a while now the welcome was more cordial and after the initial protocol and coffee had been ordered they settled down to business.

'What can we do for you, Lady Bishop? Nothing pressing I hope.'

'No, Mr Theaker, quite the opposite. I would like to buy all the coal you supply to the Preston Mills.'

'That is indeed a good offer but I detect another—but.'

'Mr Theaker, I am a firm believer that less is more therefore I want to buy your coal at the same price you charge BCCC for my canal business—but, and it's a big—but, I will not be selling it at the price you charge the Mills.'

'Lady Bishop, we will be losing income.'

'Very little. Currently you sell your coal at what you think these firms can afford. If you were to sell it evenly across the board there is very little difference. The money I will be saving the Mills will be guaranteeing jobs for the workers who are the people I am more interested in than profit and quite possibly an increase in output requiring more of them. Do you follow me? I might also add that L&P Rail is trying to negotiate a joint venture with the Carlisle – Lancaster Line to run through trains.'

Theaker turned to his companion Weston but without any attempt at disguise spoke lowly in English. 'Colin, what do you think?'

After a moment of chatter, Tricia butted in. 'Excuse me, gentlemen, would you like more refreshment while you talk. We get our scones from *'Katie's Parlour'* and they are excellent.'

Theaker swung towards her. 'That is an excellent idea, Lady Bishop, do you mind if we stretch our legs while we talk?'

'Not at all, Mr Theaker, feel free.'

Theaker and Colin stood and went to the other end of the room to continue their discussion, while Agnes organised the refreshments. The staff had anticipated the call and the coffee and cream scones were delivered five minutes later.

The atmosphere was relaxed so she passed the time chatting to Agnes, who said, 'When did you get this idea, Missy, is it not a bit too far?'

'I thought of it over dinner the other night while chatting to, Clifford, who told me that our Mill pays these people more than I do so I put two and two together and here we are. The money saved by the Mill from a deal here could go to improving the plight of the workers.'

Theaker and Colin rejoined them and immediately opened the conversation. 'Lady Bishop, Colin, my accountant has pointed out that the difference in our profit would be minuscule with the system we operate. How do you suggest this works?'

'To put it simply, Mr Theaker, I want a full franchise deal. All your coal is mine. I pay you the price I currently pay for BCCC for every ton delivered to Preston and I sell it on for more or less what I charge L&P.' She passed a piece of paper over to him. 'These are my figures.'

Theaker picked it up and handed it to Colin who studied it and nodded as he gave it back. 'These prices you are going to sell at are lower than what I charge the Mills, Lady Bishop.'

'I know, Mr Theaker, my husband owns a Mill. It is my plan that the workers will benefit from savings made by the Mills. I know there will be some renegades which cannot be avoided.'

'Have you the facilities. It will take a large yard to store all the coal you need.'

'I have thought of that, Mr Theaker. Why go to all that trouble. We work together and save together. Carry on delivering as you do. That is using your rail extensions etc… You won't have to reorganise, it will not cost more. To continue as you do will make it easier for your workers and train crews. I will not have to organise transport for the coal therefore also keeping the price low which is my aim. Mr Theaker! Except for my L&P deal, I will give up my three per cent discount to make this go through.'

Theaker looked at Colin, and said, 'Does any of this make sense?'

'Yes sir, it does. I admire, Lady Bishop's ideals for the workers, sir, and she is right. To leave the delivery system like it is would be better for both of us. We don't have to do anything and we will only be taking money from one customer, not fifty-three which is our current system. It will make it easier for your accountant. Lady Bishop has a good record for payment, unlike some Mills I can name.'

'And Bishop's Mill?'

'I can only say, sir, I wish they were all that good. I rather fancy we may have the driver behind it sitting before you.'

Theaker swung back to face Tricia. 'Lady Bishop, I apologise for that but I rather think we have something here. When would you like to take up this franchise?'

'The end of next month. This gives you time to advise your customers of the change and me time to speak to them. I think they will be glad of my offer but it will come with strict terms, such as paying on time. I have one circumstance that I will not accept. Any new customers you get between now and the agreement must be diverted through BCCC.'

'I understand, Lady Bishop. Can you draw up the contracts and have them delivered to us?'

'Most certainly, Mr Theaker, the scribe has all the details and will get on to it as soon as we finish here. Let us take a moment to sign across the bottom of the scribe's notes.'

'Yes, Lady Bishop, by all means.

Signatures complete they all stood up and Tricia stretched her hand out over the desk. Theaker took her hand and bowed followed by Weston and protocol over they were shown out to their carriage by a member of staff.

'Well, Agnes, what do you think?'

'You've lost me with all that business junk, Missy, but they appeared to be pleased.'

'Fingers crossed I have it right. Clifford will tell me tonight.'

―

After dinner, Clifford held up the contract. 'This is risky, Tricia, love, but if it works what a good idea. It benefits everyone and I assume you have put on your standard halfpenny charge per hundredweight to all the customers?'

'Yes.'

'Have you worked it out yet, Trishy?'

'At a rough guess, I would say I've trebled my income. My original intention was to make it easier for the Mill workers. If the Mills make enough there will be less pressure to lower wages etc…'

'Does this include Bishops Mill?'

'Of course, my love, but I will drop the halfpenny for you.'

He laughed as he stood up. 'No, don't do that. If other companies hear of it they will also demand it. Come; let us retire to the drawing-room. I'm ready for a brandy.'

'Clifford, you are always ready for a brandy. I must go and see Teddy, I will join you shortly.'

'If you read her one of your stories that could take awhile.'

'Oh! Clifford, they are only short stories.'

—

Tricia was worried about the loan she was asking from the Bank but before she took it Clifford came to the rescue and invested three-thousand pounds into BCCC and the transfer went seamlessly and it didn't go unnoticed by Tricia that Kearsley refused to do business with her even though his partners tried to persuade him otherwise.

"He would rather pay more to his own Rail Company than buy it from me. That explains a lot about his running of the Mill." She had no intention of persuading him otherwise but she was troubled about the effect it would have on the workers.

It did not take long for other Mills and businesses to find out about the lower prices for coal and they soon signed up with BCCC who were, in effect, a middleman taking a small profit from both sides. This suited Tricia who had trebled her income from coal and she was now able to donate money to the school, which was increasing its numbers.

—

It had not been a good year weather wise but the English landscape was able to recover from the **1846** devastation, unlike Ireland where crops still failed. They were not helped by blight and famine that was widespread. Autumn into winter was very much the same, wet and windy.

Weather aside, Tricia was looking forward to Christmas but organising the event in the Manor was a new experience and she called on Agnes for help. There would be no cavorting down to the London residence this year for any of the family because it had been a sad year and they decided that Christmas Eve and Christmas Day would be a close family affair and that New Year's Eve would be the usual extravagant mixture of friends, relatives and family.

When they had decided on the finer points and Tricia was sat before the fire with Agnes, she said, 'Agnes, promise me you will not stay on your own in the cottage. You must come up to the Manor and mix with the staff. I want to organise little gaps where you and they can have a Christmas dinner. Have a rota where one of you is on call and then rotate while you eat downstairs. We will have a drinks cabinet up here in the dance hall and keep some sweetmeats ready if they are required. Is that possible?'

'Yes, Missy. We are lucky. The Bishop family have always had the staff in mind, unlike some places I've heard of.'

'I can't promise on New Year's Eve though. Things get a bit wild especially the men.'

'It is something we are used to, Missy, but people are so drunk we are usually able to have a little sing-song downstairs.'

'Good. Speak with Mary and make sure we have all the accommodation ready for the extra staff and overnighters.'

'Will do, Missy.'

On Christmas morning, they were joined by Hilda and Constance and their husbands and although the greetings were friendly Tricia could feel an underlying resentfulness. Although it was the accepted passage when members of the family passed away they were jealous of Tricia's sudden promotion into the higher echelon.

Clifford had warned her about this and told her to carry on as normal but to make sure that she made no mistakes either morally or in etiquette, 'After all,' he said, 'it wasn't planned just nature taking its course. Treat them as you did before and they will accept you once more,' was his advice.

After Church they gathered around for lunch and gifts were exchanged in a more formal manner but this was understandable after the events of the last year which had taken everyone by surprise.

Following lunch they all went about doing their own thing before retiring and preparing for the evening's entertainment which was not the lavish affairs that Lord Abraham loved. More guests arrived but no business partners, only relatives who had foregone the arduous journey down to London.

Tricia and Clifford didn't stint on the wine or the lavish meal and as the evening wore on the atmosphere brightened and people began laughing. After dinner, the ladies retired to the drawing-room to rest with a drink of their choice while the men remained for their brandy and cigars.

Tricia circulated through the guests and then approached Hilda and Constance with a little apprehension. They went to stand up but she raised a calming hand, and said, 'Stay seated ladies, we are after all related, you even more so. How is your evening going?'

They both agreed that they were having a good time despite the overhanging memory of the loss of their father and the food was wonderful. 'Have you a new chef, Lady Bishop, enquired Constance?'

'Oh, please call me, Tricia, ladies. We are a family despite our titles and it is a family-friendly occasion, and no, we have the same chef but with his extended kitchen staff, he can branch out more. He is in his element so to speak and his new assistant is coming on in leaps and bounds. I will have to watch her as someday, somebody is going to pinch her.'

'She was a kitchen hand wasn't she?' said Hilda.

'Yes, but I insisted that she be taught how to cook and she has worked her way up after a lot of hard graft.'

Hilda looked across at her sister. 'What a frightfully good idea, Constance. I must do that come the New Year.'

'I think it helps with their upbringing,' replied Tricia, 'it makes the drudge of their daily duty less depressing when they have something to aim for. My current staff are going through the same process.' She could feel the tension lessening as the conversation went forward, and she continued, 'Enough of that. How are you pair managing at home these days?'

'Very much like yourself, Tricia,' said Constance, 'my husbands' family Mill is expanding and is looking to take over another Mill shortly,' looking at her sister, 'and you, Hilda, is not your husband's firm planning something similar?'

'They were, but his father had to retire with an illness and he is currently running the Mill. He's now wishing he had paid more attention to the business instead of trundling down to London wasting our income on gambling.'

'Oh, dear,' said Tricia, 'he hasn't put you in debt, has he?'

'Very close. His gambling was curtailed and things are looking up.'

'Oh, good.—Hilda, Constance, I do want us to be friends and I must admit my circumstances are exceptional but this must not come between us and I look forward to your experience to guide me.'

They both stood up and reached for Tricia's hand. 'Oh, Tricia,' said Constance, 'you are our sister and any time you need help just call on us but right now I think we need your guidance on fashion. You look wonderful as always and I cannot speak for Hilda but I feel rather stuffy alongside you.'

'Constance,' said Tricia, 'I prefer the freedom of movement and have virtually given up on all those bones they try to wrap you in. Go to *'Elegance'* and speak with Mrs Rose and ask her to show you my technique. It is so nice. You can breathe again.'

'I will do that, Tricia, thank you so much.'

'I must leave you for a short while ladies. I'm going to see, Edwina. I hope she's asleep by now.'

'Oh, how is she, Tricia,' said Hilda,

'She is getting more vociferous by the day, Hilda, and naughty. I may have to hire a helper for Nanny.'

'Is she taking after her mother?'

'I couldn't possibly answer that, Hilda, although Mam said I was a handful and wouldn't stop eating. Excuse me, I must go.'

When she returned ten minutes later she played the pianoforté and they danced and sang before enjoying a light supper after which enthusiasm for the celebration dwindled. A few hardy drinkers hung on but gradually they left for home and Clifford and Tricia dragged themselves off to bed with Christmas Day only a few hours away.

A long table was set out in the dining room for the multi-guest breakfast and the various dishes kept warm by small candles were laid in silver dishes along the top of the room for the guests to help themselves.

Tricia was in the middle of her favourite boiled eggs and toast soldiers when the dining room door burst open and Edwina rushed in and around the table with her arms outstretched. 'Mammy! Mammy!' she shouted.

Tricia scooped her up. 'Teddy, what on earth is the matter?'

She looked at Nanny Peters who had followed Edwina into the room. 'What is it, Nanny?'

Nanny shrugged and held her hands out. 'Nothing, she just wanted to see Mam and ran away.'

Tricia hugged Edwina. 'So you wanted to see me? Well now you have me young lady and here you shall stay.' She looked over to Nanny. 'Nanny, layout Teddy's Sunday clothes and she can come to church with me today.'

Nanny curtsied, and said, 'May I come to the Church also?'

'Of course, Nanny.'

'Thank you, ma'am,' She took a step back and left the room.

Tricia cuddled Edwina, and said, 'Now young lady would you like something to eat or drink?'

Edwina didn't answer; instead she picked up one of Tricia's toast soldiers, dipped it into one of the eggs and began eating. 'Mmm! Yummy,' she said, 'can I drink some of your tea, Mam?'

'Yes, Teddy. Have what you like.'

Between them, they got through another egg when Edwina came up with a real surprise. 'Mammy, can I have a bacon butty?'

Tricia smiled to herself as it took her back to her childhood.

'Of course, you can, Teddy, I will ask Rogers to fetch one.'

She called the footman over and asked him to bring the said butty from before she carried on talking to Edwina. A few minutes later Rogers appeared with the bacon sandwich neatly cut into child-sized portions and they shared it.

Tricia was in awe at the quantity of food Edwina ate but what her mother had said about her in her childhood came back to her and she looked heavenwards and thanked the Lord that she could afford it unlike her mother who had found it difficult to feed Tricia.

Breakfast was over they wrapped up against the cold and Tricia took Edwina for a walk around the gardens while pointing out to Edwina the different flowers and shrubs. When they stood still and listened to the birds Tricia was able to tell her which birds they were but Edwina was transfixed by the two playful red squirrels leaping around the bird table in the middle of the garden.

Time was moving on and Tricia was loath to drag Edwina away from the natural life around her but it was nearly time to go to Church, but Nanny had everything ready and getting Edwina dressed was not a difficulty. Edwina was fascinated by the routine of her mother who was being helped by Jill the new maid who had replaced Mary who had taken over the duties of Agnes.

—

Throughout the service, Tricia whispered explanations to Edwina and when they sang carols Edwina stood on the pew with Nanny holding her but five minutes into the Vicars sermon Edwina fell asleep and Tricia didn't stop her as Christmas sermons tended to drag on, her father-in-law Isaiah being a good example.

Tricia was glad when it all ended and tried to keep up with Edwina as she skipped along the gravel path from the Church to the gateway. Clifford, meanwhile, was shaking hands with his friends as he strolled down the path and he joined them where Orris was waiting to help them aboard.

Half an hour later, changed out of their Church attire they settled around the long table to a luxurious lunch prepared for them by Cook and her helpers. Tricia thought Cook had done a wonderful job considering she had requested as many staff as possible should be allowed to go to Church.

After lunch gifts were exchanged and then they retired to prepare themselves for the evening's celebrations. Tricia who was enjoying a full day with her Teddy took her once more for a wander around the gardens. Had there been more time she would have taken her for a ride and promised herself that in the future she would spend less time with business and more time with Edwina.

Tricia and Clifford had been trying to give Edwina a companion but nature had decided it was not to be but they would never give up and if she was honest with herself being a tactile person she enjoyed their many efforts at reproduction.

The skies darkened and the wind blew stronger and sensing that rain was imminent Tricia took Edwina back inside and when she saw Nanny waiting for her Edwina ran across and hugged her around the knees and went up to her room for an afternoon nap.

After checking with Mary that preparations were in hand for the evening's entertainment, Tricia followed her daughter's example and retired with a cup of tea to lie on the bed. She did not question where Clifford was. She presumed he was out with his friends roaring around the countryside doing an annual check on all the Alehouses in the district.

—

The evening's entertainment was a prolonged affair. After all the guests arrived and had partaken of a pre-evening drink the dinner that followed lasted close on two hours before the ladies retired to the drawing-room.

When the string quartet began playing they assembled in the Entertainment Hall and being the hosts Clifford took Tricia's hand and they opened the dancing and fortified with alcohol the whole room joined them and a jolly evening was had by all.

It was after one a.m. before the last of the guests left or retired and Tricia was glad to crawl into bed. Clifford was also pooped and after a brief cuddle and a kiss they fell asleep.

—

At ten-thirty the next morning there was a gentle knock on the door and Clifford with his head in his hands made his way blindly into his room. Having left an appropriate length of time for this to happen, Jill entered with a large pot of tea and a covered tray with Tricia's breakfast. Even after the overindulging the night before she always enjoyed her tea and boiled eggs.

When she was dressed and preparing to go downstairs outside on the landing she met Carr, Clifford's valet, and he assured her that Lord Clifford would not be partaking of any pre-lunch activities so she quickly organised to take Edwina for a ride.

The murky grey weather of yesterday had dispersed and overnight there had been a light dusting of snow but the morning had brought a crispy frost and clear skies and suitably dressed with Edwina sat in front of her she guided *Caterina* around the quiet country lanes pointing out quirks of nature as they went.

Remembering the lessons she had from her tutor and her parents she was determined that Edwina should also benefit from early learning. She was helped in that regard by Nanny Peters, a good informative education having been one of the qualifications required for her employment.

They were making their way home when Edwina, said, 'Mammy! Can we go to church again.'

'Yes, darling, did you like it yesterday? You fell asleep.'

'I like the singing, Mammy.'

'You may join me after lunch, young lady when we go to church. Daddy will be ever so pleased.'

'Oh, thank you, Mammy. I will be on my best behaviour.'

Tricia looked down at her daughter who was speaking in a grown-up manner. "My, my, she is coming on," were her thoughts.

Back at the Hall the groom was waiting and helped Edwina down before Tricia unhooked her leg and slid down gracefully.

She thanked the Groom and took Edwina's hand and they skipped into the house where they were greeted by an anxious Nanny who was worried about her precocious charge.

'Hello, Nanny,' said Tricia, 'Young Teddy here wants to go to Church again. Will you join us?'

'Yes, ma'am, it will be a pleasure to get back my religion.'

'Very good, we will see you shortly.'

'Ma'am,' said Nanny, 'it would be no problem for me to take Edwina to Church if at any time you are unable to do so.'

'I made a promise to myself, Nanny. I am going to give Teddy more attention but if at any time I cannot do so feel free. She loves singing even though she doesn't know the words.'

'I believe she takes after her mother.' Nanny's hand shot to her mouth. 'Sorry, Ma'am, I didn't mean it like that.'

Tricia laughed. 'I understand and thank you, Nanny, do you play the pianoforté?'

'Yes, ma'am, but nothing classical.'

'Nanny, you have my permission to teach Teddy.'

'It will be a pleasure, Ma'am.'

—

The St. Stephens Day service was less demanding than the Christmas service and Edwina stayed awake but she didn't like the hymns that day but Nanny promised they would sing some nice Christmassy songs when they got home. Brown as usual was up to the mark and he loved his new charge who giggled and laughed as he lifted her down from the coach. The happy bond built between himself and Tricia in her early days was still there despite her newly established position and he bowed deeply as she alighted.

'Thank you, Brown,' she said, 'an excellent journey.'

'My pleasure, M'lady,' he replied, smiling, 'we aim to please.'

'We shan't be needing you anymore, Brown, go and entertain your prospective wife and tell Orris to take time off, but be ready.'

'Will do, M'lady, enjoy the rest of your day.'

After a nice lunch, Tricia took her Teddy into the drawing-room and together they tinkered with the pianoforté until Teddy began to feel tired and Tricia took her upstairs and with Nanny in attendance tucked her into bed.

The evening's entertainment was quiet compared to the previous evening and Tricia and Clifford were able to retire just before midnight exhausted from the celebrations but with only four days to prepare for New Year's Eve when many of their business partners had been invited.

—

Many rooms had been prepared for the guests and their staff and early in the afternoon they began to arrive met by Clifford and Tricia with Archer, Mary and the other staff in line ready to assist.

Things were going smoothly and Tricia was able to rest in between arrivals. It was a little after four o'clock when Jill called her to announce another carriage coming up the drive.

'Do we know who it is, Jill, arriving this late?'

I'm not sure, Ma'am, but it is a highly polished six-horse coach with a Coat of Arms and two outriders.'

'Thank you, Jill; I'll be down in a moment.'

'I should hasten, Ma'am, they were galloping at speed when the stable lad spotted them turning into the gates.'

Tricia got up from the *chaise longue* and patted herself down and Jill helped her on with her cloak and together they made their way to the front entrance just in time to see their new guests climbing from the coach.

Tricia was able to see the Coat of Arms and let out a quiet sigh of resignation. 'Oh my, the Kearsley's, what will he have to say this time?'

She stood next to Clifford and Jill straightened her dress and cloak before retiring inside and with bated breath, she waited. The gentleman and his attractive blonde wife were introduced to Clifford and Tricia was able to get a closer look at his face and she said to herself, "That's not Kearsley."

The instant he stood in front of Tricia, he bowed deeply at the same time as she curtseyed and held her hand out. He was about to kiss it when he looked at her, and said, 'Tricia?' at the same time, she said, 'Harry?'

They stood looking at each other for a few seconds in disbelief then they both smiled. He clenched both her hands in his, and said, 'Tricia, how well you look, you must tell me about yourself. Father said he had met you.'

'Harry, it is good to see you also, introduce me to your wife.'

He turned to his wife and took her hand. 'Gloria I want you to meet, Lady Patricia Bishop.'

Both ladies curtseyed and touched hands. 'Lady Bishop! How

nice to meet you. Do you two know each other?'

Tricia looked at Harry and nodded, and he said, 'We go back a long way into our childhood, Gloria.—Lady Bishop, may we talk later?'

'Of course, let us get you inside and settled and then we can chat over tea. You won't mind if my husband joins us?'

'Definitely not, it will be a pleasure to meet the man who snared you.' He looked towards Clifford, and said, 'You, sir, are a very brave man. It will be a pleasure to talk later.'

Clifford called Archer forward to organise the mountain of luggage while he showed the Kearsley's up to their suite and a little while later they joined the other guests for high tea.

After both Clifford and Tricia had done their duty to the other guests they sat with the Kearsley's in a quiet corner of the room while enjoying a glass of wine. Harry was the first to speak. 'Lady Bishop or may I call you, Tricia?'

'You may call me, Tricia, but I will call you, Harry.'

Clifford butted in. 'Lord Kearsley! You see what I had to put up with?'

'Yes, sir, I do, but first let me explain to you and Gloria how I know this young lady. She rescued my brother Stephen from drowning when we were children for which I will be eternally grateful.—Tricia! Tell me how you reached your true position and one you deserve?'

'Harry, I made unusual progress through life a lot of which I owe to Miss Hardcastle and it was because of her I managed to obtain the job as a school teacher in the Isaiah Bishop Charity School where I was introduced to Clifford. We were attracted to each other but we were, because of circumstances, unable to live a life of a young married couple for very long and accelerated to our current position. Clifford was very kind to me and allowed me to continue with a little business I had set up to help poor families to provide schooling for their children. Other businesses heard of it and it became BCCC.'

'So you are BCCC? I can well imagine my fathers' frustration. No matter how much we tried, he would not move on his decision.—Tricia! We must talk before I leave tomorrow.'

'By all means, Harry, you may stay as long as you like.'

'Thank you. Stephen often spoke of you and said you were Miss Hardcastle's pet.'

'How is he, Harry?'

'You changed his personality and because of you and Miss Hardcastle, he is now doing well in the Military. He is one of the youngest Captains in Prince Albert's Own 11th Hussars.'

'Oh! I am glad, and your father? What happened to him?'

'He had a seizure at the Mill and fell down a flight of stairs. Some say he was pushed.'

'I am sorry, Harry, regardless of any bad feeling between your father and me, it is not nice when anyone passes away, but now we must retire and rest before the madness tonight.'

Clifford was quick to chip in. 'Harry, join me in a brandy.'

'By all means, Lord Bishop, or may I call you Clifford?'

'Clifford!'

―

The evening was a little on the wild side. The men had been drinking before dinner and the jollity continued throughout the seven-course meal with the provision of many types of wine. The ladies took a break for coffee and tea while the men topped up on the compulsory brandy before the ladies joined them once more in the Entertainment Hall where the string quartet exhausted their quota and started again. There was a call for Tricia and Clifford to show their talents but they declined then there was an enormous 'BONG!' as Archer struck the gong on the stroke of midnight.

There were many hugs and kisses all around and when Harry bumped into Tricia although a bit on the wobbly side, he said, 'It has been lovely to meet you again, Tricia. I look forward to our get together later this morning.'

'Harry, it has been a pleasure.'

He bowed deeply. 'At your service, Ma'am.' He spun away to look for more well-wishers preferably of the female kind.

Tricia laughed quietly to herself. "Men!" she muttered.

―

The following morning before breakfast she lined the staff up and with Teddy's help, she rewarded them all with a leather pouch and Archer presented her with a piece of coal and a bundle of gifts from all of them.

Teddy stayed with them for breakfast and as the lady guests came in they were all making a fuss of her which she took in her stride and it made her even more hungry. Harry came in looking definitely under the weather accompanied by Gloria, who said to Tricia, 'Oh! Lady Patricia, she takes after you with that lovely bundle of black hair. How lucky she is.'

'Thank you, Lady Gloria, but it becomes a handful as she gets older. I'm lucky, I have a wonderful Maid who indulges me.'

'When shall we meet, Tricia,' said Harry.

'I am going to take Teddy for a ride so you rest your weary head and I should be ready by midday. Will that be suitable?'

'It will be too late for us to leave will that be alright?'

'Harry! You and your beautiful wife can stay as long as you want. I must go now, the horses will be ready.'

Edwina was engrossed by the squirrels leaping magically in and out and up and down the trees and it was nearer one o'clock by the time Tricia joined Harry and Gloria. They enjoyed a light lunch together exchanging pleasantries but when the staff had cleared it all away, Harry said, 'Tricia or should I call you, Lady Patricia, as I want to talk business now?'

'You call me Lady, Harry, and I will call you, Lord, but how stuffy. Tricia will suit me fine. Now, what is it you wish to discuss?' She turned to Harry's wife. 'Gloria, can I get you a glass of wine or something?'

'I would like a nice sherry, please.'

'Harry! What about you?'

He nodded his affirmation and Tricia pulled the cord and moments later Archer stepped into the room. 'Yes, Ma'am, can I get you something?'

'Yes, please, Archer, three glasses of sherry.'

He backed out of the room and closed the door and, Tricia, said, 'Now Harry, what is it you wish to ask of me?'

'Before I travelled down I spoke with the board of L & P and we would like to accept your offer if it is still on the table.'

Tricia said, 'It is still on the table and in my interest as well as yours, Harry. If you wish to sign a temporary agreement I will arrange for it to begin in two weeks and the full contract with you in three days. Will that be acceptable?'

'More than acceptable, Tricia, thank you so much and are you still able to extend a branch line across the dock?'

'We have only to open the fence to be operational, Harry, and I was not surprised by your father's decision. All that is behind us now and we move on.'

'Thank you, Tricia. Have you any news of your father?'

'No, Harry, but it is my wish that one day I can go and seek him or find out what happened to him.'

'Good luck, Tricia, and I can only apologise for the unfortunate silly incident that led to his demise. They are seeking to stop transportation as there is a lot of opposition coming from Sydney, Australia. Your father must have been one of the last to go I guess because of his expertise in agriculture.'

'I have plans to expand our family, Harry, and then hopefully I may be able to seek him out. Will you join us for high tea?'

'Most certainly, Tricia.'

~~~~~

CHAPTER 18

1848

When the last of their guests departed the following day and the standard routine of the household was able to continue. With the contract with Harry and L&P now in place Tricia was able to spend more time with Edwina who was thrilled when the early snowdrops came and the shoots from the daffodils showed their heads but nobody foresaw the February weather which was probably the wettest in history. Tricia felt sorry for the thousands of Mill workers, frosty dry weather or even snow was better than rain. When it rained you were wet all day.

Spring was an improvement and April was one of the warmest and the pleasant weather lasted until the end of May when the heavens opened and did not stop until early September making the harvest one of the worst on record which did not help the famine in Ireland.

News down the grapevine told, Tricia, that the L&P had managerial problems and were struggling and that the Canal Company had a yearly franchise agreement to run it but investment was low and the Lancaster & Carlisle Rail Co. had taken advantage of the situation and ran illegal trains from Carlisle to Preston. There was no one person in charge of L&P safety and proper signalling was ignored. On the plus side, they did take advantage of the coal deal which boosted her income. Add that to the extra demand from homes for more coal because of the weather the school funds were doing nicely.

Clifford for business reasons used the trains as it was quicker and he could do a business trip to Lancaster in a day whereas before he had to make a three-day trip and so it was in late August he took a train to Lancaster to discuss a possible takeover of a Mill to expand the family business.

The sky was overcast and the red stop flag was hanging limply unseen by the train crew and the train was lolloping along at forty miles an hour when it braked suddenly. There was an almighty crash as the through Express ran into a stationary local train. Passengers were sent plunging from their seats and bags were bouncing in all directions. Clifford was thrown face-first across the carriage and into the opposite wall and as he slid down unconscious a bag crashed down onto his head doing further injury as the carriage lurched sickeningly sideways.

It went eerily quiet before there was moaning and groaning as the passengers sought to pick themselves up but Clifford remained still. One of the passengers reached down to him and as he moved him Clifford's head flopped to one side. The passenger shook his head. Clifford's neck was broken.

The news reached Tricia two days later and she was devastated to the extreme. She screamed in tearful agony and pressing her handkerchief to her face she ran upstairs to her room and lay crying bitterly while hugging Clifford's pillow.

Life had dealt her another crippling blow and it was two days before she got a grip on her feelings. Jill and Mary had tried to soothe her but it was Agnes with the help of many hugs from Edwina who finally, after much encouragement persuaded her to eat her breakfast.

Edwina sat on the bed alongside her and even helped her eat her toasted soldiers and when she had taken her second cup of tea she gave Edwina a tearful hug, and said, 'we have to move on, Teddy, let's go for a walk and let life begin again. It is going to get busy from now on.'

She pulled the cord and Jill came in, 'Yes, ma'am.'

'Jill, I want to get dressed and I am going for a walk around the gardens with Teddy regardless of the weather but first I want to see Clifford. Where have they placed him?

'He is laying in State in the Entertainment Hall, ma'am.'

'Good, and after I have paid my respects I want Brown to take me into town and I would like you to accompany me,

Jill bobbed. 'Yes, ma'am, I have a tub ready for you. While you get ready I will take Edwina to Nanny.'

Tricia hugged Edwina and sent her with Jill to Nanny while she bathed and got dressed. An hour after her visit to the entertainment Hall they stepped outside onto the patio. The rain had stopped and they enjoyed half hour looking at the flowers and listening to the birds singing their welcome and encouraging her back.

She wanted to walk longer but the urgency of her situation made it necessary to get on top of things quickly and at two o'clock Brown pulled up outside the Bishop Law Office.

On this occasion, he was solemn as he helped her down and he stood with his hat across his chest as she waited for Jill. 'Thank you, Brown; I shall try not to keep you too long.'

He bowed. 'Thank you, Ma'am,' he replied.

Tricia led the way into the office and on seeing her, the staff all stood with their heads low. The senior clerk stepped forward to the counter. 'What can we do for you, Lady Bishop?'

'I am going to my husband's office and I would like to speak with the partners, please.'

'Please go through, Ma'am, and I will inform them.'

He opened the end of the counter and opened the door for her and as she made her way to Clifford's office he called on the Partners.

She was sat comfortably with Jill behind her when Richards and Colston the partners entered. She went to stand and they held their hands up and persuaded her to remain seated. When they were seated, Richards said. 'Lady Bishop, commiserations for your loss. We shall miss him and his enthusiasm. What can we do for you, M'lady?'

'Good afternoon, gentlemen. What I wish to know is my position. What do I have?'

Richards and Colston looked at each other and shrugged before Richards, said, 'In a word, M'lady—everything!'

Tricia looked puzzled. 'What do you mean by everything?'

'Lord Bishop must have had a vision as he made a Will only a month ago and he left everything to you. That is, the Mill, the Manor, New House and the London residence and all the family effects, the family riches passed down to him from his father and you even, own us.'

'Oh, dear, what do I do now?' She sat for a moment contemplating before, she said, 'Gentlemen you are my guardian angels. You will guide me as Clifford did and I am open to your suggestions which will help me over the coming months. How much is in the family coffers for instance?'

'I'm sorry, M'lady, but this is in confidence. Could you ask your companion to leave? The front staff will look after her.'

Tricia looked around at Jill. 'Jill, could you leave us, please. They are very good here and do a wonderful coffee and cake.'

'Yes, Ma'am,' said Jill.

Richards showed her to the door and took her down to the front office before he rejoined Colston and Tricia.

When he sat down, he said, 'I don't know if you're ready for this but you have just inherited over half a million pounds plus the value of the Estates, Houses and the Mill which combined could be as much as eight hundred thousand pounds or maybe more not to mention your own significant income. The Longbottom title ends with Lord Clifford as he had no male heirs but you will be recognised as Lady Bishop for the rest of your days.'

Tricia's hand shot to her mouth and for a moment she was speechless before, she said, 'Gentlemen, may I suggest that we wait a reasonable time after the funeral and I want you to keep an eye on things to do with business? Can you do that?'

It was Colston's turn to speak, and he said, 'I think so, M'lady; it is what Clifford would have expected. Do you have any idea of your future plans?'

'I must sell off the Mill as I have no idea of the industry and I am going to dispose of my BCCC business. Could you advertise the Mill and the Manor plus the London residence for sale?'

'We know that Clifford was travelling to Lancaster to look at expansion but he did have an offer from Horrocks only two weeks ago. Shall we pursue that?'

'Yes, please do. I would like to see it but make sure and check that you are getting good value, and gentlemen, if I detect the slightest whiff of treachery this lady will be the bain of your life if you have one. You said I own this practice. If you want to own it try your best and I will sell it to you for one sovereign.'

On those words, she stood up and as they bowed in acknowledgement, she left the room.

—

On the 28th of August, Tricia bade farewell to her beloved husband and with deep sadness once more in her life it gave her a vision she had wanted for many years. She was now going to search for her father but first she must do right by her family.

On the 25th of September, she arranged a family meeting and when they were suitably seated and refreshed in the drawing-room she began…

'Ladies and Gentlemen, on this sad occasion I wish to tell you of the plans or arrangements I have made.' She held up an official-looking document. 'I have here Clifford's Will and in it he left everything and I mean everything, to me, to do whatever I wish and here are my decisions. Constance and Hilda, you will receive £10,000 each. Lady Felicity and Lady Eleanor you will both receive £10,000 and residence in the New House until you leave this mortal coil but you will be responsible for looking after it. Constance and Hilda, after they have gone the New House I will bequeath to you, maybe! As for the Mill I have had an offer from the Horrocks people which I have accepted. The Preston Town Council wish to purchase the Manor and its grounds which they are going to use as Council offices and the grounds they are going to open as a Public Park except for my housekeeper Agnes's cottage which I have bequeathed to her. She will also receive a small annual income for the rest of her natural. Myself, and my staff, are moving into the Manor annexe plus the stables and you ladies are free to go to the Manor and take what you wish of the family heirlooms. You have a month to do this. Consider tonight a late Wake if you like and you are welcome to stay. There is dinner and entertainment laid on for this evening so the gentlemen will be free to absorb their brandy while we ladies talk about them. Has anyone anything to query about my suggestions?'

They all looked at each other and there was much shaking of heads and a few grumbles but all were in agreement with what they had been told. That amount of money was not to be sniffed at.

It was after dinner when the ladies withdrew to the drawing-room that the first grumble came out. They were sat around the fire, when Hilda, said, 'Lady Tricia, why can you not bequeath New House to us now?'

Tricia had been expecting this and was ready with the answer. 'Ladies, as you well know when we acquire something it becomes the property of your man. Is that not right?'

Hilda and Constance looked at each other before Hilda, replied, 'Yes.'

'I am following the wishes of not only Clifford but his father and grandfather who both desired that Lady Felicity and Lady Eleanor should be looked after and not be the prey of gamblers or any other unlikely event that may occur. That property remains mine until they pass away and then we shall see. I may want to live there when I return. Is that clear?'

Constance and Hilda both sat with their mouths open unable to respond.

—

The following morning she went to the Devlin residence and when they were sat comfortably around the fire with a pot of tea, Tricia spoke. 'Uncle Tom…' 'Oh! This sounds serious,' he muttered. '…Uncle Tom, I have made a decision about my future. I am selling BCCC to the Colliery. I believe it was coming to an end anyway. The railways are taking over but to help you and your sons and Cartwright & Devlin, I am giving you £10,000. With this, you will buy this house and run the business and my share will be paid as usual into my bank. You will provide my ex-housekeeper, Agnes, with all the coal she needs and take it out of my money. I will be away for a long time, maybe two years, but I will subsidise the school through the bank.'

Tom looked at her with concern. 'Tricia!—£10,000? That's a lot of money.'

'Uncle Tom, life has been both cruel as it has been kind. I cannot say more, but you need have no worries on the financial side. I shall not be leaving for a while so I will see you before I go.'

She got up to leave and as she slipped on her gloves, she said, 'Uncle Tom you will make sure that my Billy gets a slice of that?'

He took her hands in his. 'Yes, baby, I will, and you take care. Both Edie and I worry about you. When you came into our life you were a gift from heaven. Our spirits were lifted and you gave us the will to carry on. Where are you going that takes two years?'

'I am going to seek my father in Australia.'

She gave him and Edie a hug and with a tear in her eye, she left. Brown was waiting patiently outside and could see that she was upset and courteous as ever he helped her into the carriage but remained silent.

In late October news came that the London residence had been sold for a considerable profit as Eaton Square had become one of the favoured addresses for the aristocrats and with the help of Colston and Richards she began research into travel to Australia. She settled for a ten per cent share of the partnership for one sovereign and the name Bishop to remain on the books.

—

On the second Sunday of November after they had returned from Church she was sat before the fire enjoying a cup of tea when she asked Jill to join her.

'Take a seat, Jill, would you like a cup of tea?' Jill was a little unsure how to respond and looked a little nervous when Tricia, said, 'Don't worry, Jill, I will enjoy your company and I want to ask you something. Please, take tea.'

Jill poured herself a cup of tea and sat on the sofa opposite Tricia and when she was comfortable Tricia, said, 'Jill how would you like to join me on an adventure around the world?'

'In what manner, Lady Tricia?'

'I am planning on going to Australia next year and I would like you to travel as my lady's maid. I have heard that the journey by sea can be rough but don't worry; you will have a cabin and not be mixing with the steerage passengers. Nanny Peters is coming also and you can share.'

'Oh! That was a bit sudden, I'm not sure. I would have to leave my family and my mother is not well.'

'I can understand, Jill, and if you decline I will give you excellent references. Speak with your family first.'

Jill put down her cup and stood ready to leave when Tricia said, 'Jill, on your way out can you send a message out to Brown to join me.'

Tricia swore she saw Jill's eyes brighten but said nothing. Jill curtseyed and left and Tricia poured herself another cup while she waited. Five minutes later there was a knock on the door and Archer stepped in. 'You asked to see, Brown, M'lady?'

'Yes, Archer, show him in.'

Archer stepped to one side and held the door and waved Brown in and closed the door behind him.

'Brown!' said, Tricia, 'come and make yourself comfortable. I won't bite, I promise.'

Brown crossed the room and Tricia held her hand out and pointed to the sofa. When he was settled, he said, 'What is it, M'lady?'

'Brown, how do you feel about a trip to Australia as my bodyguard, groom and servant all rolled into one?'

Brown didn't hesitate. 'When do we leave, ma'am, but I cannot reach Archer's standard with the servant bit.'

'You are familiar with pistols and such like?'

'Yes, Ma'am.'

'Good, I don't expect you to use that skill but you never know. Is there anything I should know that may deter you, like a relationship with a certain person?' Brown looked at his feet and rubbed his face not sure what to say, when Tricia added, 'I have spoken to Jill and she is going to speak with her family but she appeared interested when I mentioned you.'

Brown smiled. 'You can't keep anything secret. We have started to see each other, ma'am and I like her very much. If she doesn't go then I may have to think twice about it.'

'Brown, if she does go you must promise not to get her in the family way at least while we travel. I know it is difficult when two people fall in love but I don't know what this trip is going to achieve. When we reach the final destination feel free to do what you will. I will pay for a wedding if that's what you wish.'

'May I speak with her first, ma'am?'

'Of course. If you come you will have your own cabin and Jill will share a cabin with Nanny Peters. Your first job is to watch over me and the ladies. Jill will continue as my maid and Nanny of course will help me with Edwina.'

'When do we expect to leave, ma'am?'

'I am advised that the best time to sail will be sometime in May. That way we get the calmer waters both here and in the southern hemisphere before their winter sets in. That is the plan but you know the weather. I expect to be away for two years, but who knows? Meanwhile, Brown, carry on with your good work and let me know as quickly as you can.'

He stood up and did his dutiful acknowledgements and left. Tricia felt a little deflated as between now and her departure there was nothing to do apart from another stilted Christmas which this year was not her responsibility.

It was on the following Thursday that both Brown and Jill requested to see Tricia and immediately after lunch she called them in and when they were sat comfortably, she said, 'I can see by the smile on your faces that this may be good news, am I right?'

'They both looked at each other, Jill nodded, and Brown spoke up. 'Lady Tricia, we both would like to join you on your Australian trip under the circumstances you described.'

'Oh! Thank you both, but first, let me explain. I received information from an unlikely source that the journey by ship can be an onerous one which could take up to a hundred days but you will be on the upper deck in a cabin which will give us the freedom to walk around and even play which I hope to do with Edwina, and the food is better. You will of course be eating with me and the other upper-tier passengers. I am arranging to travel on a ship that will have many stops which will allow us to go ashore and stretch our legs while they take on new provisions but it will extend the journey time. In that time you will carry on with your duties. You, Brown, will watch over us both while sailing and ashore. Our final destination is Sydney and then I have to enquire of the authorities where my father went and then we organise the final part of our journey. You will be paid and there will be no extra expense on your part. Are you happy with that?'

They looked at each other again and both nodded vigorously before Brown answered, 'Yes, ma'am.'

'Good. I will keep you informed but until we sail your duties are as normal and you can pack as much as you like. I'm sorry to have to restrict your way of life in the manner I have but I wish for continuity. I have every sympathy with you as I went through a similar ordeal, very frustrating to say the least.'

'M'lady,' said Jill, 'I have the support of my family, my mother ordered me to go and it gives us both great pleasure to work for you and to travel on this adventure is a dream and our wish is to see you find your father.'

Tricia stood up and went across to them and held their hands. 'Thank you both and do not worry, I will look after you.'

Jill and Brown stood and did the dutiful acknowledgements and Tricia watched as they left the room with a twinkle of a tear in her eye she said to herself. "I am lucky to have such wonderful staff,"

Relieved from the task of organising Christmas she was able to spend more time on her journey preparations. As she expected Christmas fell to Hilda and it was rather a boring affair but Constance did better with the New Year celebrations but Tricia couldn't wait for May to arrive when suddenly it was upon her.

Uncle Tom provided a cart driven by his two sons to carry their many trunks and bags to Liverpool while Tricia, Nanny, Jill and Brown travelled down in a carriage driven by Orris relieved of his duties at the New House for two days.

After travelling all day, they arrived at the Adelphi Hotel in the evening and once settled overnight accommodation was found nearby for Orris and the two lads who were tipped generously by Tricia for their hard work.

Tricia was in a modest suite with Edwina while Nanny, Jill and Brown were in staff accommodation on the top floor at the back but Tricia had organised that they ate together for their evening meal. Edwina was loving it, even though she was tired. Like her mother, she was always keen on new experiences but they retired to bed early tired after the long day's drive.

The following morning Brown watched carefully as the trunks were taken down to the ship and loaded and Tom's two lads and Oriss were allowed to go home after a final handshake. At two o'clock they received a message from the ship that they were to board the following morning by eleven o'clock and sail with the afternoon tide…

~~~~~

Part 3

Australia

CHAPTER 19

May 1849

Tricia shuddered as the *'Goodhope'* moved further into the Irish Sea. The breeze became stronger and from a south-westerly direction making their journey to Cork in Ireland more difficult. To progress against the breeze the ship had to tack out towards Ireland and then back again in a zigzag pattern making the journey longer. The swell was modest but going across the breeze the boat leaned away from it.

As cabin passengers, Tricia, Edwina with Nanny along with the others in Cabin class were able to take advantage of the poop deck, and being an open-air person she was enjoying it. She held onto Edwina so that she did not slide on the sloping deck while pointing out the seabirds and other ships and only when they changed tack did they have to move while the crew altered the sails as the ship went from right to left and back again an hour later.

A couple of hours into the voyage they were called for evening dinner in the modest dining room and although it was plentiful all the passengers pushed it away in disgust as the quality was poor. After dinner, Tricia helped Nanny put Edwina to bed before putting on her cloak and going up on deck to speak with the First officer.

'Yes, madam, what can I do for you?'

'I would like a word with the Captain if that's possible.'

'Can I ask you what it's about, ma'am, maybe I can help?'

'It is rather personal but should only take a few minutes.'

'If you could wait a few moments, ma'am, I will speak with him. Who shall I say is requesting this meeting?'

'Lady Patricia Bishop.'

The officer knuckled the peak of his cap. 'One moment, M'lady.'

He was gone two minutes before he was back and requested Tricia to follow him down to the Captain's cabin and after a knock on the door he stepped back and allowed Tricia through. She was surprised at the size of the cabin. It stretched across the stern of the ship with a bedroom branching off and made their modest cabins feel quite small.'

Captain Fairweather stood up from behind his desk and stretched his hand out. 'Sorry! Lady Bishop, I did not know of your title you having booked the journey as Mrs Bishop. Please take a seat. What can I do for you?

She sat down and made herself comfortable before she said, 'Captain Fairweather, I don't know how to say this so I shall come straight to the point. That dinner tonight was disgusting and I am enquiring if that is going to be the standard for the rest of our voyage? I can't imagine what it was like for the steerage passengers.'

He looked at her and rubbed his chin before replying, 'My apologies, M'lady, but I also had an indifferent meal. Our cook was taken ill just before we left and I had no time to hire another one so the second mate took over the duties and in doing so made me a man short never mind the meals.'

'What are you going to do about it, Captain?'

'I am hoping in the twenty-four hours we have in Cork to take on another cook.'

'Captain Fairweather, may I make a suggestion. Could you enquire amongst the other passengers if we have a qualified cook on board? I will hire them to cook for us and assist your mate.'

He didn't answer straight away but after a moment's thought, he said, 'I will do that, M'lady. It will be tomorrow morning before I get any response.'

'Very well and I want to interview whoever we find.'

She stood up and he did likewise and with a slight nod, he took her outstretched hand and gave it a cursory peck before she turned and left the cabin.

—

It was a little after ten o'clock the next morning that she was called to the Captain's cabin and when she arrived she was introduced to a young man in his twenties wearing a worn brown tweed outfit that was nevertheless clean.

'Lady Bishop, meet Rory Maguire who tells me he is a chef.'

She sat down opposite Maguire. 'Good morning, young man, tell me about yourself.'

He raised a hand to his mouth and coughed slightly before replying in a strong Irish accent, 'Good morning, M'lady, I am Rory Maguire and I was a trainee cook or Chef in Cranberry Manor near Liverpool.'

'Have you any references, young man, and why are you on this ship?'

He reached into his pocket and withdrew some papers which he handed over to Tricia. 'Those are my references and I am travelling to Australia seeking a new life.'

Tricia read the references and when she had finished, she said, 'These are very good, Mr Maguire. What made you want to leave?'

'I saw an advert by the Governors of New South Wales sponsoring tradespeople and entrepreneurs, so I said, 'Why not?''

'How much did you earn, Maguire, and don't lie, I ran a Manor house which employed many staff so I know.'

'I was as a second chef on £40 per annum. I was offered £45 to stay.'

'Maguire, I will pay you £4 per month while the journey lasts. Is that acceptable?'

'Yes, M'lady.'

'It will not be easy. You will run the First-class cookhouse on this ship and oversee the steerage kitchen. You will order what supplies you like.' She looked across at Fairweather. 'Captain, when we reach Cork, Maguire will go ashore and order supplies to supplement what you already have for which I will pay and at every port, we stop at. In addition, I want you to provide four barrels of white wine vinegar to be distributed amongst all the passengers to wipe down their bunk spaces. That includes Cabin passengers.'

'I have no objections to that, M'lady, so long as it does not delay us but I do clean down the vessel in between each journey.'

'Very admirable, Captain, and much appreciated.' She

diverted her attention to Maguire. 'Maguire; fetch your stuff and move in with my man Brown. Come with me.'

She stood up and acknowledged Fairweather before leading Maguire from the cabin. She searched around and found Brown swanning with Jill on the upper deck and called him over. 'Yes, M'lady,' said Brown, 'what can I do for you?'

'Brown, meet Rory Maguire, he is going to be sharing your cabin for the rest of the voyage. I want you to go ashore with him in Cork and get him dressed to my requirements plus any Chefs gear he requires. While you are there he will be buying foodstuffs to enhance the menu for our journey.'

Brown shoved a hand out, 'Brown.'

Rory did likewise. 'Glad to meet you, Brown. Call me Rory short for Gregory. Have you got a first name?'

Brown put an arm around Rory's shoulder. 'Come with me mate and we'll chat while we get your stuff.'

Brown nodded to Tricia and led Rory away but they hadn't gone more than a few paces when Tricia called out. 'Maguire! Get down to the kitchens. I'm starving and so is my daughter.'

Brown laughed and waved over his shoulder as he and Rory continued talking, but first, he leaned across, and said in Maguire's ear, 'Don't be fooled, matey, underneath she is as hard as nails so don't cross her and you will survive. You respect her position and she is generous. You can see that because we are in the upper tier with her.'

Rory nodded. 'Got that, brother, what did you say your name was?'

—

Things improved after the Cork stop where Maguire was able to add his little extras to the official amounts required for each passenger. Maguire was also not happy with the water on board and kept a large pot of boiled water for drinking only in both sectors.

Fairweather was known for his clean ship and made a note of the little tweaks being made and Tricia was invited to the Captain's table for meals but she only took advantage of this for protocol sake preferring to remain with her 'family' as she called them.

The trip across the Bay of Biscay was lumpy bumpy with the prevailing wind being from the West. Seasickness was prevalent but all the hatches were able to stay open to allow air circulation and the mattresses aired but once across the Bay the weather favoured them and the passage on to Tenerife was enjoyable but longer than usual because of the calm seas.

It was during this relative calmness that Tricia began taking evening strolls around the deck before retiring to bed. There were no lights other than the lanterns on the poop deck and one hanging around the crow's nest but there was enough light to negotiate any obstacles. It was during these walks that the idea of teaching came to her. During the day she had seen the parents trying to entertain the children and she thought, "Why not open a little school. There are only a dozen of them. That and the services we have on Sundays will help them in this new world we are going to."

With that in mind, she went to see Fairweather to request the use of the dining area as a mini-school and did he have any facilities like a blackboard and chalk etc…

'By all means, Lady Bishop, it is something that happens quite often. Chalk we use all the time to mark our cargos and we also have slates leftover from other journey's. I will get the crew to bring them up to the dining room. It is getting warmer and maybe teaching on deck might be more favourable.'

'I will keep that in mind, Captain, but we will start in the dining room. Can you spread the word that school starts a ten o'clock tomorrow morning?'

'It will be my pleasure, M'lady; it will get the little beggars from under our feet for a while.'

Happy with the outcome she went to speak with Nanny Peters who would look after the tiny ones including Edwina and she would look after the older ones.

—

One bonus at this time was that the off duty crew were able to catch fish to add to the diet and the passengers saw plenty of dolphins, flying fish and the occasional shark. Edwina was saddened when the crew caught a dolphin but Tricia was able to guide her away so that she didn't see what happened to it but it was on the menu that evening.

In Tenerife, they had a thirty-six hour stop during which time the passengers were able to stretch their legs and write letters home which were carried by a sister ship travelling north.

During the stop the crew scrubbed down the steerage passenger space and all the mattresses were dragged up on deck and aired. Barrels of extra water plus lemons and oranges were loaded along with other herbs and spices used to enhance the plain diet and with an eight-knot breeze blowing over the starboard rear quarter they set off south for the Equator fully refreshed.

Seven weeks after leaving Cork they crossed the Equator. The passengers were spared the torture of taking part in the celebrations but there was a lot of rough horseplay and jollity amongst the crew. The Captain allowed them one mug of grog and set them back to work.

The breeze stiffened to ten knots and they bowled along with porpoise and flying fish for company and the crew caught a ten-foot shark which boosted their rations.

After three days of good sailing the wind dropped and the temperatures shot up which made sleeping at night difficult for the steerage and some of them opted to sleep on deck. This did not worry Tricia because she took her walk early and she was able to step around them. Things began to change as they moved further south. The breeze turned more to the west and became cooler and eventually Tricia had to wear her cloak.

Three weeks after crossing the Equator a few days out from Cape Town, Tricia was meandering along the leeward deck on a moonless evening admiring the stars and the planets when a hooded figure leapt out of the darkness and grabbed her dragging her towards the deep shadows in front of the poop deck. She screamed and at the same time a single shot rang out and her attacker dropped to the floor. She rolled over and over and came to an abrupt stop against the side of the ship as an upright figure stepped from behind a mast.

She looked up, and said, with both a hint of surprise and relief in her voice, 'BROWN!'

He pushed a .36 Paterson Colt back into his belt and bent down to help her up as the ship's 2nd Officer and two crewmen one holding a lantern ran towards them, shouting. 'Stop! Hold it there, or we shoot.'

Brown was helping to brush down Tricia when 2nd Officer Robins grabbed him and pulled him away and pushed a pistol into his stomach. 'Got' ya, don't move or you're dead.'

Tricia stepped forward quickly and pushed her arm between them. 'Officer! Leave him! He's my, Man, my guardian. He saved me.'

Robins lowered his weapon and stepped back before crossing to the inert body on the deck. He rolled the body over with his foot and called the seaman with the lantern over and had a closer look before standing up and saying, 'It's that plonker we took on in Cork. Never did like him.' He turned to the seaman. 'Get your mate and toss this over the side and get back to work.' He turned to Tricia. 'I'm sorry, M'lady, but it is hard to choose your crew in a foreign port. I will speak with the Captain. Are you alright?'

'Yes, yes, Mr Robins. A few bruises but nothing compared to what it could have been if it hadn't been for my man, Brown.'

'You got yourself a good one there, ma'am. I'm sure the Captain will want to speak with you at some time.' He bowed and knuckled his cap and turned his attention to, Brown. 'Mr. Brown, tell me, what is that weapon you have there? It appears a lot more efficient than ours.'

Brown pulled it out and showed him. 'Be careful with it,' he said, 'there are still four more shots in it.'

'It has five shots. What is it?'

'It is an American Paterson – Colt manufactured in England. I hear they are making a better one with six shots.'

'I like it. I must tell the Captain. Where did you get it?'

'A pawn shop in Liverpool complete with ammunition.'

He handed it back to Brown. 'Very nice, I'm sure the Captain will want to see that.'

The onlookers began to disperse and in the background, a

splash was heard as the body was disposed of without ceremony although one of the crew did cross himself. Brown joined Tricia and escorted her back to her cabin. When they got there Tricia paused at the door, and said, 'Brown, I can't thank you enough, you saved my life or maybe something much worse. Have you been following me every night?'

He took a step back and with a hand across his heart, he said. 'It is my job, M'lady, and I was doing no more than was asked of me.'

'Brown, I knew I could trust you. How do you get on with our chef?'

He smiled and blushed slightly. 'Very well, ma'am, he keeps us, that is, Me, Jill and Nanny well supplied with extra food.'

'You sound better fed than me, Brown.'

'I'm sure we can fix that, ma'am. Did Edwina not tell you she also eats well, in fact, she never stops?'

'The little tyke, she never said a word. Did you swear her to secrecy?'

'No, ma'am, I held my finger to my lips and said she must not tell anyone. By that, I meant the rest of the children or passengers.'

'Or me? Brown; Feel free to continue and maybe a sneaky surprise under my pillow might not go amiss. Like my daughter, I will say nothing. Meanwhile, Brown, thank you again. I will never forget it.'

He bowed, and said, 'Good night, M'lady, and sleep well. I shall always be watching out for you.'

'Good night, Brown.'

—

The next morning Captain Fairweather requested Tricia's presence at her convenience and she joined him for a cup of tea close to eleven o'clock. When she was sat comfortably he walked backwards and forwards behind his chair a few times, deliberating on what he was about to say. He stopped, and grabbing the back of his chair he turned towards her.

'Lady Bishop, my apologies. I do not know what to say. My 2nd Officer has told me everything and I can only ask for forgiveness for the events that took place.'

'Apology accepted, Captain Fairweather, the circumstances were unforeseen and your Officer did the correct thing in the circumstances.'

'But he was forceful with your man.'

'He saw my man with a gun and acted accordingly, but when he was given the full story of events he apologised and was very helpful and my welfare was his prime concern and later he had a long conversation with my man, Brown about his new handgun which I did not know he had.'

'Brown takes his job seriously, M'lady. That we all had staff like that.'

She stood up. 'I am lucky, Captain Fairweather in my choice of staff in all aspects but I must go now I have a class to attend too. I understand we are close to Capetown?'

'We shall be stopping there tomorrow for about three days. It is our halfway point and we will be loading a lot more stores this time as there is no stop before Adelaide which usually takes six to seven weeks depending on the wind. I might add that the weather so far has been kind to us even the doldrums were not doldrums. From now on the weather is rougher although I tend to keep to the northern edge of the westerly's which makes the journey longer but more, how shall we say—easier.'

'Thank you, Captain, and you need not worry about the incident any longer although you may give your choice of crew more consideration in the future.'

They did the protocol acknowledgement and she left the cabin with the purser holding the door for her as the ship leaned with the wind. Fairweather watched her, the subtle rebuke foremost in his mind.

They anchored in Capetown in the late afternoon and someone remarked that it was like an early English summer's day but they could feel the evening chill moving in and there were many trips down to the hold for some warmer clothing.

Over the next few days some of the passengers took the

opportunity to go on land, Tricia and her adopted family amongst them and their diet improved immensely but when they returned to the ship the livestock taken on board and kept in a pen forward of the hold and below the foredeck including live chickens in cages, surprised them. Little did they know that this was their diet over the next seven weeks?

They slipped their moorings on the evening of the third day. The weather was cool with a steady wind as they headed south towards the much talked of roaring forties with a new crewman on board and when they awoke the next morning they could feel the difference in the attitude of the ship. It was her type of sailing. A rear quarter twelve-knot wind tilting her over at roughly twelve degrees and pushing them along at a good nine knots. If this kept up they would do it in six said the Captain.

It was a little after ten in the morning on the first day when the 2nd Officer approached Tricia as she prepared to read a story to the older children.

'Yes, Officer Robins, what can I do for you?' she asked.

'Apologies, Lady Bishop, but the Captain would like to know if you can spare him a few minutes of your time?'

'Is it important?'

'I don't know, M'lady, he has a new passenger with him.'

'Tell him I shall be there in a few minutes. I must organise my class. The children come first.'

'Thank you, M'lady, I shall pass on your message.'

He knuckled his cap and returned to the bridge while Tricia arranged with Nanny Peters for her to take over the story reading and accompanied by Jill she went to the Captain's cabin where she was greeted by the Purser who knocked on the door and held it open for her to enter.

Alongside Fairweather who was sat at his desk was a good looking well-dressed man in his early forties with thinning dark hair who stood to one side as the Captain stood up to greet her.

He nodded, and said, 'Good morning, Lady Bishop, are you well this morning?'

She bobbed, and replied, 'I am well, Captain, I am getting

used to standing at a funny angle now. What can I do for you?'

'Lady Bishop, your man Brown, who I have no doubt is close by, tells us that you speak French.'

'I am familiar with that language, yes!'

'Allow me to introduce, Monsieur Louis-Etienne Armand. He is a new passenger but unfortunately he speaks very little English and I wonder if you could help us?'

She acknowledged Armand, and said, in his mother tongue, 'Good morning, Monsieur Armand, welcome aboard. How may I be of help?'

He bowed slightly, before replying, 'Good morning, Madame Bishop, I have an issue with our accommodation. I cannot possibly sleep in the same cabin as my Nanny. My children must sleep with her.'

'How old are your children, Monsieur?'

'My two girls are ten and eight.'

Tricia informed Fairweather, who replied, 'It would appear, M'lady, there is or was a mistake with the initial booking. A language difficulty that is all. They thought it was man and wife with two children.'

Arrangements were made to swap the cabins around and when that was settled, Tricia said, 'Captain Fairweather, may I speak with Monsieur Armand alone?'

'Not in my cabin, M'lady, Feel free to do what you wish elsewhere, and thank you.'

'You're welcome, Captain.' She turned to Armand. 'Monsieur Armand, please join me in the dining area where I am sure my Chef has laid on some coffee.'

'If I may, Madame, may I join you in half an hour? I want to oversee the changes and congratulations on your French. You could be one of us.'

'I had an overzealous teacher and I enjoy your language.'

—

An hour later after Tricia ensured that the children were being looked after they met in the dining area at the other end of the room and Tricia was the one to start up a conversation.

'Monsieur Armand, may I call you, Louis?'

'Madame Bishop, you may of course call me Louis, we are after all going to be confined on this ship for six or seven weeks.'

'Oh, good, it is much more relaxing. I would like to talk about your children. We have on this ship education classes for the fourteen children we have onboard and as we are going to an English speaking community how would you like to enrol your two girls?'

'Madame Bishop, I would love to. Does your teacher speak French?'

'I am one of the teachers, Louis. I do the older children while my Nanny teaches the younger ones. I would initially give your girls separate lessons for a few weeks and then put them in with the others. Oh, and do call me, Tricia.'

'Madame Tricia, When can they start?'

'If you have no other plans, Louis, bring them here to the dining area this afternoon. What are the girl's names?'

'The oldest is Adele and the younger, Celeste.'

'Thank you, Louis, I will look forward to seeing them this afternoon meanwhile lets us enjoy the skills of my Chef who has such a meagre pantry to play with.'

After lunch when the children were assembled in the dining area Tricia was surprised when Louis asked if he could join them as he too would like to learn English in readiness for his venture into an English speaking world.

She was stuck for words but when she spoke it was with earnestness, she said, 'It will give me great pleasure, Louis, but you will have to be patient as I divide my time with the other children. Can you by any chance provide writing material?'

'I most certainly can, Madame Tricia, if you will give me a moment to retrieve it from my trunk.'

'I will continue with my older children while you fetch it.'

She sat Adele and Celeste to one side and gave them a copy of one of her Henrietta books to look at while they waited and continued with the education of her other children and it was fifteen minutes before he returned patting his brow and looking quite flushed.

'Pardon, Madame, this climbing of steep steps is quite labouring.'

She looked on him with sympathy, and smiled, when she said, 'You should try it with skirts.'

He sat down and acknowledged her wit as she gave him the last copy of her Henrietta book. Satisfied the others were well occupied she started reading and explaining simple words but all in English the reverse of what her tutor Miss Hardcastle had done to teach her French.

Tricia found it a little disturbing when half an hour into their lessons she saw Louis watching her and not his book which she had instructed them to do. She ignored it and carried on but as the days passed it became slightly off-putting that her pupil had an alternative reason for wanting to learn English. It was flattering but disturbing nevertheless. That he had not approached her more openly led her to believe that he may be shy.

The Captain ventured further south to capture the wind and the vessel became a little bouncy as it picked up speed on the upper fringes of the roaring forties and the Sunday morning service had more than a little humour in it as people swayed and staggered with the rhythm of the ship. When the service was over young Adele staggered and slipped and Tricia being close at hand was quick to respond and she was comforting Adele when Louis joined them and he and Tricia met eye to eye. Tricia blushed and looked down while wiping a tear from Adele's eyes. Putting a hand under her shoulder she helped her stand up and hugged her.

While she was crouched down tidying Adele's hair and wiping away another tear she felt the warmth of Louis come down beside her, and he said, 'Madame Tricia, may we walk together when we have the children settled?'

Tricia had been expecting something like this and did not respond immediately but continued fussing with Adele. After a few moments she looked up and said, 'Of course, M. Louis, I think this young lady is alright now,' and speaking English, she said, 'Come, Adele, let us walk with your Daddy.'

She stood up and patted Adele's clothes straight before holding her hand and saying with a hint of humour in her voice, 'M. Louis, do we take the long route today or the short one?'

He replied in his broken English, 'I think we go the long way.'

Taking the hand of Celeste and keeping a respectable distance from Tricia they began the unsteady walk around the deck. They had only walked ten yards, when Tricia said, 'Tell me, M. Louis, why are you taking these lovely girls to Australia?'

'I am a vintner of many years experience with many acres of vineyard and I have been asked by some inexperienced farmers of New South Wales to monitor the maturity of their grapes to ensure their quality and to determine the correct time for harvest and other general things to do with making wine.'

'What were you doing in Capetown?'

'There was no ship from France to Australia so I wait in Capetown for the first ship and how lucky I was.'

Tricia squared up to him. 'M. Armand! I am flattered by your attention but what about the mother of these children?'

He took the hand of both Adele and Celeste and bent down to speak with them. 'Girls, there are some of your class friends playing on the forecastle. Go and play with them while I talk with your teacher.'

'Aah, Daddy, Must we?' whinged Celeste.

'Yes, it is only for a little while. Now run along.'

They left reluctantly and holding hands walked slowly towards the bow and when they had gone out of earshot he turned to Tricia and speaking in his natural tongue which in the light of the circumstance was the correct one. 'Madame Tricia, It is with regret that I must inform you that my children do not have a mother. She died when Celeste was born and I have had no interest in romance since that time.

Tricia's hand shot to her mouth and she took a deep breath in surprise. 'Louis, I did not know.' With her hand on her heart, she said, 'My deepest sympathies and grief over your tragedy. What can I say?'

'Nothing, Madame, and I might ask you, why do you travel with your daughter?'

Still holding her hand over her heart, she looked at him, and said, 'Touché! It is a cruel world, M. Louis, and I, like you, are in grief. I lost my husband last year and I go to Australia to seek my father who was transported irresponsibly by our terrible justice system and I also do not seek romance.'

'You seem to have trustworthy staff with you. Your man, Brown, is never far away or is that a shadow I see?'

'Oh! You know the name of my watcher. He, M. Louis, is very trustworthy and I would not step out of line if I were you. You see, I treat my staff as family. Always have and will do so in the future. They are after all human like us.'

'I know of Brown's reputation but my intentions toward you, Madame Tricia, are honourable.'

At that moment the ship lurched as it crashed into a larger wave and thrown off balance she stumbled forward into him and he held her in his arms. He looked down at her and she looked up into his eyes and shook her head. The ship was once more stable, he let her go, and after a few moments, while she tidied her clothes he stepped back to a respectable distance and from the corner of his eye, he saw the figure of Brown moving away.

He paused long enough for her to regain her composure before, he said, 'Are you alright, Madame Tricia?'

She nodded. 'Yes! I used to think carriages and coaches were rough but this puts them in the shade in that department.'

'My sentiments, entirely, Madame Tricia.'

Tricia considered her next words for a moment before she said, 'M. Louis, I wish to continue our friendship and therefore you should call me, Tricia, but I will call you Louis in return.'

'Tricia it is, Madame.' He laughed. 'It is so hard to get rid of the protocol so this new style may take some time.'

'In exchange, Louis, while I teach you English, you may tell me about the wine industry. It sounds quite involved and something we do not have in England or rather it is something I know nothing about.'

'Let us walk, Tricia, and I will give you your first lesson about that delicious nectar we call wine.'

The weather became increasingly squally and Fairweather eased the ship north-easterly. He reckoned it was quicker to keep a steady rate of knots than to go crashing through high waves even with the wind behind you.

The relationship between Tricia and Louis remained socially friendly. Her knowledge of the wine industry broadened, although she had no idea what use it would be in the future. His English, apart from his delicious accent, as she described it, improved to the extent where he spoke it freely as his second language and after a couple of weeks his daughter's were able to intermingle with their English counterparts.

Four weeks into their long hike across the Indian Ocean in mid-morning when Tricia and Nanny Peters were doing their teaching stint there was a scream coming from the steerage deck below. Nanny Peters reacted immediately and dashed off while Tricia took over the whole class but a few minutes later a teenage girl came running in calling, 'Lady, Lady, come quickly.'

Tricia stopped what she was doing and hurried after the girl wondering why they were calling her. She knew what the problem was. One of the married women who was pregnant at the start of the voyage was giving birth and this was something she knew nothing about.

The screams were getting louder and it was plain that she was in difficulty and when Tricia arrived, Nanny Peters and the French Nanny were there with another woman who said she was a midwife. Between them they were doing their best, but it was a breech birth and nothing could be done to stop the haemorrhaging.

After a couple of hours, the woman died. The husband was devastated as were the passengers but the biggest crisis was feeding the baby. None of the women on board were able to express milk and it was Rory who came to the rescue.

'We have two goats left from the initial livestock. We were about to kill one to add to our meat supply but we can use their milk for the baby instead. We should have enough fodder to feed them.'

'But how do we feed the baby,' said one of the onlookers.

'Have any of you ladies got a spare glove? A silk one would be best as the seepage is slower.'

There were mumblings amongst them before Tricia stepped forward. 'I will have Jill bring one from my trunk, Rory. Can you show us how to milk the goats?'

One of the women from the steerage pushed her way to the front. 'There is no need. I am a farmer's wife and I will milk the goats if he can show us how to use the glove.'

'Easy,' said Rory, 'pull four of the fingers inside out so that there is just one dangling. Snip the tiniest of holes in the end and then fill the glove with milk and let the baby suck.'

This idea worked, but it was the ship's sailmaker who stitched a piece of canvas to make a holder for the glove with just one finger dangling which stopped the drips from falling onto the clothes of the holder.

There was sadness around the ship and a funeral was held for the unfortunate woman the following day. The body was stitched into a weighted canvas bag and laid out on a board with one end poking over the rail.

As Captain Fairweather read out the words, '*Unto Almighty God we commend the soul of our sister departed and we commit her body to the deep.*'

Two seamen took the inboard end and tipped the board and the body slid over the side while soft weeping could be heard from fellow passengers.

They first spotted Australia when they approached Cape Leeuwin when Fairweather changed course south and then east to cut across the Australian Bight taking them directly to the mud hole that was Port Adelaide where a dozen passengers disembarked. After a one-day stoppage to refill with water and edibles they moved on through the choppy, dangerous waters of the Bass Strait but luck favoured them and after one hundred and five days at sea on the **27**th of August **1849** they turned into the bay that was Sydney Harbour.

~~~~~

CHAPTER 20

They had to stay on board for one more night but Maguire went ashore and brought in extra supplies and that night all the passengers enjoyed a real meal.

The following morning they were pulled into the quayside and the long process of unloading began. Before they were ready to leave, Tricia took Maguire to one side. He knuckled his cap, and said, 'Yes, Ma'am, what can I do for you?'

'Maguire! Have you any plans?'

'No, Ma'am, I came here on speculation and I am hoping to pick up a job in a hotel or something.'

'Would you like to stay with us? You and Brown get on well and I need an extra man on my team. You will help Brown and when I set up a home you can cook for us.'

He didn't need to think about it. He immediately replied, 'I would love to. When do I start?'

'You never finished, Maguire. You work with Brown looking after our luggage and then you are our guardians. Acquire a handgun. Do you know how to use one?'

'The old type, yes. I will have to learn the new one.'

'Good. Tell Brown, and, thank you.'

'My pleasure, Ma'am.'

The weather was cool in Sydney and she dug down into her trunk and put on her finest outdoor attire hoping to impress. On the quayside, Brown was waiting with a hackney with Jill already aboard. He helped, Tricia in, and whispered, 'I am told, M'lady, the *Colonial* hotel is the best.'

'Thank you, Brown. Have you spoken with, Maguire?'

'Yes, Ma'am, and a good choice he is.'

'Thank you again, Brown, you can stay.'

He bowed in the exaggerated way he had adopted with her and stepped back from the cab.

Tricia leaned forward and spoke with the driver. '*The Colonial Hotel*, please.'

The drive across town to the hotel did not take long and the doorman of the hotel helped her and Edwina off the hackney before he held the door for Jill and Nanny.

There was an old-world grandeur about the place and the smell of wood and polish enhanced it. The wooden floors and the long mahogany reception desk had almost been polished beyond their natural life but the glow from the chandeliers helped to embolden it.

While Jill was overseeing the unloading of their luggage the young girl on reception enquired of, Tricia, 'What can I do for you, ma'am?'

She did not remonstrate, but said quietly, 'It is, Lady Patricia Bishop and I want a suite for me and my child and good rooms for my staff.'

The girl stood open-mouthed for a second before saying, 'Excuse me, M'lady, I will speak with the manager.'

She disappeared into an office behind her only to reappear two minutes later with a grey-haired thin man with a beard. He came around the counter, and half bowed. 'Good morning, M'lady. My name is Rodgers and I am the manager. What is it you require of us?'

Although her patience was curdling inside, she said, 'As I explained to the young lady here, I require a suite for myself and my child and rooms for my staff.'

'My apologies, M'lady but we only have the large Sydney suite left for which we charge eleven shillings per night.'

Tricia thought that was disgusting but she did not concede, instead, she said, 'that will do nicely, and my staff?'

'How many are there, M'lady?'

'My maid, my Nanny plus my two guardians. They have been cooped up aboard a ship these last three months so I want the best for them. They will of course have the same menu as me when dining.'

'I will arrange that, M'lady, if you would be so kind as to follow one of my porters he will show you, your maid and Nanny with the little girl to the suite.'

'I wish to see my staff rooms first. Meanwhile, your porter can show my maid and Nanny to the suite and take our baggage.'

'Follow me, M'lady; it is on the third floor.'

She followed him and a porter up to the third floor and was quite amused to see Rodgers in some discomfort on the last flight. The porter opened the door to a room and stepped aside while she entered. Inside she stood with her back to the wall and looked around and it took her only a short time before she said, 'This will do nicely for the men. Have you something more feminine for the ladies?'

'They would have to go down on the second floor, M'lady and more expense.'

'They are worth it. Let us go and look.'

He took her down to the next floor and showed her rooms at the rear of the hotel with which she was satisfied with one more demand. 'Can you put a cot in one of the rooms in case I have to stay away for some reason?'

'In your suite, M'lady, there are two bedrooms one of which is laid out purely for that reason. Your governess will be able to stay there overnight should the occasion arise.'

'Excellent, but put a cot in there anyway.'

While they were going down the stairs to the first floor, she asked him, 'Can I assume, Mr Rodgers, you have storage for our vast amount of luggage which includes bedding from the voyage.'

'Yes, M'lady; this is a common request.'

'And you have a safe?'

'Yes, M'lady.'

Inside her suite, she found Edwina bouncing up and down on her bed in the second bedroom whooping with delight. 'Mammy! Mammy! Am I sleeping in this bed tonight?'

Tricia scooped her up and swung her around. 'Yes, my love, this monster of a bed is yours and Nanny will be sleeping in the other one occasionally. That whopper of a bed out there is mine.'

'How long are we staying, mammy?'

'I don't know, sweetheart. As long as it takes to find your grandfather. Now go and play while I talk to Nanny and Jill.'

Edwina ran across the room and jumped on the bed while Nanny joined Tricia and Jill in the lounge area. After calling room service and ordering coffee she sat on the armchair with Jill and Nanny opposite. 'Ladies, have a rest this afternoon until we prepare for dinner tonight and tomorrow while I am at the Bank with the boys I want you both to go to a local couturier with Edwina and get some suitable outfits for this new country. I am told it is winter here but it feels like summer. I do believe it gets cold at night. Oh! Get me one of those larger brimmed hats we see the ladies wearing. It must be something to do with the sun and bonnets would be useless.'

When they had finished their coffee Jill and Nanny left and Tricia went through to Edwina's room and found her asleep so she curled up beside her and wrapped in the luxury of a proper bed had forty winks.

She was disturbed by the arrival of Brown and Maguire with their day-to-day luggage and they assured her that the heavier stuff was well stored and the money chest was safely in the hotel vault.

Soon after they had left, Jill and Nanny Peters came to help her unpack and prepare for the evening and she advised them to be prepared for a meal with an extravagance of meat and few vegetables as they were difficult to acquire. On the stroke of seven she went down to the restaurant with Edwina.

When they had settled down and she was perusing the menu the maitre d' approached. 'Excuse me, M'lady, but the gentleman over there has asked me to enquire if you and your daughter would join him.'

She looked at where he was pointing and on the other side of the room was Louis Armand with Adele and Celeste. She waived, and said to the maitre d', 'Please tell, M. Armand that he is free to join us as I much prefer this table. It is more private.'

The maitre d' left only to return two minutes later with Louis and his daughters who were delighted to meet their friend Edwina.

Tricia stood and greeted him and he took her hand, bowed and kissed the fingertips. When they were sat side by side with Edwina alongside her Tricia had a quiet word with the maitre d' while the sommelier was taking their order for wine.

'Maitre d', did my staff have the same menu?'

'Yes, M'lady, exactly as you requested.'

'Let them have whatever they ask for but go easy on the drink.'

'I will pass that message through, M'lady.'

'Thank you.'

They once more set about searching the menu and discussing with the girls what they would like.

Orders out of the way, Louis said to Tricia, 'Have you settled in yet?'

'Oh, yes, and what a change from that dingy cabin and the beds are so comfortable but a little behind our hotels back home methinks.'

'You must not forget, Lady Tricia, that it is only a few years ago that this was a penal colony and I think they have come a long way in that short time.'

'You are right of course, Louis, I wonder what long-distance travelling is like here?'

'I have yet to find out but I am travelling north soon.'

'Do you know where?'

'Hunter Valley. It is the wine-growing region in this State.'

'Best of luck, Louis, I am yet to find out where my father was sent.'

Light conversation continued through the meal as Tricia helped Edwina carve up the lovely juicy fillet steak on her plate. Served as a child's portion, at home it would have served an adult. Edwina didn't mind. To her, it was just food.

When the meal was over Louis asked her if they could meet for drinks in the lounge later but Tricia declined. It had been a long day and the comfort of a proper bed inviting. His invitation to dine the next evening was accepted.

—

Enquiries at the Concierge informed her where the bank was but also the department she must go to seek the whereabouts of her father and armed with that knowledge she joined Brown and

Maguire who were waiting with a carriage.

'Where to, M'lady?' enquired Brown.'

'Good morning to you too, Brown.' She handed him a slip of paper. 'We are going to the bank first and then the Colonial Secretary's office.'

Brown had a word with the driver and climbed in alongside Maguire who had the small money chest between his feet and in a cloud of Sydney dust they set off. The journey was not long and they were shown into the Bank manager's office with little delay.

He stood and acknowledged her with the usual protocol and when she was sat down he returned to the deep leather chair behind his desk. 'Mr Connaught, M'lady, what can we do for you?'

She delved into her bag and withdrew a rolled-up document tied with blue ribbon and handed it to him. 'Mr Connaught, I wish to open an account and deposit the contents of that casket with you and this is a Financial Guarantee from the Bank of England should I require further funds.'

He unrolled the letter and had only been reading for a few seconds when his eyes widened and he raised his head and looked at her over his *pinz-nez*. 'And how much pray, is in the casket?'

She reached across, took a pen from his ink tray, dipped it into an inkwell wrote something on a piece of paper and gave it to him. He read it and shook his head in disbelief before reaching behind him and pulling on a cord.

There was an instant knock on the door and a clerk stepped in. 'Yes, Sir?'

'Take this casket, Ellis, and count its contents.'

Brown stepped forward. 'I'm sorry, sir, but we count it in here.'

Connaught sat open-mouthed for a second and thought better of what he was about to say, and said meekly, 'That is alright, go down to that side table with my clerk and you can do it there.'

Brown nodded and touched his brow. 'Thank you, sir; I have M'lady's best interest at heart.'

Brown and Maguire took the casket to the other end of the room and Brown gave the clerk the key. In silence, they counted the numerous notes and coins and it was fifteen minutes before the clerk came over to the Manager and whispered in his ear.

Words were exchanged and the clerk left the room before he addressed her. 'Lady Bishop, all is in order and I am glad to accept your cash and the Financial Guarantee from your bank. It will only take a few minutes to get the paperwork sorted and then we are in business. Tell me, do you intend to stay in Sydney?'

'I don't know, Mr Connaught, I come to Australia to seek my father who was despatched here a few years ago so who knows where I'm going?'

'Go to the Colonial Office and ask for the Principal Superintendent of Convicts. They keep a note of all arrivals and their individual sentences.'

Before she could answer the clerk returned with a bundle of papers and the next few minutes were taken up with signing and reading and exchanging notes. When the last piece had been signed and stamped, Connaught said, as he slid it over the desk. 'It has been nice doing business with you, Lady Bishop, and here is a promissory note from us should you need to travel to other places. We are recognised as the major bank in Australia and other smaller local banks will happily oblige.'

Tricia stood up, and replied, 'Thank you, Mr Connaught, you have been very helpful. May we continue to do business in the future?'

He came around the desk and he obligingly showed her through the bank and out to the waiting carriage.

After he had helped her into the carriage, Brown enquired, 'Where to next, ma'am?'

'That took longer than I thought, Brown. Take me back to the hotel and we shall have a relaxing half-hour with coffee before we go to the Colonial Office and hire this carriage for the rest of our stay. I'm sure he will appreciate it.'

Brown knuckled his brow and climbed up alongside the driver.

———

Having got rid of the main burden of her security only Brown accompanied her to the Colonial Office and she was shown into a small office where a local clerk was assigned to help with her enquiry. After a few minutes of talking over the situation and making notes the clerk disappeared leaving Tricia and Brown to chat amongst themselves for over ten minutes before he returned.

Once settled behind the desk, he said, 'Lady Bishop, sorry to have kept you but I have found one, Edward Cartwright, a head Gardner, who arrived here in 1843. Does that fit?'

'Oh, yes, that is my father,' said, Tricia, 'the date and his profession fit.'

'His profession served him well, ma'am. He was assigned to an agricultural farm in the Hunter Valley district and after two years was given a Ticket of Leave which is parole in any other language. However...' Tricia hated that word but remained straight-faced as he continued, '... after a short while he was given his Certificate of Freedom which leads me to believe he is still in that area as that is his last known address.'

'Could you enlighten me a little more?'

'Yes, he was living on the Heathdale Estate in the Lovedale area. You will have to go to the local offices in the town of Cessnock for further information.'

'Could you write that down for me, please?'

'By all means, Ma'am.'

He duly obliged and gave her the note with added information as to how to get there.

She read it and sighed. 'We must catch a boat to Newcastle?'

'Yes, Ma'am, it is the safest and the quickest way to travel and more comfortable but you must arrange transport for the forty-odd miles across to Cessnock and the Lovedale locality.'

She slipped the note into her bag and stood up. 'Thank you, you have been most helpful.'

He half bowed. 'My pleasure, Ma'am.' He then came around his desk to show her out. Outside the carriage was waiting and whisked them off to the hotel and on the way she handed the note to Brown, and said, 'What do you think?'

He looked at it and after a few moments replied, 'A bit of

both. By boat and across country. I think we should do the boat and organise the cross-country bit when we get to Newcastle. A few days to organise the boat or do you wish to rest awhile?'

'I don't know, Brown. My heart says let's go and my brain says, take your time.'

'I think your brain is most definitely correct, Lady Bishop. Let us get used to the way things work here and seek information about the country at the same time, and hopefully, we won't rush in blind.'

'Brown! You are so wise. So be it. Have you made any plans for your future?'

'It is early days yet, but Jill says to wait and see as it would be awful to do that trip home.'

'I can understand that Brown, it must have been terrible for the steerage passengers. Brown!'

'Yes, Ma'am.'

'Get me to my destination and then you can do as you wish and if you get married I will pay as promised.'

Brown cupped his chin in his hand and shook his head, before he said sheepishly, 'Thank you, ma'am but both myself and Jill wish to stay with you and we will see what the prospects are when you are settled.'

She pointed to the driver. 'And while you are seeking information chat to our driver. He looks as if he's been around awhile.'

The hotel Concierge was their best informant and following his advice the ferry was booked to take them to Newcastle and then cruise up the Hunter River to a little town called Morpeth from where they would travel the remaining few miles to Cessnock and the Lovedale area.

Four days later Brown and Maguire had their work cut out to get the luggage down to the terminal for 8.00 p.m. but they managed with minutes to spare and as the paddle-wheeled steamer pulled away from the quay they were distributing it into the cabins.

Outside the harbour heads they experienced choppy seas but a fair wind wafted them merrily along and immediately after breakfast on Saturday morning when they went out on deck they saw the Newcastle Heads. The sixty-mile journey had taken only eight hours and it was a little after six o'clock when they docked.

It being low tide the steamer could not proceed on an upward river course until after 10.00 a.m. To pass the time after breakfast they disembarked for a stroll around the quayside.

They left on time and a mile or so above Newcastle the river is barred by flats where vessels constantly become grounded. To prevent such a casualty they went at a steady pace at not more than half speed. Over the flats, the Hunter River spreads itself into a magnificent lake spangled here and there with miniature islands of no great beauty in themselves but attractive as agreeable features in a pretty landscape of which the distant mountains bathed in purple dyes are the most varied and captivating. The different bends at these flats looked like many rivers but they are merely several channels and on one of the banks left dry by the receding tide a large flock of pelicans were sunning their wings and rejoicing in the genial warmth that had succeeded the cold and blustery weather of the past few days.

For weary miles the banks of the Hunter are lonely, monotonous and unprepossessing, the first indication of industry and civilisation being discernible at a spot called Tomigo. The scenery began to improve and became more evident as they advanced. There were many circular islets but they had to take shelter from the rain that descended in torrents at a time when they were threading through the cultivated shores of the Hunter.

They passed the village of Raymond Terrace a pleasant spot at the confluence of the William River and the Hunter. The charm of the landscape around the village was marred by a vast number of decayed spindling trees on the banks on either side although the area appeared densely populated by farms.

The limit of the Hunter River to which the steamer could go is Morpeth, rising in picturesque liveliness from the water's edge and they arrived at 3.30 p.m. with storehouses and Inns dotted here and there and the lowlands around were like the Broads of England.

It was late and they hired a local teamster to transport their luggage to the *Globe Inn* which had been recommended to them by the Captain of the steamer. They managed to squeeze in the last three rooms available but a bonus was the large storage facilities for the luggage.

The Inn had recently been renovated and Tricia was pleased with the accommodation and typical of Australia the food was good but meat-based. Brown, Rory and Edwina loved this and Brown and Maguire enjoyed life in the Bar later mixing with the locals. While they were jollying they enquired after Tricia's father but nobody had heard of anyone by the name of Cartwright but they found a local haulier who would transport them for as long as they wished to their eventual destination.

After breakfast, the next day he was waiting with a cart for the luggage and a carriage for the ladies to take them to East Maitland a journey of only five miles but the roads were of dried mud and sand and negotiated at a walking pace.

Brown was upfront with the driver while Maguire travelled with the luggage cart and an hour and a half later they arrived in East Maitland. On the journey, Tricia had noticed an increase in the diversity away from arable farming towards areas of vines.

"That explains why, Louis, was sent for," was her first thought, "They need his expertise."

They stayed long enough to have some refreshments and make enquiries around the Inns and shops but yet again, no one had heard of a Cartwright. They continued their journey to the township of Cessnock but this time Edwina insisted on sitting up front between Brown and the driver and it seemed like she spent most of the time asking questions but Brown was patient and responded with vigour with hoots of laughter coming frequently towards Tricia and the ladies. They arrived a little after 4.30 p.m. and booked into a large, stone, two-storey Inn cum hotel called the *'Wheatsheaf Arms'* a substantial building which boasted a lofty coffee-room and they found the accommodation most pleasant.

The coffee room was their first thought and they enjoyed a light tea and coffee before retiring to their rooms prior to making themselves ready for the evening, but before she went Tricia enquired of the receptionist if he knew of the Heathdale Estate and Edward Cartwright.

'Yes, ma'am, I certainly do,' he responded, 'Ted Cartwright comes here often when he does the monthly shop. May I enquire who is seeking him?'

'His daughter, Patricia, and I have just arrived from England. Can you tell me how to get there? We shall venture out that way tomorrow.'

'Yes, ma'am. You travel from here on the North Road towards the Lovedale area. When you are almost there watch out for the road westward to Broke. Heathdale Estate is a few miles along it and I hear they are doing well unlike a lot of others.'

'Thank you, that sounds like a good day out tomorrow.'

'You will be staying here then?'

'Yes, I intend to use this as my base until we can find permanent accommodation.'

'And your staff?'

'They will be staying also and will be treated as guests. It took a lot of courage to leave their homeland and remain faithful to me, so they deserve it.'

'So be it, ma'am. Enjoy your stay. Oh! Before you go I have a note for you left by a French gentleman earlier.' He reached under the counter, fished out the note, and handed it to her. 'Here you are.'

She took it and walked a few paces from them before she read it and was not surprised to see it was from, Louis. 'I'm sure he's following me and now he invites me to dinner tonight.'

She had a little smile to herself and continued upstairs.

That evening she asked Nanny Peters to be her companion so that Brown and Jill could enjoy each other's company albeit with Maguire in attendance and as soon as she entered the dining room she was met by a waiter who showed her across to Louis.

Louis stood up and kissed her outstretched hand, 'Good evening, Lady Tricia, a pleasure to have your company.'

'Good evening, Louis, it is a pleasure to be here.'

The waiter held her chair for her while she made herself comfortable. Nanny and Edwina sat opposite with Adele and Celeste. When she was settled, Louis said, 'I took the liberty, Lady Tricia, to order the wine having remembered your taste from our last meeting.'

'You are welcome, Louis, how did you know I was here?'

'I was making enquiries at the desk when I saw your entry in the register. Is your father near here?'

'Yes, he is about ten miles up the road. Let us eat. Nanny, order what you like and partake of the wine if you wish.'

Nanny nodded and mouthed, 'Thank you.'

Their meal was savoury and delicious with wasteful extravagance which was too much for the ladies but the men enjoyed it as they did the blooming barmaid with long corkscrew ringlets.

As time went on Tricia saw Edwina yawning and she spoke to, Nanny. 'Nanny, can you take Edwina up to bed? I want to discuss some business with Louis. I will only be few minutes behind you.'

'Yes, ma'am, I will ask Jill to help.'

She went across and had a word with Jill, who stood up to leave when Brown and Maguire decided to retire also and accompanied the ladies out of the room. They had only been gone two minutes when there was loud screams and two gunshots were heard. There were more high childish screams and crying and another shot was fired. Alarmed, Tricia stood up as did Louis and they made for the door in time to see Brown run down the stairs with his gun in his hand and dart out of the main entrance. A minute later there was two quick shots and silence.

Tricia picked up her skirts and ran for the stairs with Louis behind her. At the top, she turned to the right and ran along the corridor where she could see her room door open and Nanny leaning against the jamb her head in her hands sobbing.

'What is it, Nanny?' shouted Tricia. She ran to her. 'What is the matter?'

Nanny pointed into the room, and said, 'It is Edwina and Jill.'

Tricia let go of her and just as she was about to enter the room,

Maguire came to the door and holding her by the shoulders he stopped her from entering. 'Don't go in, Ma'am, please. It is not nice. Jill and Edwina have both been shot. Jill is dead.'

Tricia was shaking and crying. 'Edwina! I must go to her.'

She wriggled and pushed past him and almost fell into the room and she stopped in her tracks at the sight that met her. Jill was lying stretched out as if she was reaching for Edwina who was curled up, crying and holding her tummy. By the open window lay a tramp like figure shot through the head.

Tricia dropped to her knees and cuddled Edwina who screamed when she was moved. 'What is it, darling,' said Tricia, 'show mammy.'

Edwina just cried and rolled from side to side holding her tummy unable to speak when Tricia saw the bloodstain below Edwina's hand. She gently moved the hand and saw the blood running freely and the stain getting larger.

'Somebody help,'she shouted. 'Get a Doctor!'

A suited man with a large moustache and sideburns pushed his way into the room and knelt beside Tricia. 'Doctor Malone, ma'am. Let me see.'

Tricia moved to one side and as she did so she heard a long sigh from Edwina. The doctor felt for a pulse and leaned forward with an ear to her mouth before he looked up at Tricia and shook his head. 'I am sorry, ma'am, she has just passed away. It is most likely loss of blood.'

Tricia knelt with her chin on her chest and wept before she reached down and pulled Edwina to her and cuddled her.

At that moment there was a noise in the corridor. It was Brown making his way through the gawping onlookers followed by two policemen. He pushed through the door and went over to Tricia. He eased Edwina away and helped Tricia to her feet and she threw herself into his arms and wept. He held her close but said nothing, feeling her grief passing over to him and binding with his as he was also grieving the death of his beloved, Jill.

He put an arm around Tricia's shoulder and led her out of the room collecting Nanny as he did so. He caught the eye of the manager and called him over.

'Get me another suite for Lady Bishop.' He flicked his head backwards. 'That one is finished with.'

'By all means,' he said, 'use this one,' he pointed to the one opposite. 'I will send for the key.'

A heavy hand landed on Brown's shoulder and he looked round to see who the offender was. It was a sergeant from the Military Mounted Police. 'One moment, sir, you were here for the incident and you have a gun?'

Brown nodded. 'Yes.'

'Give me your gun and come with me,' said the Sergeant,

'Can you give me a minute, please, sergeant, I wish to take Lady Bishop to her room where she can rest. I am her guardian.'

'Give me the gun,' was the sergeant's abrupt reply, 'and when you're done get yourself over to me.'

Brown reached inside his jacket but the sergeant was taking no chances and held his own gun ready as Brown handed his gun over butt first. 'Don't lose it, sergeant.'

The sergeant took it off him and turned his attention to Maguire who was being held across the corridor just as a housemaid appeared with a key. She unlocked the door and stood to one side. Brown scooped Tricia up and went in followed by Nanny. They took her through to the bedroom and Brown laid her gently on the bed. From here on Nanny took control and put a cover over Tricia who was weeping uncontrollably.

'Brown,' said Nanny, 'you can go now, I will look after her. How about you? Are you feeling alright?'

Brown nodded towards, Tricia. 'Now that she's safe I'm not sure. Jill and I were going to get married. Now I have nothing.'

Nanny put an arm on Brown's shoulder. 'Don't worry, she will look after you when she gets better. She is still your baby like you once said.'

'You're right, Nanny, and you have a new job. We had better call you by your real name, what is it?'

Nanny blushed, and said coyly, 'April.'

Brown allowed a smile. 'Not an Aries are you?'

'Yes,' said April.

'I'd better watch it,' said Brown, 'Rams are dangerous. I've got to go now; we don't want the fuzz in here.'

She conjured a smile from somewhere and waved him away as Tricia groaned and sobbed fitfully, pounding the pillow.

A constable was waiting for him and he took Brown downstairs and into a side room where Maguire was being held and the Sergeant greeted him. 'You're, Brown, are you not?'

'Yes, sergeant, I am.'

Give me your version of events, Brown.'

'On the request of our patron Lady Bishop, Sergeant, we were taking the child, Edwina to bed…'

'Does it take four of you to take a child to bed?'

'… We were all retiring. Myself, Maguire and Jill who is, sorry, was the companion and lady's maid to Lady Bishop, were just tagging along with Nanny. Edwina ran on ahead as she does. Jill ran after her and they got to the door together and at the very moment Jill turned the key Edwina burst into the room with Jill close behind. Edwina screamed and Jill went to grab her when one of the bastards shot her. Maguire pushed his way in and shot him while the other fiend was trying to get out of the window and as he did so he took a wild shot under his arm and shot Edwina and slipped away before we could stop him. I ran downstairs and outside just as he rode around the side of the building. I fired two shots which were effective.'

'They certainly were, Brown. Your version matches that of Maguire, and you have nothing to worry about.' He gave Brown and Maguire their guns and handed Brown a leather saddlebag. 'That's what they stole from the room, and let me add, you have done the State a favour. Those two bushrangers were high on our wanted list. May I ask what you are doing here in Australia?'

'Lady Bishop is here to find her father and we are her staff. We have been here just over a week and landed in Morpeth only yesterday. Some welcome that was!'

'Who is the lady's father?'

'I believe it to be, Edward Cartwright,' said Brown.

'Cartwright. I know him. He lives out Lovedale way on the Broke road.'

'That is the information we have, yes, sergeant.'

'You can go now Brown, and you, Maguire, and with shooting like that, Brown, do you fancy joining the police?'

Brown shook his head. 'I have a mission to accomplish, sergeant, and she is my first thought.'

'You must think a lot of her, Brown?'

'I do. We all do.'

'Nice to hear.'

When they arrived back upstairs the mortuary people were there and carrying Jill's body from the room. Brown stopped them. 'Let me see her one last time, please.' They nodded approval and he pulled the cover from her face. With a deep sob, he kissed his fingers and touched her on the forehead. 'Love you, baby.' He turned away quickly with a tear in his eye and they continued with their sorrowful mission. They returned to take young Edwina's body away and the police were satisfied their investigation was complete and they left leaving April, Maguire and Brown to clean up and transfer Tricia's wardrobe and other goods to the other suite.

Tricia had fallen into a fitful sleep and Brown stepped up to the plate. 'April, you sleep in the maids room. I will stay in an armchair here with Lady Tricia. Rory, you're on your own in our room. Is that alright?'

'Do you want a break during the night?'

'No, Rory, I'll be alright. I will probably fall asleep anyway.'

Rory and April set about getting things ready and when she was finished Brown extinguished the candles except for one and stretched out in the armchair on watching brief.

April was the first to rise and she went about her business quietly. When she was ready she gave Brown a nudge. He rubbed his eyes, pushed himself into a sitting position, and whispered to April, 'How is she?'

'Not good, she is not taking this very well. I looked in a few times and she was tossing and turning and I think having nightmares but as you can see she sleeps now.'

'April, call room service and set up breakfast for you and Lady T. Rory and I will go down to the dining room. Is that alright?'

'Yes, Mr Brown, I have everything ready. You buzz off and I will tend to Lady T as you call her.'

'Thanks, Na…, April. I'll leave you to it.'

An hour later, Brown, Rory and April gathered in the lounge area of the suite. Brown was the first to speak. 'April, how is she? Did she take breakfast?'

'No. I tried everything. She will not drink or eat and she wouldn't even let me clean her up. She just cried and battered the pillow and told me to go. What are we to do?'

Brown rubbed his chin and took a walk around the room deep in thought when he stopped. 'I know what we'll do. Rory, hire a horse and take a message out to her father. Tell him the story and ask him to come quick. She needs to drink if nothing else. April and I will look after her, Can you do that?'

'Yes, but how do I pay for the horse, Browny?'

'We put it on the bill. Let's go and see the manager and he can help us. Paying will not be a problem.' He turned to April. 'April, is there anything we can get you for Lady T or yourself?'

'Send for some smelling salts. It is worth a try. Brown—Why don't you go with, Rory?'

He pointed to the bedroom. 'My job is to protect that one and that's what I'm doing. I should have done it yesterday.'

'But you couldn't. You were not to know, and normally I would have been on my own. I owe it to Jill that I am still alive.'

'He stood in front of her and patted her on the shoulders. 'You are right, April, but you have to feel for Lady T. She brought her child all this way to see her granddad and this happens. What sort of country have we come to?'

'A new one, Brown, and just as ugly as the one we left.'

'We don't have bushrangers in England.'

'Point taken, Brown, now get on with it.'

'I'll be back shortly, April. Smelling salts, you said?'

—

The road north from Cessnock was good having been recently constructed and Maguire accompanied by the hired wagon driver who had volunteered to go with him made good time. They reached the junction with the road out to the town of Broke in an hour and a half and were glad to see this road was equally well made although not often used as was obvious by the overgrowth.

A few miles further on and a small battered sign directed them to Heathdale Estate and they arrived at the modest but well built colonial style house after two hours.

They had been spotted approaching and a well-built man with thinning hair and a barrel chest was stood on the veranda waiting for them.

He was in no hurry and waited until they mounted the steps before, he said, 'Good afternoon, gentlemen, what can I do for you?'

Maguire held his hand out. 'Good afternoon, sir, I am seeking a Mister Edward Cartwright.'

'I am he, sir.'

'Mister Cartwright, I have some stressful news for you. May we go inside and speak?'

'Of course.'

He made to go into the house when Maguire stopped him. 'Could you give my companion some refreshment, sir? We have travelled non-stop for two hours to reach you.'

Ted pointed towards some chairs on the veranda. 'Take a seat there, matey, and I'll send something out.' He went indoors and Maguire followed him and when they were seated inside a small study Maguire wasted no time. 'Mister Cartwright, I come with news of your daughter, Patricia.'

Ted leaned forward wide eyed. 'And what of her, what has happened?'

Maguire told him the story of events the previous night before finishing, '... And this morning she is in deep distress and lies prone in her bed and will not eat or drink no matter how much we coax her so we decided that our only course of action was to find you.'

Ted stood up. 'Give me time to get ready and I will come with my rig but first I must tell my family.'

An hour later, they set off at a steady trot for the long journey back. Because of the rig, it took them a little longer and they arrived a little after seven o'clock.

Maguire left the horses with the driver and showed Ted through the hotel and up to Tricia's room. A light tap on the door and they went in to see Brown sat holding his head in his hands and April fussing about straightening cushions.

Brown jumped up, and April crossed the room and joined him and Maguire introduced them. 'Mister Cartwright, this is Brown, M'lady's guardian, and this is April, her maid and companion, formerly the Governess for young Edwina her daughter who sadly died in the incident which you have been told about?'

Ted looked puzzled. 'Yes, I was informed but did you say, M'lady. Who is that?'

'I am sorry, Mister Cartwright, you didn't know?' said Maguire.

Brown jumped in. 'Mister Cartwright, your daughter's full title is, Lady Patricia Bishop. She was married to the late Lord Clifford Bishop of Longbottom, a wealthy Mill owner from Preston. He sadly died and Lady Tricia made up her mind to come and look for you. We were part of the household staff and she engaged us to accompany her.'

'I think she has a lot to tell me when she's well. Lady! I can't believe that. I knew she was good but, Lady! Where is she? I must go to her.'

'She is in the bedroom, Mister Cartwright,' said April, 'if you will come with me. She was asleep when I left her.'

Ted smiled at her, and said, 'I don't know whether to bow or not.'

'She may have a title, Mister Cartwright, but she is one of us and I don't think it worries her one jot.'

She went to the bedroom, turned the doorknob slowly, and

peered around the door. She looked back at Ted and with a nod of her head signalled to him to follow her in. April stood to one side as Ted approached Tricia and sat on a chair close to her. He stretched out a hand and stroked her hair, and whispered, 'Tricky, wake up, it's Daddy.'

There was a moan from Tricia and she sleepily reached up and rubbed her head where Ted had touched her. 'Wake up, Tricky, it's your daddy,' he said once more.

She moaned again, and said, 'Go away, I don't want any.'

'Come on, Tricky, it's me, your Dad. You come all this way and you tell me to go away. Wakey! Wakey!'

He leaned forward just as she opened her eyes. She stared for a moment before reality took over. She jerked upright and looked again before she reached out to Ted, calling, 'Daddy! Daddy!'

He wrapped his arms around her and pulled her towards him and while he was looking over her shoulder, he signalled April to bring a drink. She poured a glass of water and brought it around to, Ted. He looked at it, and said, 'Is it good stuff?'

'The management insists it is boiled fresh water. Only the best for someone in her position, although she demands that we have the same.'

Ted picked up the glass and held it to Tricia's lips. 'Come on, lass, get some of this down you.'

She tentatively took a sip and Ted pushed her to take more. 'You must drink, love. It is dry in this country and water is a necessity especially in the summer.'

She drank some more and said, quietly to Ted, 'Daddy, I'm happy to see you. My life has taken a bad turn. Your beautiful granddaughter has been taken from us. She was so looking forward to seeing you.'

He put the glass down and hugged her. 'There, there, baby, I will miss seeing her also. When you feel better, you and your crew come with me and she will be laid to rest under a beautiful tree where you can visit every day. Now you must eat.'

'I want a cup of tea first and then Jill can help me dress.'

'Tricia, darling, Jill was taken from us also. Your good lady,

April has assumed her duties.'

Her head flopped onto his shoulder, and she sobbed. 'I had forgotten about that.'

Ted beckoned April over. 'April, get Tricia a cup of tea and then we will organise dinner. You and the lads must be starving.'

'I will send the lads, as you call them, to dinner and I will get room service to fetch us something. Will that be alright?'

'Don't ask me, love, you're in charge. Can madam afford it?'

April nodded and left the room.

A warm bath and a change of clothes freshened her up but feeling rather crestfallen Tricia only managed a light dinner, while Ted, on Tricia's encouragement, indulged in a good fillet steak. April was more conservative and like Tricia had a light meal of local fish and salad. Dinner over, Brown and Maguire joined them for an update which had been discussed over dinner.

'Tomorrow,' said Tricia, 'my father is going on ahead to prepare for us. I'm assured there is plenty of room in the house. When we are ready, we will follow.'

'Why don't you travel with your father, Lady Tricia?' said Brown.'

'He tells me that the carriage is much more comfortable than a jolty old rig. I think he wants to tidy up first.' They all laughed despite the feeling of hidden grief hanging over them, and she continued, 'and I am told you already have your sleeping arrangements for tonight. As for now, you, Brown, and Maguire can go and enjoy the bar while I have a natter with my Dad. April did you want to go with the men?'

'No, M'lady, I will stay hidden in the background.'

During their chat, Ted told Tricia of his new relationship from which he had two children a boy and a girl, which came about when the Master of the estate had died and, Ted, who had his, Ticket of Leave, and arable land experience helped his former mistress and they fell in love. He explained to Tricia that they were living over the broom, which was a term for living together.

'Daddy,' she said, 'you can get married now and I look

forward to meeting her. Mam would be pleased for you, as I am.'

He hugged her. 'Thank you, baby, I hoped you would but I didn't know how to tell you. I couldn't come home and I knew Kearsley would kick you out so I didn't know where you were. It's bedtime now, I have an early start.'

'Is your room alright, dad?'

'Yes, love. Can you afford all this?'

'I will tell you more when we get settled.'

Tricia went through to her bedroom with April and Ted left only to be replaced by, Brown, who settled into an armchair with his feet on a stool and his gun handy on a side table.

—

Ted, true to his word had an early start and Tricia still feeling depressed did not rush and it was after lunch before they set out for the ten-mile drive to Heathdale. Brown was upfront on the carriage and Maguire stayed with the cart and their belongings.

It was a steady drive and after a little over two hours there was a huge sigh of relief when they finally turned up the dusty drive of the Heathdale Estate.

Tricia saw the acres of vines and she wondered how their wine business was doing because Louis had told her they needed help. Around the house, were a few acres of arable farming, which she guessed was necessary to survive. No wheat just row upon row of vines. When they stopped she stood up in the carriage and looked around and she liked the rolling countryside with the Blue Mountains on the horizon.

Brown opened the door and helped her down. 'Do you like it?' he said.

Tricia kept hold of his hand, looked him in the eye, and said, 'Brown—you are my rock. Thank you for all you have done. I don't know how I would have managed without you.'

Brown coloured slightly and went suddenly shy. 'I... I don't know what to say, M'lady.'

'Keep it to yourself, Brown, but I want you to stay. I will look out for you but give me time to sort things out, and, yes, I do like it here. It looks peaceful but I expect it is hard to survive. I'm rather looking forward to the challenge, and, Brown. Buy that carriage and horses from the carter will you? I will give him a promissory note, which he can take to the New South Wales Bank. I think we're going to doing a lot of travelling.'

He watched her as she walked across to Ted who was waiting on the veranda with an attractive comfortable woman with long grey streaked hair. Ted hugged Tricia and asked how she was before he introduced her. 'Tricia, this is Shirley my intended, and this young man is, Thomas, my step-son who is six and then Carrie who is three and Tiddles on the end, who is two. They are my children or rather our children.'

He put an arm around Shirley's shoulder and gently eased her forward. 'Shirley, this is my daughter, Patricia, who, I can assure you is twice as tall as she was when I last saw her.'

Tricia took hold of Shirley's hands. 'It is lovely to meet you, Shirley. Dad told me all about you last night.' Shirley hesitated, unsure how to reply when Tricia sensing her uncertainty, said, 'Don't be alarmed, Shirley, you may call me Tricia. We are family. That posh tosh is only for when it suits me.'

Shirley visibly relaxed, and said, 'Welcome to Heathdale, Tricia, I hope you will be happy here, let me show you around.'

'Shirley!' said, Tricia. 'You don't mind me calling you, Shirley, do you? After all, you are going to be my step-mum.'

'As you said, Tricia, we are family.'

'Oh, good, can I meet the children?'

'Most certainly, let's go inside and you can talk to them.'

She led the way in, the children followed, and when they were safely inside Ted spoke to Brown. 'Thank you for looking after her, Brown. You and your gang take the cart around to the barn, and then we will show you your lodgings. The carter and his buddy will be leaving tomorrow I take it?'

'Yes, Mister Cartwright that is what they wish. They both have families in Maitland.'

'We have a comfortable shack by the stables which is where they will be staying tonight and we will unload first thing in the morning.' He was about to go inside when he saw April who was still sitting in the carriage. 'Miss Peters,' he called, 'come and join the ladies inside. Let the boys sort that lot out.'

She collected Tricia's things, took Brown's hand, and climbed from the carriage and followed Ted.

Inside, she was shown into the lounge where she found Tricia sat on the floor playing with the children her teaching skills once more coming to the fore. Tricia looked up at April and blushed. 'Oh! April, I am sorry.' She scrambled to her feet. 'Come and join us. Take a seat there on the sofa.—Shirley! This is April my friend and travelling companion. She is also a very proficient Governess who has been acting as my Lady's maid.'

Shirley stood. 'April, sit by me. Would you like tea or coffee?'

April sat next to Shirley and replied, 'Tea, please. It's such a long time since I had a good cup of tea.'

'You will get that here. Tricia's father was a good teacher in that respect as well as a gardener.'

When she had settled Ted left to check on the lads and Shirley rang a lobster pot bell. The housemaid entered. 'Yes, miss?'

'Abbey, dear, take the children out to play.'

'Yes, miss.'

When the children had gone, they sat for five minutes swapping small talk about weather and travel when Tricia, with a complete change of subject, said, 'April, in light of the current circumstances would you like to become the Governess to Shirley's children?'

There was a pause while April unravelled her thoughts, and then said, 'Lady Tricia, it is with regret I have to say that I have been offered a position of Governess by someone else which I accepted on the understanding that you were safe first.'

Tricia sat open-mouthed for a moment before she responded. 'Don't tell me. It wouldn't be a Frenchman by any chance?'

April nodded. 'I am sorry, Lady Tricia, but he approached me on the day we were waiting for your father. I told him it was too early to make a decision but it would be on the understanding he could wait.'

'April, that is wonderful news,' said Tricia, 'he is a lovely man and I am sure you will be happy. I must hurry and sort myself out.'

At that moment there was a knock on the door and Ted burst into. 'Tricia, a messenger has delivered a letter from the Funeral Directors and they have arranged the funeral for next Monday.'

Tricia's hand went to her heart, she took a deep breath, and while crying inside with just a solitary tear appearing, she said, 'Shirley, I must go for a lie-down, I feel quite faint.'

Shirley turned to face, Ted, and said sternly, 'Edward! You could have been a little more discreet.'

He knew he was in trouble when she used his full name and he backed tactfully from the room while they gathered Tricia's things and Shirley took her up to her room.

—

After dinner, they sat out on the veranda that went all round the property. Tricia and Ted sat apart from the others as she gave him a quick rundown on her life after he was transported and when she had finished, she inquired, 'Dad, how are things on this estate?'

'We are holding our own as are other landowners around here. What makes it hard is the brewing of the wine. Don't get me wrong we can brew the wine but then we have to transport it to Sydney. We do that by boat but we are each doing it in small quantities and the profit is small and the wines are all different. We need to improve our output somehow and get a balance of the brew so that we can sell the name. I must add that I do have a customer in Sydney that likes our wine.'

Tricia sat for a moment deliberating before, she said, 'Dad, I think I have an answer to your problem. April's new employer, M. Armand, will be our help. I will set up a meeting with him after the funeral on Monday. I need one of your workers to take a message to him.'

'How can he help, Tricia?'

'He is a wine expert. A vineyard owner sent for him to advise them on improving the growth of the vines. He told me a lot but you must speak with him. Meanwhile, I have to find a replacement for April and we must also increase your household staff while we are here and I have to find employment for Maguire.'

'Tricia, there are vineyards all around us for sale because of our problem. Would you like to buy one?'

'I must consider that, Dad, but first I must speak with M. Armand.'

'This Maguire, what does he do?'

'He is an extraordinary chef. I employed him on the ship and then took him on to assist, Brown.'

'Can he help out in the kitchen here? He might teach our cook a thing or two.'

'You can ask him. He is on my staff so I will pay his salary. Before we join the others tell me about these little bungalows you have around the property.'

'It's a bit of a long story, Tricia, but many years ago land here was allotted to genuine immigrants by the State Governors and they were also allotted convicts to work for them for no wages only their upkeep so huts were built for them.'

'You were one of them, Dad?'

'Yes, but I was a lucky one. I was, because of my skills, allotted here and they were one of the better employers who looked after their staff and even gave us pocket money and good lodgings. Because arable farming was unsustainable they changed to vines, and I came into my own and this estate became a success. You know the rest and how I came to be with Shirley,' he pointed over to his left, 'see that second bungalow there? That was mine in the early years. I heard of some convicts who had to live in hollow trees and were given no clothes. Some ran away and became bushrangers.'

'In the peak season when you have to pick the grapes how do you manage?'

'I have my three permanent workers and in the picking season I employ the local indigenous people and a lot of people come from Sydney and Newcastle for the extra money. We use the bungalows and shacks to house them. The locals make their own camp and they work well but they do have a peculiar trait, especially the younger ones. They tend to wander off and disappear for a couple of days. They call it a walk-about. You get used to it. They just come back as if nothing happened.'

'These indigenous people, do they speak English?'

'Broken English learned through time. They have been here for thousands of years and have many tribes that speak their own dialect. The local tribe in the Newcastle - Cessnock district are the Wonnerrua, with sub-tribes who have been reduced in numbers by smallpox and tribal in-fighting.'

She sat for a moment making mental notes before, she said, 'That is interesting, but Dad, apart from that, there is one thing that bothers me.'

'What's that, Tricia?'

'What if, Mam, were still alive?'

'I wondered when it would come to that.—Tricia, dearest, I remained above the temptation to wander until one day I had word down the grapevine about your mother's demise from a lady who was detained on the same prison ship. They lost half the convicts in a month because of diphtheria. You see the convicts are a close bunch and pass on messages and the like amongst themselves. After that, I made enquiries through my employer and when on a visit to Sydney he was able to corroborate the facts. I've been worried sick about you ever since but getting back to England before my fourteen years was up was out of the question.'

'But, Dad, you have been given your Certificate of Freedom.'

'Yes, lass, but that is only freedom here.'

Tricia nodded. 'Oh, I see.—Daddy, I'm glad you're happy and I like Shirley, so get married with my love.'

'Thank you, dearest. Now let's join the others.'

—

The funeral was a drawn-out affair and Tricia wondered if the Parson was related to one Isaiah Bishop who was well known for his long sermons. Later while stood at the graveside of Jill she leaned against Brown and held on to his arm with a tear merging. She was sad for the loss of Jill but she felt for Brown also.

After arrangements were made for the transportation of Edwina's coffin to Heathdale in the morning where a plot had been prepared, they retired to the *'Wheatsheaf Arms.'*

The 'Wake' was a subdued affair where friends and guests alike stood in small groups passing the time with small talk and discussed everything except the incident when Tricia with Brown close by took M. Armand to one side.

'Yes, Lady Tricia, what is it you wish to discuss?'

'Louis! I have spoken with my father about the situation in the vineyards and he needs your professional advice to improve his vines, but there is also a problem with the brewing and delivery side of it which is making profits mediocre. They have to transport it themselves to Sydney. What do you suggest?'

'A common problem, Lady Tricia, and one I think we can solve.'

'How do you mean, Louis?'

He looked around the room and lowered his voice. 'We need to invest in a Winery.'

'What are they?'

'If they grow the grapes and sell them to us and we brew the wine and sell it as a brand it will benefit both us and them. It becomes even more beneficial if you have larger estates. Could you afford it?'

'I will make it even better, Louis. You organise it and help my father and I will become a fifty-one per cent to your forty-nine per cent part-owner with you in a Winery.'

'Lady Tricia, let us go for a walk and discuss this further.'

'Certainly, Louis, I would love to stretch my legs.'

'Will your shadow be with us?'

'Don't worry, he is very respectful of his position and not one word will pass his lips.'

The evening had closed in but the weather was mild and they had only walked a short distance from the hotel when they began to talk in earnest. Many words were said and they stopped occasionally to push a point with gestures but no voices were raised and when they turned to venture back to the hotel, Tricia, said, 'I am happy with that, Louis, and it has just occurred to me that you have another job on the side now.'

'What's that Lady Tricia, you're not suggesting I would hide anything from you?'

'Not at all, Louis, but you can carry on with your current position of advising the farmers on how to improve their output which will benefit both of us. Nice one!'

'You miss nothing, do you? While we discuss additional things, Lady Tricia, did you know that the *'Wheatsheaf Arms'* is up for sale?'

She stopped and looked up at him. 'No! But I know someone who may be interested.'

'Do you now? Is the hospitality thing your forte?'

'No, but I have a chef who may be.'

They arrived at the front of the hotel and they paused on the step and Tricia, said, 'I will leave you to make the arrangements for our business, Louis. Keep me informed and I have no problem with fifty-fifty and I will get funds moved here to cover it.'

'Lady Tricia, can we shake hands on that deal?'

'My late husband always said to me, "Do not trust a handshake," but, let us do that anyway and we will arrange with lawyers to draw up the necessary documents.'

They shook hands, Tricia looked back at Brown, who nodded, and they went inside to join the other guests plus a few uninvited gatecrashers with their unimaginative celebration of death.

Later that evening when Tricia had grown weary, she retired but on her way to her suite she stopped to have a word with the manager. They exchanged a few words and after a nodding of heads, she said, 'Thank you,' and continued upstairs where April was waiting.

—

At breakfast the following morning she spoke to, Ted. 'Dad, can you arrange to interview some staff. I want a lady's maid to replace April preferably an older one. You can get a Governess for your children, plus a housekeeper, extra kitchen staff and a housemaid. Meanwhile, I am going to your lawyer to arrange a contract and later I am going to the Land Agent. We will meet here at lunchtime and after lunch we travel with Edwina home.'

'That sounds like an order. How can I refuse? What is it you're setting up?'

'I will talk about it later but it is to both our benefits.'

With Brown in tow she hired a gig and her first stop was with the lawyer who it turned out was also that of, Louis, which made things a lot easier and an hour later she was at the Land Agents office.

'Good morning. ma'am, my name is Ogilvie, what can we do for you?'

'Good morning, Mr Ogilvie, I am advised that there is land for sale around Lovedale. Can I see it?'

'Certainly, ma'am, is there any particular reason?'

She didn't smile nor did she sigh, but said rather abruptly. 'Yes! I want to buy it.'

His head jerked back and he looked at her over his *pinz-nez*. 'Oh! You had better come into my office, ma'am.' He held an arm out. 'This way if you please.'

Once settled around his desk with Brown stood in the background he laid out a map marking all the plots in the Lovedale area. Pinning it down with bits of office material, he said, 'Tell me, ma'am, which particular estates you are interested in?'

'Show me the Heathdale estate.'

His hand hovered over the map and then his finger darted down. 'There it is, but it is not for sale.'

'No, sir, I don't want to buy that estate, I want to buy everything around it north of the Broke road.'

His hand hovered and he looked sideways at her. 'That is a considerable amount of land you are looking at. There are four plots currently for sale totalling one-hundred and fifty acres.'

'Why are they for sale?'

'Three were convict-settlers who can't make a go of it and their two years is up so now they can legally sell and the other is a retired soldier who was just not into farming. Tell me! Are you not interested in Heathdale and make it one big estate?'

'No! My father owns that and I want to expand it.'

'That is a considerable expense.'

Tricia sighed, and reached into her bag and withdrew a legal document tied with blue silk. 'Mr, Ogilvie, read that.'

He picked it up, untied it and began reading. He stopped and looked at her in surprise. 'My apologies, Lady Bishop.'

'Apology accepted. Now shall we do business?'

He finished reading the promissory note from the NSW Bank before he handed it back to her and said, 'Give me a few minutes, M'lady, and I will get the necessary paperwork so that we can work out the final amount and start the purchase procedure.'

'Thank you, Mr Ogilvie, but tell me, is there a small plot of land available in or near the settlement of Lovedale?'

His finger wandered over the map as he deliberated and then he finally pointed at a square of land. 'There is one here. It is on a junction on the Broke road. It is three hundred acres and is a vineyard not far from you.'

'That's larger than Heathdale. Add that to the bundle and set the wheels in motion. I want that land quickly, before the next growing season.'

'I will set the process moving today, M'lady. Was there anything else?'

'Yes, Mr Ogilvie. Are you handling the sale of the *Wheatsheaf Arms*?'

'Yes, I am fortunate to have been handed that property.'

'Good! I want to buy that but as a separate sale. How much?'

'One moment, please.'

He left the room to return moments later with a sheet of paper which he gave to her.

She took a quick look at the figures at the bottom and in her familiar manner when doing business she wrote something down on a piece of scrap paper and pushed it over to him. He picked it up and glanced at it before he said, 'That is a little harsh, M'lady. Can we not agree to something a little closer? We are in Australia and you have quoted English prices.'

She took the scrap paper back, scratched out the original figure and pushed it over. 'That is my final offer.'

'I am sure that will be acceptable, M'lady.'

He stood up and came around the desk hiding his satisfaction at the profit he was making and bowing slightly he took her raised hand and kissed the fingertips.

Outside the Agency, she said, 'That was a good mornings work, Brown, let's go and have some lunch. You can walk me back to the hotel.'

As they started walking she slipped her arm through his, and said, while looking sideways up to him, 'By the way, have you given any thought as to your future?'

He looked down at her, and replied, 'My thoughts, Lady Tricia, are right here.'

She flushed a little and looked down at her feet, before saying, 'Brown! If you wish to return to England, I will pay your fare but I want you to work with M. Armand who is an experienced viticulturist. Learn what there is about wines etc... He has agreed to help you.'

'If that is your wish, M'lady, so be it. When do I start?'

They stopped outside the hotel and she said with a huge smile, 'Not just yet, Brown, I am only setting up the business so you're stuck with me for a little while yet.'

He faked a groan and followed her inside.

—

Tricia was shaking and trying to hold back tears as she held onto Ted's arm while Edwina's coffin was lowered tenderly into the grave. When the pastor had finished his short sermon and a few prayers, they returned to the house. Ted asked Tricia to wait while he went to his two estate workers who were about to fill in the grave and he handed them something in a small canvas bag. They nodded and said a humble thanks and he returned to Tricia and led her across the lawn back to the house.

The Pastor turned down the offer of an overnight stay and only stopped long enough for a cup of tea before he made his way back to Cessnock, and Tricia, feeling depressed retired to her room. April, Shirley, and the children excused themselves leaving, Brown, Maguire and Ted to do what men do and, Ted, started it off by asking Brown if he knew what Tricia's plans were.

'Do you know what she's up to, Brown? She hasn't told me anything.'

'Mr, Cartwright, I am not under oath but what I learned this morning remains a secret. She will tell you when she is ready. This is how she does business. I have watched it for years.'

'Are you saying, Brown, her money is not all inherited?'

'Yes, she has had her own businesses since she was seventeen as a young school teacher and would not let her husband near them. He was a bit miffed but he didn't try for which I don't blame him. She's a terror to go up against.'

Ted shook his head. 'Where did she get that from I wonder.'

'Don't worry, Mr Cartwright, my bet is she will be down here tomorrow morning and dishing it, but what I can tell you, it is to your benefit.'

'Call me, Ted, Brown. Something stronger anyone?'

He poured them a generous glass of whisky each before asking Maguire what he was up to. 'I don't know, Mr Ca… I mean, Ted, Madam hasn't told me.'

'Rory,' said, Brown, 'I think you are in for a shock and that is all I'm saying. I've said too much already.'

They moved onto more mundane things and after half-an-hours chatting, Brown, pushed the boat out when he asked, Ted, about growing vines. This was Ted's territory and it was almost dinnertime when he called a stop and Maguire excused himself and said he was going to the kitchen to help.

April took Tricia a special soup dish that Maguire had prepared before returning to join the others in the dining room. Dinner was a subdued affair and later after spending a little while playing whist they retired early.

~~~~~

CHAPTER 21

It was a repeat of her earlier nightmares. It was three o'clock in the morning when she tossed uneasily in her sleep. There was a steady insistent something that drums into your senses. Then it turned into a cold hard clatter the unmistakable click-clack of clogs over cobbles. With shawls over their heads and bent against the drizzle, crowds of faceless beings crowded down the never-ending street.

The rain gave the slate roofs a polished appearance and they glistened. The toneless clack—clack—clack became faster and faster and echoed off the walls like hundreds of horses hooves racing on cobbles. The sound of a gunshot echoed across the scene and a laughing skeleton wearing a bushranger hat and carrying a gun appeared. Over the deafening cacophony, the undeniable blast of the six o'clock siren sounded accompanied by a bolt of lightning that struck the mocking skeleton leaving a pile of smoking bones with the hat on top.

Tricia's screams blended with that of the ghostly crowd and she sat bolt upright shaking with anxiety. Holding her head in her hands and leaning forward onto her knees, she wept. Despair had overtaken her when a voice inside her head, whispered, 'Tricia, my love, this country is your destiny. Let your heart lead you and favour the colours in your mind and pass on my love to your father.'

Her eyes shot open and she looked around in the darkness but as in other times, she saw nothing. Only a feeling of homeliness pervaded.

She knelt by the bed and said a quiet prayer for Edwina, Clifford, Jill and Auntie Gertie before she ended with a special prayer and thank you to her mother who had been her inspiration.

—

Her sleep was sound for the rest of the night and April woke her with a cup of tea just after eight before she joined the others for breakfast feeling refreshed and a new person.

When breakfast was over she asked for a meeting with all of them and at ten-thirty they were gathered on the veranda enjoying the southern spring warmth.

When they were settled, Tricia stood up and while walking backwards and forwards in front of them, she began, 'Dad! Yesterday I started proceedings to buy all of the surrounding land so you now have one-hundred and fifty acres. My friend, M. Armand, from France, a wine expert, accompanied by a chap called Brown will be coming to advise you. M. Armand did say to me that maybe you should concentrate on varietals such as Semillon and Shiraz. While you are upgrading your grapes, M. Armand and I are building a winery in the Pokolbin area. It is looking likely to be a mile to the west of here on a junction on the Broke road. The plan is that you and other farmers will sell your grapes to us and we will produce the wine. This increases your profit margin and makes transporting and marketing the wine easier as we can do it in bulk. Does that sound alright with you?'

'I like it, Tricia, but whose land will it be?'

'Mine, Dad, but as I said, the vineyard is for you to operate. Any profit will be used to enhance it and to keep you and your family.'

'Done!'

'Good, we go into town on Friday to sign the contracts.'

She spun around with a finger pointing and stopped at Maguire. 'Rory, how would you like to run a hotel?'

Taken by surprise, he stammered, 'Err... I... I don't know. That's a big jump.'

'Would you like to try?'

'Yes, M'lady.'

'That's settled. I have bought the *Wheatsheaf Arms* and you will be my manager and Chef. I am going to upgrade it and I want the restaurant to be its centre. There is only one condition and that is you keep a suite free for me.'

Finally, she turned to April. 'April! I am going to release you from my shackles. My Father is taking on more staff and I have hired a new lady's maid who will be starting next Monday. I want you to guide her for a few days and then you can join M. Armand. I will help you obtain anything you require and transport you to his future residence. Adele and Celeste will be pleased as they like you.'

'Thank you, Lady Tricia.'

'Good, let's have some refreshment.'

Brown raised his hand, and she said, 'Yes, Brown?'

'You never mentioned me, ma'am.'

'Oh dear,' she said in mock disgust, 'I knew I had forgotten something.—Mister Brown, you can set up my father's gig after we have partaken of our refreshment and take me for a drive around Lovedale. I want to see the land where I am building the Winery.'

He did an exaggerated bow and swung a hand across his body. 'Your wish is my command, M'lady.'

Everyone laughed at the jollity of it all but had inkling there was more to it.

Although it was a southern hemisphere late spring day it felt like an English mid-summers day and it was at this time that she adopted the male bush-ranger style wide-brimmed hat.

It was a pleasant drive through the rolling countryside surrounded by fields of vines. There was a smattering of wheat but in such poor condition because the soil was not compatible that Tricia could see the reason why they were changing to vines.

After fifteen minutes, they came to a junction of the road and two tracks leading off north and south. Tricia consulted her hand-drawn map from Ogilvie and decided the land south and west of the junction was the place. On the north end of the plot surrounded on three sides by healthy-looking vineyards, there was a well-crafted two-storey colonial-style house with a veranda all around.

Brown wheeled the gig into the short drive and pulled up outside the front entrance to be met by a middle-aged grey-haired woman of modest build with her housemaid behind her. He jumped out and tethered the horse before helping Tricia down with his exaggerated boldness, which had become the signature pattern between them.

Tricia walked to the few steps that led up to the veranda to be welcomed. 'Good morning, and to what do I owe this visit?'

'Good morning,' replied Tricia, 'I am Mrs Patricia Bishop the purchaser of this property and I have come to look at what I have bought. I'm sorry if I have disturbed you.'

'Mrs Bishop, you are welcome. I am Mrs McInnes. Will you join me for a cup of tea?'

She turned to walk around the veranda when Tricia stopped her. 'Do you mind if Mister Brown my companion joins us?

'Not at all, Mrs Bishop.'

'He will be running the place and I want him to see what he is taking on.'

Tricia gave Brown a nod and a come-on with her head and removing his hat he followed the ladies around the house to a shady part of the veranda where the housemaid and a manservant were already preparing to serve up tea and cake.

Brown held Tricia's chair while she sat down and he sat alongside her opposite their hostess. The maid began pouring the tea, 'Help yourself to the biscuits and cake, Mrs Bishop, and you, Mister Brown,' said Mrs McInnes.

When they had partaken of some cake and tea, Tricia said, 'Mrs McInnes! That name is familiar. We were drinking a fine wine of that name while we stayed in Sydney. Is there a connection?'

'You are correct, Mrs Bishop, you did indeed drink wine from this vineyard. It wasn't the *Colonial Hotel* by any chance? We have a contract with them. They buy all our wine.'

'It was that hotel. Can I ask why you are selling up when you produce such good wine and you have a regular customer?'

'My husband passed away some months back and although we grow a premium brand of grapes I find it too difficult to cope.'

'Oh! I am sad for your loss, Mrs McInnes. I know how you feel. I went through a similar experience only last year.'

'Thank you, Mrs Bishop, for your condolences. What made you come to Australia?'

'I came to seek my father and having found him I like it here and wish to settle down.'

'But you want to take on the running of a vineyard?'

Tricia thought it was time to be a little tactful. 'I want somewhere to live and I like the house and the area. Brown is training to do the wine side of it. Could I look around the house and is it possible for your man to show Brown around outside or should I say the working bits?'

'Of course, you may, Mrs Bishop, but would you like more tea?'

'No thank you.'

Mrs McInnes called on her manservant and gave him his instructions to introduce Brown to the vineyard foreman, Walter Dodd before she led Tricia into the house. It was forty-five minutes later when they returned to the veranda and the ladies chattering between themselves had to wait a further ten minutes for Brown to arrive with Dodd. When they were gathered on the veranda Mrs McInnes, said, 'Would you care to stay for lunch?'

'No thank you. Mrs McInnes, I am returning to my father's place and then I am going on a tour of the Lovedale area this afternoon. Thank you for the offer.'—'Come, Brown, let's go.'

They had travelled only a few hundred yards when Tricia said, 'Well Brown, what do you think? The house itself is lovely and will be my residence.'

'The distillery and the outhouses are all in good condition,' he replied, 'and the water supply is good. What is it you intend to do with it?'

'M. Armand and I are going to build a Winery but having seen it I want to keep that special wine going and Mrs McInnes has agreed that I can keep her brand name.'

'Won't the new building take away some of the vines?'

'Not much, I hope. I will have to speak with, Armand. Meanwhile, I have agreed also to keep all the staff except the housemaid. Her foreman will be my manager and it also means I have a driver so you can move in with M. Armand and learn the business. That will be a couple of weeks yet. Can you keep a secret, Brown?'

'Yes, Ma'am.'

She took his hand and squeezed it. 'Good! I will be staying in the *Wheatsheaf* every weekend and while you are with, Armand, there will be a room set aside for you.'

He glanced sideways at her with a surprised but happy face before concentrating on his driving.

While on her journey around Lovedale, she was able to survey the accommodation on one of the farms she had purchased close to the junction of the North Road and the Lovedale Road and she made a mental note. It was, she decided, ideal for her school.

~~~~~

CHAPTER 22

Two months later and the days were longer and the summer heat more than they were used to in England. Tricia was leaning on the veranda rail at the rear of Heathdale. The sun was beginning to sink behind the Blue Mountains and scattered clouds were rolling across the sky. Ted, who was sat behind her enjoying a cup of tea looked at his daughter over the rim of his cup and was feeling very proud of what she had achieved despite her setbacks.

Over the weeks, she had told him her life story. She missed nothing out and he understood her firm attitude to life. She knew what she wanted, nobody or anything was going to stand in her way from achieving it but he was concerned about her future. She was still young and attracted admirers but she treated them politely and never ventured beyond a happy evening's entertainment. She was already well known for her piano playing and singing and was not averse to learning some of the local ballads.

He put down his cup, and said, 'Tricia, dear, have you honestly got any plans for the future? When your Winery is all set up and running what are you going to do, you are still young?'

'Dad, I'm happy here in Australia. I like the way of life and most of all their easygoing fashion designed for use in ninety degrees heat. I want to settle down without all this M'lady rubbish. I want to be just me. Do not get me wrong. I appreciate my good fortune and the privileges that came my way but I want to use them for a useful purpose. Enough of that—they have finished upgrading the house at the Winery and I am moving in next week and the Winery itself will be ready soon. When I am settled I want to help the school in Cessnock and I am thinking about one for the indigenous people down the road by the junction and I want to get married.'

'Have you anyone in mind?'
'Yes, but I don't know how to approach it.'
'Does he know?'
'I think he does.'

'It wouldn't be Brown by any chance?'

'Dad, you miss nothing. I love him; I want to be Mrs Brown. He has always been there when I needed him and since we first met there has always been a mutual and humorous side to our relationship. He put his proper relationship in jeopardy to come to Australia with me and the grief both of us went through recently has pulled us closer.'

'Are you physical?'

'No, but we walk a lot holding hands and dine together.'

'Nature is cruel, Tricia, and I can't help you. You will have to talk with him as I think he is frustrated by the invisible class distinction between you.'

'But I am an ordinary person, Dad, who had a little good fortune. That is why I urged him to become a wine expert under the tutorage of M. Armand. I'm hoping that the increase in his standing might persuade him.'

'Has he got long to do with his learning?'

'I spoke with Armand only yesterday and he is impressed with Brown and said he is ready to take over the Winery and the McInnes vineyard but he will have to be with him in the run-up to harvesting. There is one other thing though.'

'And what is that, young lady?'

'He knows that I won't abide by this rule that I must give up my wealth on marriage. Don't get me wrong, Dad, he will benefit and should he live longer than me then he gets it all.'

'Can you not give him some as a wedding gift so that he won't feel, how should I say this? Under the thumb!'

'I understand, Dad.'

She leaned over the rail, looked to the West, and watched as the sun finally disappeared behind the mountains. "How beautiful," she thought, "Blue mountains and a red sky. Red and blue, that makes, Brown, how silly of me." She looked to the heavens and the vast array of stars popping through in the fading light, and said a quiet, "Thank you, Mam."

She spun around and was about to say something when Shirley joined them. Diverted from her thoughts she welcomed her.

'Good evening, Shirley, are the children safe in bed.'

'No, Tricia, the new Governess is wonderful and is reading to them. Thank you for giving us the opportunity and the books.'

The footman had been around and lit the lanterns upon which, Ted, said, 'Time to go in. We don't want to encourage the midges.'

'They are not so bad this time of year,' said Shirley, 'Let us have a glass of wine before dinner.'

She shook the Chinese lantern bell and the footman returned this time with a tray at the ready. 'Yes, ma'am!'

The wine was ordered and they settled down to pass the time discussing the day's events before the call for dinner. When the call came, Ted slapped the back of his neck too late to stop the annoying midge from biting before taking, Tricia, by the arm, and saying quietly, 'Shirley and I will come into town with you on Saturday, Tricia.'

They were sat in the lounge waiting while a waitress poured their afternoon tea when Ted, said to Tricia, 'What time does Brown usually get here?'

'It could be anytime. It depends on how far they have travelled. One week he didn't come until Sunday.'

Ted looked up at a commotion by the entrance, and said, 'Speak of the Devil.' Brown was striding over to them and he stopped behind, Tricia, and did his usual bow. 'Good afternoon, ladies and Ted.'

Ted, laughed, and replied, 'Watch it young man or I will set the ladies on you.'

Brown took a step back and raised his hands in front of him in mock defence. 'Oh, no! Not that, anything but that.'

'You had better get a seat, lad,' said, Ted.

They waited while a waiter brought another chair and manoeuvred the others around and set it up for an extra tea and when they were all settled, Ted said to Brown, 'Where've you been today, lad?'

'We were out past Broke and we called in to see the McInnes Estate on the way home. The vines there impress M. Armand. He said the McInnes's must have been well advised on the crop they acquired and the Winery will be finished by the time the crop is ready.'

'And have you looked at the crop at Heathdale?'

'We did that on Tuesday and your original vines are doing well but some of the newly acquired vines were in a neglected state. They will improve with the work we have done as you know, Mister Cartwright, but the wine this year will be blended and won't bring in much income.'

'But they won't make a loss?' said Tricia.

'No.'

'Oh, good, I won't have to wash the dishes.' Brown gave her a gentle shove on the shoulder and laughed. Tricia, continued, 'What was the hassle at the door, Browny boy?'

'It was a new footman who didn't recognise me, and silly me tried to walk straight in. That nice red-haired waitress stepped in and sorted it out.'

She slapped him on the shoulder, and said, 'Oh! You have a fancy woman. Watch it!'

They both laughed this time and Tricia looked at him her eyes shining with deep-down love.

Ted saw all this and coughed to get their attention. They looked across at him and, he said, 'Why don't you pair get married?'

Tricia and Brown immediately looked at each other and spontaneously Brown took her hands and slid down onto one knee between the chairs and said aloud so that everyone in the room could hear. 'Tricia Bishop! Will you marry me?'

There was a cheer from somewhere in the room as Tricia leaned forward and whispered into his ear. 'Only if you tell me your given name.'

He shook his head. 'You devil,' he said. He leaned forward, and whispered, 'Bernard. Could you live with that?'

She nodded and there was another cheer, as she replied so they could all hear, 'I love you, Bernard and will live with any name you have.'

He nodded and they moved closer and kissed to a cheer around the room.

Ted stood up and called a waiter and ordered champagne. The waiter was about to walk away when Tricia called him and told him to bring drinks for everyone in the room. There was increased activity amongst the staff and while that was going on Tricia went around to Ted and called him to one side.

'What is it, Tricia?'

'Can I use Mum's ring?'

'Have you got it?'

Yes, Dad, she left me all her keepsakes when they took her away and I have both her rings.'

'Have you got them with you?'

'I brought the engagement ring because I knew something was going to happen when you came along.'

'Give it to me, Tricia and I will pass it onto Brown.'

She went around to her seat, retrieved her bag, and after a few moments fiddling took out a small leather-bound box which she gave to, Ted. 'There you are, Dad. I shall pretend I didn't know.'

As she returned to her seat Ted caught Brown's eye and called him over and while shaking his hand covertly slid the box into Brown's hand as, he said, 'Congratulations, the ring in there was her mothers and you may use it with both mine and her mother's love.'

Brown opened the box to reveal a modest ruby with a blue emerald on either side on a gold ring.

The champagne and drinks were served and Ted stood up and raised his glass. 'Ladies and gentlemen, three cheers for the happy couple and may their life and love be happy and long. Hip-hip!'

'Hoorah!' shouted the crowd three times and everyone sat down the whole room buzzing with excitement. As the general hubbub died down Brown took Tricia's left hand and slid the ring on her finger, and said. 'I love you, flower.'

When the drinks were over Ted gave Brown the nod and signalled towards the door before, he said, 'That's it, ladies, us men are going for a walk. Behave yourselves.'

They left the room and as they crossed the reception area Maguire stopped them, and said, 'Congratulations, Brownie boy. You took your time.'

'I know, Rory. I always wanted to do it but I thought it was too close to our catastrophe but now I think of it that pulled us closer. Can you join us?'

'Another time, I have to supervise the kitchen. It's Saturday and always busy and the Boss likes it at its best.'

'Oh! You mean, that Boss. Now you know why I waited,' said Brown.

Rory laughed and patted him on the shoulder. 'Look after her, Brownie, she's a gift and beautiful with it.'

It was a warm close evening and felt like thunder as they hovered on the step but Ted took the lead and guided Brown to his left. 'I know a good pub this way so we should dodge any rain. You do like ale don't you and what was it she called you— Bernard?'

'Yes, to both questions.'

Two minutes later they were in the *'Black Swan'* and Ted led the way to the bar to be welcomed by a big man with a straggly ginger beard. 'Hello, Ted, who's your friend?'

'This, Geordie, is my future son-in-law, Bernard.' Ted turned to Brown. 'Bernard, meet, Geordie, who brews the best ale in New South Wales. He says he got the recipe from a friend in Newcastle, England.'

Brown shoved his hand over the bar. 'Nice to meet you, Geordie, two pints of your best, please.'

Geordie, laughed. 'Have a word with him, Ted. They're all best.'

'He's right, Bernard. He grows his own hops and then brews it. A farmer by day and a pub master at night.'

Geordie plumped the beers on the bar and Ted shoved some money over. Brown held up the glass and looked at it. 'Smaller than home, Ted.' And then took his first swig. 'Mmmm...! That's good. How come I don't know about this place?'

'She didn't let you out often enough,' said Ted, and they have their own peculiar measures here for some reason. This is called a schooner but it's only three-quarters of an English pint and half a pint is a middy.'

They stood enjoying their beer for a couple of minutes before Ted put his glass on the bar, and said, 'Right, Bernard, welcome to the family, what are your plans for my daughter?'

Caught off guard, Bernard paused and then placed his beer on the bar. 'I rather think she has got that planned already, Ted. She will be on my pedestal watching me oversee the Winery and the McInnes vineyard and assisting you with the family vineyard. I think she wants you to retire.'

'You know she loves the ground you walk on and she wants at least two children, Bernard?'

'Over the last few months when we met at the weekends she hinted at that but I didn't know how to approach it. She has no airs and graces but she is what she is and was my employer. You finally opened the door today and I must thank you for that.—Want another?'

'Yes, please.' Brown called Geordie and ordered and Ted continued, 'Tricia and I had some good talks, Bernard, and she is what she is today because there came a time in her life when she said, "Enough is enough!" An inside toughness nurtured by memories of her mother drove her on and she was determined that no one of either genre would take advantage of her ever again. That's what makes her the businesswoman she is.'

'I've watched her over the years, Ted, and I saw that, but she never lost sight of her background and she handles grief extremely well. She always thought of her staff and treated them well and looked after those who helped her.'

'You're speaking of the canal people?'

'Yes, and the school is doing well.'

'She is going to subsidise a school here you know?'

'Two, actually, Ted. She is converting one of the houses that came with the land she bought into a school for the indigenous people. An aborigine tribe chief working on the McInnes estate speaks passable English and she has asked him to organise the school and she is hiring some teachers. There is one snag and that is the low indigenous population in this area.'

'Bernard, you have a handful there but don't do anything to hurt her. She is my daughter.'

The innuendo wasn't lost on Brown, and he replied, 'Mister Cartwright, I would never do anything to harm her. I have been committed since the day we first met. Don't get me wrong, initially only as a guardian and my underlying feelings were kept on hold and I was in love with Jill and would have married her but for that diabolical incident which affected both our lives.'

They shook hands, and Ted said, 'Time we got back, lad, or do you fancy another?'

'Would I dare?'

—

They were met by the concierge at the hotel and he advised them that the ladies had retired, 'But I have a message for you, Mr Brown—Mrs Bishop, said to tell you to go to her suite when you returned, sir.'

They went upstairs and when they reached Ted's room, they shook hands once more and Brown continued along the corridor to Tricia's suite. He knocked and waited until he heard a distant voice, call out, 'Come in!'

He went in and as soon as she saw who it was, she said. 'Brown, why didn't you just walk in?' She ran across the room with her arms open and hugged him. 'You don't have to knock now. Kiss me, you big lump. That is your penalty.'

He scooped her up, kicked the door shut, carried her into the lounge area, and plopped her on the sofa where he lay alongside her and they kissed long and hard. He stopped for breath and pushed himself up, and she said, 'I never thought I would see the day. I feel so happy. Come here.'

She grabbed him and pulled him down but when things became more physical and nature's magnets were drawing them to the conclusion, he stopped and pulled away. Bernard, don't stop,' she said breathlessly, 'I've yearned for this moment for so long.'

With his heart pounding, he said, 'Tricia, my love, so have I, but I promised your father I would never harm you or your reputation and we must wait until we are married.'

Her face dropped momentarily before she looked up, and said, 'That won't be long, darling. We must put the banns up this week and we get married on the same day as Dad and Shirley. We plotted that while you were away.'

He pulled her to him and kissed her on the forehead. 'I love you and I look forward to the day. Now you rest and I will see you at dinner.'

He let her go and straightened his clothes, kissed her on the forehead again and left the suite.

—

Dinner that night was a jolly affair followed by Tricia in the entertainment lounge doing her bit on the piano and singing. The guests inspired by wine and spirits danced until late in the evening and it was after midnight before they retired.

Brown worn out by the high jinks was feeling the strain and he and Tricia wished each other a long goodnight before he crawled to his room and flopped on the bed exhausted. It could have been worse but the positions had been reversed and Tricia looked after him denying him the flow of alcohol that was thrust his way.

—

On Sunday after Church, they met Armand and he joined them for a midday brunch and throughout Tricia could sense that he had something to say so she obliged after her second cup of tea had been poured to ask him to sit with her.

When he was settled, she didn't hesitate. 'What is it you're dying to tell me, Louis?'

'Oh! Was it that obvious? Lady Tricia.' She winced a little at the title. 'I was going to tell you tomorrow but now you're here. I have secured a cargo of two hundred barrels from Portugal, which are on their way, and while I was in Sydney, I visited a bottle manufacturer and have a contract with them. It is an extension of the McInnes contract but they have upped the total.'

'How did you get the barrels?'

'It's an old contact of mine when I was in France and I wrote to him offering a good price to which he replied with a short note saying, 'Yes.' I have to speak with you about the price I paid.'

'It is a business I know little about, Louis? I trust you; we will discuss it tomorrow when you come. Will they be in time for the harvest though?'

'Yes, providing the weather stays kind they should be here just after Christmas. I think we have enough to get by on at the moment.'

'When do they start the harvest, Louis?'

'First, we have to do the blended wine and then we start harvesting the white grapes in January and then the red ones a few weeks later.'

'So we should manage the white wine and fingers crossed they get here in time for the red.'

'I could not have put it better myself, M'lady.'

'That's enough of wine, Louis. While you have been cavorting around Sydney things have taken a turn for the better here. I tell lies. It all happened yesterday. I got engaged.'

'Ah! Brown finally got around to doing something about it?'

'How did you know?'

'He's been working with me for a long time and we talked. For a strapping young man like he is, he is very shy, and he couldn't bring himself around to doing it, but I will say this for him. He worried like hell about you while he was away. The bushrangers in these parts have a troublesome reputation and he knew you would be riding about unconcerned.'

'Will you join me in a glass of champagne, Louis?'

'Yes, M'lady, but there is someone I must introduce.'

'By all means, Louis.'

'One moment.' He left the room only to return two minutes later with April and introduced her. 'Lady Tricia, my companion.'

'Oh! April,' said Tricia, 'how nice to see you. Where are your charges?'

April glanced at, Louis, before replying. 'We left them playing upstairs with that lovely Chinese housemaid you have. I hope you don't mind. The children love her.'

'You pinched her before today?'

'Only after she had finished work.'

'It's alright, April. You can borrow her as often as you like.'

She called for the sommelier and ordered champagne and at the same time, she caught Brown's eye and called him over.

When the wine was poured Louis raised his glass. 'To the happy couple. They got engaged yesterday, April.' They clinked glasses and took a sip and Louis, continued, 'when is the big day?'

'We are having a double wedding on New Year's Day along with my Father who is marrying his Shirley.'

'Let us make it a bigger day, Lady Tricia,' said Louis, 'how about a triple wedding?' He dropped onto one knee and looked up at, April. '*Voulez-vous m'épouser,* Miss Peters?

Her eyes widened and her hand went to her mouth, as she stammered, '…Err, …*Pourquoi ne m'avez-vous pas dit plus tôt. Oui, oui bien sûr.*'

'*Les hommes sont comme ça. vous devez le presser d'eux,* April,' said Tricia. She looked at Brown. 'Bernard, you didn't understand a word of that, but she just said yes, to Louis.'

Brown raised his glass.' Welcome to the club.'

'Let us all sit down now,' said, Tricia, 'it is more comfortable drinking wine when sitting down.'

They sat and April leaned over to Tricia.' I will have to buy a dress. Where do we go?'

'We will go for a long weekend to Newcastle, April, and the men can join us if they wish...' Louis butted in, '…There will be no honeymoon, ladies. We will be busy for the following six weeks harvesting grapes. Are your preparations going well?'

'With the news, you gave me earlier, even better than expected. I am arranging with the local butcher, grocer and greengrocer to put up a makeshift shop by the Aborigine school where everyone can access it. Dad tells me they run a soup kitchen throughout that period also.'

The talk changed to just general chat and it wasn't long before it was time to retire to get ready for dinner. When they stood up to leave, April, said to Tricia, 'I won't be able to attend this evening,

Lady Tricia. I have to take over the children.'

Tricia took her arm and led her to one side. 'Don't worry, April, you ask the housemaid to stay and I will provide a room for her tonight if she wants it and she has free meals. Hire her as your Governess now that you are engaged. I will find a replacement. See you at eight o'clock, and congratulations. You two were made for each other and the French language is a bonus. He's got no secrets now.'

They laughed together, and April, said, 'You don't do too bad with French either.'

'April, this was quick.'

'We became friendly on the ship, ma'am. That's why I took up the role of Governess with him as soon as you were well.'

They were about to part, when Tricia, said, 'April!—Please call me, Tricia.'

April smiled, and said, 'Yes, Ma... Tricia.'

Tricia moved house the following week accompanied by Brown who had his own rooms complete with staff. She had kept all of the McInness staff and there was such a variety of convict settlers that other staff were easy to come by. They were a little rough but help with their attire and living space soon had them back in a role they were used to before their convictions.

It was November 2nd when they went on a river steamer to Newcastle. Brown insisted on going with them and took Ted along as company while, Louis, stayed behind to oversee the testing of the grapes and preparing the winery for the harvest. They checked into the *Steam Packet Hotel* too late to venture around the town and settled for a late tea before retiring to prepare for evening dinner. Brown and Ted had other ideas and remained in the bar to test the local brew for a pint or two while Tricia did a little research on the best couturiers in town.

After dinner, outnumbered by the ladies, Ted and Brown once more retreated to the bar. They agreed that the ale was good but as Ted pointed out, 'Not as good as Geordie's.'

They rejoined the ladies after an hour for a late coffee before retiring as an early start was expected in the morning.

—

Brown was a little apprehensive as he watched the girls mount a hackney outside the hotel but he was barred from accompanying them by, 'Herself.'

Ted stood back and when the girls were out of sight, he took Brown by the arm and urged him into the hack that was next in line. 'Where are we going?' asked Brown.

'We are following the ladies to see where to find them and then we're going down to the harbour to visit a shipping company down there and then we just admire the scenery.'

'Is this to do with the wine business?'

'Yes. I used to ship my wine to Sydney through them but this year I must decline as we are now working through you. I normally use their Morpeth office but seeing as we're here?'

'That makes sense, Ted, and it fills the morning in.'

They followed the girls and watched as they dismounted and entered the *'Le Chic'* boutique.

'Looks like someone did their homework, Bernard,' said Ted.

'Why am I not surprised,' replied Brown, 'she always did her research before doing business.'

'You, my friend, have got your hands full.'

'In a way, Ted, it makes my life easier. She organises and then sits back and lets others get on with it but she never sticks to a protocol. She does it her way.'

'How do you mean, Bernard?'

'Like the way she dresses. She didn't like that starchy look as she called it so she threw away all that stuff they wear underneath. She liked the freedom, she said. Her first wedding dress was just such a case. I heard the maids talking about it. The other ladies loved it and except for special occasions she always lets her hair hang loose or in a ponytail instead of that ringlet look.'

'Sounds like my daughter, Bernard.'

'Do you think she will ever change?'

'Who knows, lad. She has a switch in her head that just clicks and she does things. You are talking about an eleven-year-old who jumped into a river to rescue a drowning boy.'

'You what?'

'You heard. Here are the shipping agents.'

They dismounted and asked the hack to wait and they went inside the company office where they were approached by a well dressed young man.

'Good morning, Gentlemen, what can I do for you?'

Ted took a card from his pocket and proffered it over the counter. 'I wish to speak with this gentleman.'

The young man picked it up and briefly looked at it. 'I'm sorry but Mister Pickwick is away in Sydney today. Can I help?'

'Yes. I use this company every year to transport my wine from Morpeth down to Sydney and Melbourne but this year I won't be doing it.'

Oh! Why's that, sir. Have we done something wrong?'

'No, son, it's just that we have changed the way of harvesting our grapes and we no longer have to ship it ourselves.'

'Let me check the book, sir. What did you say your name was?'

'Cartwright! Edward Cartwright.'

The young man reached under the counter and plucked out a leather-bound ledger and plonked it on the counter. 'Cartwright. That name is familiar. Do you come from Lancaster?'

'No, son, but close by. Why?'

'I met a girl once in Lancaster called Patricia Cartwright. She helped me to stop a factory boss removing our rights.'

Ted looked at Brown, who nodded. 'That would be my daughter, young man. She came out here to find me.'

'I remember now,' he said, 'she told me her biggest wish was to find her father. She has done it?'

What's your name, son?'

'Jack Young.'

'Mister Young, would you like to join us for dinner tonight?'

'Very much, sir. Can I bring my wife?'

'By all means. The *Steam Packet* at eight. There is just one thing, my lad?'

'What's that?'

'Treat her with respect. She is Lady Patricia Bishop now. Let's get on with our business.'

They entered the dining room and were about to sit when Tricia, said, 'It's set out for seven. I only asked for five.'

'We have someone we would like you to meet,' said Ted. 'Be seated, I'm sure they will be here shortly.'

He waived to the sommelier who came over and he ordered a bottle of white and a bottle of McInnes red wine and they had only been sat for two minutes when a waiter came over and spoke to Ted. Ted got up immediately and went to the door of the dining room and after a few seconds, he reappeared with Jack Young and his attractive redheaded wife.

April nudged Tricia, who looked up. 'Do you know them,' she said.

Tricia's hand shot to her mouth and she muttered something unintelligible and walked around the table to meet them. Young half bowed. 'Good evening, Lady Bishop, how are you?'

She hesitated before she replied. 'Good evening, Mister Young, I am well. Introduce me to your companion.'

His wife stepped forward and curtsied. 'This is Carol, my wife and the beautiful mother of my children.'

'Good evening, Carol. Welcome to our family.'

'Good evening, Ma'am. I am so glad to meet you.'

Tricia turned to Brown. 'Bernard, I would like for them to sit by me. Is that alright?'

He was a little taken aback by the request as she normally did what she wanted and to be asked was something new. He was so surprised that he muffed his first few words. 'Erm...' he raised his hand's palm upwards in a gesture of resignation, and said, 'Err... Yes.'

They shuffled their positions around and when they were finally seated and their first orders were taken, Tricia leaned towards Carol, and said, 'Carol. I get the impression that he has been boring you with details of our last meeting.'

'Longer than that, M'lady. He is always talking about the angel that saved the plight of his fellow workers. Our first daughter is called Patricia.'

'I will apologise for him, Carol. It was pure coincidence that I happened to be in the right place at the right time. Did he tell you that we both lost our jobs because of it, in a different manner of course?'

'No, he didn't, M'lady.'

'Don't worry, things have turned out for the best and our relationship was so short it is of no consequence so you are safe and enjoy your life together. How many children have you?'

'Just two daughters, M'lady, but he wants a son.'

'Carol, it is a pleasure to talk to you but, please, call me Tricia. I am marrying Bernard and in future I will be plain Mrs Brown. Now let us devour this mountain of food and I must talk with, Jack. We will catch up later when the men disappear for their ritual brandy.'

'My pleasure, Lady Tricia.'

Tricia touched her hand and smiled. 'It is so hard, Carol.'

Dinner was served and in between courses, she had a few words with Young, the first of which, was, 'What happened to you, Jack, I heard the scuffle and when I got there you had gone.'

'To keep it brief, Lady Bishop…'

'Call me Tricia, Jack. My title is only an honorary one as my husband died and I am marrying, Bernard in the New Year.'

'Very well, Ma'am, Tricia, it is. As I was saying—I was kidnapped and dragged off to a ship that set sail that night. They kept me locked up for three days and then I had to work my passage through the worst weather you can imagine for one-hundred and twenty-one days. Scaling those masts in bad weather is quite scary and I made my mind up that sailing was not for me so I jumped ship in Sydney and made it to Newcastle where I landed an office apprenticeship and now I am a representative of a shipping agent.'

'And you met my father, how?'

'He came to cancel his contract as are a lot of wine producers.

It seems they have a new method of shipping wine. The name Cartwright seemed familiar and as they say, the rest is history. Here I am.'

They carried on with their meal and while they were waiting for the sweet to be served she said, 'I must apologise for the loss of your wine contracts. It is my fault. Can you negotiate new contracts?'

'No, that is down to the boss. I find them and he wangles them.'

'Can he get here in the morning? Let's say nine o'clock.'

'He should be back tonight, so I think so.'

'Join me for breakfast at eight-thirty and we will speak with your boss at nine. Let's eat.'

—

Tricia went down early for breakfast and found Jack waiting for her and while they were eating, Tricia said, 'Do you know the total wine cargo of all the farmers, Jack?'

Taking a pencil from his pocket he started scribbling on a table napkin. When he stopped he showed her the figures.

'As much as that? What if I were to do that in bulk?'

'That would guarantee a full cargo and be much cheaper.'

'Give me a price, Jack.'

He pushed his plate to one side and turning the napkin over while talking to himself he began to do some sums. After a few minutes, he stopped and drew a line under the final figure and pushed it across to her. 'How's that,' he said.

She looked at it and pondered and then reaching over and taking the pencil she scribbled her own figure and pushed it back to him. 'That's better,' she said.

'Tricia! That is scraping the barrel, excuse the pun.'

He wrote something else and showed her and she did her usual thing by striking it out and putting her own figures in. 'My final offer, Jack.'

He looked at her, shook his head, and said, 'Are you really, Tricia Cartwright? I can accept that but I don't think my boss will. Speak of the devil.'

He stood up as a large portly man walked towards them. He stopped at the table and shook hands with Jack who stepped in quickly. 'Mister Pigeon, allow me to introduce, Lady Patricia Bishop.'

He was taken aback for a moment before he bowed and reaching across kissed her fingertips. 'Good morning, M'lady. To what do I owe this early morning call?'

'Please take a seat, Mister Pigeon. Would you like some breakfast or just partake of a cup of tea?'

'Tea, please.'

She poured him a cup and went directly to the point. 'Mister Pigeon, I have been discussing with your assistant here a possible contract for the bulk shipping between Morpeth and Sydney of wine. He has impressed me with his knowledge and I am in complete agreement with the figures he gave me. She pushed the napkin across to him. The bottom figure is mine and that is what I am prepared to pay when the time comes.'

He picked the napkin up and while he read it he wiped his brow with a kerchief. Putting the napkin down, he said, 'That is a little low. You will need to add another fifteen per cent on that.'

'I will bear that in mind, Mister Pigeon, meanwhile I shall shop around. It was nice doing business with you.' She turned to Young. 'I am sorry, Jack. It has been lovely meeting you again. I shall look you up next time I am in town but I have to go now.'

She stood up to leave when Pigeon spoke. 'Lady Bishop, may I offer a conciliatory price. How about a two per cent increase?'

She looked directly at him. 'One per cent.'

Pigeon shrugged, and said, 'When can we draw up this contract?'

She took a card from her purse and gave it to him. Get your lawyers to draw it up and have Young here deliver it to me at that address. I will pay his return fare.'

'When do you expect your first shipment, M'lady?'

'We have already purchased the fermented stocks from the growers and my partner, M. Armand, says we can begin blending quite soon. While we're at it, I think you should recompense Mister

Young for his tactful negotiating. I was aiming to pay a lot less until he advised me of certain pitfalls. With this price, I was guaranteed good service. I have to go now. I have a boat to catch.'

With that, she shook Young's hand and Pigeon, bowed as she left them.

Upstairs she was met by Brown. 'How did you get on with your friend, Lady Tricia? Have you been doing it again?'

'Very well, Bernard. It worked out better than I expected. It is cheaper to ship in bulk. All we need now is barrels and bottles.'

~~~~

CHAPTER 23

For the rest of November and through December they were busy blending, tasting and bottling the wine stocks they had bought from the surrounding vineyards. At one point they were overwhelmed as the amount that came their way far exceeded their expectations.

A general call for bottles and corks was sent out. Like the wine stocks, the response was good and they were able to continue. The expertise of Louis Armand was a blessing as was the skill of Walter Dodd, who, when he wasn't overseeing their premier McInnes wine came over to help.

The one thing they had overlooked was a name for this newly blended wine and there was a big discussion over dinner one night. Several suggestions were put forward but no one could make their mind up. Nothing stood out and tempers were getting frayed when Tricia stepped in. 'I have had enough of this quibbling so I have a suggestion. The wine and grapes we are buying are all from the Hunter River area and when it's all brewed it will be transported down The Hunter river so why do we not call it, Hunter River Wine?'

Dodd, who had been invited to the meeting, put his hand up. 'Yes, Dodds' said Tricia, 'Do you agree?'

'Yes and no, ma'am. You can improve on that. Call it, *Coquun*. That is the Aborigine name for the river and it's unique. No one else has used an indigenous name for their wine before.'

They all looked at each other and there were a couple of shrugs before Tricia, said, 'How do you write that? What does it look like on a bottle?'

Dodd dug a pencil from his pocket, and scribbled on a table napkin and handed it to Tricia who folded it and held it against a bottle. She held it in the light, then in the shade, placed it on the table, and then pretended to pour. 'You know, Dodd, I like that. The ladies are going into town tomorrow to do some last-minute shopping and wedding organising so we will take this to the printers. If there is nothing else I suggest we finish now and gather our strength for tomorrow.'

There were murmurs around the table as they finished the last of their drinks and said their 'goodbyes'. When Tricia and Brown had seen the last of them out she held his hand and looked up at him. 'I have an early start so I am retiring now, Bernard, and I have a little job I wish to do before I settle down for the night. Good night, my love.'

He leaned forward and kissed her. 'Goodnight beautiful. I am going to have me another brandy.'

She poked him in the chest, and said, 'You're an addict.'

Tricia turned away and with her maid in tow she went upstairs to her rooms. Her maid helped her change and Tricia excused her and she sat up in bed with a tray on her lap and some coloured inks and began drawing. She did several drawings holding them this way and that until finally, after six attempts got the one she liked best.

She slid out of bed and put the tray on a side table before retiring. She snuggled down clutching a pillow to her chest with two things on her mind. Brown and barrels.

—

The Southern summer temperatures were high but the hard work continued until Christmas Eve. Tricia called a halt mid-afternoon and wished everyone a Merry Christmas and she would see them back on St. Stephens Day.

Ted did the same with his employees but now he, Shirley and the children had to get ready to go to Cessnock for the family get together in the *Wheatsheaf*. It was a little after seven o'clock when Ted and his family arrived and Tricia and Brown were waiting for them. Ten minutes later Louis, April, Celeste and Adele joined them. Tricia thought it unwise to put the children together but they naturally homed in on each other so that's where they left them chattering away in English and French while the adults enjoyed a pre-meal glass of Premium McInnes wine and the children a glass of lemon juice.

When the food was served Shirley sat between Carrie and

Tiddles and Louis sat between Celeste and Adele. While they were waiting for the main course to be served Tricia looked around the room and was pleased to see it was full but felt sorry for Maguire who must have his hands full. A full restaurant was always her intention and she knew he was capable and she was pleased that she had arranged for nearby hotels to take the overflow of sleepover guests. "Fingers crossed," she said mentally, "but things are looking good for business."

Dinner over, they and other hotel guests retired to the Entertainment Hall. They sat around a table in a corner close to the mini-orchestra and they gave each over gifts. The children were excited and darted down to an empty floor space behind them to play with their new toys. Being amongst four girls, Thomas snuck into a corner to play on his own. The men retired to the bar leaving the ladies to talk about them.

When the men rejoined them the children retired to their beds and the evening's entertainment began in earnest. Tricia, with a little help from Louis, who, with his deep bass voice and accent was well-liked by the ladies, filled in a good half hour but soon it was time to go the local Presbyterian Church for midnight prayers which Brown was not looking forward too. Presbyterian ministers were well known for their elongated sermons especially on occasions like Christmas. He was right in his estimation of the sermon and it was close to two o'clock in the morning before they were back in the hotel.

Christmas Day was extremely hot but the morning service was well attended with many hands covering yawning mouths and weary-looking hung-over faces the sermon was a lot shorter and they got back to the hotel a little after twelve-thirty.

They had intended to travel home after the midday meal but it was decided to travel after dark. It would take longer but be cooler and a simple evening dinner was arranged.

They set off home later knowing that they would meet up on the morrow when they started work, but Tricia was worried. There was no sign of the barrels needed to mature the wine.

—

When the bottling and labelling was underway, the next day Tricia and Brown went with Dodd out into the vineyard to test and taste the grapes. This was a new experience for them and following Dodd's lead, they plucked a grape, felt its firmness and took a bite to taste it before spitting it out and then sniffing it.

He explained to them the taste in a manner that was strange to them. He used terms like fruity, currants, earthy, acidic, blackberry or vanilla but as they progressed around the vineyard they began to get the gist of what he was referring to. 'It's a bit like sniffing your wine before you drink it, ma'am. You get all the flavours. They're not ready yet but you have to do this every day now as they change overnight and when the time comes you have to pick them as quick as possible. Your father will be doing this and the annual pickers will start arriving this week.'

'Is everything ready for them?'

'Yes, ma'am, we did everything you said. They will love the upgrades to the huts and the improved deep holes.'

He was referring to the toilets, which she had insisted were the best. It was something she had done at the Borrowdale School.

Louis, Ted and Brown carried on supervising and working the long hours getting ready for the grape harvest while the three women prepared for the big day. They spent many hours making sure the barn was decorated the way they wanted for the big party and in between they were doing dress rehearsals as well as dress fittings.

Dodd's was right and the first of the annual workers arrived on the Friday at both Heathdale and McInnes vineyards. On Saturday morning the three men were dragged off to the Church for a rehearsal. They made up for this with a good session in the *Black Swan* much to the disdain of the women.

Sunday passed quietly with the usual morning Church service and lunch in the '*Wheatsheaf*' *before* the men went home for an early night in readiness for the following day.

The ladies, observing the Wedding Eve rule stayed overnight in the Hotel with their maids.

~~~~

CHAPTER 24

It had rained overnight and clouds were passing overhead on the seasonal wind which cooled the temperatures and made life a little easier for the guests. The Church was full to capacity and Ted, Brown and Louis stood patiently in the entrance checking the time and talking between themselves. The main discussion being about grapes and how this weather could trigger the breakthrough they were waiting for and the time it takes women to get ready. Fifteen minutes after the appointed hour the first carriage pulled up at the end of the pathway to the Church.

The men strolled unhurriedly down the path with Brown and Louis hanging back as it was Shirley who had arrived first. Intermittent showers were in the forecast and Ted waited with an umbrella while the coachman helped her down and her Lady's maid tidied her dress and train before he stepped forward to take her arm and lead her up the path. Before they had gone more than a few paces, Tricia arrived. Brown duly obliged and knew she was unconventional and she wore a more relaxed style of dress. As they began to walk up the path April arrived and joined the parade into the church.

The service went well and for a Presbyterian Minister his sermon was conservative. He shook hands with them as they left and he Blessed them before the guests pushed their way out of the Church and began clapping, cheering and throwing rice as they made their way to the carriages.

The drive to the Hotel did not take long and they stood in a line to welcome the guests as they arrived for a noisy post-wedding dinner. Maguire had worked tirelessly through the night to make sure that everything was perfect and Tricia could see in his eyes that he was tired when she went to thank him. When she returned to the dinner Maguire left his second Chef in charge and went upstairs to snatch a couple of hours sleep in readiness for the Wedding come New Years Eve party out at Heathdale.

He knew the guests at the party were not the oversize rich clientele of the Hotel but the hired hands and temporary workers here for the grape harvesting but he was duty-bound to his Boss and he made sure the buffet spread and the barbeque were his best.

At three o'clock everyone went home. Tricia and Brown to the McInnes Estate while Ted, Shirley, April and Louis went to Heathdale to snatch a little rest before the evening's entertainment.

—

The coachman dropped them off and Brown scooped her up and carried her over the threshold. As he did so he whispered in her ear, 'I want to make love to you.'

'You should linger over a good wine first,' she said with a provocative smile, 'the pleasure lasts that little bit longer.'

Every second was adding to his ardour for this woman and he tried to suppress his feelings worried that further delay would see an early climax to his passion but she relieved him of his torment. 'I think there is time enough Bernard, shall we retire.'

Outside her rooms, they paused. 'Bernard, dearest, I need someone to undo me. Could you oblige?'

Overcome with desire for this woman the direct invitation caught him off guard.

'Aah, hem, err…, yes,' he stuttered.

Taking his hand, she led him into the room and stopped in front of the long-winged dressing table mirror where she could watch him.

She stood on tip-toes and nibbled his ear before whispering. 'Undress me.'

He stood behind her and with shaking fingers tentatively undid the top button, then the next and the next, becoming bolder with each one. He paused, leaned forward, kissed the perfect skin between her shoulders, and allowed his tongue to brush against the lobes of her backbone. He felt her shiver as the sensation travelled down her spine.

She pulled on each sleeve and let her dress fall to the floor. Turning quickly, she grabbed his jacket and almost tore it from his shoulders and then frantically pulled off his bow tie and waistcoat.

The pile of clothes grew as the mutual undressing continued. When she stood naked before him wearing only her choker he dropped to his knees and kissed her in that most feminine place that led to heaven while his hands caressed, searched and fondled.

She sighed and writhed, her breath coming in short gasps. She pushed her hips forward to meet him and pulled his head into her as the tension mounted. Throwing her head back she dug her fingers into his shoulders and moaned. He held her at the peak of her climax, picked her up and carried her to the bed.

Their first coupling was wild, his lovemaking that of a Stag in heat, the rampant urgings of a young bull intent on propagating his harem. Twice, their ardour was uninhibited before the exhaustion of their lust made them rest.

Later, as they lay curled together like forks in a cutlery box she felt him rising again and she took control by climbing above him. Her lovemaking was slow and deliberate and she savoured him like a good wine, holding him at his peak and allowing him to caress her so that their eruption was simultaneous and intense.

Passion spent, they slept entwined in a passionate Gordian knot.

Her lady's maid, aware of the situation hammered on the door an hour later. Brown grabbed his things and scrambled to his rooms as the door opened and preparations were made for a hot tub for Tricia.

That evening, Tricia and Brown stopped first to pick up Ted, Shirley, April and Louis before going on to the Barn where they threaded their way through the many carts left indiscriminately. Inside, the crowd forewarned of their arrival and already fuelled by ale and wine greeted them with cheers and as they made their way down the centre of the Barn flower petals were thrown.

When they were sat at their table alongside the makeshift low stage the band struck up and Maguire opened up the buffet and started the barbeque which was located outside a side door and the festivities started in earnest.

There were no limitations. Everyone mixed which was how

Tricia wanted it and Ted chivvied her into playing the piano and doing a couple of songs. Food was plentiful and people took advantage of it. Just before midnight, she sent for Maguire.

As he approached their table, Tricia went to meet him. She took his hand in hers, and said, 'Rory, you have done a grand job both here and in the hotel. How can I thank you enough? Was there enough food here for the guests?'

'Yes, M'lady…'

'Rory, you call me Mrs Brown from now on.'

'Mrs Brown, 'he said, 'you will always be M'lady to me and yes, there was plenty of food. It was a gamble as we didn't know how many were coming but we managed.'

'Come it is nearly midnight. Get a drink, Rory.'

Ted swung around and pressed a glass of wine into his hand as the trumpeter played to announce midnight. He raised a glass, and shouted, 'HAPPY NEW YEAR!'

The whole room erupted and everyone hugged and shook hands when suddenly they stopped and stood in a half-circle in front of Tricia. A big man who appeared to be the leader raised his glass and said for the crowd. 'Thank you, Ma'am, for a wonderful evening and three cheers for the happy couples. Hip-hip!… Hooray! Hip-hip!…'

'Speech, speech, speech,' was the chant. Tricia held her hands up and they went silent.

'Thank you all for coming and I am glad you had a wonderful time. It has been a beautiful day for us but as we have to get up early in the morning, I wish you all "A Happy New Year." Goodnight and God bless you.'

There was a loud cheer and they began dispersing.

―

Tricia was still dreaming when there was a knock on the door. She threw an arm out seeking Brown and was disappointed he wasn't there when the knock came again and she sleepily said, 'Come in.'

There was a brief pause before the door opened and her maid popped her head in and looked around before entering properly. 'Come right in, Laura, what kept you?'

Laura came across to the bed with a cup of tea before she replied. 'It was your first night, ma'am, and I wasn't sure.'

'Quite right, Laura. Best do it every time although his lordship tends to get up early.'

'Is he a lord now, ma'am?'

'No, Laura, I just tease him. What time is it?'

'It is just after eight, which reminds me, Mr Dodds is waiting downstairs.'

'Did he give you a message?'

'Yes, ma'am. He said to tell you that harvesting has started and they are all out working in the fields.'

'While I finish my tea, Laura, go and tell him, "Thank you," and I will come over to the fields as quick as I can and tell Cook I will have two boiled eggs with soldiers today. I am feeling good.'

Laura left the room and Tricia flopped back on the pillows feeling happy inside.

It had come as a surprise to hear that the harvesting had started so soon but she dressed appropriately for a bit of manual work determined she was going to do her bit. She made her way out to the fields with a silk scarf wrapped over her voluminous hair and her Ranger hat on. She had asked Laura not to accompany her and as she walked with a spring in her step she could smell the clean air as if the grapes were releasing a message saying come and get me.

It did not take her long to get to the field and as she got closer she was surprised to see the children were working with their parents and in the last row the Aborigine people were working alongside their invaders.

Dodd's was there to meet her and he showed her how it all worked. Three carts were covering the first two and a half rows and two carts were spare ready to take the place of the others when they were full. The pickers had large buckets and a pair of shears. They inspected a bunch of grapes and if they were ripe, they clipped it off and put them in the bucket. When the bucket was full they took that to the nearest cart and put them in and then went back to where they finished, continuing where they left off. When the cart was full it went off to the winery and a spare cart took his place. The cycle never stopped.

It looked easy but the hours were long and in the summer heat, weary! When the outside cart reached the end he swung around the end of the rows to the left side of the third row and started back down the line with pickers putting grapes in from one side of the fourth row and so on, and so on.

'Show me how to do it, Dodds,' said Tricia.

He led her over to the fifth row where she was on her own and said, 'Before you start, ma'am, taste the grapes like you did the other day.'

She held a bunch in her hand and they felt heavier and were just on the right side of firm. She plucked one and sniffed it before she bit it and sniffed again. 'The tang is different, Dodds. I cannot say how. Fruitier perhaps with a little more bite.' She popped it into her mouth and began eating it, and went, 'Aah! That is different. Fuller, with a little spice thrown in. Has the rain done that?'

'Yes, ma'am. We only get that taste occasionally. This year is going to be good but we must get them picked quickly. A bit more rain would help. It will keep them fruity longer.'

'How do I pick them, Mr Dodds?'

He showed her how to hold the bunch and what to look for and if she thought they were not ripe or damaged in any way she was to leave them and they would be picked later. The good ones went in the bucket and then onto the cart before going to the winery where Brown was waiting with a gang to crush them.

'I would like to mix with the workers, Mr Dodds. Can I do that?'

'Does, Mr Brown know you're here, ma'am?'

'No, Dodds, and don't you tell him.'

He took her over to the first line, and said, 'Join this line, ma'am, there is a family up at the front.'

He walked with her until they reached the family hard at work and Dodds had a quick word with the father who waved Tricia over. 'Go there with my wife ma'am. If you have any problems just ask.'

'Thank you.'

She went over to his wife who said to her, 'Start in front of me and then we pass each other as we go along.'

Tricia snapped up a bucket and got stuck in. Every fifteen minutes or so a child would walk down the rows with a bucket of water and a ladle and you were free to drink as you wish. It was thirsty work and she like the others participated.

They were a little shy of her at first but as time progressed, their chatter increased and they swapped remarks at the wagon when they were emptying the buckets. She stopped for a breather and mopped her forehead with her sleeve. It wasn't tiredness she felt. A big weight had lifted from her shoulders. She was enjoying working and mixing with the pickers and in her mind, three things stood out. She was in LOVE! She felt PEACE! Above all else, she felt FREE!

She turned her back to the other workers and looked to the heavens with her hands clasped in front of her, and said, 'Thank you, Mam…'

As she went to get back to work, Dodds came running up waving a piece of paper.

'What is it, Dodds?'

'Your barrels have arrived in Newcastle, ma'am.'

At that moment a flock of birds flew low across the vineyard like messengers from heaven

~~~~~

Epilogue

Tricia had two children, Edward and Edwina, and every year she worked out in the fields during harvest. Her schools in both England and Australia flourished but her school for the Indigenous people of Australia did not. Increasing Government rules and the thinning of the Aborigine population made it unworkable but she did provide schooling for their children every harvest.

McInnes Wines became evermore popular but the first year of the new blended variety *Coquun* did not make a profit. The second-year turned it all around and when rail links were made with both Sydney and Newcastle and steamships became the preferred mode of shipping internationally things improved.

In 1852, M Louis Armand, April, and their enlarged family moved to the newly founded South Australia wine fields and he sold his share of the Winery and Coquun wines to Tricia.

Her father lived for another ten years but his stepson was not interested in wine or rural life so Tricia inherited Heathdale. With Tricia's help, Thomas went to a private school in Sydney and later on to University to study Law.

Maguire opened his own restaurant with Tricia's blessing and the *Wheatsheaf Inn* continued to flourish.

THE END

©2023